FORGIVING
ARARAT

FORGIVING
ARARAT

a novel

GITA NAZARETH

BETTE PRESS

Cover and interior design by Frame25 Productions
Cover art by Albert H. Teich, Vinicius Tupinamba, and Aaron Amat, c/o Shutterstock.com

Bette Press, LLC
P.O. Box 1139
Kennett Square, Pennsylvania 19348
www.forgivingararat.com

Library of Congress Control Number 2009910405
ISBN 978-0-9825605-1-8

First Edition

That *art thou* . . .

FORGIVING
ARARAT

"*I think it well you follow me and I will be your guide and lead you forth through an eternal place. There you shall see the ancient spirits tried.*"

—Dante, *The Inferno*

I do not remember anymore.

Were my eyes blue like the sky or brown like fresh-tilled earth? Did my hair curl into giggles around my chin or drape over my shoulders in a frown? Was my skin light or dark? Was my body heavy or lean? Did I wear tailored silks or rough cotton and flax?

I do not remember. I remember that I was a woman, which is more than mere recollection of womb and bosom. And for a moment, I remembered all my moments in linear time, which began with womb and bosom and ended there too. But these are fading away now, discarded ballast from a ship emerged from the storm. I do not mourn the loss of any of these; nor am I any longer capable of mourning.

I was named Brek Abigail Cuttler. I have just learned that what *is* is what I knew once as a young child and glimpsed twice in twilight as an adult. I have chosen what is from what is not. And I will always be.

PART ONE

1

I arrived at Shemaya Station after my heart stopped beating and all activity in my brain irreversibly ceased.

This is the medical definition of death, although both the living and, I can assure you, the dead, resent its finality. There's always cause for hope, people argue, and sometimes miracles. I myself used to think this way, but my views have changed. I've discovered, for example, that even if a miracle fails at the final moment to keep you alive, there's still the possibility one will come along later, at the Final Judgment, to keep you from spending the rest of eternity wanting others dead.

I didn't know I had died when I arrived at Shemaya Station, nor did I have any reason to suspect such a thing. Nobody announces that your life's over when it is. As far as I was concerned, my heart was still beating and my brain still functioning; the only hint that something out of the ordinary had happened was that I had no idea where I was or how I'd gotten there. I simply found myself alone on a wooden bench in a deserted urban train station with a high arched dome of corroded girders and trusses and broken glass panels filthy with soot. I had no memory of a train ride, no memory of a destination. A dimly lit board in the middle of the waiting area showed arrival times but no departures, and I assumed, as most who come here do, that the board was broken or there were problems with the outbound tracks.

I sat and stared at the board, waiting for it to flash some piece of information that would give me a clue about where I was or at least where I was going. When the board refused to divulge anything further, I stood and gazed down the tracks, as anxious passengers do, hoping to see some movement or a flicker of light in the distance. The rails vanished into utter darkness, either a tunnel or a black starless night, I could not tell which. I glanced back at the board again and then, forlornly, around the station: ten tracks and ten platforms, all vacant; ticket counter, newsstand, waiting area, shoe shine, all empty. The building was completely quiet: no announcements over the loudspeakers, no whistles blowing, brake shoes screeching, or air compressors shrieking; no conductors shouting, passengers complaining, or panhandling musicians playing. Not even the sound of a janitor sweeping in a far corner of the building.

I sat back down on the bench and noticed I was wearing a black silk skirted suit. The sight of this suit made me feel a little safer and a little less alone. I had been a lawyer during my life, and lawyers always wear suits to feel more confident and less vulnerable. This particular suit was my favorite because it made me feel the most confident and least apologetic as a young woman when I entered the courtroom. I smoothed the skirt on my lap, admiring the heavy weight and rich texture of the fabric and the way it glided over my stockings. It really was a beautiful suit—a suit that attracted glances from colleagues, opposing counsel, and even men on the street; a suit that said I was a lawyer to be taken seriously.

The best part of all was that I had found it on a clearance rack at an outlet store—a power suit *and* a bargain. I loved that suit.

So there I was, sitting all alone on a bench in this deserted train station, infatuated with my black silk suit, when I noticed some small stains on the shoulder and lapel of my jacket. The stains were crusty and yellowish-white, and I assumed I had probably spilled cappuccino on myself earlier in the day. I scratched at the stains with the edge of a polished but chipped fingernail, expecting the aroma of coffee to be released; but a very different scent floated into my consciousness instead: baby formula.

Baby formula? Do I have a child…? Yes, of course…a child…a baby daughter…I remember now. But what's her name? I think it begins with an S…Susan, Sharon, Samantha, Stephanie, Sarah… Sarah? Oh yes, Sarah.

But as hard as I tried, I couldn't remember anything about Sarah's face or hair, or the way she giggled or cried, or the smell of her skin, or the way she might have squirmed when I held her. I remembered only that a child had grown inside of me, had become part of me, and then left to join the world around me— where I could see her and touch her but not protect her the way I did when she was inside me. And yet, even though I couldn't remember anything about my own daughter except her name, I wasn't bothered by this in the least. Sitting there on the bench in Shemaya Station, I was far more worried about the stains on my jacket—terrified somebody would see what I had allowed to happen to my favorite "I belong" black silk suit.

I scraped more vigorously at the stains. When they wouldn't go away, I lapped at my fingertips to moisten them. But instead of disappearing, the stains grew larger and changed in color from yellowish-white to deep wine red. The transformation was subtle at first, like the change from clear afternoon to streaked and pigmented sunset.

*The dye's beginning to run...*that's *why the suit was on the clearance rack.*

But the stains started behaving differently too. They lique-fied, sending crimson streaks down my jacket, skirt, and legs. This fascinated me. I dabbed my fingers in the red fluid, tenta-tively at first, like a child given a jar of paint, then with growing confidence, drawing two little stick figures with it beside me on the bench—a mother and her young daughter. The liquid felt warm and viscous and tasted pleasantly salty when I put a finger to my tongue. A pool of it gathered on the concrete floor of the station, and I slipped off my heels and tapped my toes in it, lost in the creamy sensation.

In the middle of all this, an old man walked up to my bench and sat down beside me.

"Welcome to Shemaya," he said. "My name is Luas."

Luas had moist, gray eyes, as if he were always thinking something poignant, and an annotated, gentle sort of frog's face, flabby and wise like a worn book. The face seemed familiar, and after a moment I recognized it as the face of my mentor, the senior lawyer who had hired me out of law school.

Now what was his name...? Oh yes, Bill, Bill Gwynne. But the old man sitting next to me said his name was Luas, not Bill.

Luas welcomes everybody to Shemaya. He appears differ-ently to each of us, and to each in his own way. He might be an auto mechanic or a teacher to one, a father or a preacher to another, or maybe a madman or all of these combined. In Shemaya, we dress each other up to be exactly who we expect to see. For me, Luas was a composite of the three older men I had adored during my life: he wore a white shirt with a tweed blazer that smelled of rum pipe tobacco, the way my Grandpa Cuttler's clothes smelled; and, as I said, he had Bill Gwynne's flabby face; but when I showed him my feet and my left hand, all covered in red, helpless like a little girl playing in her spaghetti, he flashed my Pop Pop Bellini's knowing smile as if to say: *Yes, my grand-daughter, I see; I see what you're afraid to see, but I'll pretend not to have noticed.*

"Come along, Brek," Luas said. "Let's get you cleaned up."

How did he know my name?

I looked down again, but now my clothes were gone—my black silk suit and cream colored silk blouse, my bra, panties, stockings, and shoes. They had never been there actually. There had been only the idea of clothes, as I was only an idea, defined by who I'd insisted on being during the thirty-one years of my life. Only my body remained, naked and covered with blood. I knew now the red liquid was blood, and that it was my blood, because it was spurting through three small holes in my chest, and because it felt warm and precious the way only blood feels. Suddenly my perspective shifted, and it seemed as though I was watching it all from the opposite bench.

Who is this woman? I wondered. *Why doesn't she put her fin-gers in the holes and stop the bleeding? Why doesn't she call out for help? She's so young and pretty, she must have so much to live for. But just look at her sit there—she does nothing but watch, and she feels nothing but pity: pity for the platelets clotting too late, pity for the parts of her body that had once been the whole; and there—see how her brain flickers, losing reasoning first, then consciousness, con-tracting her muscles to force the blood back to her heart, slowing the beats, slowing the respiration, ordering the mass suicide of millions of cells in a wasted attempt to prolong her life. Listen. The roar of nothingness fills her ears.*

Luas removed his jacket and wrapped it around my shoul-ders. I was crying now, and he hugged me like the granddaugh-ter I might have been. I was crying because I remembered a past that existed before Shemaya Station and Luas, before the baby formula stains and the blood. I remembered my eyes, Irish green like my father's, and my hair, long, thick, Italian black like my mother's. I remembered the empty right sleeves of my clothes: pinned back, folded over, sewn shut. I remembered people wondering—I could see it in their faces—what an eight year old girl could have done to deserve all those empty right sleeves? I remembered wanting to tell them, to remind them, that God punishes children for the sins of their parents.

Yes, for one brief and unbearable moment, I remembered many things when I arrived at Shemaya Station. I remembered crayfish dying in the sun and the cruelty of injustice. I remembered the stench of decaying mushrooms and the inconceivable possibility of forgiveness. I remembered the conveyor chain on my grandfather's manure spreader amputating my right forearm from my elbow and flinging it into the field with the rest of the muck. I remembered the angelic face of my daughter, Sarah, just ten months old, young and fresh and precious like blood. I remembered formula dripping from her bottle down the empty right sleeve of my suit and the pinch of guilt for leaving her at the daycare that morning and the punch of guilt for feeling relieved. I remembered dust on law books and the bitter taste of coffee. I remembered telling my husband I loved him and knowing I did. I remembered picking up my daughter at the end of the day and her squeals of delight when she saw me, and my squeals of delight when I saw her. I remembered singing *Hot Tea and Bees Honey* to her on the way home and wondering what my husband had made for dinner, because he always makes dinner on Fridays. Most of all, I remembered how comfortable life had become for me...and that I would do anything...give anything...*stop at nothing*...to make it last.

And then my memories vanished, as if the plug had been pulled on time. There was just baby formula turned to blood,

everywhere now, all over my face, neck, and stomach, streaming down my elbow and wrist, streaming down the stump of
my right arm, turning red my legs and feet and toes, washing
away my life and spilling it onto Luas, painting us together in an
embrace, soaking through his jacket and shirt, spreading across
his face, pooling onto the floor and clotting into ugly red crumbs
around the edges.

This is how I arrived at Shemaya Station when I died.

And somewhere in the universe, God sighed.

2

Luas led me from the train station to a house not far away. We followed a dirt path through a wood, across pasture, a garden, an apron of lawn. The city I'd imagined beyond the walls of Shemaya Station didn't exist. We were in the country now.

The sky as we walked was moonless, dark violet and iridescent like a pane of stained glass. Luas led me on in silence, supporting me when I stumbled. I was still stunned from seeing myself bleed to death. Every few yards the weather raged between the extremes of hot and cold, wet and dry, as if even the heavens were stunned too and couldn't decide what to be and so were all things at once. I felt no physical pain. In an obscure corner of memory my torso throbbed and my nerves shrieked—but these were distant sensations, recollections more than feelings. More immediate was the dampness of the ground against my feet, the changing temperature of the air on my skin, the opalescence of the earth and trees. These were present sensations and the sum my consciousness could bear.

The house to which Luas led me had a broad porch with a white balustrade and wide green steps. An octagonal lamp hung from the ceiling projecting blocks of light onto the lawn, some of it green and leafy and the rest frozen over with ice and snow. The house reminded me of my great-grandparents' house along the Brandywine River in northern Delaware with the same threatening Victorian turret and gables and pretty scrollwork along the eaves and trim, like so many large homes built in the nineteen twenties. Everything about it was permanent and massive, a bulwark against fate and time: the heavy red brick and fieldstone, the slate roof, the tall windows and ceilings, the thick porch columns and solid brass doorknobs. Even the trees on the lawn and the hills beyond the trees were eternal and massive. It was too dark to see all these things, but I knew they were there in the same way I knew I was there.

On the porch stood an old woman waving excitedly in our direction. Luas squeezed my hand and stiffened to help me up the steps.

"Our guest has finally arrived, Sophia," he announced.

They exchanged polite hugs the way older couples tend to do, and I braced myself for the old woman's shrieks when she realized her husband had brought home a nude woman half his age and covered in blood; but for all the scandal and gore of my appearance, you'd have thought this was the condition in which all her guests arrived. She rushed forward and wrapped herself around me, carelessly staining her blue chamois dress with my blood before peeling herself just far enough away to see my face and caress my cheeks, laughing and sobbing, stroking my hair, her hands shaking with emotion.

"Thank you, thank you, Luas," she said, breathlessly, almost crying.

Luas winked at me and walked back down the steps into the darkness from which we'd come, leaving a trail of bloody shoeprints on the green planks.

They're obviously mad, I thought.

Sophia had an ethnic face, Mediterranean and expressive and proud, with an angular forehead and thin lips that curled like a faded purple ribbon around a box of secrets. Her tarnished silver hair coiled into a bun, and she spoke with an Italian accent that added syllables to the English words.

"Oh, Brek," she whispered. "My precious, precious child."

"Nana?"

The word exhaled from my lungs with a whimper, accompanied by the recollection of an old photograph, the face of my great-grandmother, Sophia Bellini, my Nana. She'd died from a stroke when I was three years old.

"Yes, child, oh yes," she said.

My only memory of her was from our final time together at the funeral home. I'd thrown a tantrum when my mother made me kiss Nana Bellini goodbye in the open coffin. Above my screaming, I remembered a sound, plastic and horrible, produced when my shiny black shoe fell from my foot and landed squarely on Nana's pallid forehead. The shoe bounced once and lodged in her hair like a tiara. I remembered the slap of my mother's hand across my face, and that Nana's eyes did not open, and that her smile, serene and insane, did not change.

"Nana?"

"Yes, child, " she said again, squeezing me close. "Welcome home."

I grinned and pushed myself away.

There comes a moment in every nightmare when disbelief can no longer be suspended and one must choose between waking or allowing the drama to play on, comforted by the thought that it is, after all, only a dream. A nightmare explained

everything that had happened to me: the mysterious train station, the baby formula turned to blood, the holes in my chest,
the appearance of my dead great-grandmother.

I stepped around Nana, the illusion, and ran my fingers along
the white column at the top of the steps. Sure enough, there
were my initials—B.A.C.—carved with an eight penny nail one
August afternoon when I sat on the porch drinking iced tea and
wondering whether summer would ever end and middle school
would finally begin. The scent of mothballs and garlic wafting
from the kitchen was as distinct to my grandparents' home as
the scent of lilacs to late spring. The screen door chirped twice
as it had always done, and our family pictures were arranged on
the dry sink in the hall: Nana and my great-grandpa Frank, my
grandparents and my great-uncle Gus and his wife, my mother
as a little girl and her brothers and cousins—me as an infant and
a teen, with and without a right arm.

"I'm dreaming," I said to Nana. "What an odd dream."

A smile crossed her face, the same knowing smile that had
crossed Luas' in the train shed, as if to say: *Yes, my great-granddaughter, I understand. You're not ready to accept your own death
yet, so we must pretend.*

"Is it a lovely dream?" she asked.

"No. It's a scary one, Nana," I said. "I'm dead in it and you…
you're here, but you're dead too."

"But isn't that a lovely dream, dear?" she asked. "To know
that death isn't the end of everything?"

"Yes, that is lovely," I said. "I'll try to remember it when I
wake up, and I'll try to remember you too. I can never seem to
remember your face, Nana; I was too young when you died."

Nana smiled at me, amused.

"My, this is such a long dream," I said, stretching and yawning. "I feel like I've been dreaming all night. But that's a good

thing. It means I'm sleeping well. I'm so tired, Nana. I want to sleep some more, but I don't want to be scared. I want this to be a nice dream now. Can we make it a nice dream so I won't have to wake up and chase you away?"

"Yes, dear," Nana said, hugging me again. "We can make this a nice dream. We can make this the nicest dream you've ever had."

She led me upstairs without another word, drew me a bath in the claw-footed iron tub off the main hall, and hung a thick terry cloth robe from the door. The dream was improving already. Before leaving me to soak, she paused to look at the stump of my right arm. Even though the accident happened after her death, she seemed neither shocked nor saddened by it, just curious, as though she were studying a cubist painting for the meaning of a missing limb. I smiled, as I always did when someone noticed the amputation, to put her ease. She kissed my forehead and closed the door.

Although the bleeding had stopped, I flushed red water from the tub and refilled it several times. There were three holes in my chest: one in my sternum and two through my left breast. I fingered each hole indifferently, as though I were merely touching a blemish. I could feel the soft tissue inside—torn, fatty, and swollen—and jagged edges of broken bone. My lungs expanded and contracted, sucking on my finger like a straw. I took none of this seriously. Doubting Thomas had probed the holes in Jesus' hands and come away convinced, but the effect on me was just the opposite. I knew now I had to be dreaming.

I wrapped myself in the robe Nana left for me behind the door and crept through the second floor of the old house, resurrecting memories both pleasant and sad. There was the happy photograph in the master bedroom of Nana and great-grandpa Frank posing before the Teatro Alla Scala on their thirtieth wedding anniversary. One month later, great-grandpa Frank confessed to having escorted his mistress to the very same opera house while on a business trip to Milan. Nana somehow overcame her humiliation and anger and offered him the forgiveness he sought; in return, on the papered wall between the windows, great-grandpa Frank hung a large crucifix with a large Christ whose mournful eyes watched over his side of the bed as a reminder. A heart attack took him the following year.

My grandparents moved into the house after Nana's death and their belongings now filled the room, but the crucifix remained: alert, watchful, reminding. It was really their house I remembered, not Nana's. Beneath the cross stood a small bookcase filled with hard bound volumes by Locke, Jefferson, and Oliver Wendell Holmes, and lesser treatises on contracts and procedure. They were my grandfather's law books, and after the accident with my arm and the lawsuit that followed, I began to look upon their impressive leather bindings and heft with a sort of reverence and awe. The pursuit of justice seemed to me a more noble and honest religion than the one I heard preached each Sunday in church; my grandfather's law books contained the sacred texts and liturgies of that religion, making the words of the Bible seem puny and childish by comparison. I was proud my grandfather owned them, and I read them over and over, understanding a little more each time. I ignored the things in the room that would have attracted most girls: my grandmother's collection of Limoges boxes and silver hair brushes, her treasure of costume jewelry, perfumes, and shoes. She would shake her head when she found me paging through the books and tell me to run along because young ladies shouldn't waste their time studying law.

Next door, my Uncle Anthony's room was a time capsule sealed in nineteen sixty-eight, the year after Nana died. In some of the black and white photographs on the walls he's slumped against a howitzer, the strain of fear and fatigue twisting his face into a haunted smile. In other photographs his eyes are glassy and unfocussed, the muscles of his face sagging in a narcotic stupor that everyone in the family insisted was some rare form of jungle fever but that I knew was either marijuana or heroin. Dog tags and a crucifix with the right arm broken off hung from a chain around his neck in these photos. The only color photograph in the room was taken two years prior to these. In this photograph, First Lieutenant Anthony Bellini stands gallant and brave in full dress uniform next to an American flag. My grandparents kept this picture on the dresser beside the dog tags, the broken crucifix, and the sad blue triangle of cloth presented to them at Uncle Anthony's funeral. I loved that broken crucifix: Jesus was missing the same arm as me and, when I touched it, I believed he somehow understood. Uncle Anthony died before I was born; when I asked about him I was told only that he was a hero and the subject was quickly changed.

The bedroom across the hall belonged first to my grandfather's brother, Gus, and, next, to Uncle Alex before he shipped out to Vietnam two years after Uncle Anthony. Uncle Alex returned in one piece from the war, so my grandparents had no need to create a second shrine. Instead, they used the room to store broken chairs, boxes, and clutter that couldn't find a home in the rest of the house.

My mother was the oldest of the three Bellini children. After she married, her room became the guest room, but they kept her things. The bed was white, with a dingy canopy I detested; a pair of ragged old dolls sat glumly against the pillows, yearning for affection and needing a bath. The lacy curtains she had sewn from an old tablecloth decorated the windows, and at the foot of the bed sat a pine hope chest filled with silly letters and pleated skirts and photographs of horses and kittens. It was a little girl's room, and, in many ways, my mother remained a little girl all her life. Her room was way up high in the turret where a princess would sleep—an oval-shaped refuge protected from robbers and dragons with small windows facing the front and side of the house. Mom and I lived here for an entire year after she divorced my father; I slept next to her every night in the same bed. We ate popcorn and read books, and sometimes she cried herself to sleep. I was the grownup in that bed, and this made me feel safe. Grownups were always safe.

After my bath, I had intended to dress and go back downstairs to talk to Nana, but I suddenly felt drowsy and weak, as though I were descending within my dream into a deeper level of sleep. I succumbed to the urge, sliding with the dolls beneath the crisp cotton ticking of my mother's bed and turning out the white unicorn lamp. I fell fast asleep. During this sleep, I began dreaming of my last day on earth.

3

It's early morning and I'm nursing Sarah in bed with the television on. We're watching her daddy in his first month as the new anchorman of the Channel 10 Morning News, trying to make cunning chit-chat with Piper Jackson, Channel 10's incredibly dull but incredibly beautiful new weather girl. Regardless of atmospheric conditions, Piper's tight skirts and blouses guarantee fair skies and high pressure. Bo and Piper make a picture-perfect couple on the set and smiling down together from the slick, new billboards along the highways that have helped increase ratings for the show ten-fold. I seethe with jealousy every morning—until Piper opens her mouth. Today, while talking with Bo about a tsunami that has just devastated the northern coast of Japan, she mispronounces it "samurai" and speculates that this must be how Japanese warriors got their name. Bo cringes.

"It's pronounced sue-na-me, Piper," he says, wincingly.

Piper looks bewildered, like a puppy hit with a newspaper for peeing on a rug.

"What is?" she asks.

"The Japanese word for tidal wave."

"Oops," she replies airily, her strawberry red lips ripening from scolded-girl pout into naughty-girl smile. "Well, I guess that explains why they call Japanese warriors tsunamis."

The cameraman knows exactly what to do. The shot widens to take in her low-cut top and admittedly impressive cleavage. You can almost hear the spontaneous applause of men all over central Pennsylvania and the spontaneous groans of their wives, girlfriends, and mothers. I pleaded with Bo to stick to reporting the news, but Piper and her breasts were bigger and better than the news; advertising revenue at the station increased in direct proportion to the number of minutes she was on screen and the amount of chest she exposed.

Sarah finishes nursing, oblivious to TV ratings, tsunamis, and samurais, perfectly content to see a miniature of her father talking from a box on the dresser no matter what he says. Sometimes she tries to talk back, as though they're having a conversation.

I shower quickly, planning as I scrub where to pick up with the summary judgment motion I'd been working on and sticking my head out to be sure Sarah's still on the bed. When the network news replaces her daddy at seven, we switch to Big Bird and I finish applying my makeup and put on my cream silk blouse and black silk suit. I carry Sarah into the nursery and change her diaper, dressing her in a light cotton jumper before switching to pants and a sweatshirt after remembering Piper's warning that a cold front will be moving through late in the day. Sarah's hands swing over her head and she stares at them in astonishment, as though she's seeing them for the first time, a pair of birds from nowhere, soaring and swooning to the music whispering through her tiny mind. With all my might I try to store this moment away—the wide fascination of her eyes and the delicate contractions of her fingers, the sunlight that celebrates her revelation, the polished perfection of skin on her belly—all locked up in my memory like a jewel in a safe deposit box to be taken out later and adored.

I drive Sarah to a daycare operated by Juniata College as a teaching practicum; it's an excellent facility, bright, cheery, and clean, with bright professors and students eager to try the latest methods and techniques for developing infant minds. The classes are small and Sarah never lacks for stimulation or attention; she's always laughing and playing and her pediatrician says her verbal and cognitive skills are advanced for her age (although I think he says this to every parent to keep them coming back). When I visit during the day, I'm convinced she's better off here than if I cared for her at home; but when I kiss her goodbye in the morning and she waves her little hands and looks after me with those sad brown eyes, I wonder whether I'm fooling myself—or whether I'm worse off even if she isn't. It's a debate I have with myself in the parking lot every morning but that I always resolve in favor of her exposure to other children and adults instead of being trapped all alone with one crazy woman in the same house day after day the way I was raised. While unbuckling her from her car seat, she flips her bottle upside down and deliberately squirts formula on the shoulder and lapel of my jacket.

"Hey, stop that!" I say, pretending to be angry. "Nobody messes on mommy's favorite suit, not even a cutie like you."

I reach the office by eight-thirty and wave to frog-faced Bill Gwynne, who's already on the phone with a client and whose desk, restored to order by his secretary last evening, is already a mess. Our offices occupy a historic red brick row house next to the county courthouse in Huntingdon, Pennsylvania, used first as a blacksmith's shop at the time the town was founded in the late 1700s and decorated with period antiques. I toss my briefcase and purse into my office on the second floor, pour a cup of coffee, and head up to our small law library on the third floor where I continue the legal research I've been working on for the past four weeks, trying to come up with a defense that will allow our very wealthy—and very lucrative—client, Alan Fleming, to avoid repaying the $500,000 he borrowed from a bank. This might seem like a fool's errand, if not a little unscrupulous, but it's actually my favorite part of legal practice: the intellectual challenge of winning a case that most lawyers would, and should, lose, by uncovering an overlooked fact, finding a forgotten law, or creating a novel legal argument from the thousands of statutes, regulations, and cases that constitute American jurisprudence—all to arrive at what we think of as *justice*—which, like it or not, has been defined for centuries not as the divine balancing of equities but as what the rule of law requires when applied, without bias, to the facts—and explains why the robed lady holding scales in front of the courthouse wears a blindfold. Otherwise, the theory holds, we would have favoritism and chaos rather than law and order.

This particular morning, the blind lady of justice bestows upon me a generous gift in the form of a little-known federal banking regulation from the Great Depression called Regulation U that forbids banks from making loans used to purchase securities if the securities pledged as collateral are worth less than fifty percent of the debt. The regulation was intended to prevent stock market crashes from taking the banking system down with them, but it catches my eye because Alan purchased stocks with the loan he'd defaulted on and, as I recall, pledged stocks worth only thirty-five percent of the debt—which is why the bank is now suing him for the balance. If the loan officer knew at the time he made the loan that Alan was using the proceeds to buy stocks, the bank violated the regulation by not demanding more collateral. I research further. The blind lady of justice bestows a second gift upon me in the form of a companion statute stating that if the bank violates Regulation U, it's prohibited from suing the borrower to collect the debt. In other words, a bank error excuses Alan Fleming from repaying the half million dollars he borrowed, and the bank's case against him must be dismissed. I slap the table with my hand in triumph and clench my fist. "Yes!" I shout. I feel like a football player stopped cold at the one yard line but who scores a touchdown anyway because he extends the tip of the ball across the front edge of the goal line. It's a technical argument and arguably unfair—just as extending the tip of the ball across the goal line is only a technical touchdown and arguably unfair—but the rules of the game are the rules of the game and a touchdown is a touchdown. I race back down to my office for the transcript of the deposition I took of the bank's loan officer, Jorge Mijares, to see whether he knew about Alan's intention to buy stocks with the loan.

The transcript comprises several hundred pages of testimony given under oath before a court reporter with each line of testimony numbered for easy reference. Scanning through it, I recall how, like most of the male witnesses I had confronted during my short legal career, Jorge Mijares had refused to take me seriously from the moment he was sworn in by the court reporter. That I could be a young woman, handicapped, and an attorney at the same time was inconceivable to him; that I could have delivered a baby six months earlier, and would need to adjourn the deposition to pump breast milk, was a shock from which he never fully recovered. With all the dignity and splendor his perfumed Latin masculinity could summon, Jorge wished for me to know that things are not done so in his native Chile, where women are spared the vulgarities of law and business. Jorge had emigrated to Huntingdon at the age of ten when his father accepted a professorship in anthropology at the college. He and his family returned often to their native land and maintained their Chilean accent and customs. Their dark, handsome conquistador faces and exotic voices made them a delicious curiosity in the very white, very rural, very conservative Borough of Huntingdon, population: 15,000.

On page one hundred and fifty-five of the transcript, I locate the testimony I've been hoping for—the testimony that destroys the bank's case:

> Q. Do you know why my client wanted the loan, Mr. Mijares?
>
> A. Well, you see Ms. Cuttler—you know, such formality makes me so uncomfortable. May I call you Brek, dear?
>
> Q Oh, yes, please do, Mr. Mijares. You are so very kind to ask.
>
> A. There it is again, Stephen, that look. Did you see it?

Stephen was the bank's lawyer, Stephen Russ, and Mr. Mijares was commenting to him about the way I had allowed my eyes to linger over his face and my lips to spread into a capricious smile before covering my mouth with my hand as though I were a school girl swooning in the presence of a teen idol. It was the third time I had done it that afternoon. This was not a sign of a weakening of my marital fidelity: I was not in the least bit attracted to Jorge Mijares, and I certainly wasn't thinking of cheating on my husband. This was, instead, my strategy for coaxing Mr. Mijares to answer my questions. I had discovered that rather than resent and resist the arrogance of men like this, I could more easily defeat them by flirting with them and using their prejudices against them; their unbounded conceit inevitably led them to become distracted and careless—and to say more on the record than they intended. This may have made me no better than Piper Jackson, but at least I knew the difference between a tsunami and a samurai. In any event, Stephen Russ, the bank's lawyer, saw what was coming and knew that his client—a well-known womanizer—was in deep trouble; he rubbed his sunken gray temples as though he were hoping a genie would pop out of his head and make it all go away.

Q. I'm sorry, Mr. Mijares. Please continue.

A. Thank you, dear. And, please, call me Jorge. You know, I simply must say this. You remind me, Miss Brek, of a statue at one of our most famous museums in Santiago. It is of a young princess beseeching the moon. She is, how do you say it…? Ravished? No, no…ravishing. And do you know, forgive me, the arm is missing and this makes her all the more alluring.

Q. Oh, my, how you flatter me, Mr. Mijares. I see now why you're such a powerful and well respected man in this community. Alan warned me that if I wasn't careful, you would end up deposing me. But we should continue or we will be together all night. [Jorge's eyes widened when I said this, like a child tempted with a piece of candy.] These business dealings are so confusing for a woman. I hope you can help explain them to me. Alan wanted to buy stocks with the loan, is that right?

A. Now who is flattering whom, Miss Brek? Yes, of course, I will help you with these things. It is very simple, really. You see, Alan told me he had a tip from his broker and wanted to buy some stocks, but he was a little overextended at the time and needed to finance the purchase...excuse me, do you know what I mean by "finance"? You know, to pay over time, just as you would use your husband's credit card to buy yourself a nice dress or something? You see? It's all the same thing, it's not so difficult. He wanted to buy the stocks on credit and we gave him the loan. Alan and I have done business together many years. Until this unfortunate incident, he had been a very good customer.

In truth, neither Jorge Mijares nor I understood the significance of his testimony at the time; but Stephen Russ, who had represented the bank for many years and knew all the banking regulations, understood all too well; he jolted forward in his chair as though the building across the street had just exploded and immediately asked for a recess. I thought maybe his lunch didn't agree with him and he needed to use the bathroom, but I was happy for the break because damp spots were beginning to form on my blouse and I needed to pump. And so, while Stephen Russ squeezed the bad news from his client in one room, a small battery-operated milking machine squeezed the milk from my breasts in another. I kept up this torture and humiliation for a couple of months after returning to work from giving birth to Sarah before switching, mercifully, to baby formula most of the time; I read all the studies saying breast milk is best—and I believed those studies and did my best for as long as I could— but I was a lawyer, not a milk cow; I had survived on formula and so could she.

Back in my own office now a few months later, I finally realize that Jorge's testimony is fatal to the bank's case and cinches our defense. I take the transcript and the regulation over to Bill's office and lay them on the last open patch of mahogany on his desk. He's buried in a file and doesn't look up as he speaks.

"Yes?" he grumbles.

Bill's always irritable in the morning, and this morning even more so because he's preparing for hearings in two cases at once; his large frog's eyes dart from file to file as if hunting insects, fingers snapping at the papers like a sticky tongue. He's wearing a conservative gray suit and matching vest, white shirt, and maroon tie. He's old school and never takes off his jacket in the office, even in the middle of the summer.

"Read it," I say proudly.

"Why?"

"Because it's how we're going to win a case we're supposed to lose."

He glances up at the regulation. "What's this got to do with anything?"

"Alan used the loan to buy stocks and pledged stocks as collateral. Regulation U says the stocks had to be worth at least fifty percent of the loan. Alan's stocks were worth only thirty-five. Mijares testified he knew. The loan's void and unenforceable as a matter of law. We win."

The frog eyes dilate and the fingers snatch the transcript from the desk. There's silence as Bill reads the testimony, then he starts laughing. "Jorge got a little carried away with himself, didn't he?"

"He's very charming," I reply.

Bill puts down the transcript, picks up the regulation and reads it. "He won't be so charming when he finds out you outfoxed him in the deposition," Bill says. "I'm glad to see you know how to handle men like that…. By the way, I've seen the statue he's talking about; I went to Santiago when I represented the grape growers in the cyanide case."

"You handled that case, too?" I ask, always amazed at Bill's remarkable legal career. I was in college during the public scare over red Chilean table grapes being laced with cyanide; when the news stories broke warning people not to eat them, my dorm roommate promptly started snacking on them by the bunches. She hated red grapes but her boyfriend had just broken up with her; she said she didn't have the courage to slit her own wrists and figured grapes would be the easier way to go.

"I thought you only represented plaintiffs back then, not defendants," I say.

"The growers were the plaintiffs," Bill replies. "There was no cyanide. The scare was a hoax but the Chilean farmers lost everything—thousands of tons of fruit was embargoed and destroyed. Jorge's father, Professor Mijares, asked me to take the case; the Mijares still own vineyards in Chile. We sued the government to lift the embargo and we sued the insurers to pay the claims."

Outside the window beside Bill's desk, the morning sun strikes the bright yellow fall leaves of a maple tree, making the tree appear as though it has burst into flame. A small sparrow lands on a branch, risking immolation.

"There's an interesting myth behind that statue," Bill continues. "Legend has it that when the princess was a young girl, the king forced her to eat her vegetables. To spite him, she shoved the arm she used to hold her fork under a millstone and it was crushed. Now she pleads with the heavens for forgiveness."

I consider this strange tale for a moment. "I think the heavens should plead for her forgiveness," I say.

Bill arches his bushy eyebrows. "The king only made her eat her vegetables, Brek; he didn't force her to marry the old pervert running the kingdom next door."

"What law says she has to eat her vegetables?"

Bill smiles and shakes his head. "Let's have this conversation again when Sarah turns six." He waves the regulation at me. "Any cases on point?"

"None," I say, but I'm unwilling to drop my defense of the one-armed princess just yet; I know how much she's suffered and how she's been judged by every person who sees her, because it's human nature to assume that another person's misfortune must be some form of divine retribution. "You know," I say, "maybe it had nothing to do with eating vegetables. Maybe her father was ignoring her and she was just trying to get his attention."

Bill doesn't respond and an awkward silence follows. I realize I'm rubbing the stump of my own right arm and he's watching me. The bird in the maple flies away having survived the inferno.

"When can you finish the brief?" he asks.

"Rough draft by Tuesday."

He puts down the regulation and starts in on one of the files in front of him. "I'll be in court all afternoon and then I have a board meeting," he says. "Have a nice weekend."

"Thanks. You too." I gather my materials and get up to leave.

"It's a creative argument," he says without looking up. "Few lawyers would have thought of it."

"Regulation U or the princess?" I ask.

"Both."

I turn to leave but stop. I'm gratified by the rare compliment but suddenly remorseful about the outcome. "So, Alan Fleming keeps five hundred thousand dollars that don't belong to him because of a technicality?"

The frog's mouth frowns as if the insect it has just swallowed tastes bitter. "Yes, and with any luck this afternoon I'll put an arsonist back on the street. But next week I'll have an innocent man freed on the same technicality, and a legal technicality will win an injunction against the landfill that's discharging dioxin and killing all the bass in Raystown Lake. You can't have one without the other, Brek; justice wears a blindfold because she isn't supposed to see who's loading the scales."

"Or with what."

Bill ignores my wisecrack and goes back to his work.

"See you Monday," I say.

4

I return to my office and begin outlining my summary judgment brief on a legal pad, stopping to look outside at the pale green film of the Juniata River dappled with the reflection of scarlet and jasmine leaves on the trees, each a unique frame of autumn. Bill's right. I've done nothing wrong; in fact, I've done my job perfectly. The system is working exactly as designed, which is more than can be said for the system that maimed the princess in Santiago—or the system that allows someone like Piper Jackson to do weather forecasts. Which reminds me to telephone Bo at the studio.

"Hi," he says. "I was just getting ready to call you."

I yawn, rather loudly and unexpectedly. "Wow," I say, "sorry about that. It's been a long morning.... So what's the latest? Did they ever catch that samurai warrior who attacked the northern coast of Japan? I heard he did a lot of damage."

"Very funny," he says.

"Sounds like he really *sakéd* the coast."

Bo groans. "I've heard that one three times already this morning—interestingly, all from women. You people can be so jealous and mean—or you just love making puns out of rice wine. How did Sarah's drop-off go?"

"You people? Jealous and mean? She's a babbling idiot! How can you stand her?"

Bo hesitates, pretending he's trying hard to find a reason. I know he likes her even though she's an embarrassment. Finally he says, as though helpless before an irresistible force: "Well, she does have beautiful…weather forecasts."

"You're a pig, Boaz," I respond. He hates it when I call him by his first name. His parents named him Boaz after King David's great-grandfather and the American soldier who rescued his mother's family from the Nazis during World War II. "With all the money the little weather tart is bringing into the station, you'd think they could find her some clothes that fit and maybe arrange to give her another shot at elementary school since the first time didn't seem to take. Sarah was fine. She spilled formula all over my suit."

"She loves doing that. I'm on my way to Harrisburg. Holden Hurley is being sentenced this afternoon. They want me to cover it since I broke the story."

My secretary, Barbara, sticks her head in to tell me Alan Fleming's on the line. I tell her to take a message. "When will you be home?"

"Around six unless things get crazy," Bo answers. "I should still be able to fix dinner."

"What are we having?"

"Any requests?"

I start glancing over the outline of my summary judgment brief again and don't hear his question.

"Hello?" he says. "Food? Any ideas? I can tell you're working on something."

"What? Yeah…the brief in the Fleming case. Sorry. No, I can't think of anything, whatever you want."

"Hurley's skinhead buddies from The Eleven will be protesting at the courthouse. Did you shave yours this morning?"

"No, but I'm very cute bald," I reply. "You've seen my baby pictures."

"You know," Bo says, baiting me because Bill and I are members of the American Civil Liberties Union, "I value free speech as much as the next guy, particularly because I'm a reporter, but rallies advocating the subjugation of ethnic groups go a little too far, don't you think? Why should they have the right to use public property to incite hatred and violence?"

I lose my train of thought and have to go back to the top of the outline.

"Really, I want to know," Bo presses, actually sounding agitated. "How can you defend them?"

"We've been through this before," I explain. "It's fascinating how you liberal Jews suddenly get conservative when the subject is anti-Semitism."

"Hurley's not just any anti-Semite; he diverted public school funds to finance a white supremacist group intent on starting a race war. Would you defend a group of men who come out to demonstrate in favor of legitimizing and encouraging gang rape?"

"Oh, you mean the financial industry…? Look, I would be among the first to organize a counter-protest to shout them down; but, yes, I would defend their right to say it. Who decides what speech is okay and what speech is forbidden? Using your theory, Jews should be banned from demonstrating in favor of Israel because Israel subjugates the Palestinians. That it's a state instead of a small group of extremists is only a matter of degree. Your mother lived through the Holocaust and even she thinks anti-Semites have the right to express themselves. Maybe you should listen to her once in a while."

"My mother's biased. And crazy. She tells everybody you're a better Jew than I am because you went to Rosh Hashanah and Yom Kippur services with her this year. Do you have any idea how difficult you're making life for me?"

"I like challah bread. Besides, it's the Day of Judgment and the Final Appeal; there's nowhere else a lawyer would rather be: the most important cases before the highest court in the universe and lots of desperate clients willing to pay anything to get off. For lawyers, Rosh Hashanah and Yom Kippur are like the Olympics, Super Bowl, World Series, World Cup, and Stanley Cup all rolled into one."

Bo muffles the phone and I hear him talking to someone.

"Sorry," he says, "the crew's waiting for me in the van. I've gotta get going. When are you finishing tonight?"

"Around six."

"You're pushing it kind of close with the daycare, don't you think? Even with two salaries I don't know how much longer we can afford the five dollar per minute penalty for picking her up late. At some point, they're going to kick her out and then what will we do?"

"Don't worry about it, I'll be there on time."

"Okay. Bye. I love you."

"Have fun. I love you, too."

I hang up and look at the photograph on my shelf of Bo and me at his sister, Lisa's, wedding. He's wearing a yarmulke and looks so sweet and happy.

I had actually assumed Rosh Hashanah, the Jewish New Year, would be a festive and gay celebration, like New Year's Day, but it turned out to be just the opposite—brooding and ominous, the day God judges the lives we've lived during the previous year. The *shofar* blasts calling the congregation to worship inside the synagogue were terrifying—the voice of God condemning the entire human race—but the liturgy for the day, the *Musaf tefillah*, had the effect of reaffirming my belief that God and justice are inseparable and one, and that as a lawyer trained in pursuing justice I had an inside track on redemption.

Still gazing at the photograph and recalling the Days of Awe, as the ten days between Rosh Hashanah and Yom Kippur are known, I acknowledge to myself for the first time that I married a Jew for the same reason I had become a lawyer: to be closer to justice. I suppose I had always known this, but I concealed it from myself and from my Irish-Italian Catholic family—who were not particularly pleased with my selection of a mate, but not unbending either. In arguing with them that I loved Bo as a man and that religion shouldn't matter, I had been less than completely honest; religion did matter—very much so—just not in the way they were thinking. For a Catholic girl raised in a community of fundamentalist Protestants, Bo's Jewish heritage, with its stories of struggle and heroism and promise of being chosen by God, glittered like an exotic jewel; I found myself attracted to him in the same way I would have found myself attracted to a rock star, an actor, or a professional athlete—because he could give me inner access to a rare and alien world and the status in life I desired. I fell in love with Bo Wolfson for all the normal and best reasons—because he was incredibly handsome, wonderful, sensitive, and caring, a man who made me feel special, loved, and complete, and who even accepted my disability as a charming attribute rather than a cause for fear and revulsion. It's just that his religion made the package, for me, irresistible. The Catholic Church and Jesus' teaching of turning the other cheek—which, to me, formed the bedrock of Christianity—made no sense in a world filled with warfare and violence, a world filled with people like Holden Hurley, a world that allowed an eight year old girl to lose her right arm. I thought Moses had it right with "an eye for an eye and a tooth for a tooth;" this rule better reflected my personal experience and understanding of the way the things worked. I sometimes thought I was a Jew trapped in a Christian's body, like one of those poor souls who believes they're a woman trapped in a man's body or vice-versa; only in my case I was not a transsexual but rather a "transspiritual." Marrying Bo enabled me to experiment safely with being a member of the opposite religion without having the theological equivalent of a sex-change operation—a full religious conversion.

I focus now on the yarmulke Bo wears in the photograph—the universal symbol of Judaism, which suddenly recalls for me, as a Gentile, not the blessings of a chosen relationship with God but the horrors of five thousand years of tragedy—and I feel frightened. I think of Bo's mother, Katerine Schrieberg, at the age of seventeen fleeing through the German woods with her family, wondering whether they would survive the night. I think of Bo's grandfather, Jared Schrieberg, who died in those woods, and of the heiress, Amina Rabun, whom Bill and I sued for reparations on behalf of the Schriebergs because her family made their fortune by constructing the incinerators at Auschwitz and robbing the Schriebergs of their Dresden home and movie theaters. I think of Holden Hurley and The Eleven, trying to re-ignite the hatred of the Nazis and, perhaps, the incinerators. I imagine how it would feel to be hunted and murdered across the centuries. Am I brave enough to bear that pain? Do I want it for my daughter? And then, I wonder whether my name was sealed in the Book of Life or the Book of Death at nightfall on Yom Kippur.

I go back to my summary judgment brief, working through lunch and stopping only when I realize I have ten minutes to get to the daycare to avoid the dreaded five dollar per minute fine. When I arrive, Sarah is the last child there, gumming a Nilla Wafer into a sticky brown paste on her face and watching a videotape of *Barney the Dinosaur*. The shame of being the last mother to pick up her child spoils my joy at seeing her. She's covered with dull red paint stains, all over her little sweatshirt and sweatpants, hands, neck, and face. She toddles toward me as fast as she can, arms outstretched, smiling and cooing. I kneel down. Miss Erin, the day care intern from the college, grins.

"Hi baby girl," I say to Sarah, sweeping her up into my arm and kissing her face, inhaling the sweetness of her hair. I look up at Miss Erin. "How was she today?"

"Great," Miss Erin says. "She's been a very good girl."

Miss Erin is a junior at the college and has definitely found her calling. She looks like a cartoon come to life with two small black dots for eyes, thin sticks for arms and legs, and freckled cheeks framed by long ropes of braided orange hair; she wears a trademark yellow smock with the sun embroidered on it. She *loves* little kids, and they love her.

"Sorry about the mess," Miss Erin says. "I'm going to miss her so much. She was my favorite."

"Are you leaving?" I ask, assuming from her response that she won't be seeing Sarah again.

"Well, I am going home for the night," she replies, puzzled by my question.

"But when you just said you were going to miss her and she was your favorite…. I guess you meant for the weekend."

Miss Erin looks at me strangely and gives Sarah a kiss. "Goodbye sweetie," she says. "I love you."

Sarah gives Miss Erin a peck on the cheek.

"Thanks for taking good care of her," I say, grabbing Sarah's bag of nearly empty milk bottles and art projects and glancing over her activity sheet for the day. "Have a nice weekend."

I carry Sarah out to the car, buckle her in, and slip a cassette of *Hot Tea and Bees Honey* into the tape player. As we drive away, I glance at Sarah in the rearview mirror and ask her how her day went. She pretends to answer with cooing and babbling sounds.

We stop at a convenience store on the way home to buy milk. The parking lot is empty. An autumn breeze freshens the car when I open the door. It's not even six-thirty yet but it's already dark as midnight. I unbuckle Sarah from her car seat. She reaches for my hair and I tease her by tilting away; she giggles, exposing a single tooth; her hair falls into her eyes, dark and full of curls like her daddy's. Carrying her across the parking lot, I'm humming the song we had been listening to on the cassette.

We enter the store and head for the dairy case in the back. I have to juggle her with one arm as I pick up a half gallon of milk; she giggles at nearly falling. We turn and head back toward the counter through the pastry aisle. Sarah reaches out with her tiny hand and knocks a row of cupcakes onto the floor. As I stoop to pick them up, the overpowering smell of decaying mushrooms fills the air. How strange, I think. I turn to locate the source but, suddenly, find myself back at Shemaya Station, on the bench beneath the rusting steel dome. Sarah's gone. I'm sitting next to Luas, covered in my own blood.

5

Dead people doubt the finality of their own deaths. We either don't believe it's happened or we hope for some miracle to change it. We learn to accept it only gradually, at our own pace and on our own terms; but this creates confusion, because we extend the torn fragments of our lives into the open wound of the afterlife, grafting the two together. For sensitive souls—the souls of saints and poets who lived their lives in the knowledge that truth exists only in the spiritual world—the transition to Shemaya might seem perfectly seamless and immediate; but for the rest of us, including people like me, who placed their faith in logic and reason and what could be measured with instruments and seen with our own two eyes, the transition from life to death takes much longer. We resist, deny, and explain away our mortality at every turn. Thus, the very first thing we forget when we die is how it happened, or, more accurately, this is the very first thing we choose not to remember, because to remember such a momentous event is to concede the inconceivable.

The next morning, which was my first morning in Shemaya, I awoke to the smell of coffee and cinnamon. These were the aromas I'd become accustomed to on Saturday mornings during my life, and as far as I was concerned this was just another Saturday morning. Bo would get up early for a jog and bring breakfast home from the bakery, slipping quietly out of the house and returning with a bag full of sticky buns and other goodies. I loved him for this. While he was gone, it was my privilege and vice to linger in bed with my eyes closed, drowsy, warm, and contented beneath the covers. That morning in Shemaya, I lingered in bed just this way, in the blissful state on the border of sleep, unable to discern the meaning of the bizarre dreams about the train station, Luas, and my great-grandmother, trying to commit them to memory before they dissolved into the noise and distractions of a new day. *What was it she said that I wanted to remember...? I'd forgotten already. Dreams can be illusive that way.* The house was quiet, Sarah still asleep. The surreal images from the night and the possibilities of the day floated through my mind like fireflies and I chased after some and let others get away. It would be a beautiful autumn weekend. Friends had invited us on a hike up Tussey Mountain and later to an apple orchard for cider and a hayride; Sarah would fall asleep in her backpack to the rhythm of Bo's steps; there were leaves to rake, floors to vacuum, and groceries to buy. And, I'd have to return to the office for a few hours on Sunday to work on my brief.

The thought of winning Alan Fleming's case was the brightest firefly on the lawn of my mind and off I went. Lying there in bed, I considered the possibility that I might just be turning into a good lawyer after all—despite being a woman and a mother and having only one arm to carry a briefcase and shake hands. What a wonderful feeling to wake up to. I reanalyzed Regulation U and the cases in my mind and outlined the sub-arguments;

I thought again about the hike and the hayride and breakfast, and chased away doubts about the fairness of my client keeping money that didn't belong to him; by that time I realized I'd completely forgotten the dreams and Nana, and that it was time to get up and nurse Sarah.

I pushed back the covers and opened my eyes. There was blood everywhere, all over the sheets and my body; I screamed and jumped out of bed, banging my head against a post that didn't belong in my bedroom—the white post of my mother's canopy bed in my grandparents' house in Delaware. *How clever,* I thought, rubbing my head and trying to calm myself down. *I've awakened from the second dream but not the first.*

I went to the window facing the front of the house and peeked outside. Only a dream could explain what I saw. Half of my grandparents' estate glowed golden, orange, and umber in the fading colors of autumn, while the other half shimmered in the fluorescent greens and pastels of spring. Sunflowers wilted and pumpkins ripened at one end of the garden as daffodils and tulips blossomed at the other. Red squirrels gathered acorns among robins searching for earthworms; two flocks of noisy Canada geese flew by overhead, one going south and the other north, separated by a dissonant zone in between where a fierce winter blizzard exhausted itself beneath a scorching August sun. I marveled at the merging seasons, struck by the enormity of their compression in space and time. It explained the hot and cold, wet and dry I'd experienced walking up to the house with Luas the night before; yet the more I stared into the continuum, the more it acquired the unfocussed *Wizard of Oz* quality of an illusion in two dimensions cast on a screen: the squirrels and geese made the same series of motions; leaves swayed in repeating patterns; squalls unleashed by the blizzard swirled in a constant velocity vortex.

Nana must have heard my scream; she entered the room without knocking, dressed in her pajamas and a flower print bathrobe. Through the hall window behind her, the faint gray shadows of dawn dissolved into a morning blue sky streaked orange with the rays of four different suns rising over the Brandywine Valley through the prism of four different seasons and merging into one brilliant fiery ball. It was beautiful.

"Are you ok, dear?" she asked with concern in her voice.

"It isn't real," I said calmly, pointing out the bedroom window. "It's scripted and mechanical…a dream…like you."

Nana opened the window, allowing the scents and temperatures of the four seasons to flood into the room in equal and opposite waves, canceling each other into one temperate climate.

"But it's not a dream, dear," she corrected me, dusting small mounds of yellow tree pollen and powdery white snow from the windowsill. "During your life you only dreamed of being awake." She started making the bed, ignoring the fact that the sheets were soaked with blood. Pulling the comforter taut, she said: "Let's go downstairs and have breakfast; I made carrot muffins just the way you like. We can go on that hike up Tussey Mountain later today. I know you were looking forward to it."

I watched her, amused by the dream. "But it isn't morning and I'm not awake yet," I insisted. "If I were awake, you'd be gone, so I think we'd better change the subject." Nana placed her hand on my arm—an old woman's hand, wrinkled and rough against my skin; she was trying to convince me that I wasn't dreaming; the effect was authentic, but I wasn't impressed. "Dead people don't talk to each other," I said. "And they don't have eyes to see each other or bodies to touch each other."

She squeezed my arm. "That's true, dear," she said. "But it's easier now for you to think of death that way. You aren't ready yet to let go of life."

"But I'm not dead," I said, "look—"

I jumped up and down, doing a little jig in the bedroom and waving my arm around to prove it.

Nana indulged me with a smile. "You know," she said, "I remember the shoe. Your mother shouldn't have slapped you like that; I would have been scared too. I can't imagine what she was thinking. Making a three year old kiss an old dead woman? Yuck."

I looked at her in sheer horror. This was one of those nightmare moments just before waking when the thing you've been dreading is about to happen and you know you're powerless to stop it—the moment that produces maximum terror, causing you to scream out in the middle of the night—which is exactly what I did. I ran down the stairs shouting "Nooooo!" at the top of my lungs. Through the kitchen and out the back door I ran, past the sink cluttered with baking dishes and the table with the plate of fresh carrot muffins. I stopped on the back porch and closed my eyes, hoping it would all go away; I even imagined reaching across the bed for Bo and finding his hip with his boxer shorts bunched up, and his legs, warm and downy, pulled up to his chest. I nuzzled close, contouring my body to his, the way a river conforms to the shape of its bank, defining itself by what it is not; his skin smelled masculine and strong and his whiskers thrilled my arm when it brushed his chin; I kissed him on the back of the neck and adjusted my breath to the gradual expansion and contraction of his chest. He stirred and smacked his lips softly. It must have been two or three in the morning because I swore I could hear the faint laughter of the college students who lived on our street returning home from their Friday night parties. But when I opened my eyes to see the clock on the dresser, I found myself still standing on Nana's back porch in Delaware with the seasons—and my sanity—colliding.

"Bo! Bo!" I yelled.

"Brek, honey, it's ok," Nana called from the kitchen. "I'm right here."

"Bo! Hold me! Hold me!"

But I couldn't feel him anymore. I leaped from the porch and raced around the house, hoping a sudden burst of exertion would jar me awake. Through winter, summer, spring and fall I ran, past the oak with the tractor tire swing, around the herb garden simultaneously leafy and barren, through beds of tulips dripping with dew and chrysanthemums covered with snow. I tripped over the hump of a root surfacing through the soil beneath the white pine at the northern end of the house and landed face down on the soft needles, my robe spread out around me like the wings of a fallen dove. I stayed there for a moment, catching my breath, inhaling the sweet pine scent and searching for answers—logical, material answers. *What was happening to me? Why couldn't I wake myself up?* It was the most terrifying dream I'd ever had.

I brushed the needles from my robe and looked around. The convulsing seasons had transformed the lawn into a paradise of climates—an entire year of days condensed into a single, dazzling moment of nature in rebellion against time. The apple tree I'd climbed as a child extended its limbs through all four seasons at once: some branches in blossom, some leafy, others tipped with ripe green apples and still others bare, like an unfinished painting. I reached from spring into winter, scooped up a handful of snow, and watched in amazement as the summer sun melted it into water that evaporated and began falling as rain on the other side of the lawn. Even more wondrous than this was the light produced by the coupling seasons: the rays of four suns, describing four distinct arcs across the sky, fusing into a shimmering aurora that passed through the objects it touched like an X-ray, exposing every darkness and allowing no possibility of shadow.

The light was a feeling more than a physical phenomenon—a pervasive sentiment of brightness, uninhibited by the laws of physics and obedient only to the lawlessness of joyful emotion. I rose to my feet and twirled with my head back, dissolving into the light like my handful of snow, drinking in its warmth, allowing it to flush away my fears.

When I stopped spinning I saw my car, for the first time, parked behind the rhododendrons. The magical light retreated, taking with it the idea that this was all a dream, as if reason itself had been a passenger trapped in the car, waiting to be released by my glance. Hot and cold, night terrors, hallucinations. *A fever? Yes, of course. A fever would explain everything that had been happening to me!* I even remembered not feeling well on Friday and wondering whether I was catching a cold, that my skin had felt cool and damp. I gazed around the lawn again and up at the house; I looked down at my legs and feet and flexed my left hand. Everything was right where it was supposed to be, and everything worked as it was supposed to work. Only the seasons were out of place, and that surely could be the result of a fever. *I must have driven to my grandparents' house in some sort of delirium and collapsed.*

Nana was gone when I went back inside. The dishes in the sink were put away, the counter cleaned. A thin film of dust coated everything, as though it hadn't been used in weeks. The oven was cool. Not even the aroma of the muffins lingered in the air. *I had made it all up after all. I really was at my grandparents' house in Delaware.*

I ran upstairs to the bathroom and looked at myself in the mirror. There was my black hair, intact but disheveled, and ashen skin and bloodshot eyes. Carefully, I pulled open my robe. The holes in my chest and the red stains were gone. I laughed ruefully for having even looked. I took the mercury thermometer from the medicine cabinet and slipped it under my tongue: it read one hundred and six, confirming my self-diagnosis. I obviously needed to get to a doctor, but equally obvious: *I was alive.*

I went into my grandparents' room and phoned home but got the answering machine: "Bo, it's me," I said, "are you there? Bo? I don't know what's happened…I think I'm really sick. I've got a fever and I guess I blacked out; I'm all the way down in Delaware at my grandparents' house. I don't know how I got here, I can't remember anything after picking up Sarah at the daycare yesterday; oh, my God, I hope she's all right. She's not here with me, nobody's here…I'm so sorry. She must be starving, there's formula in the cupboard…. I don't know whether to come home or try to see a doctor here…. I think I'm feeling a little better so maybe I'll try to make it home and see how I do. I can always turn around. Ok…I'll be there in a few hours. Give Sarah a kiss for me…. I love you. Bye."

My clothes were piled beside the guest room bed—my black silk suit with formula stains—no blood—on the lapel and sleeve, my blouse, stockings, underwear, and shoes. I dressed quickly and left a note for my grandparents that I'd been there and would explain later.

6

The fall sun warmed the interior of my car, dry-roasting the confetti of autumn leaves on the hood even as budding trees and blooming crocuses swelled in the same sunlight at the opposite end of the driveway. Between them, a snowstorm melted into the sultry vapors of a midsummer day. I must have contracted some sort of rare tropical disease like Dengue fever. Whatever it was, it was better than being dead.

I inserted the key into the ignition and held my breath, still not certain my fever had broken and worried there might be more surprises in store. "Thank God!" I said aloud to myself when the engine roared to life. My car had always been my sanctuary, the one place in the world where, despite a missing arm, I was equal to everyone else and in control. I didn't have special license plates, and I didn't park in the special places close to stores, but my car was in all other respects a vehicle for the handicapped. My parents gave it to me for my high school graduation and Grandpa Cuttler made the necessary alterations himself in the tool shed behind his barn. He bolted a rotating aluminum knob to the steering wheel so I could turn it with one hand and moved the ignition switch and stereo to the left side of the column. Extenders on the shifter, wiper stalk, and heating controls enabled me to operate them with the stump of my right arm. I refused to wear a prosthesis, but I wasn't ashamed to drive one. The day they surprised me with it was among the happiest days of my life, and theirs as well; the car purchased for me the independence I'd dreamed of and, for them, a penance for the sin of my disfigurement at such an early age.

I took a deep breath and nudged the shifter into gear. The car accelerated forward smoothly and I actually enjoyed negotiating my way through the seasons, blasting through the alternating bands of rain, slush, snow, and dry pavement. The drive from northern Wilmington to our home in Huntingdon took about three hours, arcing west along the Lincoln Highway through the flat farmlands of Lancaster County, then turning north at Harrisburg and crossing the Susquehanna River on Route 322, following the Juniata River Valley into the Allegheny Mountains. I tried to remember the trip down to Delaware from Huntingdon the night before—what I'd seen, what I'd been thinking, what I'd been listening to on the radio. I couldn't recall anything. I'd always had an excellent memory: I remembered the first chapters of the novels I read as a teenager, and the holdings of the Supreme Court decisions I read as a law student; I remembered the lyrics to old TV theme songs and all the birthdays in my husband's family to three degrees of consanguinity; but I couldn't remember anything after picking up Sarah yesterday at the daycare and stopping by the convenience store on the way home.

The gas gauge indicated the tank was full when I left Delaware and it didn't move the entire drive home. Strange, but no more so than anything else that had been happening to me. The trip was otherwise uneventful: the typical number of cars and trucks occupied the highway and did the typical things cars and trucks do; the landscape, sky, road signs, buildings, and billboards looked as they had always looked, except everything was wrapped in variegated bands of winter, summer, spring, and fall. The mountains crawled along the banks of the Juniata River like gigantic striped caterpillars, their deciduous forests alternately ablaze in reds, oranges, and yellows, snow covered and white, just budding and speckled green, and deep leafy jade. Gorgeous. Another pleasant but unexpected aspect of the drive was the serendipitous way the radio stations seemed to play the music I wanted to hear, when I wanted to hear it, without any DJs or commercial interruptions. All in all, things looked brighter for me with every mile, and I believed an end to my misery was near; but as I turned toward Huntingdon on Route 522, an anxious feeling overcame me that washed my optimism away. I began to worry about the nature of my illness and what it might mean. *Maybe I had a brain tumor?* I worried. *Or maybe my hallucination of being dead was a premonition of the real event to come?* Bellini women from my great-great-grandmother on down swore they were visited by an angel in the middle of the night to prepare them before somebody close was about to die. Was Nana Bellini that angel, coming to prepare me for my own death? Suddenly the possibility of a terminal illness was more unbearable than the possibility of already being dead. I imagined receiving the news from the doctor and falling to pieces, then telling Bo and holding Sarah close, knowing I wouldn't see her grow up. Who would braid her hair, or make her Halloween costumes, or teach her to bake cookies? Who would introduce her to Louisa May Alcott and Harper Lee, or take her camping or to the ballet, or comfort her through puberty and adolescence? Who, but her own mother, could convince her that there's nothing in life that she, as a girl, or a woman, couldn't do? I was nearly hysterical by the time I turned down our street.

Bo's car was parked in front of the house and I screeched to a stop and ran inside. Everything looked as I'd left it Friday morning, but no one was there. Bo's cereal bowl with a puddle of milk in the bottom sat on the coffee table next to the unread back sections of the *New York Times*; bagel crumbs and empty jars of strained peaches and pears cluttered the kitchen counter; our black Labrador retriever, Macy's, food bowl was half full, but she didn't bark when I entered and was nowhere to be found; our bed was still unmade and the romper I'd decided not to dress Sarah in that day was still draped over the rail of her crib. I checked the garage and found the jogging stroller, so they couldn't be out for a run. There was no note by the phone. The only message on the answering machine was the one I had left from my grandparents' house. I called the Channel 10 studios but nobody answered the switchboard—worrisome, but not necessarily uncommon for a Saturday. There was no answer at either my mother's or father's, no answer at Bo's parents either. I went back outside and looked around the house and in the garage. Nobody. The entire neighborhood was deserted.

We lived on a Lilliputian street in Huntingdon near Juniata College with small brick homes dwarfed by old sycamore trees shaped like giant broccoli. Having been born and raised in Brooklyn, Bo insisted on living in a town with a college; it was his only hope of transitioning from Manhattan to Appalachia. His dream was to be a reporter and news anchor in New York City, but the television stations there told him he needed small market experience before they would even consider looking at his audition tape. This disappointed and terrified him. He thought of small market television as a forsaken third world of vacuum tubes and static that existed somewhere between the

Hudson River and the Hollywood Hills. Applying to Channel 10 in Altoona was my idea, actually; it was one of the stations I had grown up with on visits to my Cuttler grandparents' farm in the fertile valley outside of State College, one of only two stations with VHF transmitters strong enough to reach the arrowhead antenna strapped to the brick chimney on their house in Warriors Mark. Channel 10 in Altoona was just about as small market as you could get. Central Pennsylvania is mostly dairy farms where the land is tillable and coal mines where the mountains rise up—still populated by black bears, white tail deer, elk, and more cattle than people. Schools and businesses there close for the first day of buck hunting season; and, in contrast to the skyscrapers of Manhattan, silos and coal tipples are the tallest manmade structures. When Bo got the job, I called Bill Gwynne, the lawyer in Huntingdon who had represented me and my family after the accident with my arm. Although Huntingdon was even deeper in the middle of nowhere than Altoona, Bill was considered one of the top trial lawyers in the state and he happened to need an associate. The timing and location seemed just right, almost destiny.

I heard music playing in the house next to ours and went over, hoping to find somebody who might have seen Bo and Sarah. Nobody answered the door when I knocked. I pounded on the front doors of all the houses on our street, some with frosted windows, the sidewalks in front covered with slush and snow, and others baking in the afternoon heat; nobody answered, and I started to get worried. I walked over to Washington Street. The hoagie shop and bookstore were open but empty—no customers or employees. The entire commercial district was strangely silent except for the occasional sound of passing cars and buses. Growing more frantic, I ran down the sidewalk past bicycles chained to parking meters and cars parked at the curb, looking in the doors of vacant shops and cafés for any sign of life. It made no sense. This was the busiest part of town on a Saturday in the fall. I eventually ran out to a line of cars queued at the stoplight to ask if anybody knew what was going on, but as I approached and peered inside the windows, I saw no drivers or passengers in any of them. Even so, when the light turned green, they revved their engines and proceeded on their way down the street in the normal flow of Saturday traffic. Astonishing—and creepy. I thought back over my drive from Delaware and realized that I'd passed hundreds of cars and trucks that stopped, turned, yielded, and accelerated, but I'd been so preoccupied with my thoughts of fever and death that I hadn't noticed drivers or passengers in any of them.

A tormented howl suddenly shattered the eerie silence of the street. I looked around to see where it was coming from and discovered it was coming from *me*. It was the sound of madness. I made a wild dash through the cafés and shops, throwing things from tables and shelves, smashing dishes and glasses. I wanted someone, anyone, to come and restrain me. When no one appeared, I tore out into the middle of the street without looking, daring the cars to hit me. On cue, they screeched and smoked to a halt.

"Where is everybody?" I screamed at the top of my lungs. "Why won't somebody help me?"

I climbed onto the roof of one of the cars to get a better view and watched in disbelief as traffic backed up in both directions through the changing seasons: some cars had their windows down, some up, wipers and lights on and off. Two police cruisers raced to the scene, red and blue lights flashing and sirens blaring but no officers emerged; the cruisers just pointed menacingly at me.

I broke down sobbing on the roof of the car. There was nothing left to do. I'd been frightened this badly only once before, as a child in the emergency room of Tyrone Hospital when the attendants laid me on a gurney and placed my severed forearm inside a lunch cooler beside me. I had been amazingly calm until that point; I believed my Grandpa Cuttler when he promised me in his pickup truck racing to the hospital that if I kept my eyes closed everything would be all right. But then they started wheeling me down the hall and I saw the anguish on his face and tears pouring down his cheeks; the gurney crashed through the swinging doors and deposited me into the nightmarish hell of an operating room. I was crazed with terror. They slashed away my clothes, stabbed needles into my wrist, and removed my severed arm from the cooler and held it up to the light like a wild game trophy. The arm didn't seem real at first: the skin was slimy and dishwater gray, the white elbow bone protruding from the end like the plastic connector of a doll's arm, tinged with smears of cow manure and blood, the fingers—my fingers—gnarled into a grotesque fist. I fought the nurses until they forced an anesthesia mask over my mouth and I lost consciousness.

Losing consciousness…howling on top of the idling car in the middle of gridlocked Washington Street, this was all I hoped for now, losing consciousness and awakening on the other side, in a hospital room where my mother and father would be there to hold me and tell me everything would be all right. But it wasn't to be. I stayed on top of the car that first afternoon in Shemaya until the sun overhead divided back into four suns, each setting over the mountaintop at different points and different times, torching the sky into a blaze of pink and gold flames. Inconsolable, I crawled down and walked back home. The traffic jam cleared as the cars continued on their way to nowhere.

When I reached our house, I heard a voice.

"I'm sorry, child," Nana Bellini said. She was sitting in the rocker on our front porch, enjoying the beautiful evening as though she'd just stopped by for dinner. I was certain now that I'd be locked up soon and sedated. I was obviously insane and dangerous. I talked to her while I waited to be taken away.

"How was your drive?" I said flatly, adopting her *everything's normal and we're all happy to be here* attitude.

"We're not there, dear," she said.

"We're not where?"

"Do you remember when you were a little girl and your bedroom turned into a palace and knights rode beneath your windows on great white horses?"

"Who are you?"

"Remember, child? You pretended to lounge in long flowing gowns, dreaming of the prince in the next castle. You created a world within the world that had been created for you; you painted its skies, constructed its walls, and filled its spaces; like a tiny goddess, you caused a land to exist with nothing more than your mind; but as you grew older, you found the existing structures of time and space more convincing and put aside your own power to create in favor of the creations of others. The power to create wasn't lost, Brek. It can never be lost. It's natural at first for you to re-create the places that have been dear to you."

"Where's my husband and my daughter?" I demanded. "Where is everybody?"

Nana smiled—that patient, knowing smile of hers and Luas', as if to say: *Yes, my great-granddaughter, reach now, reach for the answers.*

"We're not there anymore, child," she said. "It was a wonderful illusion, but it's gone; you've returned home. You won't see them again until they come home too. Free will is absolute; we can't direct the movement of consciousness from realm to realm—"

She was scaring me again. "Leave me alone!" I shouted. I ran back down the walk toward my car.

"Wait, child," she said. "Where are you going?"

I didn't know where. I just knew I had to find Bo and Sarah. I had to get help. Maybe it wasn't Saturday, maybe it was still Friday and I could pick Sarah up from daycare and start all over. *It's all just a dream,* I kept telling myself, *just a bad dream; you have a fever and you're sick.* I climbed into my car and started the engine. Nana called out to me:

"What would the daycare look like?"

As soon as I thought about it, I was there. The house vanished, and with it my car, the trees, the street, the entire neighborhood. The rough brick wall of our neighbor's house transformed into the daycare's smooth white wall decorated with paper blue whales that Sarah and the other children had colored with Miss Erin's help. Bright, freshly vacuumed play rugs now covered what had been the lawn; the cubby I'd crammed with fresh crib sheets, diapers, and wipes on Friday morning stood where the passenger seat of my car had been; colorful plastic preschool toys were stacked neatly near the curb; a craft table with boxes of Popsicle sticks, bottles of glue, and reams of colored construction paper sprang forth from the porch steps; and a row of shrubs became shelves holding clipboards filled with blank activity sheets for each child, ready to document the food consumed, bowel movements produced, and fun had during the day. The scent of baby powder and diaper rash ointment filled the air. But there was no laughter in the daycare, no squeals or cries. Not a child. Not a teacher. Not a sound. Nana stood in the doorway, watching me explore the space, probing it for hidden gaps, searching for the wizard behind the curtain. The movement between locations had been seamless, immediate. I wasn't transported: my surroundings simply evolved, and I caught on quickly.

The next thought that came into my mind was the set of the morning news where Bo had tried to banter with Piper Jackson. As quickly as the memory arose, the wall of colored whales metamorphosed into the sunrise mural of the Horseshoe Curve that served as a backdrop for the newscasters. Studio cameras with TelePrompTers stood where the cribs had been; lighting racks dangled from the ceiling, and a green background for the computer generated weather map emerged from a closet; coffee mugs with large "10"s on their sides steamed next to sheets of script with last night's sports scores and the latest national news. Fresh doughnuts and fruit covered a small table behind the cameras. Like my neighborhood and the daycare, the set was deserted.

I thought of my law office next. My desk, computer, files, bookshelves, treatises, diplomas, and pictures of Bo and Sarah surrounded me instantly. Then came Stan's delicatessen on Penn Street and my Bellini grandparents' beach house in Rehoboth Beach, followed by my Cuttler grandparents' barn in Warriors Mark and my bed in the physical therapy ward at Children's Hospital of Philadelphia, where I watched Bobby Hamilton, with both arms amputated, learn to tie his shoes with a long crochet hook in his mouth. I revisited the cinder track behind my high school where I'd won several races against two-armed opponents and amazed myself and the small crowds. I sat at the bar at Smoky Joe's on Fortieth Street near the University of Pennsylvania in Philadelphia where I had danced the night away with my girlfriends during law school. I knelt before the altar at Old Swedes Church, where my best friend, Karen Busfield, who had become an Episcopal priest, asked whether I would pledge my troth to Boaz Wolfson before God and a rabbi and pronounced us husband and wife. I wept in the delivery room at Wilmington Hospital where my mother had given birth to me, and then again at Blair Memorial Hospital in Huntingdon where I'd given birth to Sarah and Bo's tears dropped onto my lips. Each room and space from my past came as fast as I thought of it, as though I were plunging down a shaft cored through the center of my life.

I went back to linger, walking the sands of the Delaware shore, climbing the hay mow in my grandfather's barn, pulling on the Nautilus machine that strengthened my left arm to do the work of my right. I revisited not only the locations but the reality, every detail: the sinewy saltiness of Stan's corned beef, the burning smoke and stale beer of Smokey Joe's, the warm rain on our wedding day, the cold stirrups of the delivery room bed. Nana accompanied me, but did not interfere. Her fascination with how I had lived my life nearly equaled my fascination with the power to re-create it; but the exertion of doing all this exhausted me, and soon portions of one space began blurring into others: ocean waves lapped at the corn crib on my grandparents' farm three hundred miles from the coast; Bo's anchor chair sat behind the high altar of Old Swedes Church, and in it sat the ornate gold altar cross, staring into camera three as if delivering news of the Judgment Day. The images, the realities, congealed into a single nonsensical mass that finally ground to a halt under its own weight.

And then, everything went blank and filled with an indescribable light that seemed to emanate from nowhere and everywhere. Through this light Nana extended her hand to me in a gesture of love, smothering the blaze of fear that had nearly consumed me.

"You're dead, child," she said. "But your life has just begun."

PART TWO

7

"You are not prepared for what you would see, so we must limit what you will see, which is only possible, Brek Abigail Cuttler, because you insist upon what you believe is your sight to see."

Luas spoke these words while placing a felt blindfold over my eyes in the vestibule leading back into Shemaya Station. He was like my father on my wedding day at the rear of the church before giving me away, ironic and wistful, lowering the veil over my face and offering riddles for advice before escorting me into the unknown. He wore the identical gray suit, vest, shirt, and tie Bill Gwynne had been wearing at the office the last day I saw him. The resemblance between Luas and Bill was uncanny, as was his resemblance to my grandfathers, and he sometimes seemed to be all three men at once, shifting physical features like a hologram depending upon my memories and mood. For my part, I looked as fresh and presentable as I did on my wedding day. Nana fussed over me all morning in a mother-of-the-bride sort of way, making certain my hair and makeup looked just so;

but instead of a wedding dress, I wore my black silk suit, from which she had managed to remove the baby formula and blood. The suit had become my uniform in Shemaya: the garment that represented my identity, the proof that I had lived a life, and the symbol that I intended to return to that life. Biding time until I was cured of whatever disease had seized control of my mind, I acquiesced in the fantasy that I was in heaven while secretly knowing it was just that—a fantasy.

Nana had explained that I would be spending the day with Luas but gave no hint of where we would be going or what we would be doing. It would be my first day away from her since arriving in Shemaya. While primping my hair in the bedroom mirror before leaving the house—her house in Delaware, my grandparents' house—I asked her if Luas was my great-grandfather Frank, whom I had never met.

"No, no," she said in her Italian accent, amused by the suggestion. "Luas isn't your great-grandfather, dear. He's already moved on. Luas is the High Jurisconsult of Shemaya."

"What does that mean?" I asked. "High Jurisconsult?"

"It means he's the chief lawyer here."

Another contradiction. I pounced. "But I thought we were in heaven," I said. "Why would there be lawyers in paradise?"

Nana looked surprised. "You don't think God would allow souls to face the Final Judgment alone, do you? Even murderers on earth have a lawyer to represent them and the outcomes of those trials are only temporary. The stakes are higher here. Eternity."

I was speechless.

"Luas will explain everything," Nana assured me. "But let me tell you a little secret. He needs your help. Don't tell him I told you."

"He needs *my* help? I'm the one who needs help."

"Yes, dear," she said, "and by helping Luas you'll be helping yourself."

"What, exactly, does he need my help with?"

Nana paused for a moment and looked at me in the mirror. "He wants to leave Shemaya, but he can't find the way out."

"How long has he been here?" I asked.

Nana thought for a moment. "I think it's been nearly two thousand years," she said. "Come along now, it's time to go."

Luas continued his instructions to me in the vestibule: "The train station is crowded now with new arrivals," he said. "You will hear nothing but you will feel them brushing against you; you must make no attempt to reach out to them, and do not, under any circumstances, remove the blindfold. The entrance to the Urartu Chamber is at the opposite end of the station. We'll be going straight through. Are you ready?"

"Why can't I see them?" I asked. "And what is the Urartu Chamber?"

"I'll explain later," he said, tugging at the blindfold to be certain it was tight. "If we don't get going, we'll miss the trial. Can you see?"

"No."

"Then you're ready. Follow me."

He grasped my left elbow and urged me forward, stiffening against the weight of the doors. Entering the station, I immediately sensed a great throng of people milling about in ghostly silence; bodies began brushing against my hips and shoulders, but heeding Luas' warning, I made no attempt to reach out to them. Even so, halfway through I could no longer resist the temptation to peek beneath the blindfold. What I saw is difficult to describe: the train station was not filled with people but rather their *memories*: disconnected sensations, emotions, and images arcing through the air like bolts of electricity inside a novelty plasma globe. These were raw memories, not the sanitized recollections we tell each other over cups of coffee or even the more honest accounts we record in our secret diaries, but life itself as experienced and remembered by those who lived it; and because I came into direct contact with these memories without the protective filter of another person's mind, they became *my* memories. Suddenly, like a character actor viewing scenes spliced together from a lifetime of films, I found myself reliving the experiences of people whom I had never known but who seemed in a very real sense to be *me*, remembering events of their lives both minor and momentous, brief and prolonged, moments of numbing boredom and exhilarating excitement, excruciating pain and indescribable pleasure. At one instant, I'm working a sewing machine in a sweat shop in Saipan, the next I'm climbing the catwalk of a grain silo in Kansas City; I'm careening through the streets of Baghdad in the back of a taxi cab, tending the helm of a trawler in stormy seas off Newfoundland, strolling the rows of a vineyard in Australia, driving a front end loader from a mine shaft in Siberia, severing the head of a Tutsi boy with a machete in Rwanda, kissing the neck of a lover in Montreal. I was more than mere spectator. My fingers cramped as the fabric slid beneath the needle, I choked on clouds of dust billowing over the dry wheat, my body leaned as we swerved to avoid a pedestrian crossing the street, I barked orders to my crew on deck and saw the fear in their eyes as the waves crested the bow, I slipped a fleshy red grape into my mouth and savored the tart explosion of juice, I felt the warm spray of blood as I thrust the machete again into the convulsing corpse, I whispered softly while indulging the desires of my lover. Alien memories surfaced in my mind as though I were emerging from a lifetime of amnesia, leaving me confused and lost. Soon Luas strained against another pair of doors and we passed out of the station.

"Are you all right?" he asked as the doors slammed shut behind us.

I was unable to respond, my body trembled.

"Here," he said, "you may remove the blindfold now, sit."

We were in a remote, vacant corridor of the train station now and sat down together on a bench. Luas brushed away the hair that had fallen into my eyes and smiled. "I knew you would peek," he said. "You're not one to obey rules, even when they benefit you." He gazed toward the doors through which we had just emerged. "You see them for who they are, Brek Abigail Cutler. You have the gift."

I was barely able to understand his words. My memories had merged and deepened into the larger pool of humanity: lives rushed through me in intoxicating bursts of light and sound, joy and horror, the fragments of other lives expanding the life I had remembered in ways both tender and terrifying. It was as though I'd been raised on a desert island without music, books, television, or maps and suddenly been given a glimpse of the world. I wanted to see more; I needed to see more. I got up from the bench and turned toward the doors.

"Not yet," Luas warned. "It's too soon. You're not ready."

"Who are they?" I asked. "Who am I?" I grasped the door handle.

"No, Brek," Luas spoke sternly. "You must do exactly as I say or you will lose who you are. Do you understand?"

"Who am I, Luas?" I said, confused and lost. "Or, should I say, who was I?" I pulled on the door.

Luas tugged on the empty right sleeve of my suit jacket, causing me to turn toward him.

"You did it on purpose," he said, indicating the empty sleeve. "Quite bold, actually. Why, there isn't a child who hasn't comforted herself to sleep knowing that if pushed too far she could simply deny her parents what they treasure most of all. Children play the same dangerous game adults play on the tips of ballistic missiles, but unlike adults most children recognize the futility of trying to win by losing. Not you, Brek Cuttler. No, you heard your grandfather's instruction to stand clear of the conveyor chain as an invitation to trade a pound of your own flesh for the pleasure of the pain on your parents' faces and the sorrow in their voices."

It all came back to me, my own darkest secret, never shared. The secret of the princess in Santiago. "How did you know?" I asked.

"I know many things about you, Brek Cuttler," Luas said.

"Then you know they were getting a divorce," I said, "and that my mother was an alcoholic and my father hit her and he…. You know I thought I'd only get a cut when I reached into the machine and maybe be taken to the hospital for a few stitches, not that I would lose my arm. I just wanted them to listen. I just wanted them to stay together. Is that too much for a child to ask?" I glared at Luas as if he were my own father. "You have no right to judge me," I said. "I've been punished my entire life for the sin of trying to keep my parents together. I've more than paid for my crime—if you can call wanting a family a crime. You know many things about me? Do you know about the phantom pains, when you think your arm is hurting even though you don't have an arm? Do you know what it's like not to be able to hug another human being because you're missing an arm to hug them back? Do you know about bathing, dressing, eating, and sleeping with only one hand, and about the jeers of children and the cruelty of adults? Do you know about the awkwardness of every new meeting, about the shattered hopes and dreams? Do you know about clothes with useless right sleeves?"

"All that was forgiven long ago," Luas replied.

"Forgiven? Really? I don't remember forgiving anybody."

"Please, Brek," he said, "sit down."

I released the door and sat back down with him on the bench. Two sculptures had been chiseled into the stone wall opposite the bench: one of a Buddhist temple in the foothills of Tibet and the other of a synagogue in the foothills of Mt. Sinai. Luas noticed me looking at them. They seemed out of place in a train station.

"Have you heard of the Book of Life and the Book of Death?" he asked.

I nodded.

"They don't exist," he said.

I exhaled in relief, prematurely.

"God doesn't maintain them. We do. Each one of us. A record of every thought, word, and deed in our lives. The storage is quite perfect, actually; it's the recall that's incomplete. Not that this is a defect. Important reasons exist for narrowing the field: forgetting traumatic events helps one cope, and there's the exquisitely practical need to discard portions of an ever-growing body of experiences to avoid being consumed by them. Memory isn't the defective tape recording you've been led to believe it is; memory is the tape player itself, playing back the tracks of music we select—and sometimes those we don't. Replayed on the right machine—a high quality machine—the music can be reproduced with great fidelity and precision, nearly as perfect as when it was first produced."

Although hewn from solid rock, the stone reliefs on the wall metamorphosed as Luas spoke, reworking themselves into brooding animations of viscous stone. Two elevated thrones surrounded by great mounds of crumpled scrolls replaced the temple and the synagogue, in front of which queued long lines of people, naked, their faces erased from their egg shaped bald heads. Thin, fat, young, old, male, female, tall, small, each person carried a scroll, some bulging and heavy and others compact and light. Upon the throne sat an orb like the sun with rays emanating in all directions, and at the foot of the throne stood a robed soul who received the scroll from the next person in line and appeared to read aloud as the parchment unspooled. When the end was reached, the scroll was cast by the reader onto the pile and the bearer disappeared without direction or trace, replaced by the next in line for whom the process was repeated. Luas paused to watch the somber procession.

"You've been given the privilege, and the responsibility, of replaying the tape for others," he said.

"I don't understand."

"That is what we do here, Brek," Luas explained. "It's why we've been brought to Shemaya, to read and dissect the record of life and plead to the Creator the imperfect case of the created, as oil and canvas would, if they could, explain to the artist flaws of texture and color, or as string and bow would, if they could, explain to the composer disturbances of pitch and tone. We've been appointed to tell the other side of the story, Brek—to explain their fears and regrets, their complicity and victimization, their greed and sacrifice. We're here to make sure justice is served at the Final Judgment."

As I said earlier, I had not accepted my death at this point; to the contrary, I had been playing along, biding my time, waiting and watching for an opening to rejoin the life I had once led. My earlier thoughts of fever and illness had turned into the possibility that I'd been in a terrible accident and suffered a serious brain injury. *Maybe I had been in a car crash, or fallen off a cliff during the hike up Tussey Mountain? Maybe this is what a coma is like?* When Nana dressed me for my big day, I even imagined she was my nurse preparing me for surgery and Luas was my neurosurgeon, speaking about things I couldn't understand but telling me to trust him and everything would be fine. The blind-fold he lowered over my eyes became an oxygen mask to keep me alive. I clung with all my might to these hopes now as Luas explained things, terrifying things, I could neither comprehend nor accept—things that could not be unless I was, in fact, dead.

"Oh, I think I get it now," I said, skeptically playing along. "You're pretending to be my lawyer and you're trying to help me avoid being sent to hell for sticking my hand in the manure spreader, right? Can't you get me a plea bargain or something? Credit for time served?"

"Hardly," Luas said. "Why did God promise not to flood the earth again?"

A puzzled expression flashed across my face.

"Come now," he said, removing a pipe and a pouch of tobacco from his jacket pocket and packing the bowl. "Surely you know the story. Things only got worse after the fiasco in Eden. Cain murdered Abel, and later one of Cain's children murdered a young child. Humans began mating with animals and engag-ing in every sort of debauchery. God was furious—and rightly so. He decided to destroy the lot of us, as justice demands, but when the flood waters receded, He felt remorse. Imagine that. God regrets what God's done. Strange. He makes a promise: 'I'll never do it again,' He says, hanging rainbows from the clouds as a reminder. One day extermination of the human race is the final solution—to borrow an ugly phrase—but as soon as humanity has been driven to the brink, all is forgiven and our survival is guaranteed, even if we return to our wicked ways. Why the change of heart? Why even spare Noah in the first place?"

"I guess because Noah was the only one who obeyed," I said.

Luas paused to strike a match and light his pipe. "Yes," he said, "and if Noah had disobeyed?"

"He would have been killed with the others."

"Correct," Luas said between puffs. "Divine justice. A good case could be made, could it not, that God is the greatest mass murderer of all time and Adolph Hitler was a petty criminal by comparison? Hitler was once a presenter here, by the way. One of the best."

"Adolph Hitler was here?"

"Yes, but let's stick to the point; we're talking about God now, and there's still the matter of His last-second change of heart. It's because of this astounding about-face that beyond those doors at the end of the corridor, inside the Urartu Chamber, there will be argument for many souls today that they have a place in the Light and, for those same souls, the Dark. They'll learn their fates today and greet their eternities. You see, every birth on earth is a potential crime and a pending trial. It's the Urartu Chamber, not a pot of gold, that sits at the end of God's rainbows. God promised us those rainbows would guarantee a place for man in the world of sun and clouds, but He said nothing about the worlds to come."

Luas rose from the bench and gestured for me to follow.

"Of course," he continued, puffing on his pipe, "we do not deal here with bodhisattvas or saints, caitiffs or fiends. The conclusions for them are foregone, the judgments obvious and unassailable. Our concern here in the Urartu Chamber is for the rest of humanity—the good people who sometimes cheat, the bad who sometimes do good, the billions who failed to sacrifice everything to become priests or prophets but resisted the temptation to become demons or demigods. We put on no false airs here. We do not ask whether there has been renunciation for the

Hindu, awakening for the Buddhist, reckoning for the Muslim, salvation for the Christian, or atonement for the Jew. These are mere obfuscations of Divine Law. There is only one question to be answered during the Final Judgment of every human soul, and it is the same question that concerned God before the Great Flood: What does justice demand?"

We approached the doors at the opposite end of the corridor.

"Accounts rich and grave are reconciled beyond these doors, Brek Cuttler," Luas said. "Could you speak honestly of yourself there? Could you damn yourself if damning is what you deserved, setting aside fear and hatred for truth? Could you stand before the Creator of energy, space, and time and save yourself? Could you pass through those doors knowing your experience of eternity would be forever shaped by what you said and left unsaid? Could you explain what, during your entire life, defied explanation?"

I began to panic. I couldn't have made up these words if my brain had been knocked around inside my skull during a car accident or riddled with cancer and fever. And I couldn't have made up the memories I experienced passing through the train shed either—they were too vivid, exotic, real. The possibility of my own death was becoming more inescapable.

"You're taking me to be judged, then?" I said, backing away. "I really am going to hell for putting my arm in a manure spreader?"

"Judged? You?" Luas said, genuinely surprised by my question. "Of course not! I told you all that was forgiven long ago. I'm taking you to receive your heavenly reward, Brek, not to send you to hell. You've always hoped and prayed you would come here. Shemaya has been the motive behind your every decision, the basis of your every interaction from the first moment of your life to the last; it has been your longing and your dream, just as it has been the longing and dream of almost every human being since the beginning of time. You knew it most vividly after your accident, when you realized you suffered not because you would never again be able to dangle from monkey bars on a playground or swing a softball bat or play a violin, but because it was unjust that millions of other girls could."

Luas removed his hands from my shoulders and puffed his pipe.

"A member of the bar, not the clergy, offered you justice after the accident, isn't that right? And so you discovered at an early age that the legal system provides the redemption religion can no longer afford, and that lawyers are the true priests and judges the true prophets. You craved justice more than anything else in your life. Growing older, you felt the same sting when somebody cut you off in traffic or said an unkind word, as when a drunk driver wiped out a family or a tornado flattened a town. Although different by degree and implication, you knew in your heart neither of these was more or less capricious, and neither was more or less unjust.

"On the day your childhood friend, Karen Busfield, told you she was accepted into a seminary to become an Episcopal priest, you were filled with despair, not joy. You were already in law school by then. Do you remember how you mocked her while cross-examining her motives? You said: 'When a child with bruises all over her body tells you her father did it, Karen, what will you do? Ask her to pray and put it in God's hands? And when she tells you she's been praying every night for ten years, but the beatings still continue, what will you say then? God's hands can't be bothered with children, Karen! If you really want to save people's souls from sin—not just the sin of hating others and themselves but the sin of hating the God who breathed life into them and then abandoned them—you won't pray for them, Karen. You'll give them one of my business cards and tell them to call me.'"

I stared at Luas, trying to understand how he could possibly know all these things.

"And do you remember Karen's reply?" Luas continued. "She said you didn't let her finish; she was planning to join the Air Force, like her father, and become a military chaplain. 'The Air Force doesn't call lawyers when somebody misbehaves, Brek,' she said. 'They drop bombs on them. Now *that's* justice.' And you said to her: 'They'll never take you, Karen. They'll see right through you.'" Luas puffed his pipe. "You understood the great truth of life, Brek Cuttler. You understood that the pursuit of justice is the purest form of religion and the highest human aspiration. You became a disciple of justice. Now, as I said, the time has come for you to receive your reward. You have been chosen to join the elite lawyers of Shemaya who defend souls at the Final Judgment. I was being facetious when I asked you if you could defend yourself in the Urartu Chamber. That always gets the attention of new arrivals; one's own jeopardy helps focus the mind. No, the only question now is whether you can walk through those doors if *someone else* depends upon what you say and leave unsaid? If you speak for humanity, not yourself. But this question was answered about you long ago, was it not? My job is not to assess your fitness but to show you the way."

Luas emptied his pipe into an ashtray on the wall, then slipped his hand into his vest pocket and removed a golden key from which dangled a sparkling Magen David, the crescent moon of Islam, figures of Shiva and Buddha, the Yin and Yang, and a crucifix. "This is yours," he said, handing me the key. "It's the key to the Urartu Chamber."

I refused to take it.

"This isn't the time for fear and indecision," Luas said. "You've been waiting for God to smite the evil and reward the righteous since you were eleven years old and you put those boys on trial for murdering crayfish. To you, even crayfish deserved justice! How wonderful! Rejoice, Brek Abigail Cuttler! Your prayers have been answered! There *is* justice after all! Finally, praise God, justice!"

The memory of the crayfish trials came rushing back to me. Little did I know then how important those trials would become to my life—and my afterlife.

8

Behind my best friend Karen Busfield's house in Tyrone, Pennsylvania, beyond the ash piles left over from the old coal furnaces and the small abandoned building with the words "Tyrone Casket & Vault Co." fading from its side, glistened the wide pleasant stream known as the Little Juniata River. The Little Juniata flows north out of the Allegheny Mountains, draining the small creeks and springs that bless the hills and valleys with life, then due south when it reaches Tyrone, where my father's family, the Cutlers, who were simple farmers, are from. When the Little Juniata reaches Huntingdon, it spills into the big Juniata River, which is a big river only during twenty year hurricanes and at other times just normal sized, not wide, not deep, and not fast. The big Juniata River continues south until it empties into the Susquehanna River at Clark's Ferry near Harrisburg, and the Susquehanna River, which is a big river all year round, continues south until it reaches Harve de Grace, Maryland, where it flows into the Chesapeake Bay. There is a marina there, where my mother's family, the Bellinis, who were more wealthy and better educated than the Cuttlers, docked their sailboat. And so it was that my father's and mother's families were connected in this way, by the rivers, long before my parents married or met. I remember being astonished when I discovered this relationship on a map, like suddenly recognizing the shape of a connect-the-dots rabbit. I wondered about its meaning, and, like an astrologer searching for signs in the heavens, I began reading all kinds of maps for signs of what my future might bring. After that, when I waded into the Little Juniata River, or sailed the Chesapeake Bay with my grandparents, I could not resist wondering where the water had come from and where it was going and whose lives it would bring together.

The Little Juniata River is shallow in midsummer and has a limestone bottom of slippery, moss-covered river rocks; Karen and I could walk for miles through its knee-deep, clear waters wearing cutoff shorts and old sneakers, stumbling, slid- ing, drenching ourselves, and laughing merrily. We carried our lunches with us and ate along its banks, pretending to be early explorers charting the river for the first time. The aboriginal tribes we encountered, which is to say the boys from the dif- ferent neighborhoods along the river, tracked our movements warily, as if we really were from a faraway land. Girls never played in the river, but Karen and I were different from most girls— not because we were more tomboyish or brave, but because we thought of things differently. For example, we thought the river was interesting and full of possibilities, which most girls did not, and we believed we had equal right with the boys to play in it, which most girls would not. Ours was a difference of curiosity and perspective. And fairness.

One hot July afternoon, while Karen and I were exploring the river, we shocked ourselves and the boys by catching crayfish with our own bare hands—no easy feat for a girl with only one arm, which made catching things like bugs, baseballs, crayfish, and boys, a challenge. Little Juniata River crayfish, in particular, are difficult to catch. Like handicapped girls, they're timid little creatures, seemingly aware of their vulnerability and embarrassed by their bizarre bodies. You must approach them from behind without casting a shadow, while they're sunning themselves in shallow waters on the mossy green river rocks they try so hard to imitate. They dart backward when frightened, vanishing in a cloud of silt into the nearest crevice. You must be fast, and you must grab them by the large middle shell to avoid their sharp pincers—like lifting a snarling cat by the scruff of its neck. Held this way, they're perfectly harmless; but make a mistake, and they'll give you a painful snip and you'll drop them back into the water.

Karen and I proudly waved our crayfish high in the air that afternoon, cheering and hollering with the excitement of biologists discovering a new species. We examined them up close, noticing how their tails curled into a ball to shield their soft underbellies and their pincers strained to reach back over their heads to nip at our fingers; we stroked their antennae and clicked our fingernails against their hard shells; and finally we returned them to the river, worried they wouldn't survive if we kept them out too long. Ethically, there isn't much more you can do with a crayfish. You might shake it in the face of a boy to make him wince, but you could embarrass him this way only once, and the consequences for the crayfish were dire. When the boys saw we were still alive after handling the nasty things, they bravely attacked the river and a fierce competition set in. Soon buckets were filled with crayfish and records made of who caught the most and the biggest. This is where the minds of girls and boys turn in opposite directions. Karen and I were content to study the crayfish for a minute or two and set them free. The boys, on the other hand, weren't satisfied until they'd tortured and executed the lot of them. Their buckets became killing grounds. The crayfish snapped ferociously to defend themselves, but in the confined space of the buckets they succeeded only in maiming each other, not their captors. A thick algae of amputated pincers, antennae, and other body parts soon floated upon the water; each new crayfish added to the hoard set off a fury, and when things settled down the boys stirred the buckets to see them go after each other again. When the crayfish became too exhausted to fight, the boys tore their bodies apart with their hands and tossed the fragments back into the river.

Karen and I were horrified. We pleaded with the boys to end the competition and spare the crayfish. We tried to wrestle the buckets away, but the boys were too strong; we threw rocks at them and called them names; we even offered to let them kiss us—and threatened to kiss them if they refused to stop—but it was no use. There must be something genetic in boys that makes the suffering of living creatures an endless source of fascination and amusement.

Even though we couldn't liberate the crayfish, I was determined to bring the boys to justice for their crimes, so I established a courtroom of rocks and logs along the riverbank and held trials. I had seen my Pop Pop Bellini, valiant and righteous, cross-examining witnesses in court, and I had testified about the accident with my arm, answering the questions Mr. Gwynne asked as carefully as I could, so I knew just how to do it. I appointed myself prosecutor and told Karen she could be the judge and the jury. To my shock and dismay, Karen betrayed both the crayfish and me by refusing to participate, claiming that punishing the boys wouldn't do any good. I thought she was sweet on one of them, probably Lenny Basilio, who kept running up to show her his crayfish. Even the boys doubted Karen's motives, but to their credit they knew they'd done wrong, and they'd gotten bored with the killing and thought trials might be fun. Since Karen wouldn't help, they offered to sit as the jury for each other, promising to listen impartially to the evidence and render a fair verdict. I would hear none of it, but Karen, relishing her role as spoiler, reminded me that a jury is supposed to be composed of the defendant's peers, leaving me no choice but to agree. I would be both prosecutor and judge, and Karen would sit by and watch.

I put Lenny Basilio on trial first to spite her. Lenny was the fattest boy and the weakest, the one always being pushed around. He was also the nicest. He'd been afraid at first to catch the crayfish and had to be teased by the others into doing it, but once he got started he became very efficient and caught the largest crayfish of the day—a wise old granddaddy of a crustacean the size of a small baby lobster. Although by far the biggest and most powerful crayfish in his collection, it was too heavy and slow to defend itself against the younger ones and became the first casualty in Lenny's bucket. Lenny looked genuinely remorseful when the big crayfish died. I knew he'd be easy to convict for the murder.

I called him to the witness stand—a flat piece of river rock resting on a platform of sticks—and told him to raise his right hand. We recognized no right against self-incrimination along the banks of the Little Juniata River; all defendants were forced to testify.

"Do you swear to tell the whole truth, Lenny Basilio, so help you God?" I said.

Lenny shrugged his shoulders and sat down.

I placed his bucket before him, fetid and stinking, filled with crayfish parts. "Did you put these crayfish in this bucket?"

Lenny looked into the pail and then over at his buddies.

"Remember, Lenny," I warned him, "you're under oath. You'll be struck dead by a bolt of lightning if you lie."

Lenny let out a whine. "But the crayfish pinched me first!"

"Yes or no?" I said. "Did you fill this bucket with crayfish?"

"Yes."

"That's right, you did. And after you filled it, you stirred it up so the crayfish would snap at each other, didn't you?"

Before Lenny could answer, I dredged through the water and pulled out the lifeless granddaddy crayfish, already turning white in the heat like a steamed jumbo shrimp. Its right pincer had been amputated, just like my right arm. I showed the crayfish to the jury and made them take a good long look at it; although a few of them snickered and made coarse jokes, the expressions on most of their faces suggested that even they were appalled and saddened by what had happened. Then I showed it defiantly to Karen, who shook her head silently, and turned back to Lenny.

"You did this, didn't you Lenny Basilio?" I said. "You killed it. You put it in your bucket and killed it. Now it'll never see its family again. What if somebody reached down here right now and pulled you off that rock and put you in a bucket?"

"But I didn't mean to," Lenny pleaded. He looked like he was about to cry.

I dropped the crayfish into the bucket and turned toward the jury in disgust. "The prosecution rests."

"Guilty! Guilty!" the boys all cheered.

"Wait a minute," I said sagely. "You've got to vote on it to make it official. We have to take a poll. John Gaines, what say you?" I spoke the way the courtroom tipstave spoke while polling the jury during my trial.

John Gaines glared at Lenny. "Guilty," he said, leaning forward and barring his teeth for effect. "Guilty as sin."

"Mike Kelly, what say you?"

"Guilty!" he said with enthusiasm.

"Ok," I said. "Robby…I don't know your last name."

"Temin."

"Robby Temin, what say you?"

Robby looked sympathetically at Lenny. "Guilty," he whispered.

"Jimmy Reece?"

Jimmy threw a rock at Lenny and laughed. "Guilty…and he's a crybaby too!"

The boys all laughed.

I slid behind the judge's bench and banged a stone against the river rock. "Order in the court!" I hollered. "Order in the court!" The boys became silent instantly. I was impressed with my newfound power.

"Wally Nearhoof, what say you?"

Wally glared back at me, full of insolence and venom. He was the biggest and meanest boy, the bully of the bunch. Everybody was afraid of Wally Nearhoof, including me. He had a look of malice about him, and he held it for a long time on me, boring through me like the twist of a drill.

"Not guilty," he said, keeping his fixed eyes on me.

My jaw dropped. Before I could protest, the other boys chimed in: "What? Not guilty? No way! He's as guilty as the devil!"

"I said, not guilty," Wally insisted.

Lenny Basilio's face brightened. By some miracle, Wally the bully had actually come to his rescue. It was a first. With a warm smile of gratitude and friendship, he virtually danced over to Wally to thank him; but as soon as Lenny got there, Wally cocked his arm and thumped Lenny hard in the chest with the heel of his hand, knocking him to the ground. He leered at the other boys. "Just kidding," he said. "Guilty. Guilty as hell! Let's hang him!"

The boys broke into a riot of cheers. "Guilty! Guilty as hell! Hang him! Let's hang Lenny!"

Lenny scrambled to his feet and backed away. He looked terrified; tears poured from his eyes.

I clapped the river rocks. "Order! Order!" I said. "Order, or I'll hold you all in contempt and end this trial right now!"

The boys quieted down and I turned to Lenny, staring back at me with miserable, desperate eyes. I felt no sympathy for him. I was still thinking about what he'd done to the crayfish.

"Lenny Basilio," I said gravely. "You've been found guilty of murdering crayfish."

Lenny hung his head low.

"Murder is the most serious crime there is," I continued, "but since everybody else did it too, we can't hang you."

Lenny perked up but the boys started booing.

I slammed the rocks together again. "Order!"

"We can't hang you, Lenny, but you've got to be punished...." I thought for a moment what his punishment should be, then I picked up his bucket and shoved it in his face. "As the judge of this court, I hereby sentence you, Lenny Basilio, to spend the rest of your life inside a bucket, like the crayfish you killed!" I emptied the crayfish parts on the ground and put the bucket over Lenny's head like a dunce cap.

"Life in a bucket! Life in a bucket!" the boys all laughed and cheered.

Lenny pulled the bucket off his head. Hatred filled his eyes. "One-armed freak!" he screamed at me. "It should have been you that died in the bucket, not the crayfish!" He punched me as hard as he could in the stomach, knocking the wind out of me, and ran home.

I didn't cry when I got my wind back. I didn't care about the punch or the insult. Justice had prevailed. It was the best feeling

I'd ever felt in my life. At the age of eleven, I'd won my first trial and the battle of good versus evil. It was a glorious moment. I smiled smugly at Karen, who looked on without saying a word.

But then Wally Nearhoof, the bully, spoke up. "Now it's my turn," he said, taking the witness stand. "Bet you can't convict me."

I wanted to save Wally for last, but flush with righteousness and invincibility, I accepted his challenge. I couldn't wait to put the bucket on his dumb, ugly head. I told him to raise his right hand.

"Wally Nearhoof, do you swear to tell the whole truth, so help you God?"

"Yeah," he said, sneering and patronizing.

I pointed to the rusty, old paint can he used to hold his crayfish. Wally had caught the most crayfish of all, and he'd also been the most cruel, pulling their legs and pincers off and crushing their soft underbellies between his thumbs, breaking their squirming bodies in half and pouring the contents into the water. I hated Wally's big murderous face and his big murderous hands. I wanted to convict him more than any of the others and went straight for his throat.

"Did you put these crayfish in here?"

"Nope."

"You're under oath, Wally," I warned him, "you have to tell the truth. You put these crayfish in this can, didn't you?"

"No," he said. "And you can't prove I did."

I guess I wasn't surprised. Wally was a murderer, after all, why wouldn't he be a liar too? I stood for a moment thinking how to prove his guilt, then the idea struck me. It was obvious.

"No further questions," I said, cutting my losses.

Wally started hooting and hollering like he'd won, but he got quiet real fast when I called Jimmy Reece to the stand. Jimmy was Wally's lackey, the littlest kid of the bunch, who traded his dignity for Wally's protection. He had held the paint can and laughed while Wally dismembered the crayfish. Jimmy had more bruises on his body from Wally than anybody else, and he knew that after his testimony he would have more. He looked petrified when I asked him to raise his right hand.

"Jimmy, do you swear to tell the whole truth, so help you God?"

Jimmy glanced over at Wally, who was menacingly smacking his big fist into his big hand.

"I…I guess so," Jimmy said with a tremor in his voice.

"Did you see Wally put crayfish in this can?"

Wally smacked his fist harder.

"Ah…Ah…."

"You're under oath, Jimmy," I said. "You were holding the can for Wally. Tell the truth. You saw him put crayfish in it. You saw him tear them apart, didn't you?"

"No."

I was stunned. In my naiveté, I didn't think he would lie. I called the rest of the boys to the witness stand. They'd all seen Wally fill the can with crayfish, they'd all seen Wally disembowel them, but one by one every one of them denied it. Karen had seen him too, but when I called her she refused to testify. I was furious.

"Cowards!" I screamed at them. "Liars! You're letting him get away with murder!"

Karen was sitting on a rock a near the judge's seat. She said to me: "You don't think it's right for crayfish to spend their lives in a bucket, Brek, but you just sentenced Lenny to life in a bucket and now you want to do the same thing to Wally. They didn't know any better when they hurt the crayfish, but you do."

"Not guilty! Not guilty!" the boys cheered.

Wally strutted up to me and smiled. "I told you you couldn't prove it," he said. "You one-armed freak."

I tried not to burst into tears but I couldn't control myself. "I hate you!" I screamed. "I hate all of you!" Like Lenny, I ran away.

Later that afternoon, I went back to the river. Karen was burying the crayfish in a mass grave she had dug in the moist, dark soil of the riverbank. After covering the grave, she offered a prayer for their little crayfish souls and a prayer for the souls of the boys who persecuted them. Afterward, she wiped her hands on her legs and said to me:

"I guess everybody wants justice. My mom and dad when they're fighting want justice; teachers when we don't listen in class want justice; bullies on playgrounds want justice and their victims do too. But every time somebody says they want justice, what they really mean is they want to hurt somebody; it's ok to do that, they say, because they're doing justice. But how does that make it any better? We shamed the boys, so the boys got mad and started hunting crayfish; the boys made fun of Lenny, so Lenny got mad and caught the crayfish; the crayfish got mad for being caught and pinched Lenny; Lenny got mad and killed the crayfish; then you got mad at Lenny and convicted him; then Lenny got mad and hit you; then you got mad at me when I wouldn't testify against Wally; and Wally got mad and called you names. It's weird, you know? Everybody wants justice, but justice is what makes everybody angry and unhappy in the first place. Why do we want it so bad, if it's what hurts us?" Karen made a little cross on the grave with some pebbles. "The only way I could figure to stop all the fighting was to just forgive them."

9

I inserted the golden key Luas had given me into the lock of the massive wooden doors leading into the Urartu Chamber. Suddenly the doors, the walls, and the train shed itself vanished, leaving me standing beside Luas in an immense space bounded only by energy itself. Instead of unlocking the doors, the key seemed to have somehow freed the unknown numbers of subatomic particles that cling together to form stone and wood, leaving behind only the latticework of magnetic and gravitational pulses that had bound them together, like knocking all the bricks from a wall but leaving the mortar—or converting mass to energy at the speed of light squared. The wall of energy surrounding the space was palpable, translucent, and, if it could be said to have had a color, glistened like water in a crystal decanter on a sterling silver tray.

At the opposite end of the Chamber, the energy condensed itself into a triangular monolith several stories tall, seemingly working Einstein's theorem in reverse. The slab was both dark and luminescent, composed of what appeared to be the finest sapphire, with a triangular aperture near the top through which light entered but did not exit, allowing nothing of the interior to be seen. A semicircle of pale amber light radiated outward from the base of the monolith in a broad arc, and this light formed the floor itself. At the center of the floor stood a simple wooden chair, absurdly out of scale in substance and size. Behind this chair, but beyond the circle of light and exactly opposite the monolith, sat three more chairs. Luas ushered me toward them and insisted I take the one in the middle. He took the left chair and, after seating himself, placed his hands on his knees, closed his eyes, and said to me: "Tobias Bowles will be presenting the case of his father, Gerard."

A moment later, the presenter arrived, standing in the same spot where we had been standing, a golden key like mine still turning in his fingers. He was only a young boy, perhaps eight or nine years of age; his skin was dark and his features middle eastern, with a prominent wanderer's nose and soft brown eyes that seemed to have seen and understood too much for his years. He wore his hair long and unkempt; a light colored robe draped from his shoulders to the floor. Luas rose to his feet when he saw him, looking disappointed.

"Oh, it's only you, Haissem," he said, frowning. "We were expecting Mr. Bowles.... Well, here we are anyway. Haissem, this is Brek Cuttler, the newest lawyer on my staff. Brek, this is Haissem, the most senior presenter in all of Shemaya. I must say, Haissem, she's arrived not a moment too soon. We just lost Jared Schrieberg and now, it seems from your appearance, Mr. Bowles as well."

Haissem reached out to greet me with his left hand—a perceptive gesture, as most people reached by instinct for my right hand and were embarrassed to come up with an empty sleeve.

"Welcome to the Urartu Chamber, Brek," he said, bowing politely, his voice high and prepubescent. "I remember sitting here to witness my first presentation. Abel presented the difficult case of his brother, Cain. That was long before your time though, Luas."

"Quite," Luas agreed.

"Not much has changed since then," Haissem sighed. "Luas keeps the docket moving even though the number of cases increases. We're fortunate to have you, Brek, and you're fortunate to have somebody like Luas as your mentor. There's no better presenter in all of Shemaya."

"Present company excepted," Luas said.

"Not at all," said Haissem. "I only handle the easy cases."

"Few would consider Socrates and Judas to have been easy cases," Luas replied. "I'm just a clerk."

Haissem winked at me. "Don't let him fool you," he said. "Without Luas, there would be no Shemaya."

"Wait a minute," I said, bewildered. "Cain and Abel? "Socrates and Judas? What are you talking about. What's the joke?"

Luas turned to me impatiently. "Do you believe theirs were clear cases about which there could be no doubt?" he said.

"I, I guess not..." I said. "I really have no idea, but my point is that you couldn't possibly have— Well, what happened to them, then? What was the verdict?"

Haissem patted Luas on the back. "I must enter my appearance and prepare myself," he said. "I trust you'll explain everything." Haissem reached again for my left hand and, for an instant, his eyes seemed to focus on something inside me that was much larger than me. "We will meet again, Brek," he said. "You'll do well here, I'm certain of it." He walked toward the chair at the center of the Chamber and Luas motioned for us to take our seats.

"We present only the facts," he whispered as we sat down. "Our concern here is not with verdicts."

"But if they were really put on trial, then surely you must know—"

"Nothing," Luas interrupted. "We know nothing about the outcomes. The Chamber never speaks. One might speculate, of course. There are instances when a presenter feels the result should go one way more than another, but it is strictly forbidden. The consequences for a presenter who attempts to alter eternity last all of eternity. We must not seek to influence the result."

I stared at him, trying to see through him, behind him, still unwilling to believe, still clinging to life as it used to be, searching for explanations for what was happening. "The surgery isn't going well, is it doctor?" I said. You're making me worse. I'm even more delusional."

"Nonsense," Luas said. "Look, Haissem has taken his seat. You'll see things more clearly after he presents his case."

Haissem sat on the chair at the center of the Chamber, adopting the same position as Luas, hands on knees, eyes closed, waiting. I kept my eyes open, watching. Suddenly, a powerful tremor rocked the triangular monolith, rippling its smooth surface. From the center of the monolith, from its solid core, emerged a being like the one on the animated sculpture in the hallway, human in shape and size but without hair, face, or features, dressed in a charcoal gray cassock. The creature approached Haissem without moving its limbs, buoyed, it seemed, on a cushion of air. Haissem maintained his position and the creature stood before him for a moment, then returned to its dark home without a sound. When the tremor subsided, Haissem rose from the chair and, standing at the exact center of the Chamber, raised his arms up from his sides in a broad arc. The energy of the walls and floor pulsed violently and surged toward him from all directions, seemingly compressing the space around him like an imploding star. The shock wave struck Haissem's body, instantly vaporizing him, leaving behind in the vacuum only his voice, detonating like a great cosmic explosion: "I PRESENT TOBIAS WILLIAM BOWLES . . . HE HAS CHOSEN!"

The Chamber went dark. No light. No sound. No motion. Then the Chamber disappeared altogether.

I'M CROSSING A DIRT road now, in another time and another place. My body feels heavy, tired, anxious; my face feels thick and rough, covered with whiskers and grime; my mouth tastes unfamiliar, like a first kiss. My arms, two of them now, feel powerful but detached, as though I am operating a machine. There is an aggressiveness I have never felt before, a heightened wariness of my surroundings and other people. My thoughts and reactions are accelerated and more analytical, my emotions and ability to comprehend subtleties, dull and unused. I reek with body odors that seem both comfortable and unpleasant. My head aches from a hangover.

I'm wearing a filthy green Army uniform and new black boots. This is my second pair of boots this month, which I know for a fact but don't know why or how I know it. I know too that I can have as many boots as I want, that there are enough boots at my disposal to outfit two armies. They're nice boots, shiny, black, and warm, but you can't keep them clean here in Saverne. The dust takes the shine off as soon as you put them on, and there is nothing here but dust, darkening the sun and fading the colors. Everything is dust brown: the clothes, the tents, the once white requisition forms; in Saverne, the food tastes brown, the water washes brown, the stars sparkle brown, the air smells brown, and, when the dead arrive at the morgue here, they bleed brown onto the brown ground, ashes to ashes, brown to brown. I even dream in brown. The only thing not brown in Saverne is greed, which tints the eyes and fingertips a vibrant glossy hue of green.

Crossing the brown dirt road, I'm debating in my own mind whether to low-ball Collins or give him a fair offer and make him think I'm doing him a favor; but when I reach the middle of the dirt road, somebody yells: "Toby, lookout!"

From the corner of my eye, I see an olive green Army truck racing toward me at breakneck speed, plowing a tantrum of brown dust into the air. The dust looks startled for a moment, as if it has just been awakened from a nap. I leap out of the way, spinning a pirouette in my new black boots and giving Davidson a thank you slug in the shoulder for the warning. "You gotta be more careful, Toby," he says. "You're gonna get yourself killed."

"Me, killed? No way," I tell him. "Not by no goddamned truck anyway. It'll take a French maid to do me in."

Davidson guards the entrance to a brown tent that was once olive green. Dirt blown from the road piles into drifts against the canvas, re-creating in miniature the blowing and drifting snow in the mountain passes to the south that make the Alps impenetrable at this time of year. Early winter cuts crisp and cold over the peaks and down into the French valleys, pruning the wounded and the diseased from the battlefield and encampments, the villages and cities. A mountaineer lucky enough to reach the summit of the Alps would see war on the horizon in all directions.

The tent is warmed by a well-stocked wood stove and insulated with boxes of medical supplies stacked from floor to ceiling with dusty red crosses painted on their sides. Each box is worth two hundred dollars on the black market, making the tent into a bank vault. They form an aisle through to a desk at the center and a kerosene lantern producing a thin drizzle of light; behind the desk sits a lean, powerful looking black man. His left chest bears the name Collins, and his shoulder the stripes of a corporal. We are of equal rank. He crushes the cigarette he's been smoking and lights another without offering me one. The white smoke from his cigarette fears the dust and latches onto his head and neck like a small child among strangers.

"Scuttlebutt says Patton's crossing the Rhine near Ludwigshafen," I say. "Two Divisions are moving up from southern Italy to join the party. Price of boots and gloves just tripled."

Collins' mouth curls. "Where are they?" he asks.

"Keeping warm in a chateau."

"Don't be playin' no games wit' me, Bowles," he says, speaking like he just escaped from a plantation. "I ain't got no time for it now."

My stomach churns a sour broth of hash and coffee up into the back of my throat. *I'm finally gonna get a piece of the action*, I keep telling myself. Just a piece of what everyone else has. *I didn't want to come here. I wanted to stay home and work on cars; that's all I ever wanted. I got a right to a little comfort, and I'll be damned if any nigger from Kentucky is gonna get more than me.* They assigned me to the quartermaster after I played up an asthma attack during basic. It wasn't that bad, and I wasn't that good of an actor, but who was I to argue?

"Somebody's got to keep guys like you happy and it might as well be me, right Collins?" I tell him. "What do you want, I got it all: uniforms, tents, food, booze, utensils, tools, radios, movies, office supplies, sundries." It's all true. In the quartermaster, I'm a walking department store and everybody's my best friend. As soon as the bees figure out where the clover is, they swarm and rub themselves all over to get it. Officers, GI's, locals—they're nicer to me than to the docs who cure their syphilis. They shake my hand and talk to me about me: Where'd I come from? Got a girl? Sure, good lookin' guy like you's got a girl. Ten of 'em, and pretty, too, I bet. They show me pictures of their girls, mothers, fathers, and kid brothers and sisters. I'm just a regular guy like you, they're all sayin', and us regular guys gotta stick together if we're gonna make it. Got any extra whiskey stashed back there? Helps me sleep better at night.

"You ain't got nothin' I want, Bowles," Collins says. "I'm the one who's got what you want. You're standing in my personal piggybank, and my man Davidson out there, he's the guard. Now do you want to sign for a loan or do I have to tell Davidson to throw your ass outta here?"

I stand there for a minute, deciding whether to low-ball him. Collins just came in with the Surgeon General's command and somehow got put in charge of the medical supplies. He's got no connections in the area, but he knows he's sitting on a fortune. I came in behind the invasion force and worked up some rela-tionships with a few French doctors who have backers all the way south to Marseilles. I decide to low-ball him to see how he'll react.

"Twenty-five a box, unopened, and I'll throw in a crate of boots and gloves for every two medical."

"Davidson!" he hollers. "Get this lump of dog shit outta my office!"

"Look Collins," I counter, backtracking a little. "You couldn't move this stuff if you set up a booth under the Eiffel Tower. I'll give you three boots and gloves for every two medical. I can't go any higher."

"One-fifty a box, Bowles, and you can keep your damn boots."

"Fifty."

"One-twenty-five."

"Seventy-five."

"Hundred."

"I got costs, Collins," I tell him. "No way you're comin' out ahead of me. Seventy-five, take it or leave it."

"I'll need a deposit."

"How much?"

"Thousand."

"What?"

"You ain't the only one interested, Bowles. You the third white guy been sniffin' round here today. One thousand in cash, final."

"I got five hundred on me," I say, reaching into my pocket. "I'll give you the rest tonight."

Collins thinks it over. "You know," he says, his thick lips parting into a toothy greed-green smile, "I like you, Bowles. Get the rest here by 18:00."

I give Collins the money and walk out of the tent doing the math in my head. I can move at least a hundred boxes a month; at two hundred bucks a box, that's twenty thousand gross, twelve-five net, minus grease money for the motor pool and perimeter patrol, maybe a thousand max. I just made eleven grand! I nearly skip over to the enlisted club to grab a beer and celebrate; but on my way I see two men opening the rear panel of the truck that almost hit me, parked now about fifty yards away. They crawl up inside and begin unloading empty black body bags onto a folding litter, stacked twenty at a time. I stop to watch them. The guys in the morgue detail pretty much keep to themselves and everyone else stays away from them. A guy will deny any belief in superstitions and walk out of his way to avoid getting anywhere near the morgue. I wonder whether the bags are new or whether they just reuse the old ones over and over again. It doesn't seem right reusing them; violates the privacy of the first guy and insults the second. They gave their lives for chrissake; the least the Army can do is spring for new bags.

Eleven grand...eleven... freakin'... grand!

The body bags slap onto the litter like stacks of crisp, new script hitting a counter.

Surplus, Toby. Just surplus, I tell myself. *The stuff's just sitting there while some French kid dies because his doctor can't get enough sulfa and penicillin. A fellow ought to get paid when he puts himself on the line.*

Turning into the enlisted club I hear boots racing toward me, pounding like hooves. Before I can see what's going on I'm knocked to the ground. There's a sharp pain in my back; I try lifting my head, but it won't move. *Oh, my God, they're shelling us and I've been hit!*

"Help!" I yell. "Help! Medic! I've been hit! I've been hit!"

The pain in my back increases, like a great weight is bearing down on me.

"Stop your damn yelling, Bowles," a voice says, close behind, just above me. "You're under arrest for theft."

Two MPs pull me off the ground and cuff my wrists behind my back. Over their shoulders, I see Collins in the door of the tent, shaking hands with another MP and handing him my money.

HAISSEM IS SITTING AGAIN on the chair at the center of the Chamber. I feel the same sense of confusion and exhaustion that overwhelmed me after passing among all the souls and memories in the train station. I am not just watching Toby Bowles' life, I *am* Toby Bowles. The rough cotton of his uniform chafes my skin; the cold, dusty air and cigarette smoke burn my lungs; the fatigue and fear of being near the front weigh heavy. I soar when the deal is struck and feel the MP's knee in my back when he's arrested.

"Can you hear me now, Brek?" Luas says.

"Yes," I say, barely hearing him, as though he was far away. "What do you mean *now?*"

"I was talking to you during the presentation," he says. "When you didn't respond, I asked Haissem to stop."

"Oh…," I reply, lost, trying to separate my identity as Toby Bowles from my identity as Brek Cuttler. "I'm sorry. It just seems so…so…real, like I'm remembering my own life."

"Yes, it is that way, isn't it?" Luas says. "When Haissem begins again, listen for my voice. At first you'll hear me speaking through the people in the presentation; what I say will seem out of context. If you fail to respond again, I'll bring up the circumstances of your disfigurement again to bring you back. Unfortunately, it isn't possible to instruct you on how to separate yourself from the soul being presented; you must learn this by doing, which is one of the reasons for having you watch."

"What other reason is there?" I ask.

"To prepare you to present souls yourself."

10

Luas nodded and Haissem stood again at the center of the Urartu Chamber to continue the presentation of the life of Toby Bowles at the trial of his soul.

I'm in the parish hall of my church during coffee hour after the service, and I'm seething with rage. "How dare you tell them that!" I whisper to Claire through clenched teeth so no one else will hear. She gives me her stupid *I don't know what you're talking about* look, and I stomp ahead through the parish hall doors, letting them swing back hard against her as she comes through behind. I hope they knock her flat on her ass.

Alan Bickel smiles at me and sticks out his hand.

"Mornin'," I grunt, pushing past him without shaking his hand or making eye contact. The guy's thirty-five year old, got two kids, and he's still pumping gas at the Sinclair.

I walk out into the parking lot, climb into our car, start the engine, and light a cigarette, drawing the smoke deep into my lungs and holding it there with my rage until they both can be contained no longer. I still can't believe she said it. I exhale loudly, talking to myself:

"'I'm sorry, Marion, but money's tight right now. We just haven't any extra for the building fund.'"

How could she? To Paul and Marion Hudson? And there they go now; every year a new Cadillac. From a dry-cleaning store? The guy must be running something on the side or cooking the books. I bend down and pretend not to see them. The rear door of our car opens and Tad and Todd climb in, then Susan and Katie.

"Dibs on the window," Tad calls. There's a big commotion and Tad starts crying. "Dad, Todd hit me and Susan won't move. I called dibs first."

"Knock it off back there or I'll take off my belt!" I yell. "For chrissake, Tad, you're the oldest. What are you, nine now? And still cryin' all the time like you was a baby. If you don't like what Todd and Susan are doin', then give 'em one across the mouth; that's what I used to do to your Uncle Mike when he crossed me. It's time you started actin' like a man, son, and I'm tellin' you right now you're playin' football come August. Period. I don't want to hear another word about playin' in no fairy marching band." I take another drag on my cigarette. "You're playin', right Todd old boy?"

"You bet, dad," Todd says. "Mr. Detterbeck says he's startin' me at linebacker and quarterback." Even though he's a full year younger, Todd stands two inches taller than his brother and weighs at least fifteen pounds more.

"Atta boy," I tell him.

Claire slides into the passenger seat beside me. "I really don't understand why you got so upset," she says.

I'm furious. I throw the cigarette out the window, yank the gear selector into drive, and mash the accelerator before she can close the door. We roar out of the parking lot.

"Toby, for heaven's sake!" Claire screeches, "I haven't got the door closed and there's kids in the car!"

"No!" I holler over the engine, "There's a bunch of cryin' ingrates in this car and a woman who embarrasses her family in public and don't even have the sense to know it." My chest tightens and I feel the veins in my neck swelling. As usual, when I catch Claire she refuses to respond. "You got nothin' to say? You ain't got no idea what I'm talkin' about?"

"The souls come in through the Urartu passage," she says, "and wait in Shemaya Station, just like you did, until I come to get them. A presenter is assigned to meet with each postulant before the trial, then they wait in the train station until their case is called and a decision is made. Since they're not permitted to attend the trial, the presenter must acquire a complete understanding of the choices they've made during—"

"What the hell did you just say?" I ask.

"Do what you want, Toby!" Claire yells. "Everyday it's something. I've broken one of the invisible rules in your invisible rule book; you're swearing in front of the kids on Sunday and driving like a maniac; I have nothing more to say."

I explode. "'Money's tight right now, Marion?' 'Toby can't take care of his family, Marion?' 'We barely make ends meet with his job on the railroad, Marion?' Don't think I haven't seen the way you look at Paul Hudson. But you know why I don't worry? Because there's no way Paul Hudson would give up what he's got for big, ugly thighs like yours."

Claire starts crying. "I hate you, Toby!" she screams. "I hate you! I want you out. Just get out and leave us alone."

"It's none of their damn business whether money's tight!" I yell. "It's nobody's business. You got that? Nobody's. Off they go in their big Caddy to their big country club. I'll bet they're Red, too; there's commies all over the place, Claire, and the niggers are helpin' 'em. They're after regular guys like me; that's why I ain't got a good job and never will. Marion Hudson's laughing at us and you don't even know it. Don't you get it? She knows we don't got extra. That's why she asked, to hear you say it. That's how they get their kicks. How can you be so stupid?"

"Mrs. Hudson's not like that, daddy," Susan speaks up from the back seat. "When I stay over with Penny, they always ask about you and mommy and they're real nice."

"I don't want you kids over there again!" I holler. "Do you hear me? My God, Claire, they even do it to the kids. I can just hear it now: 'How's your mother and father, Susan? My, aren't your shoes old…and that dress. What, they haven't taken you shopping in Manhattan? Such a shame.' And that Penny Hudson: I don't want her comin' over to our place anymore either. New bikes. New dresses. She's always got something new. She's a spoiled brat."

I can't control myself. Embarrassment, jealousy, hatred: they pour out of me as if there's nothing else inside, as if I am nothing else. I want to give my kids and my wife new things. I want to be respected in the community. I want to live where the Hudsons live and eat where the Hudsons eat. I whip down Greenwood Avenue, barely stopping at the lights.

When we get home, I call Bob to see if he'll pick me up early, then I go upstairs and start throwing things in my duffel bag for the week: work lights, flares, two pairs of work pants, some t-shirts, and two pairs of work gloves. Claire stays downstairs with the kids, fixing them lunch, trying to keep them quiet. I take off my dress slacks, shirt, and tie and fold them neatly into the bottom of my bag along with a bottle of Aqua Velva. Sheila likes it when I dress up and wear cologne for her. She thinks I'm an important businessman; I don't have the heart to tell her the truth. I can't wait to see her. She's the only one who understands me. I zip the bag closed and put my Wolverines on top. Claire calls up from the kitchen.

"Do you want any lunch before you go?" Her voice is cold, emotionless. She's still upset but prides herself on not showing it in front of the kids. She knows damn well Bob's on his way over but asks anyway.

"No. Bob and I'll grab something on the way to Princeton Junction."

"When will you be back?"

"Not 'til Friday."

I carry my things down the stairs. "We're runnin' empty dump cars up to Scranton and full ones on to Pittsburgh."

Katie toddles into the living room with a coloring book and crayon, her most prized possessions. She's just eighteen months old. "Daddy, what happened to your right arm?" she asks. "Did you do it because you were mad at your mommy and daddy?"

"Sure, I'll color with you, sweetie," I say, feeling miserable for having yelled and gotten everybody so upset. "Climb up here on my lap."

"Brek, do you hear me?"

"Luas?"

"Ah, there you are," he says. "Finally got through, good."

My personality splinters in two. Half of me carries on a conversation with Toby Bowles' daughter; the other half carries on a conversation with Luas. I exist simultaneously in two worlds and two lives.

"This is a circle, Katie. Can you say circle?" She looks up at me with wide brown eyes and rosy cheeks, melting my heart.

"Cirsa."

"Concentrate on your memories," Luas says, "Bo, Sarah, your job."

I think of Sarah and her crayons, not much younger than Katie, and of Bo, who sometimes yells at me the way Toby did, and my mom and dad. The distance between selves grows until two distinct lives emerge: mine, which has depth, substance, and nuance; and Toby Bowles' life, which I know well but only episodically. I feel his emotions and see through his eyes, but I understand now that he is not me even though he's someone I have experienced more intimately and completely than I've ever experienced another person before.

"So," Luas says, "what do you think of our Mr. Bowles?"

I can hear Luas but not see him. I see only the Bowles' living room. It's as if Luas and I are commenting on a televised sporting event from the press box, eyes focused on the field.

"I don't much care for—" I catch myself. "I thought we weren't allowed to make judgments about other souls."

"Well done," Luas says. "But a little too far. We're forbidden from making judgments, if you will, not observations. A lawyer may disapprove of the actions of his client but nonetheless remain an advocate for his client's rights. Wasn't that so with Alan Fleming?"

Bob pulls up in front and honks his horn. Toby wraps Katie in his arms and gives her a kiss. He hates saying goodbye, and it's worse now because of the awful way he's behaved. Claire, Susan, and Todd approach timidly. Toby wishes he could take it all back, but an apology would be empty and they wouldn't understand. He kisses Claire tenderly and she responds with a lingering hug, at once absolving him of his crime and, at the same time, wounding him with the generosity of her forgiveness.

"I'll bring you all back something nice," he whispers remorsefully, still convinced material possessions are what they want from him. Todd and Susan give him hugs but Tad stays in the kitchen playing walk-the-dog with his yo-yo, unwilling to forgive his father and muttering goodbye only after his mother orders him to say something. Toby doesn't know how to handle Tad anymore. "I'll bring him something special too," he mumbles to himself, "maybe the cap gun and holster set he's been wanting." Toby knows he's been hard on Tad, but it's been for his own good: Toby's father was the same way before he abandoned the family when Toby was eleven. At least Toby hasn't done that. The horn honks again; Bob's waiting. Toby waves, picks up his things, and walks out the door.

"Haissem is re-creating this?" I ask.

"Yes," Luas replies. "Remarkable, isn't it?"

Nine years later. Toby Bowles is now staggering under the weight of middle age. The regrets of lost youth, the deterioration of his body, the fear of approaching death, the vain search for meaning and reaffirmation—all these things sour his life, making him restless and depressed. His hair has thinned and his worry lines have deepened.

He walks up to a small garden apartment in Morrisville, New Jersey, letting himself in with the key Bonnie Campbell leaves for him under a loose brick. The apartment is dark. He turns to lock the door as he's always careful to do, but Bonnie has been waiting and goes quickly for his ears, sending gusts of hot breath into the sensual pockets of his mind. His hand drops from the knob and they move quickly into her darkened bedroom before his eyes can adjust from the glare of the midafternoon sun.

Bonnie's robe falls to the shabby gold carpet, revealing a middle-aged body of creases and folds desirable to Toby only because the candlelight is forgiving—and because Bonnie's attraction to him refutes what he sees of himself in the mirror. The sheets are thrown back and their bodies embrace, fingers and lips uniting all that is opposite, other, forbidden. The delights are exquisite, suspending time. But bliss is fleeting, shattered suddenly by the distinct metal-on-metal click of the front door knob cylinder. Toby bolts upright out of the bed and Bonnie rolls beneath the covers, popping her head out the other side like a groundhog peering from its hole. A dark silhouette fills the doorway to the bedroom.

"Claire, honey?" Toby says in a voice trembling with remorse, shaken by the overwhelming surge of guilt that has been consuming him during his six month affair with Bonnie Campbell. Yet he's almost relieved now that it will all finally be over; he'll be able to confess his crime and beg her forgiveness. The candles on the dresser flicker low in an unseen draft, then brighter in its wake, illuminating tears streaming down the intruder's face.

"That's not Claire!" Bonnie screams, pulling the covers up to her chin. "It's Tad!"

Bonnie Campbell had known Tad since he was a little boy; in fact, she had been close friends with Toby's wife, Tad's mother— Claire—making the humiliation of the encounter for Toby even more complete than if it were Claire herself. Bonnie owned the only pet shop in the small town, and as Tad grew older he purchased at least one of every creature she sold, climbing the evolutionary chain in step with his ability to care for them: an ant farm at first, then a fish, a lizard, some gerbils and hamsters, a rabbit, cat, and, finally, a dog, a German Shepherd. He even worked in her store after school. Tad knew her son, Josh, who was much younger; he knew her ex-husband, Joe; he had eaten many meals at their home.

Bonnie switches on the nightstand light, indignant and remorseless, full of pride for what she has accomplished, daring Tad to speak. But Tad does not see her. He sees only his father: naked, panting, stunned. Tears flood down his face, but he says nothing. He turns and leaves the apartment without saying a word.

Toby's guilt and remorse vanish as quickly as they arose, replaced by rage and a sense of betrayal. He feels ashamed now, not for his own conduct but for his son's. He could understand why Claire would track him down, but Tad? His eighteen year old son? And to stand there crying the way Claire would have done? This embarrassment crowns all the other embarrassments and disappointments Tad has caused Toby over the years: his lack of interest in sports, his lack of friends, his weakness and inability to stand up for himself, his defense of his mother against Toby's abuse. Tad had judged Toby and turned on him at every opportunity, but now he had crossed the line. Toby turns out the light and slides back into bed. He takes Bonnie now with a passion he has never before expressed, but not because he wants her. In fact, he finds her suddenly ugly and repulsive. Instead, he takes her to reestablish who is the father and who is the son, to reclaim his biological position as accuser and Tad's as accused, to reassert his authority to judge what is right and what is wrong, and who is right and who is wrong. And Toby vows to himself to have Bonnie more often now, and to boast proudly of it and rub Tad's nose in it—for, Toby believes no conduct can be sinful if it is done in the open and to teach a lesson. He will dare Tad to say otherwise, dare him to tell his mother and risk destroying her life. And if that moment comes, Toby resolves not to deny it because, in the end, it is Claire's fault that he has turned to another woman, not a weakness of his own.

The light is back on now in the bedroom and Toby is pulling his boxers up to his flabby waist. He's drenched in sweat. He promises himself that he will never forgive Tad. Ever. And then he vows to destroy him, as only a father is capable of destroying a son.

Suddenly the Urartu Chamber emerges into the foreground, displacing Bonnie Campbell's seedy apartment. Haissem bows solemnly before the monolith, then walks over to join Luas and me. The glittering walls of the Chamber vanish just as magically as they appeared. The three of us—Luas, Haissem, and I—are left standing in the vacant corridor of the train station in front of the large wooden doors and near the animated stone sculptures on the wall.

Haissem turns to me and says: "The trial is over. A verdict has been reached."

11

After the trial of Toby Bowles, I knew I no longer existed in the living world to which I had once belonged—your world, there on earth. Something momentous had happened to me, something so altering and absolute that reality itself was replaced by a new archetype of existence that could no longer be postponed or denied. It wasn't a matter of voluntarily accepting the fact of my death, any more than one voluntarily accepts the fact of one's life. It was more basic than that: a simple acknowledgment that this is what is now, and the other is no more.

Oddly enough, accepting my death wasn't terrifying; it was, in a way, liberating. I no longer had to rationalize the bizarre things happening around me and to me; I no longer had to search for a cure to an illness or an injury that did not exist. And I realized I no longer had to carry the many burdens of life: I no longer had to go to work, shower, brush my teeth, eat, sleep, exercise, or take care of my husband and daughter. Death is the ultimate vacation away from *everything*.

Even so, I found admitting my death to be deeply shameful and embarrassing. In the end, death is the ultimate failure in life, the condition we fear, fight, avoid at all cost, that our every biological instinct and emotion abhors and resists. No one is admired on earth for having accomplished the feat of one's own death; even the words used to describe it are pejorative: you've either "lost" your life, as if you've somehow been careless and misplaced it, or your life has been "taken," "stolen," "forfeited," or "given up." I was one of the losers now. The fact that all of the people in history who had come before me were losers too—and that all the people who would come after me were losers in waiting—didn't make my being dead any less humiliating. Even though I had a pretty good excuse for not taking care of my husband and daughter anymore, I was still away from them. I had abandoned them. Even worse, I had abandoned *myself*—Brek Cuttler: human being, mother, wife, daughter, granddaughter, friend, lawyer, neighbor, American, all no more.

The more I thought about everything I had lost, the more angry I became. The injustice of dying after only thirty-one years of life galled me like nothing I had ever experienced before; it was a hot anger that burned hotter because I had no way to express the enormity of my loss, particularly to my Nana. She listened patiently, but she could not, I thought, understand my condition because, unlike me, she had died after having lived a full, complete life, raising her children to adulthood and seeing her grandchildren and even her great-grandchildren.

I also discovered that, like life, the afterlife is governed by a law of special relativity. This law holds that, from the perspective of the one who has died, one's own death feels not like the death of oneself, but rather like the death of the billions of others who remain alive but can no longer be seen. It was as though I was the lone survivor of a nuclear Armageddon. From my perspective, I had not been taken away from my family; my family had been taken away from me. I lost even more than this; I lost my entire world—the earth that had sheltered me, the waters that had nourished me, the sky that had inspired me—all vanished into a lyrical, haunted oblivion.

What finally broke me, though—the thing that drove me into the prolonged silence of grieving that replaces and becomes anger's surrogate—was not the gnawing despair of having lost everything, but the sarcastic resemblance of the afterlife to life itself. There was no release in my heaven, no salvation, no comfort, no "better place" to which I had gone after my death— there was, instead, only a perverse continuation of the discordant strands of my old life, freed of physical laws and boundaries, as if life and death were merely potential states of the same cynical mind. Where was the reward? Where was the eternal repose promised by the prophets? I had come full circle: the burdens of life had been replaced by the burdens of death. For my thirty-one years of effort, I was being trained for a new job at a new law firm: Luas & Associates, Attorneys-at-Divine Law.

The chilling trial of Toby Bowles had the incongruous effect of both deepening and lessening my own misery by showing me that things could actually be worse. On the way out of the train station after the trial, Haissem told me that only a fraction of Mr. Bowles' life had been presented, and a misleading portrait of his soul had been created. Yet he seemed perfectly content with this, and Luas shared his indifference, seeming almost amused by my concern. I asked Haissem what he would have offered in Mr. Bowles' defense if the trial had continued.

"Oh, many things," he said nonchalantly. "For example, Toby was actually a very kind and caring man. When his train stopped at the Altoona rail yard, he would change into his Sunday clothes and hitchhike into the mountains to visit with his sister, Sheila, who lived in a beautiful private home for mentally retarded women on the shore of a small mountain lake. She lived at this home instead of the wretched public asylum to which she had been confined since a child because every month of every year since the war, Toby Bowles paid the bills that allowed her to live there—even though he would never own a new car or a home as grand as Paul and Marion Hudson's. Sometimes he and Sheila played together, walking through the rooms of the home on imaginary journeys she created; Toby would be her customer in a store selling only hugs, or the passenger on an airplane flying to the ends of rainbows; they would climb trees and relax in the clouds, or paddle across the lake, which she thought the most exotic place on earth. He was always patient with her, and Sheila would always take Toby up to her room before he left and show him the black and white photograph of their mama and papa with their forced smiles on the day she was born, holding their baby Sheila not too close because of the deformities in her face and limbs that are the clinical signs of Down's syndrome.

"Toby suffered many injustices during his life as well," Haissem continued. "He was eleven years old when Sheila was born and that photograph was taken; it was the last photograph they had of their father, Gerard Bowles, who came home from the hospital that day with his face dark with disgrace and loathing; he told Toby his mother had done something very wrong and that God had punished her for it and he must leave and never return. Toby was relieved by his father's departure at first, because Gerard Bowles had been cruel to Toby and his mother, sometimes beating them with his belt the way Toby sometimes did with his own children—all the while quoting passages from the Bible about sin and the purification of the soul. But Toby soon learned what the loss of a father meant when his mother wouldn't stop crying and packed up their things to go live with his grandparents. This was when his new sister Sheila was taken away as a ward of the state. Lying in bed late at night, Toby worried for Sheila's and his father's safety; he prayed for their return, asking God to please forgive his mother for whatever she had done wrong to cause their family to split apart.

"In his teenage years," Haissem went on, "Toby's unrequited longing and love for his father turned into hatred of the man who had never once written a letter to let them know he was still alive—or to ask if they were still alive. At his most violent moments, Toby fantasized about meeting his father on a street, introducing himself as his son, and pulling a revolver from a pocket and shooting him dead between the eyes; at other moments, when the possibilities of the future seemed expansive and bright, Toby imagined becoming a great success and one day being stopped on the street by his father as a beggar and shoving him aside without recognition or pity. There were few times in Toby Bowles' life when he did not feel the pain of his father's abandonment; but his sister Sheila became the beneficiary of this broken relationship, receiving the love Toby would have given his father; she desperately needed such a champion because her mother blamed Sheila for all that had gone so terribly wrong. When the time came, Ester Bowles gladly handed Sheila over to the state as though she were handing over a carrier of typhus or a common criminal. Ester Bowles lived in a gloom from which she rarely ascended, replacing her need for a husband by suffocating Toby with jealous affection. Toby became as protective of Sheila as he was of his own daughters; he would have gladly gone to jail or bankrupted himself to win her escape from the asylum, and he nearly did both. All the extra money he raised by stealing and selling supplies in the Army went to Sheila, not for his own use—not even to feed and clothe his own young children.

"The only other photograph in Sheila's room, next to her bed, was taken by the director of the home on the day Toby brought her a terrier puppy she named Jack that went to heaven a year later when it crossed the road. Arm in arm, Sheila and Toby stand grinning for the photograph with the furry bundle— proud sister and wealthy businessman from the big city (for who else, she thought, could afford such an extravagant gift?).

"Sheila Bowles died in her sleep one year before Toby's affair with Bonnie Campbell began; Toby buried her on a brutal February morning in a small cemetery near the house by the lake, not far from the tiny wooden cross with the word 'Jack' carved into its surface by her hands. In a voice breaking with grief and love across the wind-swept knoll, Toby handed his sister over to her Creator, and he told her Creator, his family, and the few mourners from the house, that the earth would never again be graced by such innocence."

"But God heard none of this!" I protested to Haissem. "The moment of truth arrives for Toby Bowles, but his life unspools bad to good instead of good to bad and he's hurled into hell without appeal…without a trace? What kind of God would conduct such a trial?"

"A just God," Luas said. "The God of the Flood. Haissem presented the case through Mr. Bowles' own thoughts and actions. Could any of it be denied?"

"No," I conceded, "but only his sins were presented."

"Then only his sins were relevant," Luas answered, irritated by my challenge. "It was the Judge who ended the presentation. Who are we to weigh the gravity of Toby Bowles' offenses and determine what is just and unjust? I warned you not to speculate."

"I think it's good that Brek wants to hear Toby's story," Haissem interjected. "Understanding the mistakes and triumphs of his life may help her when she enters the Chamber on behalf of her first client." He turned to me. "There's more. Would you like to hear the rest?"

Luas wasn't willing to let it drop. "My point wasn't that Toby's story is irrelevant," he said. "I only meant to say that justice is God's, not ours, and that justice will be done."

"I understand, Luas," Haissem said curtly. "And my point is that justice has nothing to do with it at all."

Luas regarded Haissem suspiciously. "Then I respectfully disagree," he said.

Haissem ignored the comment and turned back to me. "Let me finish the story," he said. "You haven't even heard the most important part yet. You see, the truth is that Toby Bowles touched the lives of many people. To avoid a court martial for stealing the medical supplies in Saverne, he volunteered for a combat unit. Out of eight men assigned to that unit, all but Toby were shot dead or drowned in the Elbe River on the final push of the Allies to Berlin. Toby, himself, was hit in the leg while carrying his wounded sergeant up the river bank. He limped away, bleeding and stunned, and collapsed outside a small cabin in the woods near Kamenz. When he awakened, he found himself inside this cabin, feverish from an infection, surrounded by the family who lived there: a father, mother, teenage daughter, and two younger sons. They gave him food and water and he slept another twenty-four hours until he awoke again, this time to the sound of gunfire and screaming as the mother and children fled into a tunnel beneath the floorboards of the cabin and the father ran from the house with a shotgun.

"Toby hobbled along after the man to help, and they came to the edge of a clearing where they could see a very large house through the misty afternoon rain. They kneeled behind some bushes and watched as a platoon of soldiers with red stars on their sleeves drove the inhabitants from the house and out into the driveway: an elderly man, two middle aged women, a teen-age girl, two younger boys, and two younger girls, all dressed in party clothes. The leader of the platoon barked an order in Russian and the old man and the young boys were separated from the others and shot on the spot. When the women lunged toward the victims, they too were cut down in cold blood. It all appeared to Toby as in a dream, through the fine mist, distorted by fever from the infection, bodies dropping like shadows into darkness, continuing the savage nightmare begun earlier along the banks of the Elbe River. The man from the cabin, still kneel-ing beside Toby, jumped up and charged the platoon, firing his shotgun wildly into the air. The platoon returned the fire, killing him instantly.

"Toby started limping back toward the cabin before realizing he had been seen and would be leading the soldiers to the man's family. To save them, he changed direction and confronted the soldiers, knowing that in all likelihood he would be killed. He put his hands over his head and limped through the clearing, yelling 'American! American!' The grass was wet and the water soaked through his pants, stinging his wounds. All the while he was thinking not of himself, but of his sister Sheila and who would care for her now, of his mother and how news of his death would plunge her deeper into despair, of his father and how news of his death might haunt him with regret for the rest of his life.

"Two Russian soldiers came forward with their guns raised, but as they neared Toby and saw his uniform, they lowered their weapons. 'Amerika! Amerika!' they cheered, embracing him. Then the soldiers saw the cabin in the distance and advanced toward it. Toby knew the only hope for the family was for him to convince the soldiers that he had already taken them pris-oner. He limped along behind the soldiers as fast as he could; when they got to the door, he slid past them, pulled out his sidearm, and motioned for them to stand back. One of the soldiers grabbed the pistol from Toby's hands, but Toby pushed the door open, yanked up the floorboards and ordered the frightened family out of the tunnel. They were white and shaking with fear; they glared at Toby for having been betrayed after they had saved his life. Toby pointed at them and then himself and said to the soldiers: 'My prisoners! My prisoners!' He grabbed the mother and slammed her against the wall, then the daughter and the two boys. He pointed to a medal on one of the Russian's chests and then his own chest, where a new medal would be placed if he brought them in.

"'My prisoners! My prisoners!' he said again.

"The Russians finally understood. They smiled, slapped him on the back, and gave him back his gun. Toby put the gun against the temple of the mother, completing the charade. The soldiers lowered their rifles and laughed.

"'Amerika! Amerika!' they said, shaking their heads as they walked away.

"Toby saved their lives that afternoon, but they were no longer safe in the cabin; he convinced them to gather their things and flee into the woods. Late the next day, after Toby first checked to be sure the Russians had left the area, he led the mother back to the clearing to retrieve the body of her dead husband. Unable to speak German, he attempted to comfort the distraught woman as best he could, using his hands and showing her the corpses of the people from the house to attempt to explain that her husband had been brave to confront the soldiers and try and save their lives. The mother began to understand, and only then did she begin to comprehend what Toby himself had done to spare her family the same fate.

"Toby carried the lifeless body of the man back to the cabin and helped the boys dig a grave. The family's anguish overwhelmed him and at times he cried with them because he too had lost a father, just as they had. But Toby wept also out of a desperate and mournful jealousy of these children, who had at least known their father, could bury him, and would remember him as a father who had loved them enough to sacrifice his life for them and others. Although Toby couldn't understand their strange prayers, when they placed a yarmulke upon the man's head and nobody made the sign of the cross, he realized these were Jewish prayers, spoken in Hebrew. He made the sign of the cross anyway, whispering a prayer for the man and for his own father, and the entire world as well. But upon seeing the cross, the daughter, hysterical with grief, began wailing 'Amina! Amina! Amina!' She removed a small gold cross of her own from her pocket and made the sign on her chest. Horrified, the mother reached over to slap her, but suddenly a deep and profound understanding flashed across her face; she bowed her head and began to weep even more violently. Toby did not understand what had happened between the mother and daughter but helped them fill the grave.

"The group began walking west toward Leipzig, where Toby hoped to find Allied troops. At Frieberg, they came across an American infantry unit, and Toby was able with his leg wound, and a small bribe, to get them all loaded onto a truck headed further west into Allied territory. They rode together as far as Nuremberg, where they were taken to a field hospital and Toby finally received the medical care that saved his leg from amputation. The mother and the daughter were embarrassed and helpless at the moment of their parting because they had no way to repay his generosity. But then the mother's eyes brightened and she whispered something to the daughter and made a gesture, asking for a pen and a piece of paper. An orderly gave these to the mother and she carefully copied Toby's last name from his shirt, B-O-W-L-E-S, on the paper. She said to him: '*Mein erstes Enkelkind wird nach Ihnen benannt,*' but she could see that he didn't understand, so she held the paper against her daughter's womb, raising her index finger in the air as if to say 'first,' then she held her arms as if she were cradling a baby and tucked the paper into her daughter's hand. Toby finally understood what she was trying to say. He hugged them both and said goodbye."

When Haissem finished, he turned to Luas and said: "But Luas is entirely correct, Brek. We must not be tempted into judging what is and is not just. That is not for us to decide."

Luas nodded his head appreciatively.

"I must leave you now," Haissem said. "We'll meet again, after you've handled your first case. Good luck."

As Haissem walked away, Luas whispered to me:

"He's the most senior presenter here, but I sometimes wonder whether his time has passed. The things he says sometimes are very dangerous."

"What about the trial?" I responded. "The Final Judgment is nothing more than a sham where the accused is prohibited from speaking, before a tribunal nobody can see, attended by witnesses the accused can't confront, represented by a lawyer who is also his prosecutor, and ended by the judge before a defense can even be presented. There's less justice in heaven than we have on earth."

Luas glared at me. "*Never* say that again, Brek," he warned me. "This is the way of Divine Justice, not man's justice. We have no right to question it. God and justice are one."

12

My one solace in Shemaya was visiting the places that had been dear to me while I was alive. They were all there, exact replicas of my house, my town, my world—the only things missing were the people, like walking through an empty movie studio lot. These were lonely visits, but I found this loneliness, at first, to be a great comfort. I needed to get away from Luas, the Urartu Chamber, and my Nana; I needed to get away from other souls' memories and other souls' lives. So I went home. I didn't go there to grieve: I didn't dare look in Sarah's room or Bo's closet because I knew I would break down; I just wanted to be happy again, to pick up where I left off and *live*.

So, the first thing I did when I got home was go shopping. I decided that if God was going to strand me in this sadistic netherworld where everything reminded me of life's lost pleasures, I might as well indulge in some of those pleasures and enjoy myself a little. My first stop was the local mall, and, boy, did I shop. It was, without exception, the greatest shopping trip I've ever had: no lines, no crowds, no pushy salespeople; the entire mall to myself, and best of all, everything marvelously, magnificently *free*. It was, in a way, heaven. I disrobed and tried on clothes right in the middle of sales floors rather than going back to the dressing rooms; if I didn't like something, I just tossed it over my shoulder and moved on. I replaced the black silk suit I'd been wearing since I arrived in Shemaya with a cute, insanely expensive wool miniskirt and top that I robbed from a startled mannequin. I plundered stock rooms, pried open display cases, and hauled my booty around on a merry train of rolling racks weighted down with four seasons' worth of apparel, shoes, accessories, makeup, and fine jewelry. The only limit to my decadence was my ability to cart it all away. Like a looter after a hurricane, I backed my car up to the doors and crammed it full. After an entire day of this, I dragged myself to the food court and helped myself to a double cheeseburger and milkshake, which spontaneously appeared at the counter, topping it all off with five white chocolate macadamia nut cookies. Yes, heaven indeed.

By the time I returned home from my shopping spree, I was so exhausted that I left everything in the car and collapsed on the couch. To my delight, the television functioned normally and displayed any channel I selected as long as it was showing something prerecorded, like a movie or a sitcom; the live news, weather, and sports channels displayed only white static, which was fine by me. I dozed in and out, happily watching reruns of *M*A*S*H* and *All in the Family*; but as evening came on, the weekend infomercials featuring gorgeous models demonstrating exercise equipment began having their guilt-inspiring effect on me (yes, even after death). I got up, dressed in the sleek new racer-back top and shorts I'd picked up at the mall, and went to the YMCA for a workout to show them off.

Of course, the gym was empty and there was nobody to show off to when I arrived, which was rather disappointing because I thought I looked pretty hot for a one-armed girl who usually wore oversized t-shirts and baggy sweatpants during her workouts. Bo had been begging me for years to get new exercise clothes and would have loved the change. On the plus side, the fact that nobody was there meant no waiting for machines and no sweaty, smelly men grunting and ogling; it was like being rich and having my own personal health club. I climbed on a treadmill and tried to set the workout time for thirty minutes, but the digital timer, like all clocks in Shemaya, didn't work and I had to rely on the odometer. I started off at my normal pace and felt so good when I reached three miles that I continued on to six, then ten (more than I'd ever run), twenty, and so on until the indicator flashed that I'd run ninety-nine miles and was resetting itself back to zero. Ironically, being dead improved my endurance; I barely broke a sweat and my pulse remained in the perfect range the entire time. My muscle strength in death improved as well. With no effort at all I was able to lift the huge stacks of weights heaved around by the body builders and football players.

I noticed I looked better dead than alive too. In the mirrors on the walls around the gym, my muscles were as taut and sculpted as an Olympic athlete's; my stomach and thighs as tight and smooth as they had been the day I turned eighteen. No evidence whatsoever that I'd delivered a baby only ten months ago. Preening before the mirrors, my body seemed more beautiful and fascinating to me than it had ever been before. *What an exquisite and amazing creation*, I thought. I stared at it dumbstruck, as if it were another creature, not me, trying to comprehend how it had come to be here, eager to see what it would do next. It bent over and touched the floor, then recoiling against gravity rose up straight and tall, buttocks and breasts striking the perfect counterpoise, fingers fanning outward, a wave in the ocean, creating and re-creating itself, always different but always the same. Its leg tensed, then its arm, and like a cloud pushed by the wind, it reshaped itself and struck a new pose—a fractured Renaissance sculpture no less perfect for the amputation. It *was* art, music, science, mystery. I wasn't given two arms in Shemaya—probably because I could only think of myself as an amputee—but my body seemed all the more beautiful for it. When I brushed against the cold steel frame of an exercise bike, a shiver ran up my spine, reconnecting me to the body I saw in the mirror. In that moment, I regretted how foolish I'd been during my life for not having noticed all these amazing things and what a gift I had been given. This body, my body, just the way it was, had always been holy, had always been mine, and it had always been as beautiful and precious as life itself. *How could I not have known that?* I wondered. *How could I have taken it for granted for so long?*

I finished my workout perspiration and odor free, no need for a shower. Nightfall had come and I considered going to a restaurant and then a movie by myself but thought that would be just too weird. I decided to spend the evening at home, watching a movie and eating popcorn.

I changed into my new silk pajamas when I got back. Popcorn spontaneously appeared in a bowl on the coffee table, and I put on the television. *An Officer and a Gentleman* was playing—one of my favorite movies, exactly what I was in the mood to see. Because of this movie, I had willingly and blissfully surrendered my virginity during my sophomore year of college, and seeing it again triggered sweet memories of the night and the guy. As strange and implausible as it had all seemed to be dead and yet still be able to shop, exercise, eat popcorn, and watch TV, it was stranger still to be dead and feel the sudden ache of sexual desire ripple over my body in a way even more powerful and urgent than I had experienced while alive. It was far more than the carnal craving for physical pleasure and release; it was a deeper stirring of that fundamental impulse, present in every corner of the universe—present the night Bo and I conceived Sarah—to defy death by creating life. And it was also, for me—surprised but somehow unashamed to feel aroused within the darkness of my own death—a final opportunity to re-experience and reclaim all I had been and all I had lost. Submitting to the primal necessity that had moved God himself to create, alone and out of nothingness, I released the creative organs of my own body, such as they were, with the hope and prayer that out of nothingness would come life. God might have ordained that humans shall not create in solitude, but for one cathartic moment, I could see the clear resemblance of God in the fragile nobility, in the desperation and the ecstasy, of the entire human race. Then came the nagging question: *Why did I die? What happened to me?* I could no longer wait for answers.

I ran from the house still dressed in my pajamas and roared off in my car toward the convenience store and the last memories of my life, determined to re-create every detail. The fall air was fresh and cool, exactly as it was in my dreams. I retraced my steps, singing *Hot Tea and Bees Honey* on the way into the store and grabbing a carton of milk from the refrigerator case before turning down the aisle where Sarah knocked the pastries onto the floor.

It's almost six-twenty,
says Teddy Bear,
mama's coming home now,
she's almost right there.

Hot tea and bees honey,
for mama and her baby;
Hot tea and bees honey,
for two we will share.

I stooped down to pick up the pastries.

This is where all my dreams had ended since arriving in She-maya—hollow and questioning, like a failed coroner's inquest. Cause of death: *unknown.* But this time there was no overpowering smell of manure and mushrooms as there had been before. I waited at the counter with the milk carton, hoping there would be some clue or sign, hoping recollection would be stimulated and there would be an answer. None came. I remembered nothing of life beyond this moment, just arriving in Shemaya Station, my clothes stained with baby formula that turned to blood.

I threw the milk carton across the counter; it exploded white against the shelves stocked with cigarettes.

"What happened to me?" I screamed into the silence. "*What happened to me?*" I walked back out to my car in tears.

On the drive home, a car appeared in my rearview mirror—my first encounter with another car since the traffic had backed up on the street when I arrived in Huntingdon and I thought I was going insane. When we reached a long, deserted stretch of road with corn and hay fields on both sides, the high-beam headlights of the car behind started flashing and bursts from a red strobe light filled my rearview mirror, hurting my eyes. The red light came from low on the windshield; I could tell it was an unmarked patrol car and decided to pull over even though I knew it would be unoccupied. Sitting there on the side of the road with my car idling, admiring the authenticity of the virtual reality game I seemed to be playing with myself, I remembered Bo warning me he'd seen a speed trap on this stretch of road.

Of course, no patrolman appeared at my window, so I decided to get out and go have a look. The engine of the police car was running but there was nobody inside. I opened the driver's door, turning on the dome lights. It looked like the interior of a normal four door sedan rather than a police car after all; there was no police radio or any of the other equipment you would expect; the only resemblance to a police car was the red strobe light on the dashboard, connected by a coil of black cord to the cigarette lighter. Glancing in back, I saw a videocassette tape on the floor and went around to the rear door to get it. As I slid across the seat, the door slammed shut behind me and locked me inside; then the shifter on the steering column mysteriously moved itself from park to drive and the car pulled back onto the road without a driver. Looking over my shoulder, I could see my own car following behind.

I laughed. It could have been very spooky, terrifying even, but after you've accepted your own death, what more is there to be afraid of? Handwritten on the label of the videocassette were the words "What Happened?" *How appropriate*, I thought. *Maybe God speaks to souls on video and I would finally find out what happened to me.* I sat back and relaxed, as if I were on an amusement park ride, curious to see where the car would take me.

We headed south on Route 22 for a few miles. There were no other cars on the road, all the homes and businesses were dark. The seasons stopped cycling; it was autumn everywhere now and colored leaves rained down on the windshield like drops of thick, wet paint. We turned off onto a side road at Ardenheim and up an old dirt logging road into the mountains with the headlights of both cars shut off, hitting ruts and splashing through mud puddles. The car I was riding in finally stopped, and my car following behind stopped as well, then turned and backed itself off the log road into a grove of pine trees, crushing branches as it moved until it was covered with pine boughs and could no longer be seen in the moonlight. Its engine shut off and a moment later, the videocassette suddenly vanished from my lap, as if it had been a mirage all along. The car I was riding in backed its way down the logging road in the direction from which we had come and drove out onto the highway, turning its lights back on. *Very strange*, I thought, *very strange*. But I had seen far stranger things in Shemaya—and I had nothing better to do—so I decided to play along.

The driverless sedan with me sitting in the backseat continued traveling south through the night to Route 522, then along Route 322 east toward Harrisburg. This was the same route I took when traveling between Delaware and Huntingdon, and I began to suspect that Nana and Luas had somehow contrived all of this as a way of bringing me back home. The radio came on, switching itself between country music stations as the signals faded, proving to me that my mind was not in control of the car—I rarely listened to country music. When we reached Lancaster, the car turned onto Route 30 east, then south onto Route 41 through the rolling farmland of southern Chester County and toward Delaware, as I had suspected. But before crossing the state line, we turned off onto a winding secondary road, following this for a time until we turned again onto a smaller country lane. There were no streetlights or power lines now; the sky was coal black, without the hope of stars or the kind solace of the moon. The last uninhabited home passed from view miles ago, asleep in the cool harvest air pregnant with the scent of decaying leaves and apples. Finally, the pavement ended and we were traveling on a gravel road descending a steep ravine through woods and ending on rutted tracks leading through an open, overgrown field, then back into more woods and down an even steeper slope.

The tracks ended at a crumbling cinderblock building protruding from the ground like an ugly scab. Its windowless walls stood barely one-story tall and were pocked with black streaks of mold and a leprosy of flaking white paint; it resembled the shell of an abandoned industrial building and looked out of place in the country. I had the feeling I had been there before, although I remembered no such place.

The gear selector moved itself to park, the engine shut off, and the doors unlocked. I got out of the car and walked up to the building, lit by the yellow glare of the headlights. The cloying stench of manure and mushrooms—the same odor I had smelled in the convenience store in my dreams—made the air heavy and difficult to breathe. Pulling open the worm-eaten door, I was fearful now even though I knew there could be nothing to harm me. As I stepped inside, bright daylight erupted across the sky, like a thermonuclear explosion, vaporizing the building, the car, the woods, and my own body.

I find myself within the bedchamber of a great Roman palace, a chamber as immense and splendid as the Pantheon itself. White stone columns soar into the bowl of a fantastic marble dome overhead; beneath it sits a glittering golden bed surrounded by divans covered in plush crimson fabric. Standing in front of this bed, bloated and nude, is the Emperor Nero Claudius Caesar. At his feet, groaning and pleading for mercy, lies his wife, Poppaea, fully clothed and several months pregnant with his child. Her white gown is streaked red between her legs.

"You ungrateful whore!" Nero bellows as he drives his foot deep into Poppaea's abdomen. "I put Octavia's head on a platter for your amusement and this is how you repay me, by ridiculing me!" He kicks her again, more savagely, and this time her ribs give way, cracking and breaking like twigs. Poppaea gasps for air, blood drools from her mouth.

"Get out of my sight!"

Poppaea does not rise. Nero strikes another blow to her stomach, then turns and walks from the bedchamber with his hands on his hips, soaked with sweat from the exertion, his penis flapping from side to side against his heavy thighs, like a wagging finger. He orders his servants to have her removed and bring him a meal before he takes his afternoon nap.

The Roman palace vanishes just as suddenly as it had appeared. In its place emerges the outline of the Urartu Chamber with Luas standing at its center; the faceless creature from the monolith whispers something in his ear then returns to its home inside the monolith. I am sitting, now, on one of the observer chairs in the back of the Chamber. I have no idea how I've gotten from the cinderblock building, to Nero's palace, to the Urartu Chamber. Luas walks over to speak to me.

"Hello, Brek," he says. "I'm sorry you had to see that. How was your visit back home?"

"You just presented Nero?" I say, astonished by what I have just seen.

The Urartu Chamber disappears, and now we're standing in the corridor leading back to the train shed.

"Yes, foul character, isn't he?"

"But he died two thousand years ago—"

"And I've been representing him ever since," Luas says. "The presentation usually ends here, or just after he has the boy Sporus castrated and takes him for his wife. When I return to the Chamber the next day, I'm informed a final decision on his fate still hasn't been made and I must present his case again." Luas sighs. "This is my job, it seems, to try Nero's soul every day for eternity, even though a decision is never made. Seems God isn't quite ready to make up his mind about this one."

"Didn't you say we only present the close cases," I ask.

"Yes, well, there are two sides to every story, aren't there? It may seem strange, but Nero did have some redeeming qualities, not unlike Toby Bowles. I never get to them during the presentation, of course, but he had them. Anyway, ours is not to wonder why. Nero is a postulant here and we treat him like all the rest. Just be happy he isn't one of your clients."

We start walking toward the train shed, but Luas leads me around a corner and into another corridor I hadn't seen before, so unfathomably long that I'm unable to see the end of it stretching beyond the horizon and out into space. It has the appearance of a vast courthouse annex, with thousands of identical offices lining both sides of the corridor, each with tall, slender wooden doors and transoms closed tight; florescent tubes bathe the walls in the uniform and compassionless light of bureaucracy.

We continue walking. "So," I say, still stunned by the trial, "Nero and Toby Bowles are treated the same way—nothing they did right their entire lives is heard in the Chamber. What's the point of conducting a trial at all—if you can even call it that? Why not just send them straight to hell?"

"Back to that again, are we?" Luas says. "There is no Bill of Rights in Shemaya. The procedural protections in which you placed such great faith as an attorney on earth are entirely unnecessary here. No lie can go unexposed in the Urartu Chamber, and no truth remains hidden. Justice is guaranteed as long as the presenters remain unbiased and do nothing to tip the scales."

"But how can there be justice if all sides of the case aren't presented?"

"Do I need to remind you," Luas answers in a reprimanding way, "that the Judge himself was once tried, convicted, and punished unjustly? Surely He requires no lessons from us about fairness. Of course, justice has many dimensions, and we've been speaking only of fairness to the accused; you lost your arm when you were just a little girl, Nero Claudius turned Christians into tapers, and God once drowned every living creature. To know whether justice has been done, one must consider all of its aspects."

We somehow reach the end of the limitless corridor. Luas stops us at the last office on the right. A small plaque on the door reads, "High Jurisconsult of Shemaya."

"Ah, here we are," Luas announces, opening the door. "The next phase of your training is about to begin."

13

There was a simple wooden desk in the office, two candles, two chairs behind the desk, and a single guest chair in front of it. No windows, papers, files, phones, pencils, or other office items. Luas closed the door and struck a match to light the candles.

"Please have a seat here beside me," he said. "We're going to interview a new postulant together and then watch the presentation. I will be your proctor. After this, you will be assigned your first client and conduct a trial on your own."

"Am I being forced to represent them?" I asked. "I mean, what if I refuse?"

"Forced?" Luas said. "Certainly not. The choice is yours, but it's a choice you have already made. That's why you're here. You will represent them because, like all lawyers, justice is what you crave most and you won't rest until you have it."

"There's no justice here," I said flatly. "At least not the kind I crave."

Luas smiled condescendingly. "Perhaps you will introduce it to us then," he said.

I thought about this for a moment and, for the first time, considered the possibility that I just might be able to help these poor souls, that this might be the reason why I was brought to Shemaya, to fix a broken judicial system. Lawyers had a long and proud tradition of bringing about reform and restoring justice to the world. I had always dreamed of doing something truly significant and grand, like Mahatma Gandhi or Martin Luther.

"Perhaps I will," I said. "Perhaps I will." Then I looked down and realized I was still wearing my silk pajamas, from what I had thought would be a relaxing evening at home, watching a movie and eating popcorn.

"Oh, you needn't worry about your clothes," Luas said, noticing my embarrassment. "The postulants can't see us; but if you'd feel more comfortable, you may change into these." From a desk drawer he produced the black suit, blouse, and shoes I'd been wearing since I arrived in Shemaya—the ones I'd discarded at the mall during my shopping spree.

"How did you get these?" I asked, confused.

"I didn't get them," he said. "You did. Go ahead, put them on, I'll step outside."

By telling me I got the clothes, Luas meant to remind me that I was making all of this up—my appearance and his, that is, not Shemaya itself, which existed quite independently of me, and over which I exercised no control. Even so, I took the opportunity to dress, out of respect for my profession if nothing else; pajamas were not appropriate for meeting a client on earth or in heaven, particularly a client facing the Final Judgment.

Luas returned to the office and seated himself beside me behind the desk, surrounded by darkness. The dim candles gave his face a dull orange color.

"Before I invite the postulant in," he said, "I must warn you that there is a grave danger in this meeting, one for which I have been trying to prepare you. More than Mr. Bowles, more than your parents, your husband, or even your own child, will you come to know the postulant we are about to meet; only slightly better will you know yourself. To avoid losing your identity forever, you must employ the tactics I showed you earlier. No matter how difficult, you must continue to remind yourself of the circumstances of your disfigurement. Try to recall the smallest details: the smell of the air above the manure, the sound of the flies buzzing over the heap; the puzzled look of the cows as they watched you and your grandfather spreading their excrement across the fields; the way the heavy, wet dung, produced by the first alfalfa of the season, clotted in the bin like plaster, jamming the tines.

"Your parents had told you they were taking you to your grandparents' farm to enjoy some time in the country, but you had heard the viciousness of their argument when your father revealed the arrangements, against your mother's wishes, to admit her into a treatment center for alcoholics and your mother revealed her knowledge that he had been having an affair. All that had held them together was you, and you were convinced that only a crisis would hold you all together now. You considered running away, but this would only separate you from them; you had already tried modulating your grades, but the good marks only gave them confidence of your adjustment and the bad just another source for blame. Behaving and misbehaving had the same weak effect, and crying worked only temporarily and could not be sustained. You had even contrived illnesses, but doctors confirmed your health and the proper functioning of your organs."

I could no longer bear the pain of reliving those difficult days. "Enough!" I said. "Please, stop."

"You did not plan what to do next," Luas continued, ignoring my discomfort. "Your grandfather had warned you to stand clear as he worked his pitchfork through the pile; he climbed down from the bin and up onto the tractor, but he left the guard off the conveyor chain. You watched the chain hesitate for a moment under the load and then break free with a bang, whirring through the gears and cogs as the tractor engine roared and the manure flew. The thought struck you in that very moment, before he could disengage the power and replace the guard. You ran up and thrust your hand into the gears. You thought you'd only cut your finger or perhaps break it; but feeling no more than the return of a firm handshake at first, you watched in astonishment and disbelief as your forearm ripped from your elbow and hurled along the conveyor like a toy on an assembly line. You stood frozen for a moment, the way one does upon first seeing one's own reflection, watching yourself watch yourself, but not fully recognizing the image. In the moment before you lost consciousness, your body tingled—not with pain, but with the brief exaltation that you had finally succeeded in reuniting your parents and all would soon be well."

"No more, Luas," I begged, sobbing. "Please, stop."

"But there is more," Luas said callously. "So much more. This is the only way to separate yourself from the powerful memories of the postulants, and this is what must be done. Two years later, after your parents had divorced and the right sleeves of your clothes had been sewn shut, you took the witness stand in the Huntingdon County Courthouse, where you would one day practice law, and a young attorney named Bill Gwynne asked you to show the jury the mangled stump of your arm and tell them what happened. It was the most critical testimony in the case, to establish the liability of the manufacturer of the manure spreader for producing a defective product and bestow upon you and your family a small fortune in recompense. The courtroom was silent, every moist eye turned to you. You had practiced your testimony so often with Mr. Gwynne that you actually believed what you were about to say. He had promised you justice. You faced the jury and do you remember what you said?"

"Yes, yes," I cried, traumatized and ashamed. "I remember. There's no need for you to repeat it."

"Oh, but I must," Luas said. "'I was standing on my toes,' you told the jury, 'trying to see what my grandfather was doing. I slipped on the wet grass and fell against the guard. I didn't hit it very hard, but the guard gave way and my arm got caught in the gears—' You became too emotional to go on; the memory of what happened next was too painful."

Luas' relentless recounting of the story was having the desired effect; so immersed did he have me in my own memories that I couldn't possibly confuse my life with that of the postulant I was about to meet. I saw myself there on the witness stand, a ten year old girl again: the judge, robed in black, glaring down at me from the bench, old and terrifying like God; the pinch-faced stenographer yawning as she taps her keys; my grandfather, pale with guilt and remorse, nervously fondling his pipe, aching for a smoke; my grandmother waving a roll of Lifesavers at me for encouragement; my mother sitting by herself on the other side of the courtroom with her "I told you so" face, snarling at my father and grandparents; my father sucking on a Lifesaver my grandmother insisted he take, checking his watch; the defense lawyer from Pittsburgh, too slick and condescending for Huntingdon County, whispering to the vice president of the equipment manufacturer, a Texan, who crosses his legs and strokes the brown suede of his cowboy boots. To my right sits the jury who will decide the case: three farmers, a hairdresser, a housewife, and a truck mechanic. The farmers tug uncomfortably at the collars of their white dress shirts; the hairdresser, wearing too much makeup, cracks her gum, drawing the glare of the overfed tipstave with stains on his necktie; the housewife, wearing too little makeup, fusses with her hair; the truck mechanic bites his dirty fingernails, stealing glances at the hairdresser.

"It's ok, honey," Mr. Gwynne says. He's here to protect me, my knight in shining armor, gallant and handsome; I have a secret crush on him. "Take a moment to blow your nose; I know it's difficult with one hand. I'm sorry we have to do this, but the makers of the manure spreader here want their day in court, and they're entitled to it. Just a few more questions, ok? We need you to be brave now and tell the truth. Are you certain the guard was in place? I'm talking about the metal shield over the chain."

"Oh, yes, Mr. Gwynne, I'm certain."

"And you slipped and bumped into it?"

"Yes."

"And it gave way?"

"Yes."

"And your arm got caught in the chain."

"Yes. Gee, I'm sorry, Mr. Gwynne; I'm awfully sorry for all this. I should have been more careful."

"You have nothing to be sorry for, Brek," he reassures me. "We're the ones who are sorry for what happened to you. You've been very brave for us today, and we appreciate it."

The jury returned a verdict against the manufacturer in less than an hour: four hundred and fifty thousand dollars. An expert hired by Mr. Gwynne testified that if the spreader had been designed properly, there would have been no need to remove the guard to fix the problem in the first place, meaning that my lie might not have made the difference after all. One-third of the money went to Mr. Gwynne; another third put me through an expensive Quaker boarding school, four years at a private liberal arts college, and three years at an Ivy League law school; the rest paid my medical bills with some left over for other expenses, including a semester abroad in Europe. Only my grandfather knew for certain I lied about the guard, but we never spoke about it to each other. He testified that he couldn't remember whether he left it on or off, which made it seem like only half a lie.

Luas wasn't finished with me yet: "Nobody in the courtroom that day knew," he said, "not your parents, not Bill Gwynne, not even your grandfather—that you deliberately put your hand into the machine. You told only one person, Karen Busfield, and that was almost twenty years after the trial. Do you remember?"

It came back to me with the same clarity as the trial, as if it were happening all over again—as if I were seeing my own life being replayed in the Urartu Chamber. Karen called me late one night; Bo and I were asleep.

"Hi, Karen," I said, yawning into the phone. "What time is it? Are you ok?"

"2 a.m. Sorry for calling you so late. I need a lawyer."

"I told you this day would come," I quipped. The sounds of a jail echoed in the background; rough voices, the slamming echo of steel doors. "Where are you?"

"Fort Leavenworth."

"Fort Leavenworth? What are you doing there, counseling inmates?"

"I am an inmate."

I could tell she wasn't joking.

Bo rolled over. "What's going on?" he said.

"It's Karen," I whispered, covering the phone. "I think she's been arrested."

I uncovered the phone. "You're a chaplain, Karen," I said. "What could you have possibly done?"

"I can't talk about that right now," she said.

"Ok. Can you tell me what they're charging you with?"

"Assault, destruction of government property and...."

"And what?"

"Treason."

"*Treason?* Are you serious?" Bo's eyes widened.

"Yes."

"I'm coming, and I'm bringing Bill Gwynne with me."

"No, just you," she said.

"Treason is a big deal, Karen; I don't want to scare you, but it carries the death penalty. I'm bringing Bill with me—and maybe twenty other lawyers. Let me call the airlines. We'll be there as soon as we can."

"Just you, Brek, okay?" she said, desperately, on the verge of breaking down. "Please?"

"Okay," I said. "For now. We can talk about it when I get there."

"Thanks," she said. "Don't rush, take care of Sarah first. I'll be fine. I'm really sorry about this. How's she doing?"

"She's fine. It's you I'm worried about."

"I'm really sorry—"

"Don't worry about it. Let me pack a bag. Do you need anything?"

"Just you," she said. She was crying and I could hear voices in the background. "They're saying I've got to hang up now," she sniffled.

"Everything will be all right," I said. "I'll be there as soon as I can. Stay strong. And no matter what you do, *don't answer any questions, okay?* Tell them you're invoking your right to remain silent until you've spoken with your attorney."

"Okay. Thanks, Brek. I've got to go. Bye."

I hung up the phone.

Bo was fully awake and sitting up now. "They're charging an Air Force chaplain with treason?" he said. "We did some research into treason cases for an espionage story we were doing a few years ago; there have been fewer than like fifty treason prosecutions in the entire history of the United States. This is going to be front page national news."

"I know," I said bleakly. "But you know you can't be the one to break the story, right? Karen called me as her lawyer; my conversation with her was a confidential attorney-client communication."

"But—"

"Promise me, Bo," I said. "This is serious. I know you want to be the first on a story like this, but there's no way you can report it or tip anybody else about it. I can't be Karen's lawyer if I have to worry that everything I say in my own home might wind up on the wires the next day."

"Ok," he said glumly, "but get ready: you're going to be facing a lot of other reporters—guys who won't be as nice as me. You'll be on television every day—maybe even more than me."

"Great, I'll replace the weather girl."

"Let's not get carried away."

"Can you take care of Sarah while I'm gone?"

"We'll manage. I'll call in a few favors."

"Thanks. I'm going to need your help to get through this."

"You've got it, whatever you need." He kissed me on the forehead. "Go kick some prosecutor's butt and make me proud."

I hugged him and headed for the shower.

14

The next morning, I flew to Kansas City, rented a car, and drove to Leavenworth. Two female guards escorted Karen, wearing handcuffs and dressed in orange prison coveralls, into the small room with a table and two chairs reserved for attorney visits. Karen looked terrible—pale and gaunt with dark circles under her puffy, red eyes as though she hadn't slept or eaten in days. She took the chair across from me and flashed me a weak smile. The guards left the room and closed and locked the door behind them so our conversation would be confidential, but they continued monitoring us through a window.

"Oh, sweetie," I said, reaching out to touch her hand. One of the guards rapped on the window and gestured toward a sign in the room saying, "No Physical Contact Permitted." Karen scowled at the guard, but I obeyed, putting my hand in my lap. We looked at each other silently.

"I'm really sorry I dragged you all the way here," she said. "How was your flight?"

"Fine," I said, "no problems. How are you holding up? Are they treating you okay?"

She looked down and tugged on her coveralls. "They took my clerical collar."

"Don't worry," I said, "we'll get it back. I'm meeting with the U.S. Attorney later this afternoon to see if I can get this cleared up, or at least negotiate a low bail; you're a priest with no criminal history and you're not much of a flight risk." I glanced at my watch. "We only have forty-five minutes. Tell me what happened."

Karen yawned and rubbed her eyes. "They've been questioning me for two days. I haven't gotten any sleep."

"Questioning you for two days?" I said, alarmed. "Didn't they tell you that you had the right to a lawyer?"

"Yes," she said, "but I told them I didn't think I needed one."

"What?" I said, indignantly, more than a little cranky myself from having been awoken in the middle of the night to travel from Pennsylvania to Kansas. "They're charging you with treason and you didn't think you needed a lawyer? Why did you bother calling me then?"

"Please don't yell at me," Karen said.

I took a deep breath. "I'm sorry," I said. "It's just that it makes it so much harder to defend you if you've been talking to them for two days already. Did you confess to anything?"

"Of course not…at least not that I'm aware of."

"That's exactly my point," I said. "Two days with no sleep, who knows what they had you saying. No more talking, okay?"

"Okay, no more talking."

"Good, now tell me what happened."

She looked at me and then, fidgeting with her fingers, looked away. She was broken and ashamed. I had never seen her this way before.

"I can't help you unless you talk to me, Karen."

"I know."

I sat quietly, waiting, but she wouldn't speak. "Okay," I said, finally, "I'll tell you what. Let me tell you something I've never told anybody before, something *I* did wrong."

"You've never done anything wrong," Karen said.

"Yes, I have," I said. I tugged on the empty right sleeve of my suit—the same black silk suit I was wearing when I arrived in Shemaya; I wore it that day because I knew I would need all the confidence I could get to meet the U.S. Attorney. "Do you see this?" I said, showing her the empty sleeve; then I proceeded to tell her everything about how I had lost my arm, including my perjured testimony during the trial. When I finished, she smiled gratefully and compassionately—like a priest.

"You were only a child," she said, softly. "And you've already been forgiven. Do you know that?"

"Yes," I said, "I know. And *you've* already been forgiven for whatever you've done too. Do you know that?"

She smiled again and wiped her eyes. "Yes, I guess I do."

"Then tell me what happened."

"Okay," she said. She summoned her strength. "Well, since you're my lawyer, I guess I can tell you...I'm a chaplain to the missileers."

"The who?"

"The missileers—the airmen who man the nuclear missile silos; you know, the ones who will launch the ICBMs to end the world when given the command?"

"Wow," I said, impressed, "I guess I thought you were just an ordinary base chaplain somewhere ministering to fighter pilots and their families or something."

"I wasn't allowed to tell anybody what I really do," she said. "I actually requested this duty after I passed Officer Training

School. They stationed me at Minot Air Force Base in North Dakota, one of the few remaining bases that still has Minuteman nuclear missiles on alert."

"Interesting," I said. "Okay, so what happened?"

"I told them launching nuclear missiles was wrong and they should refuse to do it if they're ever ordered to."

"You mean 'wrong' as in wrong unless we're attacked first?" I asked.

"No," Karen said, "even in retaliation."

I was surprised. "So if the Russians or some rouge nation fires nuclear missiles at the United States, we're not supposed to respond?"

"We're supposed to forgive. We're not supposed to resist violence with violence."

"But that's what the military does, Karen," I said. "They resist violence with violence; that's their line of work, it's their entire reason for being. Why did you become a military chaplain if you don't agree with what they do?"

Karen looked annoyed. "Would you ask why somebody became a doctor if they didn't agree with human sickness and disease? We go where we're needed most and can do the most good. Doctors work in hospitals because that's where the sick people are. Nobody needs to learn about non-violence and forgiveness more than the military—and nobody in the military needs to learn about it more than the people who launch weapons that can destroy the world."

I was stunned—it was the crayfish trials all over again. "That's all very nice," I said, "but the best way of deterring a nuclear attack is to make sure our enemies understand they'll suffer the same fate if they ever try it."

"But if we're attacked," Karen argued, "then, by definition, nuclear deterrence will have failed, so why bother to retaliate?"

"I don't think I follow you," I said.

"Let's say we're attacked by nuclear weapons this afternoon," Karen said. "If that happens, it would be despite our threat of retaliation and mutually assured destruction. In other words, our threat of retaliation didn't work—it didn't deter the attack."

"I guess so...."

"So if it didn't deter the attack, then retaliating would be risking the destruction of the world to carry out an already failed strategy. It would be both illogical and immoral."

"Look," I said, now annoyed myself, "you've obviously given this more thought than I have. I'm not here to debate nuclear strategy; I'm here to defend you against a charge of treason. There's a right to free speech in this country, a right we protect, by the way, with nuclear missiles—and it says you can say anything you want regardless of whether others agree, so I still don't understand what you did wrong and why you're here. Telling missileers not to launch their missiles might be a breach of your duties as an Air Force officer, but it's not treason. You're not in the chain of command as a chaplain; the most they can do about it is give you a dishonorable discharge."

"There's more to it than that," Karen said. "I went down into one of the missile silos."

"Did you break in?"

"No, one of the guys I'm friends with, Sam—I mean Captain Huggler, one of the missileers—let me go with him and Brian, Captain Kurtz, during their shift in the MAF."

"What does that mean, MAF?"

"Missile Alert Facility, that's what they call the underground launch control capsules inside the missile silos. Each MAF controls ten Minuteman missiles."

"Was he allowed to bring you along?"

"He got special permission. They're normally two person crews and they stay underground for twenty-four hours, but they'd been studying whether three person crews spelling each other over longer shifts would work better, so having me along wasn't that unusual. I have the necessary clearance because I talk to them. They're under a lot of stress, you know, sitting for days on end with their fingers on the button; they've got questions and they need somebody to talk to."

"I can imagine," I said, "but that's not treason either."

Karen held her eyes on me. "They went on alert while we were down there. A satellite picked up what appeared to be two North Korean ICBMs. Sam and Brian said it was probably just a false alarm due to a sunspot or something, but it might be the real thing and they had to be ready to launch their missiles within five minutes."

"Did they ask you to leave?"

"Not right away. Since I was an officer with clearance and it was probably just a false alarm, they said I could stay."

"Then what happened?"

"It was totally surreal. The MAF capsules are suspended on huge shock absorbers in case of a nuclear blast, like an egg yolk inside an egg; the entire thing started rumbling and shaking. Sam and Brian explained that this was normal and caused by the huge steel blast doors over the missiles sliding open. We could see it on the closed circuit monitors. Within seconds, the tips of the missiles were pointing toward the sky."

"That's pretty scary."

"Yes, it is. So, Sam and Brian begin their preparations and their countdown. One minute, they're just two perfectly nice, normal guys with families, you know, but suddenly they have the power to destroy ten cities at once by pushing a few buttons and turning a few keys. When the alarms go off, their humanity is switched off and they're turned into machines. They're actually trained not to think about what they're doing or the consequences of it, to just obey their orders and launch their birds. Ironic isn't it...? They call them, birds. If the right set of numbers and letters blip up on a screen, they take a key, open a box, get another key, put it in a console, lift a panel, press a button, and in a few minutes fifty million people are erased from the planet. They're gods. The Air Force missileers are gods."

I glanced again at my watch. "This is all fascinating," I said, "but we're running out of time. What happened that caused you to be arrested and taken to Leavenworth?"

"Sorry," she said. "Okay, so the countdown winds down to two minutes before launch. The fuel and oxygen lines disconnect from the missiles; there's lots of hissing and white vapor clouds rise out of the silo on the video monitors. Sam and Brian pull out their top secret launch codebooks, strap themselves into their seats, and take their first set of keys and open their launch panels. I'm in disbelief at this point. It looks like they're really going through with it; two minutes until the end of the world. It's crazy. How could I just stand there and let them murder fifty million people?"

"Because it's not your decision to make," I said. "It's the president's decision." Karen looked annoyed again. "I'm sorry," I said. "It's obviously a huge deal and it must have been very difficult. Nobody wants to murder fifty million people. Go on."

"So I tried to reason with them and get them to stand down."

"What did you say?"

Karen ran her fingers through her hair and laughed. "You'd think at a time like this," she said, "—the two most important minutes of my life—maybe the two most important minutes in the history of the world—that I'd have something eloquent and convincing to say to save humanity, but the only words that came out of my mouth were: 'Hey, come on, guys, you're not really going to do this, are you?'—like I was trying to stop them from having a squirt gun battle or something. Unbelievable. They didn't respond, of course. They were automatons by this point, reading off their checklists; the only thing they were worried about was whether they completed everything in the correct order, as if any of that would matter in two minutes.

"Well, apparently somebody on the surface didn't like that I was down there during an alert because suddenly two armed SPs—Air Force Security Police—burst into the capsule to escort me out. I'm convinced now that this isn't a drill and they're going to launch. It's like a nightmare: I'm standing there seconds before the nuclear exchange that ends the world and I can do something to stop it. 'For God's sake!' I say to Sam and Brian, 'don't do this. What if it's a mistake? You'll kill millions of people—women, children, mothers, fathers, maybe all life on the planet. For what? For an order? For an eye for an eye? For *justice?*'

"They glance at each other but say nothing and continue with their checklists, launch codes, and buttons. The two SPs order me out, but I stall a little longer and keep pleading with Brian and Sam. At this point, a new alarm starts sounding and an ominous computer voice comes on through the speakers. I'll never forget it, it's burned into my brain: 'Warning! Warheads armed! Launch in sixty seconds! Warning! Warheads armed! Launch in fifty-nine seconds.' We're one minute from destroying the world. One minute. There's this big red digital clock in the MAF and it's counting down to the end of time. You have no idea what it's like until you're in one of these silos. They're the scariest places on earth."

"This is unbelievable, Karen," I said, riveted by the story. "It's like a movie or something."

"I wish it were only a movie. One of the SPs finally walks over to me to lead me out by the arm.... That's when I saw my chance."

"You're chance for what?" I asked.

Karen stared into my eyes. "I grabbed his gun from its holster and told Sam and Brian to get away from the launch consoles."

"Oh, my God, Karen."

"I know. Another warning comes over the speakers: 'Warheads armed! Launch in forty-five seconds!' The other SP pulls his gun and orders me to drop mine, but Sam orders him to hold his fire. I tell him I'll drop my gun only if Sam and Brian move away from the launch consoles.

"Another warning sounds: 'Warheads armed! Launch in thirty seconds!' Everybody looked scared now, but not because I had a gun; none of them had ever seen a countdown go this far. They confirmed that they had received valid launch codes, and Brian crossed himself. They were going to go through with it. I didn't know what to do. I couldn't let them launch the missiles, but I had no intention of shooting anybody either. I yelled again for them to get away from the launch consoles, but they refused. I'm no sure shot, but I had basic small arms training in Officer Training School. I steadied the gun with both hands, aimed it at Sam's launch console and fired two shots to scare them and maybe disable the launch controls. The SP with the gun pleaded with Sam for permission to fire but Sam refused."

"You could have been killed, Karen!"

"Yeah, I know. The bullets went through the metal of the console but didn't disable anything or hurt anybody. And they didn't cause Sam or Brian to move either. They stayed at their launch consoles under fire; their commanders would have been proud. At ten seconds, a new siren sounded, signaling the final phase of the countdown. We all realized now it wasn't a false alarm or drill. They were about to launch their missiles. We were ten seconds away from Armageddon."

"Unbelievable," I said. "What did you do?"

Karen smiled. "I put my gun down."

"What? You put it down?"

Karen looked past me and her face became blissful, like the face of a monk meditating. "I could see it all so clearly in that moment," she said. "Everything became perfectly calm and still. I suddenly understood what Jesus had been trying to teach us by not resisting his executioners and forgiving them. To reunite with God, we must be like God, and we must love like God. Even God wasn't going to come down from the sky and shoot Sam and Brian. He had already forgiven them for launching the missiles and destroying the world, just as Jesus had already forgiven his executioners. A great God loves without condition— even when we murder millions of people, even when we attempt to murder God Himself. In that instant, I was standing in the Garden of Eden, Brek, right there inside that nuclear missile silo." Karen's eyes glistened. "I had come home. It was the most sacred moment of my life. I got down on my knees and laid the gun on the floor as an offering. I touched the face of God."

For a moment, I thought I could almost feel what Karen was feeling, that I could almost sense her ecstasy; but suddenly some inmates started shouting at each other in the hallway and I snapped out of it. We were talking about nuclear warheads here, not beautiful sunsets. I was worried Karen might be forced to spend years in a prison or a psychiatric ward for the sake of her spiritual epiphany.

She smiled at me. "You think I'm crazy."

"I'm worried about you."

"Don't be. This was a gift from God."

"So, what happened next? They obviously didn't launch the missiles."

"At six seconds, a new mechanical voice came on telling them to abort the launch and stand down. Sam and Brian folded their launch consoles and put the launch keys away. The SPs arrested me. Five FBI agents were waiting when they brought me to the surface. They flew me here to Leavenworth that night. Two FBI agents, and a CIA agent, have been interrogating me ever since. Can you believe it? They actually think I'm a spy! They keep reminding me that treason carries the death penalty. It's ridiculous. I was set up. It was all a charade."

"Set up? What do you mean you were set up? You tried to stop them from launching the missiles and you fired a gun. I'm not saying I can't get you out of this, but I'd say they've got a pretty good case."

"They told me they'd been watching me for months. Apparently some of the missileers who I'd been meeting with and counseling that launching nuclear missiles is morally wrong reported me. No surprise there; I knew it wouldn't last long. But, like you said, they could have simply discharged or transferred me if they didn't like what I was saying. Instead, they let me keep my clearance…and go down into a missile silo knowing all along I'm morally against it? There was never any North Korean ICBM launch, mistaken or otherwise; they set it all up to see what I'd do. I'm not a lawyer, but that sounds like entrapment. I'll bet Sam and Brian will admit it if you ask them. I don't think they really believe I'm a spy. I think they want to make an example out of me to deter others. The only thing they didn't anticipate was me taking an SP's gun and shooting a launch console; but that just makes their case stronger, doesn't it? And you know what? I don't care. They can do whatever they want to me. Something happened to me in that silo, Brek. I'll never be afraid of the government or anybody else again. Let them fry me if they want. This case is going to draw more attention to the danger and immorality of nuclear weapons than a lifetime of protests."

All this came back to me while sitting in Luas' office, waiting for the new postulant to arrive. Luas said nothing more. He had accomplished his goal of immersing me in the miasma of my own past so that I could not become lost in the past of another soul. He struck a match to light his pipe, adding a third flame to the darkened room. There was a soft knock at the door and the faceless gray robed creature from the Urartu Chamber entered. In a subservient voice, it asked whether we were ready.

"Yes, Legna," Luas said, exhaling a cloud of smoke from his pipe. "I believe Ms. Cuttler is now ready. Please send in the next postulant."

15

Amina Rabun's hard life passed before my eyes, ending sixty-seven years after it began in the quiet dawn of a day that looked like any other day.

I saw nothing of her soul coming or going from Luas' office. She had no shape or size like Nana, Luas, or Haissem. Rather, I saw Amina Rabun only as she had once seen herself: reflected in mirrors brushing her long, brown hair; in the reactions of those for whom she cared, and those for whom she thought she should care; in the memories and fantasies of who she had been and who she might have been; in the photographs that could not be trusted because they were always at odds with mirror and mind. She was a woman both ugly and beautiful, as she had accepted and rejected those qualities in herself from time to time; and so, at the end of her life, when she passed on from one world to another, the *she* that passed was, as we all are, a collection of thoughts and ideas—bits of data transferred from one realm to another, like moving computer files to a new machine that can open and read them again.

Our interview of Amina Rabun consisted of sitting in her presence and receiving the record of her life. No questions were asked, no conversation took place, and none was needed. The memories of Amina Rabun came to us whole and complete unto themselves, an entire human life copied from one storage device to another. I felt full after meeting her the way one feels after reading an epic novel: having entered another world and become part of it heart and soul. Like such a reader, at first I found no difficulty in separating my life from hers. When I closed the book of Amina Rabun's life—the most wonderful book I had ever read because it contained a full and complete life with all its nuances, far more than any human author could ever hope to achieve—Legna, the meek librarian of Shemaya, reappeared to return the volume to the great hall of the train shed where it would wait on the shelf with the many others until Amina Rabun's case was called in the Urartu Chamber.

"Who are you?" Luas asked me in the flickering candlelight after Legna left.

"Brek Abigail Cuttler," I said proudly. "That wasn't so hard after all."

"Good. Very good," Luas said, standing up behind the desk and blowing out the candles. "But I want you to stay with your great-grandmother until we're certain you've adjusted fully to the burden of having another life resident inside your own."

"Okay," I replied, having nowhere else to be anyway. This was one of the many advantages of Shemaya: no plans, no appointments.

Walking back through the impossibly long corridor of offices, one of the doors opened midway down the hall and a handsome young man appeared. Unlike Amina Rabun and the other postulants inside the train shed, he had both shape and size and was the first soul I had seen in Shemaya besides Nana, Luas, and Haissem. He wore a dark suit and white shirt with a blue and gold striped tie loosened at the neck, as though he had just finished his workday, and round wire rim glasses that required constant attention to keep from sliding down the steep slope of his nose. He didn't notice us and nearly backed into Luas while closing the door behind him.

"Careful there," Luas said, stepping wide to avoid a collision and coming to a stop. "Ah, Tim Shelly, meet Brek Cuttler."

Tim extended his right hand and, seeing I had no right hand to return the gesture, sheepishly retracted it, stepping with me the same awkward dance I had stepped with countless others during my life. I broke the tension the same way: "My left hand's got a better grip than my right," I said. He laughed uneasily, as they all did, and shook my left hand. He stared uneasily at my empty right sleeve, visibly unsettled. I, on the other hand, was excited to have found someone in Shemaya closer to my own age…and, I admit, a bit smitten by his good looks.

"Brek here is our newest recruit," Luas said. "She just met her first postulant." Luas turned to me. "Tim hasn't been with us much longer than you, Brek. He's had a more difficult start of it though: poor fellow came away from his first meeting with a postulant convinced he was a waitress at a diner. Wouldn't stop taking my breakfast order—poached eggs and toast, no butter mind you, Tim. Miserable wretch brought me biscuits slathered in butter every time; and when I threatened to dock his tip, he'd grumble, take the biscuits back, scrape them clean, and return them to me stone cold. For a little fun I started ordering dishes that weren't even on the menu; he'd become irate with me and storm off to his imaginary kitchen. When I refused to order altogether, he threatened to throw me out for loitering! As I recall, Tim, it wasn't until you made a pass at me that we achieved a full separation of personalities. No offense, but you're just not my type."

Tim seemed embarrassed, but I found the story hysterical. It felt so good to laugh again; it had been such a long time.

"You'd make a good catch, Luas," Tim shot back gamely.

"Now, now," Luas said, "you mustn't tease me so. You were interested in me only because your boyfriend made conversation with a pretty woman at the other end of the counter and you were trying to make him jealous."

"I think Tim is right, Luas," I said, joining in the fun. "You'd make a fine catch."

"You do seem to have adjusted better than me," Tim said, plainly impressed. "I really was as lost as Luas says."

"Well," I, said nodding at my empty right sleeve, "Luas had plenty of material to prepare me with. He made me so preoccupied with my own past I couldn't possibly mistake it for anyone else's."

"I have something of a confession to make, Tim," Luas said. "Unlike Brek here, I dropped you in cold with your first postulant as part of a little experiment I was conducting. I couldn't tell you in advance for fear of tainting the results."

"What kind of experiment?" Tim asked.

"Well, as you know," Luas explained, "the object of every presentation is to project an accurate and unbiased representation of the postulant. I wanted to test whether this could be improved upon by removing any trace of personality of the presenter."

Tim seemed unamused. "You mean you subjected me to the memories of my first postulant without preparing me at all?"

"You, among others," Luas said. "I also maintained a control group for comparison."

"What if I wasn't able to handle it?" Tim said. "What if I'd lost who I am?"

"I knew you would do well," Luas replied. "And I was obviously correct. Besides, I kept a cache of your most important memories handy to bring you back in case of emergency."

"I guess," Tim said, resigned, but still annoyed. "Well, did you learn anything useful?"

"Yes. There's no difference among well-trained presenters— and you were well trained." Luas smiled slyly. "I also discovered that you care for me far more than I could have imagined."

I laughed uneasily. Tim stood frozen-faced.

"Well," Luas said, "I thank both of you for your flattery and would very much enjoy hearing more, but I must attend to some administrative matters. Tim knows the way out. Would you be so kind as to escort Ms. Cuttler?"

"Sure," Tim said.

"Splendid. She'll still need the blindfold before entering the hall."

"Understood."

"I'll check in with you periodically, Brek, to see how you're doing. Sophia knows how to reach me if there are difficulties. Make no effort to evaluate Ms. Rabun's case; there'll be opportunity for that later. Just get accustomed to her memories and emotions, both of which are quite powerful, as you well know. You should spend most of your time relaxing. Sophia will be with you. You're okay?"

"Yes...yes, I'm fine."

"If she starts taking breakfast orders, we'll know who to blame," Tim said, getting in the last jab and letting Luas know he was no longer angry.

"Guilty as charged," Luas said, bowing in mock apology. "I must be off."

We watched him walk to the end of the corridor, disappearing through a set of locked doors.

"How long have you been here?" I asked, eager to learn about Tim's experience and everything he knew about Shemaya.

"I'm not sure exactly," he said.

"I know what you mean," I replied. "Where are all the clocks and calendars? That's been one of the most difficult parts of the transition for me."

We started walking toward the great hall.

"Have you done any presentations on your own yet?" I asked.

"No, I've only watched," Tim answered. "Luas says the next one's on my own though."

"Me too…after Amina Rabun. Are these all presenters' offices? There must be thousands."

"Yeah, I just got mine. There are a bunch of empties down at this end. Where are you staying?"

"With my great-grandmother, at her house—or what used to be her house."

"I stayed in a tent with my dad when I first arrived. He and I used to go hunting in Canada, just the two of us. He died a couple of months before I got here."

"Sorry— Or not…you've got him back now."

"I guess. It was great seeing him at first, and he really helped me adjust, but he's gone again."

"Gone? Where? I didn't know you could leave here."

"I don't know where he went. One day he said I was ready to live here on my own, but that we'd see each other again someday. You can live anywhere you want when you're ready."

"What do you mean, anywhere?"

"Well, anywhere…let's see, I've lived at Eagle's Nest and Hitler's bunker in Berlin—I'm really into Nazi history—let's see, the White House, Graceland. If you can imagine it, you can go there."

"Wow," I said. "That's amazing. I thought you could only go to the places you've visited during your life. That's all I've been doing."

"No, anywhere you want. I'll show you when we get outside. You can't do it in here."

When we reached the train shed, Tim opened a bin near the doors, removed a blindfold, and tied the thick felt cloth over my eyes. I peeked again as we passed through the great hall, sampling paragraphs from the thousands of autobiographies cramming the room, each authored by a different hand but, like all autobiographies, revealing the same truths, pains, and joys. I closed their covers when we reached the vestibule on the other side, neither confused nor weakened as I had been before.

For the first time since arriving at Shemaya, I felt a flicker of hope rather than apprehension, the way a visit from a friend brightens the darkness of an extended illness. I flipped off the blindfold and Tim and I literally raced outside like two kids let out of school. The entrance to the train shed somehow bordered the western boundary of Nana's property; it was little more than a disturbance in the air between two maple trees that had been there all along, since before I was a child, diaphanous, like a faint patch of fog. *Could the entrance to heaven have been so near all along?* I wondered. But, of course, we were nowhere near Delaware or her home; it was all being made up spontaneously, conjured from...I had no idea if there was even air. In any case, I could see the roof of Nana's house through the trees, however it emerged, and hear the sound of light traffic along the road.

"Nice place," Tim said, looking around. "Okay, so where do you want to go?"

"Um...."

"Just pick any place, you can see them all."

"Well, okay...Tara," I blurted, of all possible things.

"I've never been there," Tim said. "What would it look like?"

All at once we were there, standing on the wine colored carpet sweeping through the foyer and up the grand staircase of the fictional plantation mansion. Crystal chandeliers tinkled softly in a gentle spring breeze that stroked the plush green velvet curtains of the parlor, carrying the sweet afternoon scents of magnolia, apple blossom, and fresh-cut lawn. With our heads turning, we walked out to the portico with its whitewashed columns and made our way to the rail fence over which Gerald O'Hara leaped but never returned, then under a giant sycamore, through the gardens and back onto the sun-drenched veranda. We examined the dining room, with its sparkling tea service and glassware, and the study lined with *Farmer's Almanacs*, English poetry, and some French volumes. It didn't matter that Tara had been only a description in a novel or a set in a movie any more than it mattered to readers of the book or audiences in the theaters. Nor did it matter that I could not remember the details as they appeared in the book or on the film: my mind instantly provided what I expected to see, feel, and smell, extrapolating outward from memory. I was panting when we reached the top of the stairs, and felt a very real stab of pain when I banged my shin into the corner of a dry sink, proving that we were not wandering through a mere illusion. Everything was in its place, except Rhett and Scarlet. I bounced on her bed, giggling uncontrollably, intoxicated by the dream turned reality. Tim had never read the book nor seen the movie and did not share my enthusiasm, but I dragged him through each room anyway like a star-struck movie studio guide: "And this is where she shot that Union scoundrel," I squealed. "And this is where Rhett left her."

We went back into the parlor; Tim sat down on the formal sofa, bored and unimpressed with the mansion, but amused by my first giddy moments at the controls of such magical powers to re-create it. I admired the porcelain figurines on the shelves and stopped to examine a miniature ship in a bottle on the fireplace mantel. As quickly as my mind recognized the ship, my thoughts replaced the plantation with ocean, and the mansion with masts and hull. Suddenly, we were deposited onto the deck of a sixteenth-century caravel on the high seas, and Tim was all enthusiasm. She was leaning-to in rough weather off the coast of a Caribbean island; there we were, dressed in our business attire like a pair of farcical bare-boat charterers. The caravel rolled sharply to port, forcing us to claw our way on hands and knees toward the starboard rail through a drenching saltwater spray; we kicked off our shoes to gain better hold of the slimy oak decking. With the next wave the ship listed heavily starboard, sending us scrambling back across the deck for the port rail. Despite the battering, the ship carried full sails on the foremast, main, and missen, and the tattered red and gold stripes of Spain. The deck was deserted. I made my way to the wheel to bring the ship under control and Tim went for the rigging to bring in the sails. He found a hatchet and cut loose the yards, sending the beams, ropes, and sails plummeting to the deck with a tremendous thud. With the reduction in wind power, the rudder responded and I was able to steer a course directly into the waves, stabilizing the ship. Tim made his way back to the transom over the heaps of canvas and rope littering the deck. He was dripping wet by the time I saw him, the long locks of his dark brown hair matted to his forehead in jagged inky stripes, his shirt, pants, and suspenders torn almost to tatters and his round glasses lost to the sea.

"Maybe you could warn me next time you're about to think about a ship!" he shouted, breathless, his ruddy face breaking into the smile of one who has shared a common peril and cheated a common fate. We fell off another crest and the ship lurched forward knocking him onto the deck. I had seen it coming and braced myself against the bulkhead.

"Next time!" I shouted back, laughing.

He collected himself and rose wearily to his feet. "Think calm seas!"

I did and the seas quieted instantly, as if two gigantic hands had reached down from the heavens to tuck and smooth the immense sheet of ocean, snapping the surface flat as a pane of glass. Tim folded back the sails and cleared a place to sit on the starboard side of the deck facing the island.

"My grandfather took me sailing on the Chesapeake Bay when I was a girl," I said. "Sometimes I'd fall asleep with him at the helm and dream I was one of the early explorers lost at sea and sailing through a storm."

A tropical breeze rocked the boat, cooling the warm touch of the sun. The mottled timbers and planks of the ship dried quickly with a powdery white brine on their surface. We floated adrift for a while with only the far-off sound of gulls and the easy slap of water against the tired wooden hull breaking the silence. I unbuttoned the neck of my blouse and Tim helped me roll the sleeves up to my shoulders for me. He seemed very uncomfortable doing this, and happy when it was over. We stretched out on the sun-splashed deck, propping our heads against a hatch cover.

I soon fell asleep in this paradise, and in my dreams I returned to the Chesapeake Bay. I was on my Pop Pop Bellini's sailboat and he was teaching me to steer. The pink skin of his bare chest and shoulders added color to the spotless white fiberglass coaming around the cockpit of the boat; a weathered, old blue captain's hat shaded his eyes as they darted from the jibsail to a landmark on shore toward which he told me to steer to make the most efficient use of our tack. The day was perfect, breezy, and warm; as soon as we sailed out of sight of Havre de Grace he allowed me to take off the life jacket my parents insisted that I wear because swimming with one arm is virtually impossible. These little signs of trust made me adore him. We talked about school and sports, even boys and music, anything I wanted. Although he was an attorney, Pop Pop Bellini's manner was informal and easy, the way men confident of their position in life tend to be. My other grandfather, Grandpa Cuttler, was more uncertain of himself and, because of that doubt, less comfortable with me after the accident. He never stopped blaming himself for what happened, and I never had the courage to tell him I'd done it on purpose to release his guilt; we didn't have much to talk about except the energy crisis and Jimmy Carter and the demise of the American farmer. But with Pop Pop Bellini, whose interests were vast, I could talk about anything—except Uncle Anthony, and my mother's drinking habits, both of which tapped into emotions so intense that even he could not control them. Regardless of the subject, he spoke of all things—politics, history, art, science, religion—in terms of right and wrong, fair and unfair. I guess this is what being a lawyer did to him. Francis Bellini, Jr., Esq. saw the world in black and white; he had no belief in gray. Neither did I, which is another reason why we got along so well. He was successful and well-respected, one of the high priests of justice upon whom God smiled; he was my role model and my hero. I loved my father dearly, but I never aspired to be like him because he and my mother had always bathed themselves in those confusing shades of gray.

We anchored at the mouth of the Sassafras River for lunch and returned to the harbor by five, a glorious day; but as we motored into the slip, the boat and the harbor faded away in my dream, and I found myself back at the convenience store, carrying Sarah up to the counter, then alone with Luas in the train shed. Even while dreaming I felt the frustration of that gap in space and time. Then my dream descended into a more bizarre realm.

My little brother Helmut and I are playing near the beautiful sandbox built lovingly by our father out of colored bricks and mortar. Papa had arranged the bricks on three sides of the box into patterns of ducks and flowers and extended the backside into a wide brick patio area, the opposite end of which turned ninety degrees straight upward into a chimney stack. Beds of roses, carnations, and begonias surround the two opposite ends of the sandbox, and our lush green lawn spreads across the front.

Despite the obsessive state of tidiness in which my father maintains our patio and yard, the sand in the box is excreting a putrid odor. I do not want to play in it until papa adds fresh sand, and I tell Helmut he should stay away too, but he plunges in without concern. Soon his legs, hips, and torso are swallowed up, as if he is sinking in quicksand.

"Help, Amina! Help me!" he cries. I reach in to grab him, but as I peer over the edge into the box I realize there is no sand after all. Instead, the arms of thousands of cadavers, tangled, blackened, and rotting, are swarming around like snakes inside the box, clutching at Helmut, pulling him down into an immense grave that extends deep into the earth, as if the box is situated over a portal into hell itself. I call to papa for help and pull as hard as I can to free Helmut, but I cannot overcome the strength of all these thousands of arms.

When the last traces of Helmut's blond hair vanish into the chasm, I suddenly awaken from the dream. Tim Shelly is holding my left arm and pulling me back onto the deck of the caravel. I had been teetering on the edge of the cargo hatch, my screams echoing out of the hold as if they were too horrified to stay below. Then the ship and the ocean disappear, and I am standing on the porch of Nana's house. Nana takes my hand, thanks Tim for looking after me, and leads me upstairs to my room.

16

Helmut Rabun died at the age of seven years and three months, but not in a sandbox. A five hundred pound bomb punched through the roof of the gymnasium at his school, killing everyone inside. The old men who had no children in school and could, therefore, examine the scene objectively, the way men do in their fascination with destruction, said it happened that way because the debris was driven outward in a ring around the blast zone; and this was not questioned by the hysterical mothers and fathers or the city elders and townspeople. Helmut liked the pommel horse and the trampoline.

The bomb that hit *Der Dresden Schule für Jungen* at 0932 hours on 22 April 1943 instantly dissected and immolated the thirty-two little boys playing beneath it, scattering many times that number of arms, legs, and other body parts hundreds of yards from where they had last been assembled. The Nazi officials who took control of the scene collected these remains and divided them into roughly equal sheet-draped mounds, one for each family believed to have had a son in gym class that day. With solemn voices during the invocation, they said the supreme sacrifice for *Das Mutterland* had been made by the children and, for that, we should all be very proud. Despite the dark hairs that curled around the edges of our little sheet, we cried and prayed over it as if it were our own little blond-headed Helmut. Mama swooned and had to be carried from the street and sedated for a week.

My nose itches. I reach to scratch it with my right hand, miss, reach again, and miss again, as if I am swatting a fly rather than part of my own anatomy. There is a throbbing, penetrating numbness in my arm. This is the phantom pain. The ghost of my forearm haunts me each night, deceiving me during sleep into reattaching itself to my body and performing the functions a forearm performs, like scratching itchy noses and swatting flies. Having set me up this way, it exacts its revenge for my careless-ness around the manure spreader by vanishing just as my eyes open in the morning, so that I am forced to re-experience the terror of seeing a bandaged stump quivering above me like a bro-ken toll gate on a windy day. The stump points indiscriminately at the eighty-seven squares of ceiling tile in my hospital room; I have counted them often and am certain of the number. The morning nurse, Nurse Debbie, comes in and eases the stump back down to my side, sending bolts of pain shrieking to my brain and from there to my vocal chords. She apologizes.

"Time for breakfast and more morphine," she says, calling me sweetie and fussing over me.

Luas and Nana sit at the foot of my bed. Their mouths move but I cannot hear them, so I ignore them. Globs of gray oat-meal dribble down my chin from a spoon held by fingers not yet accustomed to holding spoons. Nurse Debbie serves the narcotic after breakfast, injecting it directly into the intravenous tube that still replenishes the fluids I drained onto the field, my grandfather's pickup truck seats, and the emergency room floor. The poppies submerge me into a warm, perfect, opiated sleep from which I always regret returning.

At the suggestion of *Vater* Mushlitz, the parents of all the little boys killed at the school in Dresden agreed to bury their gruesome parcels in a mass grave as a sign of communal loss. All except my papa.

"My son will have his own grave!" he raged, in denial of the fact that only God himself could determine which sheet or sheets concealed Helmut. "He will not be buried like an animal! Like a common Jew! He will be buried in the family plot outside Kamenz!"

Papa ordered his staff to design a monument appropriate for the son of a wealthy industrialist, constructed, he insisted, of the gymnasium's broken concrete and twisted rods of steel so no one would forget the cowardice of his murderers.

"It must be bigger by three-fold than all other monuments in the cemetery! It must be completed immediately!"

He permitted himself only two days to bury Helmut and grieve; then he returned to Poland with the explanation that the war effort there had intensified despite our having conquered the country years earlier. "The Third Reich urgently requires the expert services of Jos. A. Rabun & Sons," he said, "to assist in various matters of national security that cannot be discussed." Papa stopped smiling after his first trip to Poland; his eyes turned darker and narrower, as if he were being hunted by someone or something.

In the half-century since *grossvater* Rabun opened the doors of his small masonry shop near Kamenz, Jos. A. Rabun & Sons had swelled into the mighty *Korperschaft* that trenched modern Dresden's sewers, paved its streets, and erected its buildings. Our little family business became the premier civil engineering and construction firm in all of Saxony province, providing for our needs very well. Because of this, its demands were never questioned by the family. We had far more than most: ample food, beautiful clothes, sufficient funds with which to enjoy dining out, the opera, and even wartime travel abroad. We lived comfortably on my grandfather's estate with its large chalet-style house, riding stables, and gardens reflecting his love of the Alps. Other less fortunate citizens of *Deutschland* sacrificed so much more.

After papa left for Poland, I met Katerine Schrieberg at our secret place on the estate—a hollow in the woods surrounded by a dense grove of pine trees and guarded by a thicket of briars and vines. She was nervous and pale as always, her fingers incessantly rubbing all the blessings that could possibly be extracted from the gold crucifix I had given her to present if she were ever stopped by the Nazis in the woods. I could see that my failure to appear during our last three scheduled meetings had made her very concerned. When I told her the sad news about Helmut, she cried as if it had been one of her own brothers, so much so that I found myself comforting her instead of she comforting me. Of course, she was fond of Helmut and felt sorry for me; but she wept also for herself and her family—for if the mighty Rabuns of Kamenz were no longer safe, where did that leave the weakened Schriebergs of Dresden? She asked if I would come back with her to her house and I eagerly accepted the invitation, welcoming the opportunity to escape, for even a moment, the pall that had descended onto my life with the Allies' five hundred pound bomb.

The house in which the Schriebergs lived was not really a house at all. It was an abandoned hunting cabin built by my grandfather deep in the immense tract of forest that stretches from Kamenz all the way to the Czech border. Before taking up residence there, the Schriebergs lived in a beautiful townhouse in the finest section of Dresden and owned several theaters, two of which, in fact, had been constructed by Jos. A. Rabun & Sons. Katerine and I grew up best friends: we had taken dance and violin lessons together since I was eight years old, and her parents and mine held seats on the boards of many of the same civic and charitable organizations, until the Nazis banned Jews from such positions. Then, in nineteen forty-two, the Schriebergs abruptly booked passage to Denmark after accepting the then-generous but insulting offer to sell their theaters, home, and belongings to my uncle Otto for thirty-five thousand Reichmarks in total, rather than allow the government to seize the properties for nothing. They had family in Denmark who had agreed to house them, but when news spread of Nazis rounding up fleeing Jews at the train stations and loading them onto boxcars headed for Poland, they changed their plans and decided to take their chances by staying and hiding. Katerine made contact with me and asked about the hunting cabin. She and I had sometimes slept in it on warm summer nights and talked about the boys we would marry. The cabin had not been used by my family since the start of the war, so I agreed and soon began these discreet visits to our meeting place with baskets and sometimes small wagons loaded with food and supplies, always honoring their constant pleas not to tell anyone of their existence—not my mother, not Helmut, and most importantly, not my father or uncle Otto. No one.

Katerine's father, Jared Schrieberg, and her younger brothers, Seth and Jacob, were industrious and immediately set to excavating a tunnel beneath the cabin through which to escape if anyone should approach. She told me they drilled their flight twice daily regardless of the weather and could silently vanish below the carefully reinstalled floorboards within thirty seconds exactly. They came and left from this tunnel, did most of their cooking at night to avoid attracting attention to the smoke from their fires, and relieved themselves far away from the cabin to avoid even the scent of habitation. It was a miserable and demeaning existence, and I felt sorry for them, but their precautions proved unnecessary. The very boldness of hiding on the property of a Waffen SS officer (the organization into which my uncle Otto accepted a commission) made life there secure for them in the way that life for certain tropical fish is made safe by living among lethal sea anemone.

When Katerine told her parents the news about Helmut, tears filled their eyes and they said they would sit *shiva* for him, which they explained to me was the Jewish mourning ritual. In my youth and ignorance, I panicked. I did not want them confusing God with their Jewish prayers into mistakenly sending Helmut to the Jews' heaven. As politely as I could, I begged them not to do this. When they insisted, I grew furious. I had helped them at great personal risk and would not tolerate their interference in such matters. My grief for my brother and my hatred of his unseen murderers found an outlet in the Schriebergs, and I yelled at them in a voice more than loud enough to remind them upon whom they depended for their survival:

"*Beten Sie nicht Jüdisches für meinen Bruder!*"

The room fell silent. Katerine stared down at the floor, biting her lip as *Frau* Schrieberg dug her fingernails into Katerine's arm. Seth and Jacob looked to their father in horror, expecting him to punish my impudence as he had so often done to them. But *Herr* Schrieberg only smiled coldly at me, revealing a flash of gold through his graying beard and mustache, unwittingly contorting his long, bulbous nose into the very caricature of a Jew mocked regularly in German newspapers of the day. As if surrendering a concealed weapon, he cautiously pulled the black yarmulke from the balding crown of his head and placed its flaccid shape before me on the battered plank table that served the family as dining area, desk, and altar. The Schriebergs would not offer prayers for my brother's soul. I glared back at the old man and thanked him with a healthy dose of teenage smugness, having for the first time cowed an adult. He had no option. I left without another word and ran quickly through the woods, regretting my resort to such tactics but intoxicated by exerting my will so forcefully and effectively against my elders. The Schriebergs' submission to my demands made me feel powerful and, for a moment, in control of the uncontrollable world around me. At least I didn't have to live like them, like animals.

The skin has miraculously knitted itself over the amputation and the bandages have been removed, but even so, I refuse to touch or even look at the stump of my right arm. It terrifies me. Dr. Farris, the psychologist assigned to all amputees at Children's Hospital, assures me this is perfectly normal.

"I've counseled many children in your situation, Brek," he says. "Victims of firecrackers, car accidents, farm kids like you, too. Most react the same way. They think that what remains of their arms and legs are monsters poised to take what's left of their bodies, but you must remember that this is the same arm you were born with. It's been terribly injured and it needs your love and compassion. You're all it's got. Can you do that?"

"I'll try, but it isn't fair," I cry.

Dr. Farris looks at his watch. "Oops, time's up for today. I'll see you next week, okay? I think you're doing great."

I find my mother reading a fashion magazine in the waiting room.

"Done?" she says.

"Yep."

We run into Luas in the hallway outside Dr. Farris' office. My mother doesn't see him. Luas smiles and extends his left hand without first extending his right, pulling me with the gesture back into Nana's living room in Shemaya.

"Sophia and I were beginning to wonder whether you would ever return," Luas says.

I look around the room, dazed and confused by the flood of images, emotions, and personalities rushing through me. Nana brings me a cup of tea, and I sit down on the sofa.

"You've been spending a lot of time with Ms. Rabun," Luas says. "She led an interesting life."

I slide my hand into the right sleeve of my bathrobe and trace the familiar contours of my arm: the shrunken, atrophied bundle of biceps; the rough, calcified tip of humerus jutting like coral beneath a puffy layer of flesh capping the bone.

"Yes, yes she did," I say.

"The Schriebergs lied, you know."

"About what?"

"They sat *shiva* for Helmut."

17

On the rainy afternoon of 23 April 1945, a Soviet scouting patrol advancing south toward Prague stumbles upon the Rabuns of Kamenz. It is the day of Amina Rabun's eighteenth birthday celebration.

The Allies hold Leipzig to the west and the Russians are massed along the Oder to the east, making escape impossible. Amina's father, Friedrich, and her uncle, Otto, had already pulled back to Berlin with the retreating remnants of Hitler's forces but advised their families against leaving Kamenz, reasoning that the Russians were interested only in Berlin, that the western Allies would soon take Dresden, and that the armed forces of the latter were preferred to the former with respect to treatment of civilians. Privately, the Rabun brothers were also concerned for their affairs and property, which almost certainly would be looted if abandoned—if not by enemy soldiers then by their own German neighbors who have suffered such privation during Hitler's desperate last stand.

Unaware of the approaching Russian forces, Amina rises early this day to begin baking for the party, but not before *grossvater* Hetzel, who has risen even earlier to slaughter a pig to roast in a pit dug several paces from the long garage full of polished Daimler automobiles owned by the Rabuns, the axles of which rest on thick wooden blocks because there is no fuel to run them. By noon, the sweet scent of pork, yams, cabbage, and fresh *küchen* tease aunt Helena's four hungry children, two boys and two girls, who have been playing hide-and-seek all morning despite a soft rain and their mother's unwillingness, in anticipation of the feast, to prepare their usual hearty breakfasts. Sensitive to the effect displays of prosperity can have during such lean times, only family members have been invited to the party, all of whom, save those living in the manor, conveyed their regrets due to lack of transportation to the country. It is thus agreed that leftovers will be delivered to the hungriest of Kamenz by anonymous donation to the cathedral. Amina also plans secretly to smuggle a portion to the Schriebergs, who have enjoyed very little meat recently and, having long ago relaxed observance of Kosher laws in their cabin, will happily accept scraps of pork.

All goes merrily and well into the early afternoon, with everything and everyone cooperating except the weather. The soft rain becomes a downpour just as *grossvater* Hetzel is removing the pig from its pyre. Everybody races inside as much to stay dry as to enjoy the feast. They assemble in the formal dining room around a large table upon which has been arranged the finest place settings and two large hand-painted porcelain vases overflowing with bouquets of wildflowers freshly picked from the surrounding gardens. Colorfully wrapped gifts are arranged near the seat of honor at the head of the table, including several packages for the birthday girl delivered by special SS courier from Berlin. The anticipation builds until finally, with considerable ceremony, the grinning pig atop a tremendous silver platter makes its debut to ravenous applause. The browned head and body of the beast remain intact, resting peacefully in a soft bed of garnishes as if it has fallen asleep there. Toasts of precisely aged Johannisberger Rheingau are made first to Amina, then the cooks, and finally to the safe return of Friedrich and uncle Otto and, solemnly, a swift end to the war. A phonograph whispers Kreisler and Bach into the air. Amid the happy conversation, laughter, and music, the revelers cannot hear the Soviet patrol approaching and, therefore, have no opportunity to defend themselves or flee.

The soldiers enter from three sides of the manor and quickly herd the Rabuns and *Herr* Hetzel out into the rain in front of the garage. After conducting a thorough search and satisfying themselves they have everyone, the soldiers segregate the old man and the young boys, ages six and twelve, from the group and without warning or hesitation shoot them on the spot before they can offer either protest or prayer, as if this is simply a matter of routine for which the soldiers assume everyone has been rehearsed. Amina's mother and aunt are shot next while running to their aid. Left standing, like statuary in a graveyard, are Amina Rabun and her stunned cousins, Bette and Barratte, ages eight and ten. The three girls' features are petrified into rigid sculptures of terror, waiting for the next bursts of gunfire that will join them with their fallen family members. The girls are spared such a fate, however.

Suddenly two shots are fired from the woods behind the house. The soldiers drop to the ground and return a fearsome barrage with their automatic weapons. Amina and her cousins stand motionless in the crossfire, afraid even to breathe. Then everything becomes silent. Amina sees a man in uniform in the distance across the field, in the direction from which the shots were fired. He has his hands over his head as if he is surrendering, and he is shouting something unintelligible that sounds vaguely like, "Amerika! Amerika!" The commanding officer of the Russians directs two of his men to roll out and circle around the house toward this man, making a pincer-like gesture with his fingers. The rest of the platoon holds its position. Many minutes pass; finally Amina hears some words shouted back from the woods in Russian and the commander gestures for his men to get up. After several more minutes, the two Russian soldiers return, one of them carrying a simple double-barrel shotgun, the kind Amina has seen her father pack away on hunting trips.

Laughing at the weakness of this threat, the soldiers present their trophy to their commander and the rest of the platoon joins in the cheering and congratulations. And then, as if the same idea has struck all of them at the same time, attentions are turned toward Amina, Barratte, and Bette, who still have not moved. The men look from the girls to their commander and back to the girls. Their eyes are hungry and wild. They cheer louder and louder, insisting that their request be granted. The commander looks at the girls and then his men and shakes his head no in mocking disapproval. The cheering becomes more frantic. Finally, like Pontius Pilate, the commander turns his back on the girls and wipes his hands. Amina, Barratte, and Bette are dragged into separate bedrooms of the manor and raped and beaten throughout the night.

At dawn, the commander of the unit orders his men to move on. Amina is certain they raped little Bette long after she had died, because when the drunken and gorged Russians permitted Amina to use the toilet, she slipped briefly into Bette's room and found her naked body cold and blue, already bloated, her face broken and bloodied almost beyond recognition because she would not obey their orders in Russian to stop crying. Even after that, Amina heard men with Bette at least three times.

I cried so long for Amina Rabun and her family. I cried for her more than I had even cried for myself after I lost my arm. I lived each horrifying moment with Amina: the bewilderment of being rushed out of the house at gunpoint, the shock and disbelief when the soldiers executed her grandfather and cousins, the terror, almost into unconsciousness, when blood began spouting from her mother's chest; I smelled the stench of the Russian soldiers as they pressed their bodies against her; I swooned in the horror of Bette's open, unseeing eyes. I believed I would die in the agony of the soul of Amina Rabun, if dying from death were possible. I was traumatized.

Nana Bellini and I sat together on her porch one evening, watching the seasons struggle with each other for space in the cramped sky, like quadruplets in a womb. She said:

"Luas introduced you to the souls of Toby Bowles and Amina Rabun for a reason. New presenters are exposed to souls with whom they have had some relationship, because in doing so they come to see the hidden relationships in their own lives. This, in turn, encourages them to search for hidden relationships in the lives of their clients, which may be decisive during a presentation."

"Katerine Schrieberg, Amina's best friend, became my mother-in-law," I said.

"Yes."

"She was in the cabin in the tunnel under the floorboards; she was led away by Toby Bowles, who saved her life; she had no idea Amina and Barratte had been raped by the soldiers when I convinced her to let Bill Gwynne and me sue them to recover her inheritance."

"That's correct, she didn't. But neither did you."

"And Amina never knew that it was Katerine's father who fired the shots at the soldiers from the woods, that he lost his life trying to save her and her family."

"Yes."

"My husband was named after Toby Bowles. Katerine had lost the sheet of paper with his name on it but remembered the sound of his name—Boaz, Bowles—and almost got it right."

"Yes."

On another day, Tim Shelly came to visit me to see how I was doing. We went for a walk along the Brandywine River behind Nana's house. I had created a row of snowmen on the riverbank in the alternating bands of winter. Portly and resolute, they watched over the river and me, keeping me company. Tim liked them and saluted each one as we passed.

Tim told me that he, too, had some connection with his first postulant—the waitress in the diner—but he didn't want to discuss it with me. He wanted to talk instead about his mother. He seemed suddenly nervous and upset. She hadn't been well since his father died, he said, and he was worried about how she was taking his own death. Tim's father didn't have life insurance and they had lost their mushroom farm when he died. His mother was too old to find a job or a husband; Tim was all she had left. Now, he was gone too. How would she survive?

We stopped in a band of spring, at a patch of wild daffodils where a large tree hung out over the river, defying gravity. "Do you ever wish you could see your husband and daughter again?" Tim asked.

"Always," I said.

"My dad told me we can't go back. We can't see the living or communicate with them."

"I know. My Nana told me the same thing."

Tim picked pieces of bark off the tree and threw them into the river. They floated away like tiny ships in the current.

"Are you all right?" I asked.

"Yeah, I'm fine."

"Are you sure?"

"Yeah, it's just…."

"What?"

"It's just that I visited her recently."

"Who?"

"My mother."

18

"Shall I take you to them?"

Elymas appeared as Tim Shelly told me he would, during a moment of despair when going forward seemed no more possible than going back. That moment for me came on the rocking chair in Sarah's room. I had not been home since my last visit there to disprove my mortality had so thoroughly confirmed it instead. Home teased me the way a casino teases a gambler, luring the eyes and the mind into a world offering pleasure and hope, but delivering only pain and disappointment. Tim's addiction had taken him back over and over to his family's mushroom farm, which was as deserted as Sarah's room, making the sudden appearance of Elymas so startling and so welcome.

Elymas was older than Luas and more poorly preserved. His withered body floated inside a pair of green plaid pants that piled at his ankles, and gathered high around his chest, held there by a moldy brown belt that drooped in a flaccid tail from the buckle. A food-stained yellow shirt sagged over his narrow shoulders, buttoned crookedly so that the left side of his body appeared higher than the right. He had a corncob face and relied for balance upon a cane with four tiny rubber feet at the bottom. He was completely blind; his eyes glowed glassy, white, and terrifying.

"Shall I take you to them?" he asked again, hovering in the doorway of Sarah's room, too vulnerable and frail to have made such an impossible, gigantic promise. A light breeze could have lifted his body like a scrap of paper and carried him off.

I had been crying, mourning the loss of my daughter and my life. "But they said it isn't possible—" I sniffled.

"You did not listen carefully. They said it is not possible to direct the movement of consciousness from realm to realm. They said nothing about you visiting and interacting with it. Shall I take you to your husband and daughter?"

"But—"

The old man banged his cane fiercely against the floor. "Do not question me! Many wait for my services. You must tell me now whether you wish to see them."

"Yes, yes desperately."

"Then open your mind to me, Brek Abigail Cuttler. Open your mind and you shall see them."

The old man's eyes dilated until they consumed his entire face from the inside out, and then they consumed me. I felt a sudden motion in the darkness of his eyes, as if I were being hurled through space. Two small points of light emerged in the distance from opposing directions, each emitting a soft, warm glow like the flames of two candles carried from opposite ends of a room, growing as I approached them. At the instant their coronae touched, they exploded into one mass of brilliant white light, and this light finally dimmed, distilling into an expanse of an azure sky, an outline of poplar and ash trees, a swing set, a slide, a jogging stroller. Then the shapes of Sarah and Bo, with

Macy barking at their feet! The playground near our home! I couldn't believe my eyes.

Sarah toddled toward me. I swept her into the air, pulling her close, burying my nose in her hair, drinking in the sweet scent of her baby shampoo. She wrapped herself around my neck and pressed her face against mine so that my tears dripped down her cheeks. Then Bo's strong long arms enveloped us both. I felt his scratchy Saturday beard against my neck and smelled the clean sweat on his back from his long run through the college to the playground. He wore his faded blue jogging shorts and a t-shirt with a large red "10" stenciled on back and a small "WTAJ" over the left breast on front. Macy whimpered and leaped into the air to get my attention.

"I miss you so much," Bo whispered. "Sometimes I don't think I can go on."

"I know," I whispered, "me too."

I turned my face to his and we kissed, looked into each other's eyes, and kissed again, longer and deeper. I could taste the salty sweat on his face and the fiery warmth of his mouth. Sarah squirmed to free herself and return to the swing, and Bo and I exchanged disappointed but happy smiles. He buckled her into the toddler seat and we took positions in front and behind to push her, her face sailing within inches of ours as she squealed with delight. Bo had her dressed in my favorite denim jumper and sneakers, with her hair tied into a fountain on top of her head.

As Sarah flew through the air, I recognized my own features in her face—my dimpled chin and cheeks, my small nose and olive shaped eyes—and behind them, an unbroken line of ancestors—of Bellinis, Cuttlers, Wolfsons and Schriebergs, of Putnams, Savellis, Stefankos, Schenks, Giampietros, Ashers, and LeFortes—a line of families whose names have long since been forgotten, marching back in history and time, waiting there to step forward into the next generation. This little girl sustained their memories and kept alive their hopes and dreams. *And mine.*

Bo and I talked over Sarah's laughter and the squeaking chains of the swing. He had just returned to work for the first time, he said. He had taken my death very hard. They had stayed with his brother and sister-in-law at first; then his mother visited for a few weeks to help out until he could get used to taking care of Sarah alone. He had put the house up for sale because the memories were too painful, and he was looking for a job at one of the New York television stations to be closer to his family. They were doing fine though, he insisted; work helped occupy his mind, and Sarah woke only twice during the night now looking for mommy. He had the roof fixed and had gotten the garbage disposal running. The Bostroms had their baby, a boy, Anders, eight pounds, seven ounces. Bill Gwynne had called from the firm to offer any help he could with settling my estate, which was kind of him. My parents called once or twice a week, but the conversations didn't last long and were filled with awkward gaps of silence. Karen came by to talk and left some books about grieving that sometimes helped.

So much to say. I tried to assemble my thoughts—not about what had happened to me since my death, but about what I wanted for their future. Bo looked so strong and handsome standing there in his shorts and t-shirt—so determined and resilient, yet so wounded and vulnerable. I fell in love with him all over again, deeper than before. I wanted to tell him that, and tell Sarah how proud she should be of her daddy. I wanted to tell her how I wanted her to be like him. And me. I wanted her to know me—who I had been, how I had gotten there, the experiences to have, the mistakes to avoid. I wanted her to live life to the fullest because I could not. But as I struggled to form these words, which for some reason would not come, the sky brightened again into the harsh whiteness that began our visit, bleaching the color from their faces and the green from the grass and leaves and the blue from the sky. They were fading from view.

"No! No!" I cried. "Bo! Sarah!"

"We love you!" Bo called back. "We love you forever...."

And then they were gone.

I was back in Sarah's room. Elymas stood in the doorway. I lunged at him.

"Take me back!" I pleaded with him. "Please, it's too soon. Please, take me back."

A toothless smile spread across the old man's face. "But of course," he said, patronizingly. "We'll go back, Brek Abigail Cuttler. In due time. In due time."

"No, take me back now!"

He turned toward the stairs. "That is not possible."

"Wait," I said. "Please, don't leave me."

He grunted for me to follow him. Using his cane to feel his way by lowering it to the next step, he slowly climbed down the stairs. When we finally reached the bottom, he said: "Listen very carefully, Brek Cuttler. Whether you see your husband and daughter again is up to you. But know there are reasons you were told otherwise. Luas is concerned about your effectiveness as a presenter. He believes you should devote your efforts to the Chamber, and he is concerned you will spend too much time with your family and that it may affect your work. Sophia is concerned that you will not be able to adjust to your death unless you let your loved ones go. It was easier for them to tell you contact is not possible. Do you understand?"

No, I did not understand. I was furious.

"I do not share their views," Elymas said. "I do not presume to determine what is best for others. The choice is yours, just as they, too, have been free to choose. I come only to present you with possibilities. I do not criticize your decisions. Now, I must be going."

"Wait, please. I want to see them again."

"But, you must understand that when Luas and Sophia learn of your decision they will be angry. They will deny that it is even possible and do everything in their power to convince you of this. They will say it is all an illusion, and they will slander me and claim I am nothing more than a sorcerer and a false prophet. They may even threaten your position as a presenter and insist that you leave Shemaya."

"I don't care," I said. "I just want to see my husband and my daughter."

The toothless smile flashed again across the old man's unseeing face. "We visit them in their dreams. Take your time, Brek Cuttler. They will be there when you decide. Think about what I have said." Then Elymas banged his cane three times on the porch floor and he was gone.

PART THREE

19

City Hall in Buffalo, New York rises thirty-two stories from the eastern shore of Lake Erie, floating upon the waves of the city skyline like an art deco frigate making a port of call. So prominent is the thick spire at the top of the building that pilots, navigating their barges laden with Midwestern grain and ore, use it to reckon their courses from twenty miles out. Inside the sturdy office tower, a different form of reckoning takes place.

As if by some tasteless architectural joke, the Marriage License Office and the chambers of the Divorce Court are both located on the third floor of the building, either making a commentary on the impermanence of marriage or, perhaps more benignly, affording one-stop convenience to people entering into, and departing from, life's most important voluntary relationship. The irony of this curious placement of governmental services is not lost on Amina Rabun Meinert while walking past the doors of the former, which she visited with her fiancé only four years earlier, and through the doors of the latter, where she now intends to be rid of him. The crisp clip-clip of her heels echoing from the vaulted, melon-colored ceiling telegraphs news of her return and rouses the sleepy young clerk—a somber man of slight build and possessing the exaggerated nasally accent peculiar to those who live near the Great Lakes, as if that water also fills their sinuses. The clerk bars Amina entry because the court, at the moment, is sitting in closed session—something about abuse of a minor and confidentiality. He explains that the case of *Meinert v. Meinert* will not be called before ten-thirty; and, no, her attorney has not signed in yet.

"When the weather is nice," the clerk says, trying to be helpful, "folks go up to the observation deck to wait."

And the weather is indeed nice, surprisingly so for early March. A confused mass of warm southern air has raced up the coast, blessing cities as far north as Montreal with three consecutive sixty degree days.

"What is observation deck?" Amina asks in her broken English and German accent.

The clerk looks puzzled for a moment, then points at the roof. "You can see the lake from the top of the building," he says, speaking more loudly now, as if the accent is an indication that Amina is deaf; he also waves his arms in a crude attempt to sign his words. "Take the elevator over there to the twenty-eighth floor."

"*Bitte*," she says. "Thank you."

Amina tucks her handbag under her arm and clip-clips her heels back down the hall, past the Marriage License Office and into the restroom to check her makeup. She presents a perfectly respectable image in the mirror: mousy brown hair bunned respectably tight, pale lipstick applied respectably light, white cotton blouse buttoned respectably tight. The reflection is reassuring. George will be fine, it says to her. He understands. You cannot be with him in that way, with *any* man in that way. You encouraged him to go to other women, which was generous. And you thanked him by giving him money to establish a business. You owe him nothing. You are doing the right thing, the reflection insists.

But you have seen him cry, Amina, and you did not know men could cry.

This plea comes from a different Amina Rabun, one of five Aminas whose views are arbitrated by Rational Amina, the one who first appeared in the mirror. This is the weak voice of Nurturing Amina. It was this voice that consoled Barratte with whispered lullabies after the Russian soldiers left the house in Kamenz. There is also Fearful Amina, who since arriving in the United States has permitted Amina to venture beyond her home only rarely and wonders at the motives of men and the sources of sounds in the night. Vengeful Amina stokes the constant rage over the destruction of her family—a rage directed against no person, for Vengeful Amina lays the blame squarely on God. She had been raised to give thanks for all good things, but logic demands that God must not take credit for the good without also taking blame for the bad. Finally, there is Survivor Amina, the most dominate of the five Aminas Rabun. Survivor Amina carried Barratte five miles to the hospital at Kamenz and then returned to the country to bury her mother, grandfather, aunt, and cousins. One month later, Survivor Amina identified the bloodied bodies of her father and uncle in a Berlin morgue and buried them too. Most importantly, Survivor Amina located her family's trusted advisor, Hanz Stossel, the Swiss lawyer who, in exchange for twenty percent, liquidated Jos. A. Rabun & Sons, A.G. and all the Rabun wealth—the land holdings, equipment, automobiles, art collections, gold, and also the Schriebergs' home and theaters—and moved the fortune to a secure Swiss bank account. It was Survivor Amina who later bribed the Russian officers into allowing her and Barratte to board a train pulled by a Soviet zone locomotive out of Berlin on 13 May 1949, the day after the blockade was lifted. And it was also Survivor Amina who overcame Fearful Amina and seduced Captain George Meinert of the U.S. Army into a bed at the Hotel Heidelberg, then onto an ocean liner with Barratte, and, ultimately, into the Marriage License Office on the third floor of City Hall in Buffalo, New York.

He is patient, urges Nurturing Amina. Don't hurt him, there's been enough of that for many lifetimes. Maybe in time—

The blue tiled wall behind Amina in the mirror fills with the brown shoulders and arms of a different man. His face is hidden behind Amina's head. A red insignia is on his sleeve. Amina Rabun knows this man well. She has been living unfaithfully with him for years, and he accompanies her wherever she goes; he is a jealous, harsh man. But she has grown accustomed to his presence and his demands, and she gave up trying to escape him long ago. She can deceive him, but for only for short periods. All of the Aminas Rabun close their eyes.

Yes, you are doing the right thing, says Rational Amina. You are doing the right thing for George and Barratte, for Bette and your mother, for your grandfather, your aunt, your father, and your uncle. For all the Hetzels and Rabuns. You will not betray them.

From the observation deck atop City Hall, Amina Rabun looks out across the vast blinding expanse of white that is Lake Erie in late winter under a cloudless blue sky. The sudden thaw caused by the warm front has caused the thick crust of ice and snow on the lake to heave and break away at the mouth of the Niagara River where the undercurrent is strongest, grinding huge ice floes against the massive concrete supports of the Peace Bridge between Buffalo and Fort Erie, Canada. If the ice refuses to break up and move downriver soon, the Coast Guard will detonate explosive charges to clear the jam for fear of damaging the bridge supports. Amina can see men with ropes cinched around their waists walking on the slabs of ice piled beneath the bridge, jabbing long poles into the crevices to set them free. Despite living so close to Canada, she has never paid a visit to that land. She is afraid of the border officials, who are rumored still to be suspicious of Germans, and she is also distinctly not curious about what she might find there; she has seen enough of the world to know that the same hatreds and fears inhabit both sides of all borders.

Two men stand at the southwestern end of the observation deck, smoking cigarettes. The men's faces are in the shadows, but as time advances and the earth turns, the sun touches the top of the taller man's hat, turning it into a gray flannel torch. The men appear very animated in their discussion; one of them keeps pointing at a newspaper folded in half on the ledge. The date on front page is March 6, 1953. Amina draws closer.

"Goodbye, comrade," the larger man says, flicking his cigarette over the rail.

Fearful Amina is startled by this term, comrade. It is a word used only by communists, a term she heard often when the Russian soldiers spoke to one another throughout that horrible night in Kamenz. Suddenly the rendezvous seems clandestine and dangerous; perhaps she has stumbled across spies.

"Yeah, good riddance," says the smaller man.

They both laugh and turn inside for the elevator.

Rational Amina picks up the newspaper. It is the morning edition of the *Buffalo Daily News* and the headline reads, "STALIN DEAD." A sarcastically benign black and white photograph of the dictator looks from the newspaper upon the assembled Aminas who race their eyes over his features and then back to the headline. They read it again to confirm their understanding, and smile in unison. Not even Nurturing Amina feels shame in such delight. Indeed, the Aminas Rabun on top of City Hall believe that all who learn this news will benefit from it, even Premier Stalin's own family and perhaps, too, the black soul of his now decaying body, which can no longer wreak its havoc upon the world of the living. The Aminas read on to learn the cause of death and their smiles fade. *A stroke in the middle of the night?* How unjust and inadequate! It should have been a bullet. A thousand bullets. He should have been made to watch bullets tearing into the flesh of his wife and children, and, only then, his own body; he should have died the slowest and most painful death in the history of the world.

But the news is good just the same. Very, very good. And the air is crisp and warm, the sky blue, the sun bright, the day hopeful. Stalin's death is certain to emancipate Amina Rabun from the nightmares, and twenty-five stories below, a judge will soon emancipate her from the strains of a marriage of convenience. Perhaps the reckoning of accounts, like the reckoning of barges on the lake after the ice melts, has finally begun for Amina Rabun formerly of Kamenz.

And here, she thinks, is a very strange coincidence. George had asked her to attend Ash Wednesday services with him two weeks earlier; she had said yes, but still did not understand why. Could there be a connection to the death of evil and a change of fortune? Certainly one had been hoped for. Amina had not been inside a church since the funeral of her father, and not once with George, making him all the more bitter. George Meinert wanted all the trappings of a family, including his beautiful wife, sitting in the pew beside him every Sunday morning in the church where he had been baptized. Amina not only denied him the physical intimacies of marriage but also these tiny morsels of relationship and respect. Yet for some strange reason, on the Tuesday before Ash Wednesday, just two weeks before their divorce would become final, Amina relented. Perhaps in apology for the times her absence had caused George such pain? Perhaps to disprove his conviction that kneeling before an altar would somehow make her a different person and save their marriage? Or perhaps she had begun to forgive God?

And why Ash Wednesday? It was such a strange liturgy, the most primitive and ghoulish of all the Christian holy days. How bone chilling for a priest to whisper those terrifying words: "Remember that thou art dust, and to dust thou shalt return," and then, to be certain his grim message was not soon forgotten, to feel his thumb coated with the ashes of last year's palms smearing an ugly black cross upon your forehead as a badge of mortification. Yet a miracle of sorts had taken place during the service: Amina heard a more subversive message that afternoon than she had ever heard before. "In ancient days," the priest had said during his homily, "Lent was observed as a time when notorious sinners and criminals who had been excluded from the church were reconciled with the congregation and God." As the priest spoke, Amina believed she could actually hear the cries of all the penitents of the world daring to ask for forgiveness, and the joyful weeping when open hands were extended, rather than fists. At that instant, Amina Rabun Meinert wondered whether this is what Christianity offered the world—not sacred marks and secret words, but reconciliation. On Ash Wednesday in nineteen fifty-three, Amina Rabun Meinert accepted that offer—on behalf of herself, yes, but, more importantly to her, on behalf of her father and uncle, whose sins committed during the war were unspeakable and who could not ask for forgiveness themselves. Indeed, on that magical Ash Wednesday, Amina Rabun sought forgiveness for all things done and left undone; and for this momentous act of contrition—because God was to blame for all she had suffered—Amina Rabun expected nothing less of God than an end to the long punishment of her family—for she believed the murders and rapes in Kamenz to be a punishment for the sins of her father and uncle—and the beginning of punishment for the men who had caused her such pain.

The sun's searing, cleansing waves wash across the observation deck, spilling over the edge onto the street below. Perhaps, think the Aminas Rabun, news of the death of Joseph Vissarionvich Stalin is a symbol of the truce reached with God on that Ash Wednesday. And perhaps, I might have added, were I standing in the Urartu Chamber presenting the case of Amina Rabun, the death of Joseph Stalin was as fine a symbol of a covenant with God as the billions of small rainbows sealed into ice crystals across the frozen surface of Lake Erie.

20

When the High Jurisconsult of Shemaya deemed that I had spent sufficient time digesting the life of Amina Rabun, he summoned me to his office in the infinite corridor, which seemed even more cheerless and institutional than during my first visit—a department of motor vehicles for souls. Luas was the chief technocrat. My only question was whether the bureaucrat, or the bureaucracy itself, was corrupted?

I resented him for not informing me of Elymas and the ability to visit Bo and Sarah. For this, I resented him a lot. He knew I had gone, of course, without me saying a word. I expected the scolding Elymas had warned me would come, but instead Luas smiled benignly from across his desk and said:

"So, how shall we present Ms. Rabun?"

We were both playing the same game of evasion. He needed my help as much as I needed his.

"Just as she is," I replied.

"Naturally," he said. He was dressed in the same sport coat, trousers, and open-collared shirt he had been wearing when he found me bleeding and naked in the train station. I wore blue jeans, a t-shirt, and sneakers—the outfit I would have worn to my office Sunday to write the brief in the Alan Fleming case. He rocked back in his chair. Three thin ribbons of smoke rose into the stale air from the two candles on the desk and the pipe he held in his left hand. "But which part of her? We can't replay every moment of her life; that would serve no purpose. Our role as presenters is more selective. We must present the choices she made."

Choices. The same word Haissem had used in the Urartu Chamber to begin the presentation of Toby Bowles: "He has chosen!" Chosen what? To wait in a train shed with thousands of other souls while bureaucrats work the algorithms of their eternities?

"What choices are those?" I asked.

"The choices Yahweh promised Noah we would make," Luas replied, gripping the pipe between his teeth and talking between them. He was obviously obsessed with Noah and the Great Flood; all his metaphors eventually began and ended there.

"Did you get here by drowning?" I asked with a smirk.

"No. I was decapitated, actually. See—"

Luas' head, with the pipe still clenched in its teeth, rolled right off his neck and onto the desk, as if the blade of a guillotine had dropped out of the ceiling and chopped it off. A gush of blood shot up between his shoulders like a small fountain. I jumped back and screamed. Having made his point, his arms retrieved his head from the desk and put it back where it belonged.

"Sorry to startle you," he said coyly, "but you did ask."

"Don't ever do that again!" I said. "How did it happen? I mean, how were you decapitated? Were you in an accident?"

Luas puffed thoughtfully on his pipe. "One must begin at the beginning to answer such a question. Why did Yahweh promise not to destroy the earth after having just destroyed it?"

Like I said, obsessed. "I think we went all through this when I got here," I reminded him.

"Did we...? Oh, yes, you're right. Sorry. I've confused you with one of the other new presenters. Let's pick up where we left off, then. What if Noah had disobeyed?"

"Already asked and answered, your honor," I said impatiently.

"He'd have been killed with the others. The price of disobedience was exceptionally high, don't you think?"

"Well, the death penalty *is* the ultimate punishment," I said. I was in a very snitty mood. I wanted him to know I was upset.

"But this was the ultimate death penalty, Brek. Not only Noah's life but his family's and the entire human race. The animal kingdom as well. Disobedience meant the end of everything, not just the end of Noah. The stakes could not have been higher."

"You're all about choices," I said. "What choice did Noah have? Build an ark or everything dies? People make him out to be some kind of hero doing God's bidding. He had the biggest gun in the world pressed against his head; who wouldn't build an ark? He was just doing what anybody else would have done to save their own neck."

Luas put his pipe in an ashtray on his desk and got up.

"Precisely. Now, how shall we present Ms. Rabun?"

"Precisely *what*?" I said.

"What's the first thing Noah did after the Flood?"

"Towel off?"

"He made a burnt offering."

"That's what the Bible says."

"Why make a burnt offering?"

"To give God thanks."

Luas began pacing the small room. "Correct, and what was it worth, this offering?"

"I guess what all offerings are worth."

"Really?" Luas said. "This man, Noah, had just witnessed the mass murder of millions of people and animals. As you said about building the ark under threat, who wouldn't have been grateful for having been spared after all that? But look at it from God's perspective, Brek. What did God really want in all this?"

"Love, I guess. Love, respect, the same things everybody wants."

"Precisely. Now, is that what billowed up from Noah's burnt offering? Love? Or was it the stench of fear? The fear of instant death and annihilation—"

"But—"

"Throughout history, the tendency has always been to read Genesis from mankind's perspective, from the perspective of the accused: *man's* fall, *man's* destruction, *one man's* obedience, *one man's* deliverance, *one man's* thanksgiving, *mankind's* guaranteed survival. Perhaps the story is told not so we understand better the condition of man, which we know all too well; perhaps it is told so we understand better the condition of *God*. Noah built the ark because the price of disobedience was intolerable and later praised God to appease God, not out of love for God. Not that we should criticize Noah...he did exactly what was his to do. But if we look more closely, we see that it was divinity itself, entangled in the greatest of all ironies, that cheapened the gesture and desecrated both the obedience and the sacrifice. The story of Noah is the story of God's need for man, Brek, not man's need for God. It also explains why, because of that divine need, the possibility of evil must be permitted to exist for there to be any possibility of love; it explains why a serpent inhabited the Garden at the beginning of time, and why it will continue to coil around our feet until the end of the age."

"I don't understand," I said.

"Look," Luas said. "What changed in those forty days was the very essence of God's relationship to man, not man's relationship to God. God changed *His* ways; we didn't change ours. Yahweh recognized the problem instantly, the moment the waters receded and the sacrificial fire was lit. By punishing man for disobeying and turning away, the Flood had destroyed love itself. For true love to exist, the option not to love—without compulsion—must also exist. When love is demanded and extorted, it becomes fear, and fear is the opposite of love. So, Yahweh had a *choice*: He could accept the possibility of sin to achieve the greater prize of love, or He could endure the false praises of creatures too terrified to do anything else. He chose the former, gifting to humanity the freedom to choose. So critical is our understanding of this act that Yahweh selected the refraction of sunlight into the many colors of a rainbow as the eternal symbol of our freedom to follow many different paths. No matter how far we may stray, no matter how much it hurts—God or us."

Luas returned to his chair behind the desk.

"Amina Rabun is an heir to that promise, Brek. But that promise is both a gift and a curse. With the freedom to choose comes the responsibility for one's choices. The Urartu Chamber is the place where those choices and responsibilities are reckoned. So, I ask you again: How shall we present the case of Amina Rabun?"

21

Elymas sits on the rocking chair in Sarah's room, pushing himself back and forth with his cane against the corner of her crib. I have made my decision: I must see them again. The toothless smile appears when he hears me enter. I'm here to see my husband and daughter, but it feels shady, like a drug deal.

"Shall I take you?" Elymas asks.

"Yes."

His eyes widen and I disappear into them. I emerge this time in a quiet country cemetery on a sloping hillside bent in prayer against the wooded pew of Bald Eagle Mountain. I have been here several times before. This is the cemetery near my grandfather's farm where the Cuttlers bury their dead. It is a pretty place. And sad. The sun this day burns warm and bright, but the graves do not taste the sun or feel its heat. A requiem of red oak trees enshrouds those who sleep here, denying them any sense of the dazzling display of fusion at work in the heavens above. Maybe it is not so dazzling after all: a paper-thin membrane of chlorophyll in the tree leaves demonstrates the easy dominance of darkness over light; but the shadows moving beneath the leaves appear to be of a different darkness and a different light; they flicker over and around the stones and dance across the grass without relation to the sway of the trees. A warm breeze stirs the memorial flags; the shadows examine them and retreat, satisfied with the crisp red, white, and blue fabric fixed with staples not yet rusted into shafts of blond wood not yet weathered.

At the end of a row of well-kept plots without flags kneels a man in his fifties. His hair is thinning and his middle thickening. He resembles Bo's father, Aaron, when I was first introduced to him, pulling weeds from the garden behind their house. The man in the cemetery hears me rustle through the grass and rises to his feet. In his right hand he holds a small silver tea cup, in his left, a black yarmulke. The cup falls when he sees me, crashing onto a sterling silver tray placed at the base of a small, granite gravestone. I cannot see the name. The collision knocks over a silver teapot and two other cups, spilling their contents.

"Brek?"

"Bo?"

We race around the gravestones to hug each other.

"I knew you'd come today," he whispers.

I look at him. He looks hollowed out, like he has aged decades, a faint shell of the man I once knew. "Are you sick?" I ask.

"No, why?"

"Because… because you don't look well. You look so different from when we met two days ago."

"Two days ago?"

"Yes, two days ago, at the playground with Sarah. Have you forgotten already?"

He holds me at arm's length. "That was twenty years ago, Brek."

"No it wasn't," I insist. "It was the day before yesterday. Remember? You had just finished your jog, and we put Sarah on the swing. You told me how you'd been staying with David and that things were starting to get back to normal. You were looking for a job in New York."

"I remember. That was twenty years ago, look—"

He walks back to the grave, pulls a copy of the *Centre Daily Times* from beneath the serving tray, and shows it to me. The headline reads, "BOWLES EXECUTED." The dateline reads, "July 21, 2009."

Bo leads me to the trunk of a large oak tree at the end of the row of gravestones, and we sit down together. He's wearing wrinkled slacks and a polo shirt that looks as if he's slept in it; his face is covered with gray whiskers. "I got the job in New York and lost it," he says dejectedly. "I haven't been able to keep a job for more than six months at a time since. No television station will touch me; they're afraid of people who tell the truth. Maybe I drank a little too much and missed a few deadlines; but television is a sham, Brek, and the news is a sham. It's all make-believe. I'm doing fine though. I'm a counselor at a homeless shelter now; they let me stay there while I get myself together. Good people. I run an AA meeting and keep an eye on things; I'm thinking about doing a documentary. I've been talking to some old friends at the station. People think the homeless are animals, but they're just like everybody else; they had normal lives, just something went wrong."

Bo reaches out to hold my hand, but I pull it away.

"Have I changed that much?" he asks.

"Yes."

"I've missed you, Brek. When I heard they were executing that bastard at Rockview this morning, I had to drive up to see it. He asked the guard to read a Bible verse and that was it. No apology. No remorse. Nothing. I loved seeing him shake when they fried him. You saw it all, though; I knew you were there. I could feel you in the room."

"Who, Bo? Who are you talking about?"

"Ott Bowles. That's why you came back, isn't it? Because it's finally over and justice has been done? We can finally rest in peace. I'm gonna make a fresh start now. Clean myself up. I'm not that old. Maybe I'll even get back into the news. I'd be a great producer. I've been talking to some old friends at the station—"

"Where's Sarah?"

In the distance, I see Elymas slowly climbing the steep gravel road that severs the graveyard in two. His feeble body assimilates each small step before taking another.

"It's time." he calls out in a dry, hacking voice. Bo doesn't see or hear him. "It's time, Brek Abigail Cuttler. Come with me. It's time."

"What do you mean, where's Sarah?" Bo says.

"Where is she? I want to see her?"

Bo's face purples as if it's been bruised by a punch. He jumps up from the grass and starts running away, weaving through the gravestones with his hands gripping his head as if he's in pain. I chase after him.

"Wait, Bo, what's wrong?"

"Why are you doing this?" he yells. "Please, please just leave me alone."

He makes a loop and staggers to the ground beside the upset tea service. Tears streak down his cheeks. Except on the day Sarah was born, I have never seen him cry.

"Come with me," Elymas says. "It's time."

"Bo," I say, kneeling beside him, "it's all right. Everything's all right. Just tell me where Sarah is?"

"What do you mean where's Sarah?" he yells at me. "Don't you know?" He points at the gravestone. Engraved into the top of the monument is a crucifix superimposed over a Star of David. The sight of this heresy startles at first, but the symbols look somehow correct together, as if the perpendicular lines complete the thought of the interlocking triangles and are their natural conclusion when manipulated properly, like a Rubik's cube. Engraved beneath them in large block letters across the polished surface of the stone are the words CUTTLER-WOLF-SON. Beneath these, in smaller letters, is this:

BREK ABIGAIL
December 4, 1963—October 17, 1994
Mother

SARAH ELIZABETH
December 13, 1993—October 17, 1994
Daughter

Hot tea and bees honey, for two we will share . . .

22

I found Nana Bellini in the garden behind her house, stooped low over a row of tomato vines sagging with ripe, red fruit. Her silver hair, pulled back in a bun, shimmered under the cloudy skies of an approaching summer storm. She hummed a tune while filling a small basket with fresh produce, aware that I stood nearby in the cool spring air watching her. Reaching the middle of the row, she twisted off a huge beefsteak tomato, so large and swollen that its skin had split open exposing its tender pink meat inside. She held it up for me to see.

"Even vegetables suffer as much from abundance as from want," she observed. "Some, like this one, are bold and flashy, taking everything they can; others sip only what they need, content to share with the community." She pulled apart a snarl of average sized tomatoes and pointed to a stunted tomato vine off by itself in a patch of cracked, barren dirt. "And then there are the ascetics, joyfully suffering without any hope of bearing fruit themselves, secure in the knowledge that their sacrifice will make the soil richer next season and they'll become the fruit of future generations." She turned around to me. "The wise farmer values them all, equally. If one is favored over the other, the entire garden suffers."

I drew closer. I wasn't there to talk about gardening. "Why didn't you tell me Sarah was dead?" I asked. "Did you really think I wouldn't find out?"

Nana stopped picking and slid her arm through the hoop handle of the basket so that it swung from her elbow. Flecks of black soil clung to her wrinkled fingers and denim blue skirt. "There was nothing to tell, dear," she said. "You knew it all along. You didn't want to remember, you weren't ready."

I left her in the garden and walked through the woods to the entrance of the train station. Flinging the doors wide, I shouted to the souls inside: "Run! Run now, while you still have the chance!" They didn't dare move. They looked at me with the same suspicion my grandfather's cattle looked at him when he was trying to do something for their own good, then they lapsed back into their catatonic march back and forth across the train shed floor. There was a time when they would have rushed through those doors, but that was when they still believed mortality was the fantasy; how very real it had become, and how very soon would the final judgment be passed on their lives. Cattle. It was the proper metaphor; like my grandfather's herd, the great herd of souls arriving at Shemaya Station each day moved obediently up the loading chute and into a packing plant for slaughter, submitting themselves to what was to come and living in the memory of what once was.

I had entered the train shed without a blindfold because I was searching for Sarah. This was a grim task. There were infants, children, and adults in every horrifying shape and condition of death: wasted away by starvation and disease, blistered and burned, gnawed and digested, shot through with holes, stabbed and sliced, blue from drowning, bloated from rotting, blown apart, hacked, crushed, poisoned; suicides, murders, accidents, illnesses, old age, acts of God. Their stories no longer affected me. Only one story concerned me now. I looked everywhere, but Sarah was not among them; although I wanted desperately to see her, like a parent searching a morgue after a calamity, I was relieved. And then terrified.

What if her case had already been called? What if she had already been judged and gone on without me?

I ran from the train shed, frantic to find her. The golden key Luas had given me turned the lock, depositing me inside the Urartu Chamber. There was no one, just God and me, alone, inside the Holy of Holies. He had taken my daughter. I had come to take her back. I was not as trusting as Abraham with Isaac. I moved to the presenter's chair and looked up at the sapphire monolith, searching the smooth surface for the slightest blemish that might indicate a hint of acknowledgment or compassion. When I found none, I asked meekly in my nakedness:

"May I see her? I gave her life."

God looked on, unblinking and unmoved, my existence too infinitesimally small to notice, my plea too insignificant to deserve a response.

"Where is she?" I screamed at the top of my lungs.

The answer came back as a deafening concussion of silence—the silence of God's love being withdrawn into the infinite vacuum of space, heard by the soul, not the ears, and mourned by the soul, not the heart. I looked around the Chamber. Its walls pulsed with the purest energy of the universe while just outside, in the train shed, the walls were spattered with the innocent blood of humanity—the blood of those judged against unattainable standards by a judge who, Himself, was guilty of the crime.

"Where is my daughter?" I screamed again. "Goddamn you! What have you done with her?"

God created all things.

God created evil.

God is all things.

God is evil.

God shall punish the wicked.

Therefore, God shall punish Godself.

I raised my arms as Haissem had done presenting the case of Toby Bowles. And in unison with every man, woman, and child since the beginning of time, I spoke:

"I PRESENT GOD, CREATOR OF HEAVEN AND EARTH...*HE* HAS CHOSEN!"

The Chamber shattered into a billion shafts of darkness.

I am.

I am creation, a first thought, a last, a beginning without end.

I am a before, an after, a space in between.

I am spirit, a single breath of God.

I am love.

"I am love! I am love!" the air sings. And the waters, too, and the creatures that swim, creep, fly, and walk. The stones whisper "I am love" as they support the soil, which whispers "I am love" and supports the plants, which whisper "I am love" and support the creatures even as they raise their heads toward the sun, which whispers "I am love" and warms the Garden through which I tread.

Another like me walks in this Garden.

"We are Love! We are Love! We are Love!" we sing. And we *are* love. Love given. Love unending. Love without condition. And the knowing we are all of this, and the knowing that this is All There Is.

And the Lord God formed man of the dust of the ground and breathed into his nostrils the breath of life; and man became a living soul.

And the Lord God planted a garden eastward in Eden; and there he put the man whom he had formed.

And out of the ground made the Lord God to grow every tree that is pleasant to the sight, and good for food; the tree of life also in the midst of the garden, and the tree of knowledge of good and evil.

And the rib, which the Lord God had taken from the man, made he a woman, and brought her unto the man. And they were both naked, the man and his wife, and were not ashamed.

Now the serpent was more subtle than any beast of the field which the Lord God had made. And he said unto the woman, Yea, hath God said, Ye shall not eat of every tree of the garden?

And the woman said unto the serpent, We may eat of the fruit of the trees of the garden:

But of the fruit of the tree which is in the midst of the garden, God hath said, Ye shall not eat of it, neither shall ye touch it, lest ye die.

And the serpent said unto the woman, Ye shall not surely die:

For God doth know that in the day ye eat thereof, then your eyes shall be opened, and ye shall be as gods, knowing good and evil.

"That is the only way, then?"

The serpent coils upon a rock so I may see him more closely. When he is not speaking, he, too, sings "I am love! I am love!" with the other creatures in the Garden. He stops his song for me again. "Yes, it is the only way. You long for the experience of love. But this experience may be had only by calling upon that which you are not, for you cannot experience that which is Love until you first know that which is Not Love. Therefore must you separate yourself from Love and enter the realm of Fear and Evil."

"But what is Fear? What is Evil?"

"All that you are not."

"And I will not die?"

"You are of God, the Eternal One. Think you God can die? Think you God would place in this Garden the fruit and the tree and call me into being without purpose? Think you this purpose is to harm you? To trick you? To murder you, His beloved creation? Think you this of God? Of Love? The Lord God said, if you eat the fruit then shall you *experience* death. For how can you experience together without having been apart? How can you experience contentment without having been discontented? Hot without cold? Love without hate? No, you shall not die, but yes, you shall *experience* death. And in experiencing death, shall you experience life."

"I am Love! I am Love! I am Love!" But what does this mean? I am as a drop of water in the ocean, unable to experience its own wetness.

I eat of the fruit, and call upon the desert, and find for the first time silence. Where is the singing of the waters, the soil, the grasses and the creatures? For the first time I hear nothing in the Garden; it is both a terrible and wonderful sound. I am one, when once I had been Many. I am Good, but for the first time I have done Evil. I take Adam's hand. He has not tasted the fruit yet and does not understand. He does not hear the silence. He lives where there is only Love, and therefore he knows nothing of Love. I cling to him because I am now apart. I tell him I need him, that I am empty and cold without him. I tell him I love him, and that the fruit is the sweetest in all the Garden.

We hear God's voice. Adam rushes me among the trees to hide. We tremble and giggle. Our bodies touch the leaves and feel their chill, but also touch each other's body and feel our warmth. Adam is large, strong, and coarse; I am smaller, weaker, and soft. In seeing and touching him, who is so different, for the first time do I experience and feel myself. We long not to join with God, but to join with each other. And then we are ordered to leave.

Adam presses his lips to mine. I melt in the taste of his mouth. Now this I whisper: "I love you! I love you! I love you!"

THEY CALL ME CAIN, son of Adam.

The wind of the earth is hot and filled with dust. I shield my eyes. I jab the point of a stick into the ground and pour seeds into the holes.

My mother has told me of a place close but far away, a beautiful place, lush and green, where there is always enough to eat and drink, where the wind is cool and clean. She told me she left this place to experience love and from that experience she produced me. She told me that when she created me, when she first laid her eyes on me, she felt what God felt when he created my father. She tells me I am created in God's perfect image because she and my father had been created so. I do not see the resemblance.

Abel came after me. My mother and father say they love him as much as they love me, but they have always made his life easier than mine. He follows the herds, while I break the soil. He brings God the fatty cuts from his best lambs, while I can offer only the meager produce from my fields. God is more pleased with Abel's gifts than mine. I hate him.

"Why are you so angry?" God asks. "Are you not also perfect in my sight?"

"Because you love Abel."

"Yes, but if you dwell on this, it will be your ruin. Even so, you may do as you please."

Abel is weak and easily fooled. I tell him a lamb is injured and lead him into the fields. He does not see me unsheathe my knife. I come up behind him and slit his throat. I watch his blood spill onto the ground. He should not have taken God's love from me.

Justice is the sweetest fruit in the lands east of Eden.

The Urartu Chamber reappears. I turn and find Luas and Elymas seated on the observer chairs, watching me.

"Come sit with us, Brek Cuttler," Elymas says. "Watch and see justice done."

Luas shakes his head mockingly. "Ha! You haven't seen anything since the day I blinded you for your insolence, you old beggar."

"That is true," Elymas replies, "but justice herself is blind and yet she sees more clearly than any of us. And you, Luas, were once blinded for your own wickedness as I recall. When will you stop thinking you're better than me? Who's next on the docket?"

"Amina Rabun."

A withered old man in not much better shape than Elymas enters the Chamber holding a golden key like mine. He is tall and frail but wears an elegant double-breasted suit in the European style.

"Ah, hello, Hanz, please come in," Luas says. "We've been expecting you."

23

The door to the publisher's office of *The Lockport Register* opens and a large, powerful man appears in the threshold. Behind him, the newsroom buzzes with ringing telephones and reporters busily typing their stories. The man in the doorway has a fierce face but looks frightened, as though he is about to encounter a foe even more formidable than himself. His lacquered black hair emphasizes the severity of this expression, together with dark wings of perspiration spreading across his blue dress shirt, which is open at the throat exposing a patch of moist skin and a few gray curls of chest hair. The temperature outside is eighty-eight degrees with one hundred percent relative humidity; the waters of Lake Erie that froth themselves into blankets of snow in January evaporate into suffocating clouds of humidity in August. Inside the office, the air is only slightly cooler and less humid but the man takes in a deep, luxurious breath and savors it, puffing his cheeks into small pink balloons. With his right hand, he mops a soggy handkerchief across his smooth forehead; with his left hand, he holds a long cardboard cylinder, the type used by architects to carry blueprints.

Amina Rabun sits comfortably behind the desk inside the office, in front of a quiet fan. She is wearing a white linen blouse and heather skirt, holding in her left hand a telephone handset into which she threatens a newsprint company salesman with cancellation of her order if he fails to match a ten percent discount offered by a competitor. The salesman on the phone, a French Canadian, barely understands the English words tangled in Amina Rabun's German accent. While the man at the door waits for the conversation to end, his blue eyes wander ahead into the office like a pair of curious bottle flies, coming to rest on a beautiful Tiffany lamp in the corner; they caress the colorful glass petals and measure their value, then fly off to the framed black and white photograph of a modest bride and groom standing in front of the Dresden's baroque *Frauenkirche*, and finally coming to rest on an engraved plaque naming *The Lockport Register* the best small-town newspaper in New York. Amina had been advised by her counsel, Hanz Stossel, to purchase the newspaper as a passive investment, but she found herself in need of something to fill the expanding emptiness created by her divorce. She decided to learn the newspaper business and soon fired the publisher and took over operations.

The office is simple and sparse, as one would expect of a small-town paper of limited circulation, but on the white wall opposite Amina's desk hangs an extraordinarily valuable work of art—an original oil painting by the French impressionist master, Edgar Degas. This treasure was a gift from a man, much like the man waiting in the doorway, who also happened to find himself in the same predicament. Degas' subject in the painting is a bristly-bearded father dressed in a light overcoat and wearing a black top hat enjoying a cigar as he strolls along the edge of a Parisian park with his two handsomely dressed daughters and their dog, all moving in opposite directions at once. The painting has a snapshot quality to it, freezing mid-stride, and waist-high, the diverging characters as portions of a horse-drawn carriage and an onlooker slip into the frame. On the rare occasions when Amina rests back in her chair to admire this work, she thinks of strolling with her own father on Saturday mornings along Dresden's broad boulevards to the offices of Jos. A. Rabun & Sons, and then to a small café for lunch. Sometimes in the café she would see Katerine Schrieberg and her father. The men would sip coffees and speak of subjects that did not interest their daughters, who in turn would sip hot chocolates and speak of subjects of no interest to their fathers.

Beneath the Degas painting stands a polished walnut case filled with copies of the four books of poetry published by Bette Press during its brief existence. The binding of each book bears in gold leaf the Bette Press colophon: a square imprint of a little girl eternally fixed in mid-swing beneath the thick branches of a poplar tree, her hair and dress rippled softly by a breeze. She laughs and looks upward, beyond the ropes that lift her toward the heavens and the branches that anchor her to the earth. The original wood carving of this colophon, still stained with ink from the first run of cover pages, rests on top of the bookcase. It is the work of master printer Albrecht Bosch, who studied at the Bauhaus School before fleeing the Nazis to Chicago. Mr. Bosch convinced Amina to print books alongside her newspaper and to employ him as her production manager. The carving did all the persuading necessary. He produced it without commission, as a prospectus, from memory of an early photograph of Bette Rabun glimpsed on a table in Amina's study. He knew only that the girl had been Amina's cousin and had died very young. Amina hired him on the spot and ordered the immediate installation of a Colt's Armory hand-fed press next to the Goss Community web press that produced the *Register* each day.

The newsprint salesman at the other end of the telephone finally grasps the meaning of Amina's words and immediately concedes the ten percent discount, all of which, he wishes her to understand, will come out of his commission. She thanks him for the gesture but feels no gratitude or sympathy; *The Lockport Register* is his largest client and he has done very well for himself. Amina smiles, places the handset into its cradle, lights a cigarette, and observes the man at the door, who does not cross the threshold until asked. They have not met before, Amina and this man, yet she finds his expression familiar. Three others like him have passed through her door, each feigning the same calm, each indebted to her but somehow indignant. Amina cannot help but see in these men the same arrogance and resentment that covered *Herr* Schrieberg like a tree bark when he removed his yarmulke in submission to her threat at the cabin in the woods. The irony of this draws her smile a bit thinner until it dissolves into a frown. These men, she thinks, these strong, brave men; how quickly they are reduced to pleas for refuge from the nightmares that haunt them. But where was *their* compassion when it was requested? Where were they when others sought refuge? Three months ago, the man at the door was Gerhardt Haber. Twelve years before that, he was *Einsatzgruppen SS* Colonel Gerhardt Haber—a fact confided to Amina in a cable from Hanz Stossel, who asked if she would be willing to help another German family as she herself had once been helped. Since the fall of the Third Reich, the Habers had been on the run, living in considerable discomfort in the Parana River valley in Argentina. The Nazi hunters had tracked them as far as South America.

"Completely false," Stossel assured her concerning the allegations against Haber, the details of which she did not want to hear. Too much knowledge, she had learned, is dangerous. Amina is unsure exactly why she accepts these risks. Perhaps as a penance for her disloyalty in hiding the Schriebergs, or maybe out of altruistic concern for the hunted, regardless of their crime, or their innocence. Perhaps for the thrill that comes from knowing secrets of life and death that induce the capitulation of those desperate to keep them concealed. Whatever the reasons, and she spends little time on their identification, she convinces herself that given the opportunity to do it all over, she would permit the Gestapo to load the Schriebergs onto the train—and the Nazi hunters to take the Habers to Nuremberg and hang them. But she does not have it to do over.

Neither Hanz Stossel nor Amina Rabun consulted *Herr* Haber in choosing his new identity; she simply told Albrecht Bosch what to print on the false passport and he did exactly that, without question, in exchange for her indulgence of his expensive appetite for more sophisticated printing equipment and additions to his typeface collections. Amina had not given birth to a child nor ever would, so she took great pleasure in bestowing new identities on the people who came briefly under her care. Gerry Hanson was a nice name, she thought, faithful at least to the first consonant and vowel of the original. And completely inconspicuous.

"Your passport, please," she asks.

Hanson steps forward and presents the forgery. Amina opens it and examines the exit stamp from Buenos Aires, which appears over the talons and tail feathers of a perfectly reproduced American eagle that bears some resemblance to Hanson himself. The document is flawless.

"Any difficulties?" she asks.

"*Nein.*"

Amina raises her eyebrows.

"Pardon me, *none*, thank you," Hanson corrects himself.

Amina gestures toward a guest chair and directs the fan toward him not out of concern for his comfort but to disperse the offensive scent of his perspiring body, which has suddenly overtaken the office. This most male of odors arouses in Amina the jealousy of the man with the red insignia on his shoulder. He appears briefly in a corner of the office to confirm Amina's fidelity, then returns quietly to his couch in the living room of her subconscious.

"What are the names and ages of your wife and children?"

Hanson tenses as if he has suddenly forgotten; his contrived calm is easily cracked by the mallet of another interrogation. "*Bitte*, sorry," he says. "Hanna, age 39, Franz, age 15, Glenda, age 13, Claudia, 10."

Amina writes these down. "Hanna?" she ponders. "Would she like Helen? Helen Hanson?"

Gerry Hanson hesitates a moment, then nods his assent.

"You're sure? We could call her something else. You must be certain, the name cannot be changed."

"Yes," Hanson replies eagerly, not wanting to insult this woman who holds so much power over his and his family's future. His face suggests he does not like the name, but Amina moves on.

"Very well then. And Franz…Franz becomes…Frank?"

"Good," Haber says. He likes this selection much better. Amina writes it down.

"Glenda… Glenda…? Gladys?"

Haber's smile sags momentarily but returns. "Yes, Gladys, she will like that."

"And now Claudia…. Oh yes, do you like Cathy?"

Haber brightens a bit more. "Very good. Yes, I like Cathy."

Amina rewrites the new names on a fresh sheet of paper and calls for her secretary, who appears immediately with a steno pad. Amina is pleased by Alice's efficiency in front of her guest. "Please take this to Albrecht in the print shop, and tell him these are the additions for the Hanson project. Tell him I need a rush. It must be completed this afternoon." She does not explain the nature of the project, and Alice does not ask.

Hanson is unable to maintain eye contact with Amina. So close now to freedom, a new identity, and a new life in the United States for his family. He is embarrassed and worried. "Thank you," he says. "*Bitte.*"

"Welcome," Amina replies. For a very brief moment, she feels sorry for the man, but she quickly dismisses this sentimentality and reverts into the shell of Survivor Amina, who has counseled her so long now and who, with Vengeful Amina, has dominated almost to extinction Fearful Amina and Nurturing Amina. "You have something for me?" she asks impatiently.

"Yes, yes," Hanson says, even more embarrassed now for not having offered first. He stands the cardboard cylinder on end, removes the cap, and extracts a long roll of dingy canvas, producing a cloud of black soot that settles evenly across Amina's desk. Hanson apologizes for the mess as he unrolls the painting, which despite charred edges is in otherwise good condition. It depicts a funeral procession under gray winter skies, a coffin being carried through a snow-covered churchyard into the shattered ruins of a Gothic chapel. The nave and clerestory of the structure have crumbled, leaving only a broken facade and a few heavy limestone columns surrounding the altar. The name at the bottom right hand corner of the work is Caspar David Friedrich. Amina smiles. She has long admired the nineteenth-century romantics, but most especially Friedrich, who lived in Dresden. The private girls' school Amina attended in Kamenz, only a few blocks away from the boys' school in which Helmut was killed, saw to it, by Nazi decree, that she knew first and most about Germany's own great artists.

"Where did you get it?" she asks.

Hanson hesitates, calculating whether to speak the truth, giving Amina another lever over his soul, or to lie. "It has been in my family," he says, choosing his words carefully. His evasiveness reminds Amina of the accusations against Haber, and she decides not to press for more information.

"They say Friedrich was influenced by Runge, but I don't see it in his work," Amina says. "Do you?"

Hanson has no response to this. He knows nothing about Friedrich, Runge, or romanticism; he knows only that certain objects have great value, measured by what others will do to acquire them. Stossel confirmed by cable to Buenos Aires that Amina Rabun would produce five passports in exchange for the painting. That, then, fixed its value and ended Hanson's concern for it.

"I trust you are satisfied," he replies.

"Yes," Amina says, more coldly now and in the manner with which she dispatched the newsprint salesman. She exhales a cloud of cigarette smoke. "I'm sure Hanz told you I would require authentication. Someone from the Albright-Knox Museum will look at it this afternoon. Assuming there is no problem, you may return at four-thirty for your passports."

Hanson looks at the painting and then back at Amina, forcing a smile from his lips.

"Yes, thank you," he says, bowing his head slightly. He turns and walks out of the office. Amina closes the door behind him.

"Victim?" Elymas whispers.

I am seated between him and Luas, watching the presentation. Hanz Stossel stands at the center of the Urartu Chamber, presenting his former client. A shaft of light courses through him, carrying away the fragments of Amina Rabun's life and splashing them into the room.

"Of what?" I respond, absorbed by the presentation.

Amina props the canvas up on her credenza, leaning books against the corners to keep it erect. She steps back to imagine how it will look when framed. From this perspective, taking more time to observe and admire, the mourners in the painting appear to her as her own family must have appeared when carrying Helmut to his tomb beneath the twisted girders and broken concrete of the memorial her father had assembled for him from the debris of his school.

"Victim of injustice," Elymas says.

Amina wipes away tears as the memory of that terrible day envelopes her. She has been so consumed with the horror of Kamenz all these years that she has rarely thought of poor Helmut. She succumbs to the unanswerable guilt of such neglect, and of having named the press for her cousin, Bette, instead of her own brother or her own mother or father.

"The creature weeps," Elymas whispers. "You feel her anguish, Brek Cuttler. But where is the compassion of her Creator? Can you feel that touching her soul? Does the throne express even the slightest concern? One tender thought or word? Where is justice? When will the scales be balanced?"

But Helmut's death was, in the final analysis, an accident. The Allied pilots could not have known their bombs would raze a school. They did not look Helmut in the eyes and execute him, and that is why she has been willing to forgive them and, therefore, to forget. But not the Russians. No, their crime was deliberate and their faces depraved. There can be no forgiveness for them. Ever.

This self-pitying does not last long, Survivor Amina will not permit it. She dabs the mascara stains from her cheeks and blows her nose. She resolves to display *Cloister Graveyard in the Snow* in memory of her brother Helmut and to tell those who ask that it means this to her. And then an idea strikes Survivor Amina. She has been planning to publish a letter in the paper, timed to coincide with the death, one year ago, of Senator Joseph McCarthy. Amina had supported McCarthy, using his rabid patriotism as a means of disguising her German heritage. Embracing McCarthy made as much good business sense to the *Register* in the nineteen-fifties as did embracing the Nazis to the economic well-being of Jos. A. Rabun & Sons in the nineteen-thirties; but there was also a deeper emotional attraction to McCarthy, for he stood alone in Amina's mind as the only one who truly understood the evil of Russia and the suffering of its victims. These understandings became the germ of Amina's forthcoming Letter from the Publisher. She would explain in personal terms what the Rabuns of Kamenz had lost to the Red hoards—and she would bravely contrast that with what they lost to the Allied bombs. It would be a moving, convincing, wonderful letter. A fitting tribute to Joseph McCarthy.

The light gushing through Hanz Stossel in the Chamber changes color, signaling that the presentation of Amina Rabun is about to shift forward in time. I am deeply concerned with Stossel's selections for the presentation. Why has he omitted Amina's life in Germany and the sacrifices she made for the Schriebergs? Why is he presenting only the dark side of her life and character? And why is Hanz Stossel, who figured such a prominent role in Amina Rabun's life as friend, confidant, and advisor, presenting her case at all?

24

The presentation of Amina Rabun continues.

Each February, Amina Rabun vacationed on the Caribbean island of Aruba. Buffalo winters could be tolerated only so long. She rented a villa on the leeward side of the island with a luxurious stretch of white sand beach owned by an executive who found it convenient when visiting his company's oil refineries at the southern end of the island. Amina favored Aruba over other Caribbean destinations for the European architecture of Orangestad and its popularity among German vacationers. Bathed in the desert island's orange sun and warm turquoise waters, the past for Amina was sanitized, the vessel of memory was freshened, and the delicious summers of her childhood, when the Rabuns of Kamenz vacationed on the French Mediterranean coast, were restored like ancient frescoes under the tender hands of a doting archeologist.

One such vacation occurs in February, nineteen seventy-four. After a three week respite, Amina returns to her drafty home in

Buffalo accompanied by Albrecht Bosch, who has enjoyed his second visit to the island as her companion. Amina and Albrecht have become intimate friends but not lovers, for Amina is adamantly asexual and Albrecht adamantly homosexual. They learned these secrets about each other the day they first met, in a bright tavern in the Allentown section of the city on the second anniversary of Amina's divorce, which also happened to be the first anniversary of the day Albrecht ended a relationship with an artist who convinced him to come to Buffalo from Chicago. And so it was a common nationality and a common fate that brought Amina and Albrecht together—but it was Bette Press that made them inseparable. Albrecht Bosch was in love with the printed word. He would invite anyone who would listen into his magical world of typefaces and printing presses and, once there, explain with an artist's passion how a simple serif can arouse anger or evoke serenity, and how paper texture and weight can be grave or lyrical, pompous or comforting. He introduced Amina to the ancient struggle between legibility and creativity that ties typography to tradition like no other art form and allows for only subtle innovation; and like Amina's early teachers of romanticism, he appealed to her Germanic pride by reminding her that Johann Gutenberg gifted the printing press to humanity. In the joyful marriage of paper and ink that followed, Amina and Albrecht experienced the harmony of opposites that had eluded their private lives.

For the past two years, Amina and Albrecht have resided in separate rooms of her small, slowly decaying mansion on Delaware Avenue, built in the nineteen-twenties by a Great Lakes shipping baron. The house is cold when the travelers arrive from their journey to the tropics, infuriating Amina because she had left specific instructions for the housekeeper to turn up the heat two days before their return. Amina asks Albrecht to adjust the thermostat and light a fire in the study, then heads for the mail, which has been stacked neatly for her on the large mahogany dining room table. She scans through the envelopes quickly, searching for anything that looks important or interesting, setting aside the monotony of bills and solicitations. Two envelopes fit the former criteria: a large, beige square of heavy cotton fiber bond addressed to "Ms. Amina Rabun and Guest," and a menacing business envelope with a return address of "Weinstein & Goldman, Attorneys-at-Law." She takes both envelopes into the kitchen, puts on a pot of water for tea, and opens the invitation first. To Survivor Amina's delight, she reads that the prestigious Niagara Society has, for the first time, requested the favor of her presence at its annual Spring Ball—*the* social event in Buffalo each year.

"Albrecht!" she calls.

"What is it?" Albrecht groans with his head in the fireplace trying to resuscitate a few fading embers. He has already gone through half a Sunday newspaper but still can't coax the wood to ignite.

"We're going to the Niagara Society Ball!" Amina sings. "Get your tuxedo pressed."

"Not if I die of asphyxiation first," Albrecht coughs.

The telephone rings as the water comes to a boil.

"Can you get that, Albrecht?" Amina asks. "The tea's on."

Albrecht takes the call in the living room while Amina pours the bubbling water into a creamy Beleek teapot. She adds Earl Gray tea leaves to the infuser; sets a tray with two matching cups, milk and sugar, the invitation, and the letter and carries the tray into to the study. After settling into her favorite wingback chair and fixing herself a cup, she opens the envelope from the law firm, finding the enclosed letter:

Dear Ms. Rabun:

I represent Mrs. Katerine Schrieberg-Wolfson in her capacity as Executrix of the Estate of Mr. and Mrs. Jared A. Schrieberg.

As you know, my client has written to you on several occasions concerning ownership of certain theaters and real property in Dresden acquired by your family from the decedents during the war for the sum of 35,000 Reichmarks, equivalent at the time to approximately $22,000 U.S. You no doubt realize the purchase price was far below fair market value and the sale was made under duress and threat of seizure of the property by the Nazi government and incarceration of the decedents in the Nazi death camps. Therefore the sale was and is, invalid.

Mrs. Schrieberg-Wolfson, on behalf of the Estate, seeks rescission of the purchase contract and return of all property. In that connection, she has previously offered in writing to refund you the $22,000 plus interest from the date of the sale. You have not responded to Mrs. Schrieberg-Wolfson's offer and she has, therefore, retained me to take the necessary steps to rescind the contract and recover the property or its value.

My research has disclosed that your family no longer owns the property, it having been sold in 1949, at your personal direction, by Mr. Hanz Stossel, Esquire. I am in the process of determining the compensation received from that sale. I also understand that although the property had been purchased by Mr. and Mrs. Otto Rabun and not you directly, the proceeds of the sale were paid to you personally, or in trust for their daughter and your prior ward, Barratte Rabun. As I do not know the location of Ms. Rabun, I ask that you pass this correspondence on to her if appropriate.

Assuming the property was sold by you for fair market value, my client has authorized me to accept the proceeds of that sale plus interest, minus the purchase price, in full payment and settlement of the Estate's claims. We believe fair market value in today's dollars would equal at least $3,500,000 U.S. If such an arrangement cannot be reached, we will be forced to initiate legal proceedings to invalidate the purchase and to recover the full value of the property. We believe the courts in this country and Germany will be sympathetic to these claims.

My client deeply regrets the need to resort to the courts, but is firm in her resolve. She is and shall forever be grateful to you for sheltering her family during those terrible years, and has expressed as much in her letters to you. This is, however, a matter of the unfair acquisition of property by your uncle under extreme conditions. As a result of that action, my client and her surviving family were forced to live in relative poverty compared to the lifestyle which you and your family have enjoyed. Mrs. Schrieberg-Wolfson seeks no more than to right that wrong; she bears neither you nor Miss Barratte Rabun any ill will.

I am authorized to initiate legal proceedings if I receive no response from you to this letter. In light of your position as publisher of a newspaper, it would seem that the negative publicity surrounding such a case would prove very uncomfortable. In that regard, our investigators have learned that Otto Rabun was a member of the Waffen SS and that your father's construction firm, from which much of your family's wealth emerged, was under contract to build the crematoria at Majdanek, Treblinka, and Oswiecim. Such extraordinary facts will be difficult to conceal from the public in litigation.

I look forward to your prompt response.

Very truly yours,
Robert Goldman, Esq.

"How dare she threaten me!" Amina fumes.

Amina had received letters from Katerine Schrieberg and thrown all of them away. She had come to see the Schriebergs as responsible for the horror of Kamenz. While the Russian soldiers murdered members of her family and raped her and her cousins, the Schriebergs remained huddled in a Rabun hunting cabin nearby and did nothing, risked nothing; when she ran to them for help the next morning, they were gone. Indeed, Amina had come to blame all Jews for these things: in her view they had sunk Germany into poverty and, ultimately, war, and their outrageous claims about death camps had defamed her father and uncle and shamed the nation. Now this, after all their cowardice, after all Amina had risked to protect them, Katerine Schrieberg repays her by threatening to ruin her? It was too much. Amina takes the letter to the hearth, ignites it with one of the matches left behind by Albrecht, and places it into the fireplace on top of the charred newspaper, warming her hands by its flames.

"What's going on in there?" Albrecht calls from the living room. "Barratte's on the phone, do you want to speak to her?"

This news startles Amina even more than the letter. She has not spoken to Barratte in nearly twenty years. The bond between cousins strained when Amina decided to flee Germany with Captain Meinert and take Barratte with them. Barratte despised the Americans for the death of her father in Berlin as much as she despised the Russians for the deaths of her mother, sister, and brothers in Kamenz. She considered Amina a traitor to Germany for marrying an American soldier, and a traitor to their family for liquidating their assets and running. Brought to the United States against her will, Barratte did not adjust well. She found the language and customs difficult, performed poorly in school, and was unable to make friends. The other children—children of American veterans dead and alive—tormented her as a Nazi in their midst, an orphaned "Kraut girl" whose parents and country got what they had coming. She never revealed to them the horrific price she and her family had paid in Kamenz. Her teen years were spent in quiet desperation; she substituted her rape with a story that she had seduced and slept with young German officers at the age of eleven, bragging about this to the other girls and, in this way, finding acceptance among them as worldly and exotic, responding to her trauma in the exact opposite manner of her cousin. She found acceptance, too, among older boys, who were pleased to find a willing, experienced partner regardless of background and accent. Barratte thus developed an unflattering reputation, and this eventually found its way to Amina, who was furious but, privately, jealous that her young niece seemingly had been able to put Kamenz behind her in this way. As her guardian, Amina punished Barratte severely for her behavior, and in response, Barratte grew colder and bided her time. Within weeks of her eighteenth birthday, she hired a lawyer, took control of her inheritance, and left for New York City. Amina knew little about Barratte's life during the years after that. The surprise telephone call on that cold Saturday in February came to her as a complete shock.

"What does she want, Albrecht? Is everything okay?"

"Everything's wonderful!" Albrecht replies. "Barratte had a baby boy this morning! Seven pounds, five ounces! She named him Otto Rabun Bowles! You're a grandmother, or a great aunt, or something, Amina! Here, come speak to her!"

The Urartu Chamber reappears. "A decision has been made," Legna announces with the hollow voice of a proctor calling time, terminating the presentation of Amina Rabun before the final essay on her life can be completed. Another postulant in Shemaya graded on less than half her work.

"Well done," Luas says, shaking Hanz Stossel's hand.

"Yes, well done." Elymas agrees. "Well done."

25

"We're going out tonight," Nana said.

It was late afternoon and we were in the study. She was reading, of all things, the *1897 Farmer's Almanac*—the year she was born—and I was needlepointing a Christmas stocking for Sarah. We had never gone *out* before. I pulled the needle through the fabric.

"Where?" I asked.

I had started the stocking when I was pregnant; it would have been finished in time for Sarah's first Christmas. I picked it back up again when I went home to meet Elymas after the presentation of Amina Rabun. I waited for days, but he never came. Doing something with my hands (hand)—doing something for Sarah—became my way of mourning, and protesting, her death. I decided to act as though she was still alive—that we were both still living. I made bottles of formula for her every morning and ran her a bath; I washed her tiny clothes and crib sheets; I drove to the daycare and then to work, and back to the daycare and then to the convenience store. The unmarked police car flashed its lights to pull me over, but I kept driving until it disappeared from the mirror. When the loneliness became too great, I returned to Nana's house and brought the stocking back with me to finish.

"It's a surprise," she said, her lips spreading into a smile. This was actually the first time we'd spoken since I came back. We had spent several days silently passing each other in the house.

"I don't think I can take any more surprises," I said.

"Elymas does have a flair for them," Nana replied. "It's part of his charm, I suppose. But I wouldn't trust everything he says and does."

I looked at her. "Should I trust you?"

"You should trust the truth, child."

"What is the truth, Nana?"

"The truth is what makes you feel calm and loved, nothing more than that."

"That's meaningless."

"No it isn't. It's the only meaning. Truth is never anger or fear. They're illusions, and Elymas traffics in them."

I looped the thread and pushed the needle back through the fabric. I was working on the toe of an angel blowing a trumpet.

"He told me you would call him a false prophet."

"He also told you that I'd be upset, but I'm not. You're free to follow false prophets if you wish. They all expose themselves eventually… and truth is never far away."

"I saw Bo and Sarah with my own eyes. I held them in my arms."

"I know, dear, I know. And you sailed on a caravel and walked through Tara, and everything around you here seems so real. But it all disappears. Things and bodies are not real. They're symbols, and symbols are impermanent. Life is impermanent."

"Bo's life has been ruined."

"According to Elymas, it has. But who's to say? Is Bo closer to the truth by working at a homeless shelter or sitting in front of a television camera?"

"What happened to her? What happened to me? What are you hiding?"

"I'm not hiding anything, child. It's you who doesn't see the truth all around you." She closed the almanac and pushed herself up from the chair. "When you're ready to see it, you will. It's time now for us to get ready."

"For what?"

"You'll need an evening gown."

That got my attention. "And where do you expect me to find one of those in Shemaya?"

She had the devious look of a grandparent teasing a child with a present. "In your closet."

I went upstairs and opened the closet in my mother's room. There were five different gowns—beautiful silks, satins, and crepes with matching stockings and shoes. I was thrilled. Nana stood at the door, watching me.

"They're beautiful," I said, holding each one in front of me. "Won't you tell me where we're going?"

"I can't," Nana said, "it's a surprise."

She sat on the bed as I tried on each gown, twirling past her. They all fit perfectly, but we liked the black satin gown with straps and the low bodice that exposed my shoulders and back the best. I was actually enjoying myself. We went through the same process in her room, settling on a gown for her with more color and a high neckline. She pulled two strands of pearls and two matching pairs of earrings from her jewelry box and gave a set to me. Standing before the mirror, we made a striking couple, and neither of us needed hair brushes or makeup. Hair and complexions are *always* perfect in Shemaya.

We left the house with the last of the four suns from the four seasons dropping beneath the treetops. Nana led me out the back door and through the woods on foot to the entrance of the train station. There were strange new sounds when we entered the vestibule, mystical and resonant—the sounds of water rushing and wind blowing, of dolphins laughing and birds singing, of children talking and parents sighing, of all creation living and dying. It was the sound of the earth rotating, if it could have been heard from space, primordial and otherworldly, as viewing the earth from orbit feels both primordial and otherworldly. It turned out to be the sounds of a band. A handwritten note on the doors read: "RECEPTION FOR NEW PRESENTERS." We walked in.

All the postulants were gone, and with them the static discharge of their memories and the sad, horrifying, but sometimes beautiful, states of their deaths. On an elevated stage near the board showing arrivals but no departures, hovered four faceless minstrels, like Legna, dressed in long gray cassocks. Two played instruments that looked like violins, one a bass, and the other a cello that vibrated in colors: auroral greens, violets, and blues. Before the band milled a crowd of formally attired men, women, and children, some off by themselves enjoying the performance with a plate of hors d'oeuvres and a glass of champagne (or milk for the children), others gathered into small groups, talking and laughing. Banquet tables had been erected in the four corners of the hall and piled high with pâtés, caviar, cheeses, fruits, and other delicacies, and next to these were bars fully stocked with wine, liquor, and other refreshments. A small army of faceless, gray-dressed creatures tended the tables and bars and collected the empty glasses and plates from the guests. A magnificent crystal chandelier and a constellation of lesser chandeliers bathed the room in a warm, sparkling light. I looked around, trying to gain my bearings. Luas emerged from the crowd, dressed handsomely in a single-breasted tuxedo.

"Welcome! Welcome!" he said, greeting us. "We've been waiting for you!" He gave each of us hugs, then turned and waved his arms over the crowd. "Grand, isn't it?"

"Yes," I yelled over the din.

"And all in your honor, my dear. You've graduated with flying colors, and you're ready for your first client. I must say, we've got an excellent group of new presenters. Time for a little play before the work begins. You both look wonderful."

"Thank you," I said. "But I really don't feel like I'm ready to graduate or represent anybody. I barely understand the process…and I don't think I agree with the results."

"Have no worries, Brek," Luas assured me. "Everyone's nervous the first time, you'll do just fine."

"Brek was very suspicious about tonight," Nana said. "She almost forced me to ruin the surprise."

"Was she now?" Luas said. "Ah, but she's an inquisitive one. That's what we love about her."

"Here's another question, then," I said. "What have you done with all the postulants? The hall was filled a few days ago."

"And a perceptive question as usual," Luas said. "Didn't I tell you, Sophia? They're still here, actually. Come, I'll show you."

We walked back out of the train shed and closed the doors. "Okay," he said, "now, open them again."

All at once the music was gone, along with the minstrels, food, tables, chandeliers, and beautiful guests, and the postulants were back—thousands of souls lurking in the dim, sulfurous light of the train station, comatose and naked, wandering endlessly over the cold, filthy floor. The soul of a teenage girl approached me, and in her I saw a doctor explaining that there is nothing he can do to stop the treatment for her leukemia from making her nauseous; her stomach hurts and she's crying, squeezing her stuffed rabbit, Mr. Ears. She returns to school thin and bald, a freak in her own eyes. Her mother has quit her job to care for her; she is a tender, loving mother, but the girl despises the woman because she is healthy and beautiful, and responsible for bringing her into this horrible world. Most of all, the girl despises her sister, who is younger and also healthy and beautiful; she plays soccer and flirts with boys, flaunting her life. She has no idea of suffering. The sick girl refuses to speak to her sister, and refuses to smile. She infects others with the blackness that infects her, for she believes no other goals are attainable, and she is alone. She would die for a last laugh. And she does.

I looked next into the soul of an old man from Congo, and from him I received magnanimous humor and love. His life begins in a shack with a dirt floor, in a village with a dirt road, and ends in the same shack with the same road and the same dirt. He has fourteen children and loves each one, although eight died before the age of ten. He loves his neighbors, his fields, and even the wild boar that gores him to death. Most of all, he loves his wife, who tries with all her strength to heal the infection that becomes gangrenous and ultimately kills him. Offered to do it all over, he would happily say yes.

"How can they be here?" I said to Luas.

"Creation is a matter of perspective and choice. What one wishes to see becomes what one is able to see. You have never seen the subatomic particles pulsating in the furnishings of your living room, nor the place of your living room in the pin-wheeling galaxies millions of light years away, but this does not mean subatomic particles and galaxies do not co-exist. Your powers as a presenter are maturing, Brek; you are seeing more of what there is to see. You are seeing through microscope and telescope."

The soul of a man with bulging eyes and a shaved head glanced up at me and turned away. He seemed familiar, like somebody I once knew, but I couldn't place him before he disappeared into the crowd of souls. From elsewhere in the crowd, the soul of a young girl stared at me with haunted, defiant eyes. She stood among a group of souls missing arms and legs. I expected to see the images of her life but saw nothing, only a void, as if she had lived no life at all. Her right arm was missing and she reminded me of me as a girl.

"Do you know her name?" I asked Luas, "the one over there without the right arm. Maybe I could represent her since we have something in common."

"That won't be possible," Luas said. "The girl already has a lawyer, and your first client has already been selected. He's at the other end of the hall, but this isn't the time or place for an introduction. You'll meet him tomorrow. This is a time to celebrate. Shall we return to the reception while there's food left?"

We exited the train shed and re-opened the doors back into the party. The music and light instantly washed away the despair of the hidden room, and I wondered whether subatomic particles and galaxies ever contemplate their existence.

26

My new colleagues—the many honorable and longstanding members of the bar of the Urartu Chamber—were eager to welcome me at my graduation party and share stories of their first presentations. Disturbingly, each of them related similar tales of trials terminated before a defense could be made, and what seemed like eternities spent trying the same soul over and over again to the same conclusion. Yet, none of them seemed much bothered by it. Constantin, for example, an older man with blackened teeth and scars on his face, told me he presented the soul of a police officer whose duty, and pleasure, it had been to torture prisoners into making confessions. "He was a singularly cruel man," Constantin explained, "but Legna sees fit to end the presentation each day before I can inform the Chamber of his fondness for abandoned animals found on the street, which he sheltered in his apartment." Another presenter, Allee, a pregnant teenager with swollen cheeks and hands, presented the soul of a young man who left his girlfriend after impregnating her. "He risked his life to save a child from a fire that swept through his neighbors' house one day," she said. "I try to bring it up in the Chamber, but we never seem to get to it. I guess God doesn't think it matters." Another presenter, a young boy named Julio with soft features and a lisp, presented a bully who beat and tormented his classmates. "I guess he wasn't all that bad," Julio conceded, "his father was sick and he helped take care of him; he even helped him use the bathroom—yuck! I can understand why God doesn't want to hear about that."

I lost Luas and Nana in the crowd and continued on alone to a banquet table. After helping myself to some pâté, brie, and crackers, I drifted off toward an amazing stone sculpture in the corner of the room that I hadn't seen earlier. It was a perfectly smooth sphere as tall as me and might have represented the earth. A miniature stone figurine of a woman with long hair and wearing a skirt stood on the surface of the sphere at the top with three miniature pairs of stone doors arrayed before her. When I looked more closely at the figurine of the woman, the sculpture somehow reconfigured itself, like the shape-shifting sculpture of the monastery and synagogue in the hallway, so that I was now seeing the three pairs of doors before me, as if I were the figurine of the woman on the sphere. Over the first pair of doors in front of me was a sign that said "SELF," over the second, a sign that said "OTHERS," and over the third, a sign that said "SPIRIT." All three pairs of doors had mirrored surfaces, and I could see my reflection in them, but the left and right doors of each pair reflected back different images of me. The left door of each pair displayed an image of me I had always wanted to see: taller, with more pronounced cheekbones, fuller breasts, and two complete arms. This Brek Cuttler was witty and sophisticated, a loving mother, brilliant lawyer, devoted daughter, exquisite lover, competitive tennis player, accomplished violinist, and wonderful chef—the perfect specimen of a woman, envied for having a perfect career, perfect body, perfect mind, perfect husband, perfect children, and perfect home. The right door of each pair mirrored back a far less glamorous image of myself. This Brek Cuttler was more round and plain, with a blemished face, thin lips, small breasts, limp hair, and no right arm. These were her only distinguishing characteristics, yet she seemed more noble and less frantic than her twin reflected in the other doors, as if there were no need for further identification and even these few features were unnecessary. This Brek Cuttler defined herself by everything the other Brek Cuttler was not: comforting rather than competitive, spiritual rather than intellectual, forgiving rather than condescending, complimentary rather than complimented, trusted rather than feared—perfectly defenseless and, thus, perfectly indestructible; dependent upon everyone and, thus, independent. The Brek Cuttler in this reflection was a creator of possibilities, not a victim of expectations, incapable of envy because she understood that everything belonged to her and she, in turn, belonged to everything.

"Love me," pleaded the perfect Brek Cuttler reflected in the left doors of each of the three pairs with the signs above them. Behind her in the mirror assembled the trappings of her success—the awed glances of men and women, the beautiful clothes and home, the powerful friends and powerful titles, the luxurious vacations, the coveted invitations, the ruthless victories. Her slightly queer little twin reflected in the right doors of each of the three pairs said only, "I am." Behind her assembled the trappings of her freedom—represented by the universe itself, from the smallest gnat to the brightest star, each perfect in its own way, and in its own time.

The magical sculpture divided my miniature avatar into three, and each of us stepped forward to make our choices

between the three pairs of doors. We were greeted at the thresh-
olds by parents, teachers, and friends: to the left they all pointed,
and through the left doors we went, finding behind them more
doors and the same sets of choices. To the left again we went,
receiving the same guidance, and to the left again, again, and
again, as we had been taught and raised, eventually choosing
on our own. We chose an occasional right door, demonstrating
our compassion, but quickly turned left again, and again, the
sculpture rotating slowly, like a boulder being pushed uphill, the
doors opening and closing. Suddenly the sculpture transformed
itself back to the way it had been, a large sphere with me no
longer part of it but standing by its side. Looking down upon
its surface, I see, as though viewing the earth from high altitude,
a labyrinth of doors, paths, and choices crisscrossing the surface
like so many rivers and highways.

A man's voice, deep but gentle, came from my right, startling
me: "A traveler who sets out in one direction eventually returns
to the place of his beginning, seeing it again for the first time."

I turned to find a strikingly exotic man standing beside me.
He was thin and of middle height and middle age, shirtless and
shoeless, with smooth, titian skin and dark, black eyes; he wore
a rainbow-colored dhoti wrapped around his waist and legs in
the style of a Hindu ascetic, and on his head a skullcap made of
small gold beads. His face was peaceful, unfathomable, like that
of a Buddhist monk during meditation. He was beautiful in the
way a gazelle or an antelope is beautiful.

"Oh, hello," I said, trying to recover from the shock of his
appearance while blushing and coughing on a cracker at the
same time. "I didn't see you standing there...." I coughed again
and cleared my throat. "Wow, pardon me," I said.

"Are you all right?" he asked.

"Yes, I'm fine, thanks. Quite an interesting sculpture, isn't it? But to me, it seems to be saying that a traveler can't maintain a single direction. Choices are constantly being made, changing her path."

The sphere rotated, and my three virtual representatives disappeared around the far side.

"But time leads in only one direction from which there can be no deviation," the man said. "If your point is that there can be many possible present moments, then I would agree. One may choose between them."

"I'm not sure that's what I meant," I said. "How can there be many present moments?"

"I believe the sculptor intended for the forward rotation of the sphere to represent the unchanging direction of time. This means that any point on the surface where the figurine happens to stand represents the present moment as experienced by her at any particular instant of rotation. If so, then stretching behind her from that point on the sphere is the past, and out in front of her lies the future. Yet, it is a sphere, so what is behind her must eventually rotate around and appear again in front of her, illustrating that the past inevitably becomes the future. From the traveler's perspective, she will be seeing it again, as if for the first time."

"You seem to know a lot about this sculpture," I said.

"I've studied it a great deal," the man replied. "Now, suppose you were to draw a longitudinal line halfway around the sphere from the present moment where she stands—a prime meridian. You would see that this line represents all possible places on the surface of the sphere where the traveler can stand and still be within the present moment. The doors represent the decisions she must make on where to stand along that line."

"If that's what the sculptor was trying to say, I missed it."

"I don't think that's all he was trying to say," the man said. "We've accounted for only two dimensions of the sphere so far—time, represented by the rotation of the sphere, and place, represented by the surface of the sphere. We've described only a flat disk, I'm afraid—half a pancake."

"I didn't do well in geometry."

The man smiled.

"There must be a third dimension giving volume to the sphere and meaning to the dimensions of time and place. The meridian line I mentioned, representing the present moment, doesn't just float upon the surface; it also extends beneath the surface, through to the core of the sphere, giving the sphere its depth and shape. This dimension of depth represents the possible levels of understanding of the traveler at any given present moment—the levels of meaning of place and time. Her perception might be very basic and primitive, in which case her understanding of her time and place would be near the surface; or she might possess a more complete understanding of her time and place and all its nuances, in which case her understanding would be very deep and near the core. Meaning is also a matter of choice, is it not? We may experience the same present reality in many different ways. Thus, although our traveler has no ability to choose her particular time—although she may indeed fantasize about the past and the future—she has complete freedom to choose both her place in the present moment, and its meaning and significance to her—her level of perception. In this way, she experiences reality in three dimensions from a potentially infinite number of locations along the line of the present moment, assigning to her reality a potentially infinite number of meanings corresponding to the depth of her perception."

He was talking way over my head. I was there to celebrate becoming a presenter, not engage in a philosophical exegesis of time, space, and perception. I scanned the crowd for Luas and Nana and a polite way out of the conversation.

"My name is Gautama," the man said, perceptively extending his left hand.

"Brek Cuttler," I said, smiling sheepishly, embarrassed at having been caught looking for an exit.

One of the faceless attendants arrived to retrieve my empty glass and plate.

"Yes, I know who you are," Gautama said. "I hope I haven't bored you. I myself am far more interested in the smaller steps along the journey, but standing back on occasion to glimpse the whole can be useful. For instance, it explains the presence of the postulants here among us right now, and our mutual inability to see each other because of our chosen levels of perception."

"Does it explain why every presentation in the Urartu Chamber is terminated before a defense can be presented? I assume this has been your experience as well?"

"I'm not a presenter," Gautama said. "I'm a sculptor... among other things."

"You sculpted this?" I asked, even more embarrassed.

"Yes, do you like it?"

"Yes, of course," I said. "It's fascinating...but a bit intimidating."

"We're not comfortable making choices; we prefer others to make them for us. But choice is what makes everything run, you know; it's the energy that powers the universe. To create is simply to choose, to decide. Even the Ten Commandments are choices—ten choices each person must make at any instant in time that create who they are and who they will become, although they can be reduced to three, which is what I've tried to do here with my sphere."

"Three?"

"Yes. The first four Commandments are simply choices about the Holy One, are they not? Will we acknowledge God—or Spirit, or Truth, whatever language you wish to use—or will we worship material things and settle for the impermanent world? Will we invoke the power of God, the creative force, to harm or destroy others, or will we love them as ourselves? Will we set aside time to appreciate Creation and Truth, or will we consume all our time in pursuit of finite ends? The remaining six Commandments concern choices about others and self. Murder, theft, adultery, the way one relates to one's parents, family, and community—these reflect how one chooses to regard others. Whether one is envious, and whether one conceals the truth, are ultimately decisions about one's self."

"Interesting way of looking at it," I said.

Gautama turned toward the crowd.

"Your understanding of this, my daughter, is essential, for these are the choices that must be presented in the Urartu Chamber. From these choices alone is the Final Judgment rendered and eternity decided. The Judge is demanding and thorough. Some might even say the Judge is unforgiving."

"The presentations are never completed," I said. "Some might say the Judge is unjust."

"Ours is not to question such wisdom; but you might ask yourself how many times the same choices must be presented before the story is accurately told."

"Since I arrived in Shemaya, I don't think I've met anybody, except my great-grandmother, who wasn't a presenter. You said you are a sculptor, among other things. What things are those?"

"I help postulants recognize themselves and their choices. That is why my sphere is located here in the train station. "

We turned back to the sphere. "I still don't understand the reflections on the door," I said. "I saw two different versions of myself."

"Are not all choices based in personal desires? And are not all desires reflections of who we are or wish to become? We could distill the three choices presented here by the three pairs of doors into one, and conclude that all things in life turn upon choices concerning Creation itself. We could distill this even further and conclude that all things turn upon Creation's choices about Creation itself. In other words, Brek, we are co-creators with God. At the highest level of reality on the sphere, at the pole from which we start, and to which we will inevitably return, there is but one possible here and now. All the rest flows from it, and returns to it, in the course of Creation—in the course of making choices. We choose who we are or wish to become, but in the end we are only one thing, permanent and unchanging, no matter what choices we make. The journey around the sphere is, in essence, an illusion."

Tim Shelly staggered up between Gautama and me, reeking of alcohol. His eyes were glazed over and his bowtie undone.

"Hey, *great rock!*" he said, slurring his words. Then he placed his hand on my shoulder and slid it down my back inappropriately. "Go get somebody else, Gautama," he said. "Brek's mine."

"You seem to be enjoying the evening, my son," Gautama replied, not bothered by the remark, or Tim's apparent drunken condition. I, however, was very uncomfortable with the way he was behaving.

"I think he's enjoying it a little too much," I said, pushing him away.

Tim grabbed me again and tried to kiss me full on the lips.

"Stop it, Tim!" I yelled, turning my face away. "What's gotten into you?"

"What's the matter, Brek? Too good for me?"

"I believe it is time for you to go home, my son," Gautama said.

"Why?" Tim said, "so you can have her?" He winked at Gautama and gave him a punch on the shoulder. "I've been watching you…I know you older spiritual guys still got it in you."

Gautama smiled but said nothing, as if he were dealing with a misbehaving child.

"Problem is," Tim continued, "she thinks she too good for you, too. She only screws Jew boys. She likes them circumcised. Well, I say it's time for her to find out what a real man looks and feels like. You wait your turn here, Gautama, and we'll see what she thinks. It won't take long." Tim lunged toward me and I screamed, but Gautama stepped in front of him and spun him around in the other direction.

"Good night, my daughter," he said, leading Tim away by the arm. "Enjoy the rest of your evening."

27

I left the reception badly shaken and walked down the long office corridor outside the Urartu Chamber to calm myself down. For the first time in Shemaya, I feared for my personal safety. It wasn't like there was a police department or I could call 911 if Tim attacked me.

But was there really anything to be afraid of? Can a human soul be raped—or harmed in any other way? Tim Shelly looked like a man with a man's body; I felt his hand on my back, on my woman's body; but none of these things existed—and yet they did. And how disappointing must it be for Jews to learn that anti-Semitism survives even death! I wasn't even Jewish, and I never told Tim that Bo was; how did he know, and why did it matter? None of it made sense. Yet, Tim's ugly words and threats were as palpable and real as if they had been made during my life; there was something genuinely cold and malicious about the way he looked at me. What happened to the sweet guy who thought he was a waitress and camped out with his father—the guy who visited Tara with me, and sailed with me on the caravel, and worried about how his mother was taking his death? Maybe it was just the alcohol talking…but how can a human soul consume alcohol, let alone become intoxicated by it?

I continued walking down the corridor until I reached Tim's office. A sudden chill came over me, but that was nothing compared to the dread I felt when I saw my name on the office door next to his, on a brand new plaque that read, "Brek Abigail Cuttler, Presenter." The door was unlocked, and I went in. The office was identical to Luas' with a small desk, two chairs, and no windows. I was not the first occupant: two white candles sat on the desk, burned unevenly, their sides and brass holders clotted with polyps of wax. It was a claustrophobic little room, not unlike a confessional in a rundown cathedral; the air hung damp and heavy, laden with the sins of those who had exhaled their lives there; but it felt safe and almost cozy—and it was mine. I lit the candles, closed the door, and settled in behind the desk to enjoy the privacy.

Then came a knock at the door.

Tim?

I slipped quietly around the desk and braced the guest chair against the door.

The knock came again, followed this time by a girl's voice, Asian-sounding and unfamiliar: "May I come in please?"

"Who is it?" I said, wedging the guest chair more tightly into place with my foot.

"My name is Mi Lau. I knew your Uncle Anthony. I saw you leave the reception."

"Anthony Bellini?" I said.

"Yes."

I pulled the guest chair away from the door and opened it. What I saw standing before me on the other side was so hideous and repulsive that I shrieked in horror and slammed the door shut again. A young girl stood in the doorway, her body was burned almost beyond recognition and still smoldering, as if the flames had just been extinguished. Most of her skin was gone, exposing shattered fragments of bone and tissue seared like gristle fused to a grill. Her right eye was missing, leaving a horrible gouge in her face, and beneath the socket two rows of broken teeth without lips, cheeks, or gums and an expanse of white jawbone somehow spared the blackening of the flames. The stench of burned flesh overpowered the hallway and, now, my office.

"Please excuse my appearance," the girl said through the door. "My death was not very pleasant. Nor, I can see, was yours."

I looked down and saw myself as Mi Lau had seen me—as I had seen myself when I arrived in Shemaya, naked with three holes in my chest and covered with blood. I opened the door again. Mi Lau and I stared at each other, sizing each other up like two monsters in a horror movie. We obviously could not communicate or even be in each other's presence if our wounds were all we could see, so we engaged in the same charade played by all the souls of Shemaya, agreeing to see in each other only the pleasant hologram reflections of life the way we wished it had been. In this filtered and refracted light, Mi Lau suddenly became a beautiful teenage girl with yellow topaz skin, large brown eyes, and long, thick, dark hair. She was a child on the verge of becoming a young woman—fresh, radiant, and pure, and dressed in a pretty pink gown, making the gruesomeness of her death all the more cruel and difficult to reconcile.

"I am very sorry my appearance frightened you," she said. She spoke in the rhythmic, loose guitar string twang of Vietnamese, but I somehow understood her words in English, as if I were listening to a hidden interpreter.

"No, I'm the one who should apologize," I said. "I didn't expect anybody at the door and then, well…yes, you frightened me. Please, come in."

Mi Lau sat in the guest chair with her hands folded in her lap. I closed the door and returned to my place behind the desk.

"So, how do you know my Uncle Anthony?" I asked. "He died before I was born."

"We met during the war," Mi Lau said, "and he is also one of my clients here."

"My uncle is on trial here?" I asked. "Can I see him?"

"Yes, you can come see his trial. I present his case every day."

"Legna ends it before you finish?"

"Yes, like the others."

"That's unfair, and it doesn't make sense. Why bother having a trial?"

Mi Lau said nothing.

"How did you meet during the war?" I asked. "What was he like?"

"Your uncle came to my village with other American soldiers, they were chasing the Viet Cong. The VC stayed with us; we had no choice; they were mostly just young boys; they left us alone and didn't harm us. When the Americans came, there were gunshots, and my family hid in a tunnel beneath our hut. Always my mother would go into the tunnel first, then my sister, me, and my father last; but the fighting caught us by surprise and this time I was last. The tunnel was narrow, and we had to crawl on our stomachs. We could hear the machine guns and the Americans shouting, and the VC boys screaming. My sister and I covered our ears and trembled like frightened rabbits."

"It must have been horrible."

"Yes. But the fighting did not last long. Soon all became quiet until a powerful explosion shook the ground. Dirt fell into my hair, and I was afraid the tunnel might collapse. My father said the American soldiers were blowing up the tunnels in our village and we must get out quickly. I crawled toward the entrance, and that is when I saw your uncle. He was kneeling over the hole, holding a grenade in his hand. I remember it clearly. A crucifix with the right arm broken off dangled from his neck; I remember thinking it looked like a small bird with a broken wing. I smiled up at him. I was so naïve, I thought Americans were there to help us, that they were our friends. But he didn't smile back. He looked at me with terrible, hateful eyes, and then he pulled the pin and dropped the grenade into the hole. 'No! No!' I screamed, we're down here!' The grenade rolled between my legs. It felt cold and smooth, like a river stone. I saw him turn his head and cover his ears and realized what was about to happen. And then it exploded."

Mi Lau spoke without anger or emotion, as if she were describing nothing more than planting rice in a field. I lowered my head, too ashamed and distraught to look at her. "I'm so sorry," I said. "I didn't know."

"I know," Mi Lau said. "I know all about your family from presenting him. They seem like such nice people. Your uncle knew your mother was pregnant with you when he died, but he was convinced you would be a boy, so I was surprised when Luas told me who you were at the reception."

"I was told he died a hero."

"Maybe he did," Mi Lau said, "but hero is something that lives in other people's minds. After blowing up all the tunnels in our village, he went off with some of the other soldiers to smoke marijuana. He said to them with a laugh: 'The best thing about blowing up tunnels full of gooks in the morning is that they're already in their graves and you can spend the rest of the afternoon smoking dope.' An hour later, he wandered off by himself and shot himself in the head. That was heroic maybe, to take his own life so he could no longer take the lives of others."

It took me a long time to absorb what she had said.

"How can you represent him if he killed you and your family?" I asked. "I'm sorry about what he did, but how can he get a fair trial? I mean, naturally you would want him to be convicted—and maybe he should be. That's probably why he's still here. "

Mi Lau's eyes narrowed and she straightened herself indignantly. "I present Anthony Bellini's life exactly as he lived it," she said. "I cannot change what he did, and I do not bias the presentation in any way. Luas monitors us closely and disciplines any presenter who attempts to influence the result."

"But how can you even face him after what he did to you?"

"He can't hurt me again, and I feel better knowing justice has been done. All is confessed in the Urartu Chamber…there are no lies. Some say Shemaya is where Jesus stayed for three days after his death, before ascending into heaven, presenting all the souls who have ever lived. I believe Shemaya is where the final battle is fought between good and evil. Evil must not be permitted to win. It must not be allowed to hide or disguise itself; it must be rooted out, and destroyed, and all those who perpetrate evil must be punished."

Mi Lau stood and suddenly she transformed back into the girl whose body had been mutilated and blown apart by my uncle's grenade. "I must go now," she said. "Welcome to Shemaya. You will be serving God here. You will be serving justice."

28

I woke the next morning to the nutty-sweet aroma of Irish porridge. It was a delicious, familiar aroma I hadn't smelled since my Grandma Cuttler made it for my grandfather and me on the farm. I went downstairs and found Nana Bellini in the kitchen, already dressed for the day in tan slacks and a red sweater. She gave me a kiss on the forehead and placed a steaming bowl of porridge before me at the kitchen table.

"You'll need your strength today," she said.

There was something different about her. Her eyes seemed distant and moist, almost melancholy. I hadn't seen her this way before.

"Thanks," I said, delighted with the breakfast. "Are you okay?"

"Yes," she said. "It's just that the time has come for me to go, and I'm sad we'll be apart."

"Go? What do you mean, go? Go where?"

"Just go, child, go on. You came here wounded and frightened, and there's still some pain and fear left in you, but it no longer controls you. You've recovered from the shock of death; that's why I was here, to help you. But you're a presenter now, and I can't help you with that. You need space to experience, to spread out your thoughts and look them over—space to study and understand. The next steps you take must be your own. You're ready, and I'm proud of you. We're all proud of you. You give us hope."

I was terrified. "Take me with you," I said. "I don't want to be a presenter. There's no justice here. Uncle Anthony, Amina Rabun, Toby Bowles…they're all convicted before their presenters even enter the Chamber. The same trials are held every day, and the same verdicts are issued. It's…it's hell, not heaven."

Nana went back to the counter to get some coffee. "Maybe you were brought here to change all that. Maybe God needs you to fix it."

"God created it, and God is the judge. He's the one who stops the trials before a defense can be made. Let Him fix it."

"That's not God's way. We all have free choice. You have a choice about the kind of presenter you want to be, just as you had a choice about the kind of person you wanted to be."

"I don't want to be a presenter at all."

Nana sat down next to me. "That choice was already made, child. You chose to come here. The question is not whether you will be a presenter, but what kind of presenter you will be. That is something you must decide for yourself. You'll feel differently when you meet your first client. The postulants need you, Brek. You mustn't abandon them."

"But, you're abandoning me."

"That's not true. I've done all I can. The rest is up to you."

My emotions quaked even though somewhere below I knew I was rooted in solid ground because I had been planted there by her, this remarkable woman who had nursed me when I passed through my mother's womb, and who nursed me again when I passed through the womb of life. "Where will you go?" I asked. "Will I be able to see you?"

"Oh, I couldn't describe it to you in a way you'd understand," she said. "What I can tell you, though, is that, like all places, I'm going to a place I choose and that I help to create. I don't know where it is, or what it will be like, but I do know that it is a thought to which I go—a thought I've been thinking that, like all thoughts cultivated and cared-for, becomes manifest in a tiny corner of the universe so that it may be experienced. Creation transcends everything, child; a million-billion acts of choice become a million-billion acts of creation."

"But I already lost you once, Nana," I said, " I can't bear losing you again."

"Shhhh, child, Shhhh," she whispered. And then she gave me what I needed most—one last brief, wonderful moment of childhood. She held me close and pressed my face against the wrinkled skin of her cheek; she allowed me to hear the strong pumping of her heart and smell the sweet fragrance of her skin. In her embrace I felt safe again. And then she said, "Haven't you learned, child? Don't you see? Visit my garden when you have doubts. Learn from the plants that live and die there and yet live again. And remember, oh child, always remember that I was here to greet you when you thought I had gone so long, long ago. You did not lose Bo and Sarah, Brek. And you will never lose me. Love can never be destroyed."

29

I wanted nothing to do with the sordid proceedings of the Urartu Chamber. I would have rather spent eternity alone than participate in them, and when Nana left Shemaya, so did I.

Although Tim Shelly had turned on me, he had done me a great favor by showing me that I had the power to go anywhere. I decided to do just that, embarking upon my own Grand Tour, seeing and doing things no person had ever done, or could ever do, in a single lifetime. I started off at a leisurely pace, recreating and sunbathing on the most exclusive beaches of Barbados, the French Riviera, the Greek Islands, Tahiti, Dubai, and Rio de Janeiro. I lived the lifestyle of the rich and famous, sleeping in the most exclusive villas and resorts, sailing aboard the most luxurious yachts, flying on private helicopters and jets, arriving in the most expensive limousines, dining at the finest restaurants, drinking the most expensive champagnes, shopping at the most exquisite jewelers and boutiques, and winning—and losing—millions of dollars at the most exclusive casinos. It was a dream life, a heaven, but eventually even the richest person in the world—which I was, hands down—grows weary of pampering and decadence. After what felt like a year of glorious, but ultimately dispiriting, self-indulgence—I was, after all, alone on the beaches, in the villas, on the planes, and in the casinos with nobody to share my good fortune or to envy me from afar— I was ready for some adventure and set out on a journey that would have made even the most intrepid explorer weep. Within a span of months, I scuba dived the coral reefs of the Galapagos, climbed the highest mountains of every continent on earth, including Mount Everest, trekked across the Sahara, sailed solo around the world, paddled a canoe the entire length of both the Amazon and the Nile, walked the Great Wall of China, visited the North and South Poles, went on safari across the game lands of Africa, made pilgrimages to Jerusalem, Varanasi, and Mecca, explored the deepest crevices of the ocean by submarine, piloted several fighter jets, drove race cars, and concluded my journey with a trip to the moon and Mars, as captain of the Space Shuttle, which I landed expertly on the surface and re-launched even though such a feat in the living world would have been impossible. After returning to earth exhausted but exhilarated, I craved another period of rest and relaxation and decided to make the great palaces of Europe and Asia my home for several months, followed by some long, meditative stays in the great monasteries and ashrams of India, Tibet, and Christendom.

Having explored and indulged in all the world I had known had to offer, I found myself bored yet again and decided to take a new journey, this time traversing both space and time. In an instant, I found myself wandering the great civilizations, from the kingdoms and dynasties of Egypt, China, Mesopotamia, and India, to the rise of the Semitic peoples, the Greek and Roman empires, the Inca civilizations of South America, the Aborigine villages of Australia, the fiefdoms of Europe, the colonization of North America, and the expansion and contraction of the British empire. This journey was a historian's dream, but a tourist's nightmare—can an uninhabited empire even be considered a civilization, aren't *people* required for that? I discovered along the way that the nature of the universe itself is loneliness, that God is lonely. It isn't like God has a family and friends to hang around with, or that there are resorts for God and God's friends where they can dine together, share a bottle of wine, and talk about their day and their problems. In realizing this, I found a strange comfort in my own loneliness.

And then one day I realized that although the nature of the universe might be loneliness, even God can't tolerate it for long. There is no greater sorrow in all the universe than having all of *this* and no one to share it with. As I traveled alone from one wonder of the world to another, from ocean to mountain to cosmos, I came to understand why God would have been willing to risk everything—even rejection, suffering, and war—for the joy of hearing just one breathless human being say, "Oh, *my God...* look at that!"

Yes, I had been able to avoid Tim Shelly, Mi Lau, Luas, Elymas, and what I considered the tragedy and injustice of the Urartu Chamber, but I needed to share my experience of the afterlife as much as I had needed to share my experience of life itself. Like God, perhaps, I grew increasingly desperate for something to create, a purpose for being, an objective to accomplish—a soul with which to share; and I understood now why the serpent had told Eve that it is the risk of failure and harm, the risk of evil itself, that makes life rich, and the experience of contentment and joy even possible. In short, I slowly began to realize that I had returned, in a way, to the Garden of Eden and found it as wanting as Eve had found it; I was ready, again, to be cast out of paradise, and to accept that risk—even the risk of being assaulted by Tim Shelly and being reminded of what I had lost: my husband, my daughter, my life, my world. I was even willing to accept the risk of souls being unjustly convicted and sentenced for all of eternity.

And so, as Gautama had said, I returned to the place of my journey's beginning, seeing it again for the first time. I returned to Shemaya Station, ready now for my first client but secretly hoping, as I had hoped every day since I arrived in Shemaya, that this would be the day I would be told it had all been a very strange and terrifying dream, and it was time to wake up.

30

Luas didn't answer when I knocked on his office door. Legna appeared in the hallway instead and informed me that the High Jurisconsult was occupied and would see me after I had met with my first client; I was to go to my office and wait.

I did as I was told, and soon Legna arrived with a postulant, closing the door behind on the way out and leaving us alone together in the darkness. I had decided not to light the candles. I wanted to postpone the exploration of my client's past as long as possible and communicate first under present conditions, one fellow soul to another, lost from a common home, left to a common fate. I would not lightly rob my clients of their memories, or demand that they wait in the other room while I negotiated eternity with their Creator; they would be given the opportunity to participate in their own defense, to explain on their own terms what had happened during their lives and why.

So there we sat in the darkness, my first ecclesiastical client and I, together on the precipice of eternity. I reached out, across the unfathomable chasm separating us from each other, fearful not for myself or what I might find, but for the soul on the other side and what lay ahead. Then I hesitated: every lawyer has doubts, and what was at stake in the Urartu Chamber was far greater than what was at stake in any courtroom on earth. I wanted to leap back through the darkness into the familiar, dull light of my own misery. How could I bear another's burdens when I could not even bear my own? How dare I attempt to reconcile another's accounts when my own debts remained unpaid? Turn back, warned instinct, turn back.

I stumbled beneath the weight of these doubts, and I did begin to turn; but from my client came a sound: a small, barely audible plea for mercy that could not be left unanswered, no matter what demons haunted me. Not only did this plea from the darkness stir my compassion, but it made plain for me, as if there all along, that this was the call I had prepared all my life to answer, and the reason I had been chosen to defend souls at the Final Judgment. The mystery of my own life, and afterlife, had been revealed unexpectedly in the suffering of another soul. I would devote myself to rescuing my clients from the desolate pit of despair and injustice. I would redeem them before the throne of God.

With the joy of this revelation, I no longer wanted to keep the soul across from me enshrouded in the darkness. I yearned to see his or her gentle, vulnerable face in the light of truth, and to learn everything I could about the life he or she had led, both the good and the bad. I would bless, not judge, and do everything in my power to guarantee my client every benefit and annihilate every doubt. I would speak out in the Urartu Chamber with the partisan voice of an advocate and risk even my own punishment, if necessary, to win justice. I would never allow to happen to this soul what had happened to Toby Bowles, Amina Rabun, and my Uncle Anthony.

These were the promises I made when I struck the match and lit the candles—promises I had made years ago, as a young girl, when a conveyor chain disfigured my body and reconfigured my life. I knew now that I had been brought to Shemaya to fulfill those sacred vows and, perhaps, to secure my own redemption. I could see now how defenders of justice are created in childhood, during tender moments of awareness when they first understand that the insects in their hands, the crayfish in their buckets, and the puppies on their laps depend upon their benevolence for their very survival; that they wield the awesome power of life and death over other living creatures, and choose not merely to allow life to continue, but to protect and nurture it no matter the cost—because they too have trembled before their own vulnerability and prayed for someone to deliver them from the careless and cruel hands of fate.

The candles flicker and burn brighter, and from the shadows emerge this beautiful, helpless creature upon whom I will lavish my devotion, my love, my eternity. But the light reveals a very different kind of face; it is the wicked face of a tormentor, not the innocent face of a victim. And there are the hands that have ground life from the innocent limbs of insects, crayfish, and puppies.

No...no, not him. Please...please, dear God, not him!

But it is too late.

The man who murdered my daughter and me has died and gone to Shemaya.

And now his soul roams inside me.

PART FOUR

31

Otto Rabun Bowles met his grandfather only twice—first during a football game when he was eight years old, and then, four years later, at the old man's funeral. Ott's father made sure it would be no more than this, and that Ott knew this was for his own good. Thus, of the life of Tobias W. Bowles played back through his oldest son Tad's bitter words and actions, his grandson Ott caught only a glimpse, and that taken from the same fraction of life Haissem had presented in the Urartu Chamber before Legna said a decision had been made.

In fairness to Tad, he honestly believed there was nothing else to know about his father, because he could remember nothing else. But in fairness to Toby, his son never tried to cultivate another belief, and never stepped back from his jealously guarded version of the past long enough to see whether a different point of view could be sustained. Tad even resented his aunt Sheila because she received from his father the tenderness and affection he believed rightfully belonged to him.

Regardless of justification or blame, the fact was that all the wounds, resentments, and indignations visited upon the son were showered down upon the grandson in a cold, steady rain; a soft rain often, just enough to germinate apprehension in the little boy, but at times a violent storm too, sometimes unintentional, and other times vindictive. What else does an angry adult child have? He can withdraw his love from his father, but that is never enough to feed the hungry flames of revenge; so he withdraws the love of his own children too, multiplying the loss by denying his aging father any connection to the future for the sake of righting wrongs visited during an increasingly distant past. Such had been the case between Toby and his own father, Gerard Bowles, who abandoned the family when Sheila was born; had this man reappeared at any point in Toby's life, Toby would have done exactly what Tad had done to him; and, indeed, Toby did make certain Tad knew nothing of his grandfather so that even his memory could not survive another generation. Thus, if one were to play back the life of Otto Rabun Bowles—and that *is* what presenters in the Urartu Chamber do—one would find four generations of Bowles—Gerard, Toby, Tad, and Ott—starring in the same morality play, reversing roles with age and taking turns personifying the vices of fathers and their sons.

But what of the grandmother, Claire Bowles, in all of this? Surely Tad allowed her sunshine to beam down upon young Ott through such menacing clouds? Unfortunately, no. This might have been the case if Claire had left Toby after his infidelity, but Toby promised to end his relationship with Bonnie Campbell and begged for Claire's forgiveness. After much soul-searching, she granted it to him and accepted him back. For Tad, who had risked everything to win his mother's love and vindicate her honor by pursuing his father into a mistress' bedroom, this betrayal was incomprehensible, and stung as deeply as the many years of his father's relentless abuse. Having unknowingly starred in a Greek tragedy of a different sort, Tad became estranged from both parents, breaking the heart of the mother for whom he had sacrificed his relationship to his father. There were attempts by the mother, all unsuccessful, to reconcile father, son, and, later, grandson. The last of these experiments involved arranging for Toby's surprise appearance at Ott's junior football game. This is when Ott Bowles met his grandfather for the first time, and the last.

Of course, little Ott understood none of this at the age of eight. He knew only that he had been hit viciously during the football game by children nearly twice his size. During halftime, he pleaded with his father not to be sent back into the game. His father, like *his* father before him, responded by belittling him on the sideline for acting like a baby and ordered him back onto the field. Yet a strange thing happens to men as they age: Toby Bowles, the grandfather and former perpetrator of such callousness, climbed down from the bleachers to make his surprise appearance by intervening on his grandson Ott's behalf, asking Tad to give the boy a break. Ott was all bruises and wonderment at this fallen angel about whom he had heard only terrible things, but who bore such a strong resemblance to his own father. Although he had never laid eyes on the man before, he suddenly seemed like his only friend in the world, and Ott loved him on contact. But Tad, the victimized son and current perpetrator, was enraged. Harsh words were exchanged between the two men—words that should have been spoken fifteen years earlier when there was context in which to understand them and love left to heal them, but that landed now like hammers on the firing pins of revolvers. When Tad could bear no more and restrain himself no longer, he shoved his father—hard enough to cause Toby to lose his balance and fall to the ground in front of the other parents, spectators, and children. Ott's wounded eyes swelled with hatred into hostile slits—eyes that Toby, sprawled on the ground, recognized instantly as his own son's eyes in the back seat of the car at church after the fight with Claire about Paul and Marion Hudson. Stunned and embarrassed, he used the bleachers to support himself, got up, and walked away, never to be seen by Ott, or Tad, again. Four years later, Tad's mother called and, in a voice both accusatory and guilty—a co-conspirator willing to testify to receive a lighter sentence—reported that Toby had died of a heart attack. By then, the opportunity for Ott to forge a bond with his paternal grandmother had come and gone.

Ott did, however, come to know his maternal grandmother well. Nonna Amina, he called her, even though she was actually his second cousin, only eight years older than his mother, and his real grandmother, Ilse Rabun, lie in a Kamenz churchyard beside the grandfather after whom Ott had been named. The close relationship between Amina and Ott was made possible by a miraculous remission in the cancerous relationship between Amina and Ott's mother, Barratte Rabun, brought about in the same manner most forms of the disease are conquered: by nearly killing the body to save it.

Bill Gwynne and I could be thanked for administering the almost-lethal dose. Acting out of a sense of continued debt and gratitude for what Amina had done for the Schriebergs in Kamenz, my mother-in-law, Katerine Schrieberg-Wolfson, did not follow through on the threat made by her former lawyer, Robert Goldman, Esq., to sue Amina and Barratte Rabun in nineteen seventy-four. But in nineteen eighty-six, I, as a freshly minted lawyer married to Katerine's only son—who was also a rightful heir to the Schrieberg fortune—convinced her to reconsider. The Rabuns had not only stolen Katerine and her brothers' inheritance—which perhaps could be overlooked because Amina had saved them from certain death—but they had also stolen the inheritance of Katerine and her brothers' children and grandchildren. This could not be overlooked. These future generations were entitled to their share of the estate created by their ancestors. As a potential mother of the next generation, who as a Christian had spoken to Katerine about converting to Judaism, and who happened to work for one of the most respected and aggressive lawyers in the nation—my arguments on this point received added weight. Bill Gwynne also loved the idea—not only because the contingency fee if we won would be substantial and I would be earning my keep as a new associate—but because it was a high profile international case filled with broader implications for the recovery of assets confiscated by the Nazis. After much prodding and encouragement by Bo, Bo's father, Katerine's surviving brother, and me, Katerine reluctantly consented.

Bill and I promptly initiated the lawsuit, making it every bit the publicly embarrassing spectacle for Amina and Barratte Rabun promised in Mr. Goldman's letter. Bill was a master, both in the court of law and the court of public opinion. I watched in awe, helping him behind the scenes. This was the type of case lawyers wait for their entire careers, but there I was, working on it fresh out of law school. From a torrent of Hague Convention subpoenas, we obtained from German archives copies of contracts signed by Amina's father for the construction of the crematoria at Osweicim and Majdanek. Although these documents bore no direct legal relevance to our claim for recoupment of assets derived from the Schriebergs' theaters and home, they made sensational copy. Soon the publisher of the award-winning *Lockport Register* was being tried in the media as a war criminal—and Jewish groups were calling for a boycott of her bloodstained paper and the bloodstained books of Bette Press.

These war contracts were the first solid pieces of evidence Amina and Barratte had seen of their fathers' involvement in the Nazi death camps, and they were devastated. Even so, they had been through far worse during the war, and in facing this new common threat they found again the mutual love and trust for each other that had sustained them during those terrible days, weeks, and months after Kamenz. Plus, now, there was young Ott to think of. With Amina's refusal to bear children, Barratte's twelve year old son held the only hope for a new generation of Rabuns. With the survival of the family at stake, the cousins held each other and turned their backs against the coming storm, unyielding even when Bill and I convinced the *Buffalo Evening News* to print portions of *Patentschrift Nr.* 881 631, *Verfahren und Varrichtung zur Verbrennung von Leichen Kadavern und Teilen davon*, issued in 1941 to Jos. A. Rabun & Sons. This patent, also obtained from German archives, had been secured by Amina's father, Friedrich Rabun, to prevent his competitors from using his improved crematoria design, first installed at Osweicim, that utilized better airflow management, ash removal conveyors, and new refractory materials to elevate temperatures and increase capacity. In the accompanying technical drawings, Amina recognized the shape of the brick sandbox built by her father for her and Helmut. This vulgar resemblance, and the photographs of thousands of cadavers in the camps, haunted Amina's dreams the rest of her life.

Yet, the Rabun women fought back against even this disgrace. In interviews and editorials, they explained how Amina had saved the Schriebergs at great personal risk; how the purchase of the theaters had been for fair value at the time, giving the Schriebergs the money they desperately needed to survive;

and how just a few hundred yards from where the Schriebergs lived under her protection, the Russians raped her, Barratte, and Bette and murdered their family. Coming from the mouths of the accused, however, and countered by the damning archive documents and the Rabuns' great wealth, these stories did little to change public opinion. Amina and Barratte Rabun were tried and convicted not for wrongfully withholding the Schriebergs' money, about which no one seemed much concerned, but, symbolically, for perpetrating the Holocaust itself.

32

The final, nearly fatal blow to Amina and Barratte Rabun came not from Bill Gwynne and me but from Amina's once-loyal secretary, Alice Guiniere. Wearing her finest go-to-church print dress one early autumn day, Alice recounted under oath before a grand jury the mysterious visit to her employer's office by a Mr. Gerry Hanson—a man known formerly, she believed, as SS Colonel Gerhardt Haber. During this testimony, she produced galley proofs of five United States passports bearing the Habers' new identities, collected from a waste bin in the print shop of Bette Press. Dabbing her eyes, she explained that something just didn't seem right that day and she thought she ought to save the proofs, just in case. It was a sense of patriotism, she insisted— not vindictiveness for her recent firing by Amina in an attempt to reduce expenses and save the paper—that compelled her to come forward now after all these years.

The grand jury indicted Amina, the Habers, and Albrecht Bosch; and the United States Attorney held a press conference.

Standing before a nearly-hysterical throng of reporters and photographers, the ambitious prosecutor confirmed Gerhardt Haber's status as an international fugitive and war criminal and unveiled several easels attached to which were fiendish photographs of the SS Colonel in full black dress uniform and photographs of the identical man, Gerry Hanson, dressed in civilian clothing, together with the galley proofs of the forged passports and the front page of that day's *Lockport Register*. Amina and Albrecht were charged with obstruction of justice, harboring fugitives, and forging official documents, for which they each could be sentenced to thirty years imprisonment. The prosecutor also disclosed that discussions were being held with the Department of State about extraditing the Habers to Germany or Israel. Not lost on a few sympathetic newspaper editors was the harsh irony that for assisting the Schriebergs in Germany in the same manner that Amina had assisted the Habers in the United States, she could have been hanged. "No good deed goes unpunished," one editorial concluded, and "whether a deed is good or not appears to be a matter of opinion at the time—primarily the opinion of those operating the levers of state."

With all energies turned to the criminal defense, Amina's lawyer called Bill Gwynne with an offer to settle the civil litigation. In light of everything that had befallen Amina, and everything that had happened in Kamenz, Katerine Schrieberg-Wolfson instructed us to accept the offer—seventy-five percent of our original demand—and end the litigation immediately.

All this had a profound impact upon young Otto Bowles, who helplessly witnessed the systematic destruction of the people he loved. The unraveling for Ott began when his mother and father divorced. The marriage was somewhat unusual and had never been stable. Barratte and Tad had met in a nightclub in New Jersey where Barratte, aged thirty-nine and still quite attractive, served drinks. Something in the younger Tad Bowles' sad brown eyes and embarrassed smile made her want to hold and protect him. At twenty-six years of age, he vaguely reminded her of her older brother, who had been executed by the Russian soldiers in Kamenz, and he seemed so different from the other young men at the bar who, having finally been given a voice by the alcohol they consumed, had nothing to say but "feed me," "where's the bathroom?" and "sleep with me."

Even so, the attraction between Barratte and Tad was primarily physical, and this began to wither for both of them when Barratte's narrow waist and flat stomach expanded after she became pregnant unexpectedly. That they married so far apart in age, background, and outlook could only be attributed to loneliness, not love, and to the sense that the making and nurturing of a child might become a panacea for the problems of the past. It wasn't to be. Until the morning Barratte delivered Ott, she had viewed men only as game to be hunted and collected, stalking them like a poacher and mounting their dumb, wondering heads on the paneled walls of her memory. After the birth of her baby, men generally, and Tad in particular, were not worth even this to her, and marriage meant only hanging up her gun. She had already harvested what little the male of the species offered the world—that precious fertilizer they squandered so recklessly. Young Ott became her finest trophy, her beginning and her end. Each contraction of her womb breathed new life into her dead family, whose existence now depended upon her sacred labor. Not for one day during Ott's childhood would she allow him to forget that the survival of the Rabuns of Kamenz depended upon *him*; he was the irreplaceable link to all those who had come before, and all those who would come after.

Ott accepted this responsibility, but his father, in no way a Rabun, was never let in on the important secret. Tad Bowles, looking always into the hyperbolic mirror of his own father, believed his wife's distance was caused by his own luminance, and he took this to be a sign that he was finally in control and, like his father, in position to wag his finger while indulging his own indiscretions. He had an affair with another woman just after Ott's first birthday, as if to mark the occasion. Barratte knew instantly; the pall of guilt smothering him could not have been missed. But she tolerated the infidelity because she expected nothing less from an animal, and because it allowed her to devote more attention to Ott, which only confused Tad; he would have been happier if she had thrown him out, as he had wanted his mother to do to his father. Worse still, he mistook Barratte's indifference for his mother's forgiveness, leading him to believe she actually cared and might even love him.

Then came the Schrieberg lawsuit, served with all the solemnity the Sheriff of Middlesex County, New Jersey could muster. The startling revelations about Jos. A. Rabun & Sons came as a complete shock to Tad. Barratte had told him only that her family was killed during the war, that she inherited a modest sum, and that a cousin in Buffalo had helped her escape from Germany before the Soviets closed the Iron Curtain. That Barratte's father and uncle had been wealthy, that they had accumulated this wealth from the death camps and the extortion of Jews, that Barratte had been raped by Russian soldiers and her family murdered, and that she had concealed all this—badly frightened him. He had never understood a woman to have such abilities to conceal the truth and to deceive. Yet the scare also had the effect of inflating Tad's damaged ego, because Barratte's lack of emotion in the marriage could now be explained by reasons other than his own inadequacies. He had married a fraud, and perhaps much worse, so it was he who pressed for a divorce even as he purchased his fourth new automobile in as many years with tainted Rabun money. Of course, Barratte would have divorced Tad eventually, just as Amina had divorced George Meinert. Tad threatened to seek custody of Ott—and might have won, given Barratte's history and the allegations against her—but she threatened to destroy him if he tried it, and he knew she could—and would. One week after Ott's twelfth birthday, Barratte packed their things and moved from their home beside Tad's insurance office in New Jersey to Amina's small mansion on Delaware Avenue in Buffalo to begin life again.

Ott tolerated the move to a new home reasonably well despite being held back a year by his new school and the difficult work of making new friends—and having to explain to them his lack of a father, whom he missed deeply in spite of the way he had sometimes been treated. Amina recognized Ott's loss and made up for it as best she could. The role of grandmother suited her well. With Barratte saddling Ott with the burden of resurrecting their family, Amina became the fairy godmother who could afford Ott the luxury to be who he wanted to be—and to love him without condition and guide him gently along the path of his dreams. She encouraged but never insisted, so that when Ott showed no interest in playing baseball, football, or hockey (a heresy in a city just one bridge-length from the Canadian border), she abandoned these without judgment. When Ott showed interest in music, Amina purchased for him a piano and retained the services of a private instructor; when he showed fascination with birds, she erected for him a small aviary behind the garage of her house. Although he was a bit old for it, she read to him nightly, in German and English, and took him to museums, aquariums, amusement parks, and movies. She also brought him to her office at the newspaper on Saturday mornings, as her own father had done in Dresden. There, her friend Albrecht Bosch—who had moved out of the mansion several years earlier after taking a new male lover—showed him how to print books and cards, and how being "different" need not necessarily mean being lonely and unhappy.

Amina and Ott thus became best friends, and she shielded him from his mother's excesses. Consumed by the past and what might have been, Barratte insisted that Rabun men should make their living excavating dirt and pouring concrete, and have their fun hitting each other on fields and killing animals in the woods. Ott's inability to live up to that standard was a constant source of disappointment, and, in this way, Barratte assumed the role of perpetrator that Ott's father had abandoned.

The details of the civil litigation with Katerine Schrieberg-Wolfson were easily concealed from Ott, but the criminal indictment exploded inside his life like a bomb, detonating upon the arrest of his beloved Nonna Amina. In an instant, he lost his dearest companion and was forced to endure his family's humiliation alone in a school, like all schools, where mercy is in short supply. What little compassion that remained at home in Barratte was depleted quickly by the ordeal of defending her cousin and operating the newspaper in her stead. Ott's only other potential source of support, his father, had remarried and was expecting another child with his new wife, leaving little room for his oldest son, who had become one of those mistakes of passion best forgotten. The time between visits to New Jersey grew longer until there was nothing left but time.

Ott turned in on himself then, to a mostly silent world narrowed to manageable proportions and insulated from causes, effects, and accusations. From this place he would emerge only as necessary, to respond to his mother when her threats became real, to scribble answers to exam questions that demonstrated a grasp of numbers well beyond his classmates, to correspond weekly with Nonna Amina and visit her once each month at the prison for women near Rochester. But Nonna Amina had become a different woman. Devastated by the betrayals of Katerine Schrieberg and nearly everybody else in her life, disgraced by her father's Nazi past, despised by the public, imprisoned, scorned, and nearly bankrupted, she became embittered, morose, and began displaying the symptoms of clinical depression. Moreover, although a plea bargain would set her free in three years instead of thirty—on the weekend of her sixty-seventh birthday, to be exact—handing over Hanz Stossel to the Nazi hunters in exchange had nearly killed her. It was not that she believed Nazis were guiltless or deserving of special protection; Amina held the more radical belief that all people deserved compassion and somebody must start somewhere. For the sake of that naïve idea, she had risked her life to help a Jewish family when they were being persecuted, and, later, a Nazi family when their turn had come. What harm was there in that? Had she shown favoritism? The prosecutors forced her to reveal confidences to gain her own freedom, and that act of treachery cut as deeply as it would had the Gestapo forced her to turn over the Schriebergs. She owed everything to Hanz Stossel; he had helped her escape East Germany and given her the opportunity to lead a new life in a new country. But on the basis of her own grand jury testimony, he was captured while on vacation in London and extradited to Israel. He lost his home, his family, his law practice, and his fortune. He died of pneumonia in an Israeli jail cell several years later.

Otto Rabun Bowles, now at the age of fifteen, had become a thoughtful, perceptive boy. He understood the significance of much of what had happened; but to make sense of it, he used the same strategy he had been taught in mathematics of simplifying equations and reducing fractions to their lowest common denominator. In his new, simplified, equation of life, Nonna Amina suffered because she had tried to help two families, one Jewish and one German. Because, in the final analysis, she was German.

33

It was the injustice of Nonna Amina's imprisonment that caused Otto Rabun Bowles to embrace his German heritage, raise it up from the filth in which he believed it had been trampled, and carry it forth for all Rabuns. Like his father before him, who in the name of honor entered the darkness of his own father's sins, young Ott, in the name of honor, entered the darkness of the Rabun past. Also like his father, however, he never quite returned from the journey.

Ott's letters to Nonna Amina in the penitentiary soon became interviews for the story of redemption he was writing in his mind. He asked her to recount in the smallest detail the lives of their fallen family, beginning with Joseph Rabun, the patriarch and founder of the company that bore his name and that had been a source of such pride and, now, shame. Amina resisted Ott's inquiries at first, finding the memories too painful to explore; but Ott was persistent and, gradually, Amina opened up, discovering that writing about her past was an effective therapy for the deep depression into which she had fallen.

Barratte, by contrast, was overjoyed by her son's sudden insatiable curiosity about his heritage and ancestors, deeming it the first step in fulfilling his destiny to become the savior of the Rabuns. So enthusiastic was she, in fact, and so determined to encourage and assist him in any way, that for Ott's sixteenth birthday she arranged a three week trip to Germany, coinciding with the reunification of the country following the collapse of communist rule and thus allowing them the luxury of freely visiting Dresden and Kamenz.

They began their tour by paying their respects at the poorly maintained gravesites of the Rabuns in a churchyard outside Kamenz, including Ott's grandmother, great-grandfather, aunt, and uncles murdered by the Russian soldiers, and also the monument to little Helmut Rabun, made from the mangled girders of his school destroyed by an Allied bomb. As heartrending as this visit was—and it was exceptionally difficult for both mother and son—the emotions released there paled in comparison to the sheer agony, and terror, that overwhelmed Barratte when they reached the ruins of the once grand estate where the Rabuns had lived and where Barratte's mother and siblings had been murdered in cold blood before her eyes, and where she, Bette, and Amina had been raped. Witnessing the indescribable wailing and anguish of his beloved mother, Ott was instantly transformed, vowing at that moment to right the wrongs of the past and restore the dignity and glory of the Rabuns, accepting his mother's mission for him as his own.

After taking two days to recover from the trauma of seeing the estate, Ott and Barratte undertook a more methodical tour of Kamenz and Dresden, searching for remnants of their family's past in recorders' offices, archives, and, often without knowing it, standing, walking, riding upon, and drinking from the sturdy concrete infrastructure constructed by Jos. A. Rabun & Sons, which had survived not only the horrific Allied bombing that leveled much of Dresden and killed thirty thousand of its inhabitants but also the dreary period of communist rule and reconstruction afterward. The only sour moments during these days came when Ott and Barratte proudly revealed their identities and heritage to aging pensioners who might have known the Rabun family, only to be greeted with silent glares or malicious comments about how the Rabuns had lived all too well while others suffered during the war, and how Friedrich and Otto had despoiled the good name of Kamenz with their involvement in the death camps. But for each one of these bitter people, Ott and Barratte also located more friendly contemporaries who were delighted to see living Rabuns and share with them sweet stories and photographs of the happy days before all came to ruin. During these conversations, Ott marveled at his mother's fluency in speaking German and eagerly demonstrated his own growing proficiency, greatly pleasing her.

After learning everything they could, and gathering all the documents and artifacts about the Rabuns they could carry, and snapping hundreds of photographs, Ott and Barratte journeyed north to Berlin and then south to Munich, and, finally, to Austria, in search of the remnants of the Third Reich that lived on in Barratte's memory and loomed ever larger in Ott's imagination. Although largely unsuccessful in uncovering evidence of the former Nazi empire—expunged by the victors during the post-war years—they did find much to be hopeful for and proud of as Germans, including thriving industry, commerce, and culture. Before flying home from Frankfurt, they concluded their trip with a visit to the *Festspielhaus* in Bayreuth to take in Wagner's

Götterdämmerung. Otto Rabun Bowles, like Adolph Hitler—or perhaps because of him—had come to worship Richard Wagner.

Ott returned to Buffalo profoundly changed, having discovered the world to which he believed he truly belonged. Unfortunately, most of this world existed only in the past, or only in fantasy. Thus, the silent world into which Ott had withdrawn himself at home and in school began filling with voices: the pleas of impoverished German workers in the nineteen-twenties; the empty hypotheses of German intellectuals and the broken promises of German politicians in the nineteen-thirties; the strategic decisions of field marshals and the brutal commands of concentration camp guards in the nineteen-forties. While Ott's classmates raced home from school to watch television or go out to movies, Ott raced to the library to read more about the history of the German people, beginning with the resplendent days of the First Reich and the coronation of his ancestral namesake, Otto I, as Holy Roman Emperor; then moving forward in time to the humiliation of Germany by Napoleon and the hopes of nationalism to restore the old Roman grandeur; then on to the second humiliation with Germany's crushing defeat during the First World War; and, finally, the fatal seduction of a bold new Aryan nationalism and, when the fever broke, the fading away of the *Fuhrer's* one thousand years dream.

Like a man starved for food, Ott gobbled down Germanic texts, histories, biographies, and novels. When written words alone were not enough to locate him in the world for which he longed, he began filling his bedroom with its objects: silvery family photographs from Kamenz, a brick from the sandbox built for Amina and Helmut by their father, brittle yellowed papers from the business records of Jos. A. Rabun & Sons. Soon the collection expanded to include memorabilia from the gigantic days of the Third Reich—a red flag with its mighty slashing crosses, maps of Europe depicting what was, and what might have been, a highly coveted Hitler Youth armband and cap. When Ott's room overflowed with these and similar items, he freed the birds and enclosed the aviary, converting it into a small museum and shrine. He also started attending gun shows instead of libraries, where word of a young, well-heeled collector interested in authentic German weaponry spread rapidly. Soon brokers and dealers were offering their wares and Ott was arming a small platoon of Aryan mannequins with German bayonets, pistols, rifles, and even some disabled German submachine guns and grenades—all war booty brought home by American troops and sold to the highest bidder.

Driven by her own demons, Barratte had no possibility of distinguishing family pride from what was becoming, for her son, a dangerous romantic fanaticism. She cheerfully endowed Ott's hobby, and with it the revival of her early childhood, using the dwindling but still considerable resources of the Rabun family fortune. She also became an active participant with Ott, repairing torn military uniforms, taking Ott to World War II conventions and shows, purchasing rare items as gifts for him, and assuring gun dealers that his purchases were made with her complete consent and fully backed by her credit. Amina, also, to whom Ott presented the entire collection as a welcome home gift upon her release from prison, could find nothing wrong with her grandson's passion. "How many thousands of boys are fascinated with such things?" she reasoned. "And besides, was it not time to embrace the past and stop running from it?"

Ott's collection of German war memorabilia, and the notoriety of Amina Rabun, gave Ott a certain celebrity status as his high school graduation approached. With Amina's encouragement, he entertained occasional visitors to the mansion—normally just curious teens, but sometimes serious collectors and even museum curators looking to expand their collections. By means of these interactions, and with Nonna Amina's return, Ott emerged slowly from the fantasy world into which he had withdrawn.

It was during one of these encounters at the mansion that he met Tim Shelly—a stocky brute of a kid, a year older than Ott, with thin lips, pale blue eyes, and a wire brush of dark hair cut close to his scalp. He arrived at the mansion one afternoon with his father, Brian, who resembled his son in nearly every detail, except age. They explained that they were passing through New York on their way home from a hunting trip in Canada to their mushroom farm in Pennsylvania; they had heard about Ott's collection at some gun shows and wanted to see it. They were willing to pay for admission.

Ott was apprehensive; Tim looked like the kind of kid who would have knocked him to the ground and kicked him in the side for fun. He tried to think of a quick excuse to say no and send them on their way, but his mind went blank and he reluctantly led them around back to the aviary. He soon learned he had nothing to worry about. When Brian and Tim entered the shrine and saw the first display—an Nazi SS officer in full dress uniform—they became immediately solemn and reverential, as though they were approaching a communion rail. With eyes wide and mouths agape, they pointed in fascination and whispered their amazement as Ott explained each item's significance and how it had been acquired. Ott relished these rare gestures of respect, rewarding them by allowing Brian to handle his most prized possession—a Luger pistol bearing the initials "H.H." and authenticated by experts as having been taken from Heinrich Himmler when he was captured by British troops. Brian bowed his head and cupped the gun in his large hands, receiving the gun as holy sacrament. Then he said something completely unexpected:

"I just want you to know, Ott, that we think what they did to your grandmother Amina was a crime."

Ott's heart leaped. It was the first time a stranger had expressed any sympathy for what had happened.

"Lies," Brian said, operating the smooth action of the unloaded handgun with an expert flick of his wrist. "And it starts with the biggest lie of all...the lie of the Holocaust."

Brian pointed the pistol at Tim and ordered him to raise his hands, but Tim knocked the gun upward and in one powerful motion yanked it from his father's hand, reversing it on him. Not to be outdone, Brian responded with equal speed and force by grabbing Tim's wrist, twisting it behind his back and freeing the gun, then placing Tim in a choke hold with the gun pressing against his temple. Ott was amazed and amused.

"Okay," Tim gasped. "You win...this time."

Brian squeezed the trigger and the hammer hit the firing pin with a hollow click.

"No mercy," he scolded his son. "You should've finished me off when you had the chance. You hesitated. How many times have I told you?" He gave Tim a violent jerk that made him gag, then released him and smiled at Ott. "There were never any death camps," he said. "The Jews made it up to take control of Palestine, and they've been using it ever since to take control of the world. We're under attack and we don't even know it. If we don't wake up and do something about it, it'll be us in the Jews' death camps."

Ott could hardly believe his ears. His dream had been to exonerate his family by proving that Friedrich and Otto Rabun hadn't knowingly participated in the gassings; but here was Brian Shelly claiming that the gassings had never even taken place!

"How do you know the Holocaust was a lie?" Ott asked, fearful the answer wouldn't be convincing.

"A friend of mine has been working on a documentary about it. He says there's no evidence of any gas chambers. It was all a fraud created by the Jews to justify the State of Israel, and the Allies and Russians used it to demoralize and pacify the German people after the war. When the documentary is finished, he's going to expose the Jews for the liars they are."

Ott invited Brian and Tim to stay and have a German beer with him and tell him more about the documentary. They accepted the invitation, but Ott ended up doing most of the talking, thoroughly enjoying himself recounting for Brian and Tim how Jos. A. Rabun & Sons had built Dresden and, embellishing here and there, how his grandfather and great-uncle had helped Hitler build the Third Reich. "The sacrifices they made for the cause!" he said. "And how the Rabuns had suffered at the hands of the Russians and Jews!"

Brian and Tim hung on Ott's every word, awestruck. They said they had never been so close to a genuine Nazi family. In their excitement, they even asked Ott to speak in the fierce syllables of German to make the conversation more authentic and then translate back. As the beer flowed, Ott was more than happy to show off his skills, engaging in outright fabrication to impress his guests, saying: "*Mein Grossvater, Otto Rabun, war ein Bauteil der SS und kannte Hitler gut. Er beriet mit Hitler auf Operationen in Osteuropa und empfing persönlich das Eisenkreuz vom der Führer.*" And then back in English: "My grandfather, Otto Rabun, was a member of the SS and knew Hitler well. He consulted with Hitler on operations in eastern Europe and personally received the iron cross from the *Führer*."

This all greatly impressed Brian and Tim, and they, in turn, revealed to Ott that they belonged to a secret, exclusive group in the United States that considered people like the Rabuns to be heroes and martyrs. A fellow like Ott, they told him, the sole surviving heir to all that greatness, a man with the right breeding and blood, might be just the type of person who could become an important member of this group, a leader even.

Ott was flattered and astonished. No one had ever spoken to him like this before. Their words reached down to soothe all the injuries and injustices of his life. In the warmth of their wide embrace, Ott opened his heart to receive and be received. He explained the frustrations of his youth and found solace, understanding, and acceptance. In return, he joined in the Shellys' ugly remarks about Jews and blacks even though, in his heart, he harbored no genuine hatred for either group—only for those who had harmed the Rabuns. It was a glorious evening for Otto Rabun Bowles, one he would long remember. When Amina came down to say it was time to close up the house for the night, Brian and Tim greeted her like a celebrity and begged her to pose with them for pictures but, being in her bedclothes, she refused.

Walking out to their car, Ott said to Brian, "You've got to tell me more about this group you keep talking about. The people who are going to fight back. How can I join?"

Brian extended his hand. "We're called The Eleven," he said. "And you just did."

34

At 12:01 A.M., two guards lace a foul smelling leather mask around No. 44371's head and face. It is almost a comfort, this mask, because it holds, like a memory, the final impressions and breaths of other men whose names have become numbers, and, in this way, the mask whispers to the next man to wear it that he is not alone. No. 44371 has been staring off into the gallery behind the glass, looking at no one in particular. He knows what to expect. In fact, he knows just about everything there is to know about the art of judicial electrocutions. More, possibly, than the executioner himself.

No. 44371 knows, for example, that the idea of electrocuting criminals originated in the city where he himself was raised—Buffalo, New York—from the creative mind of a dentist in the eighteen-eighties who began experimenting with the application of electricity to animals after witnessing the accidental death of a drunk who had stumbled onto a live wire. No. 44371 also knows that the beloved inventor of the electric lightbulb, Thomas Edison, promoted the concept of electro-cuting criminals as a means of winning control of the electric utility industry away from archrival George Westinghouse, by demonstrating the dangers of Westinghouse's alternating current transmission system over Edison's own safer but inferior direct current lines. So determined was Edison to sway public opinion against Westinghouse that he invited the press to witness the execution of a dozen innocent animals with a one thousand volt Westinghouse AC generator, coining the term "electro-cution." The next year, he successfully lobbied the New York legislature to use Westinghouse AC voltage in the first Electric Chair. No one, Edison gambled, would want AC voltage in their homes after that. Westinghouse did all he could to stop it, refusing to sell the generator to prison authorities and even funding judicial appeals for the first souls to be put to death by the device. He lost those appeals, and the condemned men lost their lives, but he did ulti-mately win control of the electric utility industry.

Yes, No. 44371 knows well the peculiar history of the Elec-tric Chair, and now all of it flashes through his mind. He looked at it long and hard until he reached the point where he could look at it and not swallow so much and blink so often, anesthe-tizing himself to the fear of his own death by bathing himself in it. Hence, he read with more than morbid curiosity about the case of William Kemmler, who, by murdering his paramour in Buffalo, won the honor of being first to sit in Edison's Chair. And this made No. 44371 wonder about the peculiar relationship the City of Buffalo bore to the dentist, the Electric Chair, Kemmler, and his own life. In the year eighteen-ninety, the United States Supreme Court denied Kemmler's petition for a writ of habeas corpus, ruling that death by electricity does not violate the Con-stitution's prohibition against cruel or unusual punishment. So sanctioned, the citizens of New York on August sixth of that year wasted no time in trying out their new device. They fitted Kemmler with two electrodes, one on his head and the other at the base of his spine, and for seventeen seconds passed a Westinghouse alternating current of seven hundred volts through his body. Witnesses reported seeing hideous spasms and convulsions and clouds of smoke and smelling burned clothing and flesh. They gave him a second dose of one thousand and thirty volts, lasting two minutes. A postmortem revealed that Bill Kemmler's brain had been hardened to the consistency of well-done meat and the flesh surrounding his spine had been burned through. Among those in attendance that historic day at Auburn Prison was a disgusted George Westinghouse, who remarked on the way out: "The job could have been done better with an ax."

Techniques improved.

No. 44371 has been assured by the guards that he will receive a lethal jolt of two thousand volts straight away, then two more of about one thousand volts each for good measure, each lasting a minute in duration and spaced ten seconds apart. His body temperature will be raised in that time to over one hundred and thirty-eight degrees Fahrenheit—too hot to touch but not so hot that he will begin to smoke like poor Bill Kemmler. His chest will heave and his mouth will foam, his hair and skin will burn, he will probably release feces into his pants—and his eyeballs will burst from their sockets like a startled cartoon character, hence the snug fit of the stiff leather mask the guards have just placed over his face.

Yes, No. 44371 knows all there is to know, and now with the mask over his face it seems like he knows too much. He knows that despite more than one hundred years of practice, perfection in the art of judicial "electro-cution" remains elusive. And so, weighing heavily now on No. 44371's mind as they clamp the cold electrodes to his shaved legs is the botched execution in the year nineteen ninety of Jesse Tafero in Florida. During the first two cycles, smoke and flames twelve inches long erupted from poor Jesse's head. A funeral director with some experience in these matters opined that the charred area on the top left side of his skull, about the size of a man's hand, was a third degree burn. But Jesse was dead, sure enough.

Also on No. 44371's mind while he waits is the glowing torch made of Pedro Medina's head a few years later in the same Florida Chair. Witnesses reported that smoke filled the death chamber again—although no one thought it impaired visibility—and argued over whether the smell was of burnt flesh or burnt sponge from the saline-soaked pad squeezed into the copper headpiece to promote conductivity. Pathologists found a third degree burn and some charred material on Pedro's skull, but at least his eyebrows and lashes had not been singed the way the flames had scorched Jesse Tafero's face.

The guards tug at the leather straps around No. 44371's chest and waist, and now he starts to blink faster and swallow harder.

At the beginning of the twenty-first century, when for humane reasons, society no longer destroys even rabid dogs this way—and the Electric Chair in most states has already taken its place in the museum of horrors beside disembowelment, the rack, burning at the stake, the noose, and the guillotine—No. 44371 need not have faced execution in such a brutal manner. In fact, four years before his death sentence was issued, the governor of Pennsylvania signed a law making lethal injection the preferred method of execution in the Commonwealth. But death by "Old Sparky," as some referred to the Chair, was the one condition No. 44371 insisted upon in his agreement with the district attorney to plead guilty to two counts of kidnapping and two counts of first degree murder and irrevocably waive all his rights to appeal. When his lawyers refused to assist him in striking such a deal, he fired them on the spot.

"Maybe an injection of drugs can dull society's conscience of what it plans to do to me," he boldly proclaimed to his fellow death row inmates, "but I won't take 'em! I hope my body bursts into flames and burns the prison to the ground! I want history to remember what happened to me and to the Rabuns of Kamenz! I won't deny my actions or my beliefs for anybody! Did the martyrs in the Colosseum deny their faith? Did Christ himself? Would the world remember any of them today if they were dealt a dreamy death with the prick of a needle? When humanity nailed Jesus to a cross, it nailed itself to the cross; and when humanity electrocutes me in the Chair, it will electrocute itself in the Chair!"

Such was the courage—or the madness—of No. 44371.

The district attorney was more than happy to seek a special order from the court to accommodate the unusual request in exchange for eliminating the risk of an acquittal by reason of insanity or the endless appeals that could delay an execution, by any means, for decades if not permanently. Yet even with the guilty plea entered in the docket and the special order signed, fifteen years had passed because neither No. 44371 nor the district attorney considered the possibility of collateral appeals being filed by opponents of the use of the Electric Chair.

Now, at long last, all those appeals have been overruled. The death warrant has been signed, Old Sparky has been removed from the museum of horrors and returned to the death chamber, the possibility of a stay of execution has passed, and No. 44371 is finally about to be granted his wish. But now *he* is having doubts. After all those years of studying judicial electrocutions, he cannot control his panic in these final, terrifying moments. The leather mask reeks with the vomit of dead men, the copper cap scratches into his naked scalp, the electrodes dig into his legs, and his waist and limbs are lashed too tightly against the rough wood. He imagines the current crashing into his skull, detonating his brain like a bomb before plunging down his spine and fusing his gut under the intense heat, imploding his bowels; he sees it leap from his legs like a crazed demon, carrying his soul down, down into the earth. Then nothing.

No. 44371 hears the heavy breathing of the guards, heavier now than even his own breath because his lungs are afraid to breathe because the next breath might be their last.

"Mount Nittany! Mount Nittany!" he mumbles despondently, trying desperately to conjure his last glimpse of the mountain from his cell window before they removed him to the isolation chamber yesterday; he had decided this view would calm him in the final moments. And, yes, yes, the paper! It's still in his fingers, a single sheet sent by his father, to whom he had not spoken in so many years but whose last name would now be forever inked into the annals of the condemned. On the sheet is a passage from St. Luke.

"Maybe," wrote his father, "it will be of some comfort to you."

But what did it say? The words! What were the words? No. 44371 has forgotten them already.

"Doug! Doug!" he cries out.

"I'm right here," says the guard, attempting to sound reassuring while trying to steady his own nerves and bear his own fear and guilt. In these final moments there is compassion even between inmate and jailer. They've known each other for so long that they wonder how they'll be able to get along without each other; but they know too there's a job to be done and each man must play his part. There are no hard feelings.

"Doug, I can't read it. Read it to me, Doug."

No. 44371, whose arms are strapped to the chair, is trying to wave the sheet with his fingers and nod his head in its direction, but he's strapped too tightly and can't move.

"Just a second," the guard says, turning toward the narrow slit in the wall where the executioner stands. "I think... Yeah, it looks like they're ready now," he says.

"Wait!" No. 44371 pleads. "Please, Doug. I can't remember the words. I haven't given you any trouble."

"Okay, okay," Doug says, "I've got to take it from you now, anyway." The guard retrieves the paper and says to the executioner, "Just a second."

"Read it, Doug," No. 44371 cries. "Read it."

Doug wipes away a small tear from his eye. "Okay, here's what it says:

> *And there were also two other, malefactors, led with him to be put to death. And when they were come to the place, which is called Calvary, there they crucified him, and the malefactors, one on the right hand, and the other on the left.... And one of the malefactors which were hanged railed on him, saying, If thou be Christ, save thyself and us.*
>
> *But the other answering rebuked him, saying, Dost not thou fear God, seeing thou art in the same condemnation? And we indeed justly; for we receive the due reward of our deeds: but this man hath done nothing amiss. And he said unto Jesus, 'Lord, remember me when thou comest into thy kingdom.'*
>
> *And Jesus said unto him, Verily I say unto thee, To day shalt thou be with me in paradise.*

No. 44371 takes a deep breath and smiles beneath his mask.

"Thanks, Doug," he says gratefully. "I remember now. You'll put it in my pocket when it's over, right, like you promised?"

"Sure, Ott," Doug replies, relieved now that the prisoner seems calmer. "Sure, just like I promised. We gotta get started now. It's almost ten past."

"Okay. Goodbye, Doug."

"Goodbye, Ott."

35

In life and in death, Nana Bellini kept lush pots of pink and white vinca, impatiens, marigolds, ferns, and a dozen other varieties on the front porch of her house. She planted ivy and wisteria vines in an apron around the perimeter and allowed them to pull themselves up the balustrade like children at play. The flowers perfumed the air, attracting hummingbirds and bumblebees that tormented the cats napping in the shade. Like the garden behind the house, the front porch was its own little ecosystem and parable of life.

That all changed when Nana left Shemaya, leaving me alone to take care of the place. By the time Luas had come to find me after my meeting with Ott Bowles, which on earth would have been equivalent to sixty years later, everything had withered and died. Only raw piles of dirt filled the pots now, littered with fragments of dried stems and roots; the banister sagged and swayed dangerously in gusts of wind created by a thunderhead that stalked the four seasons of the valley day and night like

a homicidal lover; the window panes of the house were broken, and paint peeled from the mullions and frames. The place
looked as if it hadn't been lived in for decades. There were no cats
or birds, and there was no color, just a monochromatic frame.
My Shemaya had turned to shades of gray.

I hadn't seen Luas or been out of the house since the day the
spirit of Otto Bowles entered my office and infected my soul. I
had staggered from my office in a daze, down the long corridor,
through the great hall, the vestibule, the woods, up the steps of
the porch, into the house. There I stayed, behind closed doors,
reliving his life again and again, horrified and fascinated. My
body aged with the house over those sixty earth years; I would
have been ninety-one. My hair turned gray, thin, and coarse. My
face contracted into the frightened expression of an old woman,
barely more than skeleton with absurd knobs of bone protruding from my chin, jaws, and forehead; and my lips disappearing
into the toothless crater of a mouth without definition or color,
shriveled and hardened like an earthworm baked in the sun. I
slept during the day and woke in the night wet and aching all
over, my bladder unable to contain fluids and my joints brittle
and inflamed with arthritis. This is the way I might have looked
and felt had my life not been cut short, at the age of thirty-one.
Maybe Ott Bowles had done me a favor. I knew it would be Luas
when I heard the knock on the door; there had been no visitors
during all those years. He would be coming to say I could no
longer delay the presentation: Ott Bowles was waiting in the
train shed for his case to be called, and God was waiting in the
Urartu Chamber to judge his soul.

Luas said nothing about the change in my appearance when
I opened the door. He only smiled—that knowing grandfather's
smile of his, the way he smiled at me when I arrived in Shemaya,
as if to say: *Yes, my daughter, you have suffered, and it is difficult,*

but I would only make it worse by noticing. I offered him a seat on the porch, too embarrassed to let him in and see how run down I had allowed the house to become.

"I'd pull the switch again," I said, in the graveled, quivering voice of an old woman, weak but defiant. "Until there was nothing left of him but ash."

The dark anvil of the thundercloud crossed the sky. I imagined how it would feel to be pulled hot from a fire and hammered against its flank.

"Nero Claudius committed suicide," Luas said, his face pinching into a wince while his hands groped through his pockets to find matches for his pipe. "Unlike Mr. Bowles, he cheated the world of its opportunity for justice."

"Yes," I said, "but did it hurt when he had you decapitated? I didn't die right away. I can still feel the bullets tearing through my body."

"You've got me there," Luas said. "I didn't feel a thing when the blade came down." He struck a match, and it flared bright orange in the shadows.

"So God has a sense of humor after all," I said. "Satan is a lawyer and carries a briefcase. What did we do to deserve all this?"

The white smoke from Luas' pipe bubbled over the sides, too weak to rise into the wind. "I did cheer when they stoned Saint Stephen to death," Luas said, "so I guess I had it coming. But this isn't hell, Brek. The Urartu Chamber must be certain of our fidelity and self control. If we are impartial when presenting the souls we most despise, then the Chamber can be certain we will present all postulants with dispassion. Our motives must be pure when we enter the Chamber—we can show no favoritism or emotion. The judgment is Yahweh's; He alone determines how Otto Bowles and Nero Claudius spend eternity."

A blue bolt of lightning flashed across the valley, followed by a loud clap of thunder. A doe and her fawn, tiptoeing through the band of deep white snow covering the meadow, lifted their ears toward the sky, confused by the sound of thunder on such a cold day in their part of Shemaya.

Oh, take care, I wished the doe with all my heart, one mother to another. It's not safe here. They're after your baby, and they're after you. Trust no one. Assume nothing. Run. Run!

"Did you know that the word justice appears more than one hundred times in the books of the Old Testament, but only four times in all of the New Testament?" Luas asked.

"No, I didn't," I said.

"The Messiah tried to do away with justice," Luas said. "He claimed love is the only law, and when we're wronged, we should not seek justice against our enemies but turn the other cheek instead. It came as no surprise, of course, that he died a victim of injustice, crucified by his own words."

"That's why Jews make the best lawyers," I said. "That's not a bigoted comment, by the way; it's a matter of theology and philosophy."

"As a Jewish lawyer myself," Luas said, "I completely agree. In fact, I did everything I could to bring the Messiah's supporters to justice; but then one day I found myself blinded by his ideas, I don't know how it happened. In the darkness, I convinced myself he was right. Oh, it was quite a conversion: I started preaching this to the people and criticizing them for appealing to the law courts."

"You misled a lot of people," I said.

"Yes, I did," Luas agreed. "I first realized that when I met Elymas. He was a stubborn old Jew like me, thirsty for justice. When he opposed me, I couldn't just turn the other cheek. I blinded him just as I had been blinded—he still carries a grudge about it even though I've apologized a thousand times. I went back to the old law of an eye for an eye, Brek, and I can't tell you how good it felt. But by that point, the rabbis worried that I was becoming too dangerous and had gone too far, so they convinced the Romans to imprison me as an enemy of the state, just as they did with Jesus. I wasn't about to give up without a fight the way he did; I demanded my right to a trial as a Roman citizen. When it looked like I couldn't get a fair trial, I appealed to Nero Claudius. He had a good reputation in those days; nobody knew he would turn out to be such a sadistic killer. You know the rest. Nero and I meet again here every day in the afterlife. And so we happily find that even mighty emperors are brought to justice. Jesus was wrong. Justice is the only law, not love, and justice exists only when the law courts and the lawyers thrive. The Urartu Chamber is the final proof of that. The Messiah was entitled to make at least one mistake."

The storm clouds cleared, revealing four moons in the nighttime sky: a quarter moon, a half moon, a three-quarter moon and a full moon, each set against the constellations appropriate to its season, hashing the sky into astronomical gibberish. The air cooled and I wrapped one of Nana's shawls closer around me for warmth. Bats flickered above the trees after insects, and in the distance I could hear a great horned owl and a whippoorwill, and the bark of a lonely dog—the sounds I'd heard many nights on that porch as a child.

"Ott Bowles can speak for himself in the Chamber," I said. "He made his choices. He doesn't need a lawyer."

Luas tapped his pipe against the banister to empty it of ash. "Perhaps so," he said, "but it is justice that needs our help in the Chamber, Brek, not Ott Bowles. Presenters supply the distance that makes justice possible for the accused and the Accuser, the created and the Creator. We are the many colors in the promise of the rainbow as it fades into the horizon of eternity."

"*I* am the Accuser, Luas," I said. "There's no need for a trial because I've already found him guilty. It's time for justice to be served."

36

I'm waiting for a clerk to come to the counter of the convenience store and holding Sarah in my arm. She's getting fussy and heavy, and I'm getting impatient.

"Hello? Hello…?"

"Just a minute…," a female voice calls from the stockroom.

The clerk finally pushes through the double-hinged doors, a young woman in her early twenties, overweight, with too much makeup and a too tight shirt. Flicking back her hair, she apologizes for the delay. She smiles at Sarah, extending two thick fingers and tugging at her tiny hand.

"How old are you?" she asks.

I lean in close to Sarah like a ventriloquist. "Say, I'm ten months."

"What a big girl," the clerk says. "I've got two little boys, one and three; they'd sure love to meet a little girl as pretty as you. What's your name, honey?"

"Sarah," I answer for her again.

"Hey there, Sarah. *Sara Smile*. That's one of my favorite songs. You're a cutie."

The clerk releases Sarah's hand and touches her nose; Sarah responds by reaching out and touching the clerk's nose, making us all laugh. I give Sarah a squeeze and a kiss on the cheek. The clerk pulls the milk toward the register.

"Will that be all today?"

"That's it."

"Bag?"

"No, thanks."

I pay and we walk back out to the car, picking up where we left off with the song that's been playing on the cassette: "*It's almost six-twenty, says Teddy Bear, mama's coming home now, she's almost right there. Hot tea and bees honey, for mama and her baby....*" Sarah allows me to buckle her into her car seat without fussing.

It's a cool autumn night, already dark at 6:30. We pass a couple of other cars heading in the opposite direction on the way home, but otherwise the road is empty until a single car appears in my rearview mirror and begins following us. Coming around a bend and picking up speed on a slight downgrade, we reach a long, deserted stretch of road with corn and hay fields on both sides; the high-beam headlights of the car behind us start flashing and bursts from a red strobe light fill my rearview mirror, hurting my eyes. The red light comes from low on the windshield; I can tell it's an unmarked patrol car. Bo had warned me he'd seen a speed trap on this stretch of road, and I was being careful to stay below the posted speed limit. Bringing to bear my expensive legal training, I'm already planning my defense as I pull off onto the berm. The officer couldn't have clocked me with radar while following me from behind, so he must be relying on his speedometer. I decide to request a copy of the speedometer certification from the police officer at the trial—if they have them, they're usually expired, and it's an easy way to get out of a ticket if you know to ask. Even if I did go over the speed limit, it couldn't have been for long; they have to record it for at least a full one-tenth of a mile; I'll come back tomorrow and measure the distance from the bend in the road to the point where he started flashing to pull me over, which looks like less than a tenth of a mile to me.

By the time the officer opens the door of his car, I have all my insurance and registration documents in order, and Sarah's starting to cry now that I've turned off the music. Maybe he'll give me a break because of Sarah and my arm. Against the glare of the high-beams I can see only his silhouette in the mirror with his revolver bulging at his hip. He's short, thin, and slightly bow-legged, not the large, powerfully-built patrolman you normally see. I counsel myself to say nothing incriminating and roll down the window, but strangely he stops at the rear door and tries to pull it open.

"Up here, officer," I say, always polite to the police, thinking he somehow mistook the rear door for the front.

He inserts his arm through my open window and around the pillar to unlock the back door, then climbs in and slams the door shut.

"What's the problem, officer?" I ask innocently, believing there must be some good reason for his behavior. Maybe he's afraid of being hit by passing traffic if he stands at my door.

A young male voice answers calmly: "Do what I tell you, Mrs. Wolfson, and nobody'll get hurt."

I look in the mirror and see a gun pointing at my head. The kid holding the gun appears to be in his late teens or early twenties, with soft, downy whiskers on his chin, pale skin, and thin, almost feminine lips. His head is shaved and he's wearing a camouflage Army shirt. I've never seen him before in my life.

"Get out of my car!" I yell, outraged that he has the nerve to do something like this and not yet comprehending the gun or the reality of the threat.

A savage smile darts across his face. He points the gun down toward Sarah and there's a loud crack and a bright orange muzzle flash. Time slows like a rock falling through water. I feel myself screaming but my ears are ringing because of the concussion.

"Sarah! Sarah!"

I try to reach back to her, but the kid slams the gun into the side of my face, knocking my head forward. The heat from the barrel stings my cheek, and the bitter scent of gunpowder fills my nose. From the corner of my eye I see the hammer cocked to fire again. It's an oddly shaped handgun, older, like something I've seen in World War II movies.

"Drive the car!" he orders. "Now!"

But I'm crazed with panic, and I'm still screaming, "Sarah! Sarah!" I force my head back against the gun, scraping the barrel across my cheek like a razor. I can see her now. There's no blood…and…yes, thank God…she's still crying! The shot must have gone through the seat beside her. The kid slams the gun into my face again, producing a stabbing pain through my sinus and a thin trickle of blood from my nose.

"Drive!" he yells. "Now!" He rolls down the rear window and waves to the car behind us. The lights stop flashing, and it pulls out in front of us. "Follow him."

I try to move the gear selector, but I'm shaking so badly that the stump of my right arm slips off the lever. The kid reaches up, slaps it into place with a jolt, and I pull out onto the road. We drive to a stop sign and turn left onto Route 22. With each oncoming car, the kid presses the gun against my head, warning me not to do anything to alert them. I'm searching frantically for a police car, or a gas station where I can pull off for help. All the while, Sarah's screaming at the top of her lungs, terrified from the gunshot.

"Make her stop!" the kid shouts at me.

"Please, just let us go," I say, trying to reason with him. "You can have my car and my purse, whatever you want; just, please, let us go."

"This isn't about money," the kid says. "Keep driving." He uses his free hand to cover Sarah's mouth, which only makes her cries louder.

"You're hurting her!" I shriek, hysterical that he's touched my baby. "There's a bottle in the diaper bag on the floor. Give her the bottle, and let her go."

The kid finds the bottle and puts it in Sarah's mouth. She drinks the stale formula left over from her afternoon feeding, cries out, drinks again, then finally begins to settle down.

Everything is happening so fast I have no time to think. We turn off a side road at Ardenheim and up an old dirt logging road into the mountains. The car we're following shuts off its headlights, and I'm ordered to shut mine off too. We drive into the woods in darkness and stop. The driver of the car in front gets out; in the moonlight I can see that he's about the same age as the kid in back but taller and more muscular; his head is shaved and he's wearing camouflage Army clothes as well, and he's carrying a gun in one hand and a videocassette in the other. He opens my door and yanks me out of the car, wrenching my left arm. The kid in back climbs out with Sarah and hands her to me, then takes the videocassette from the bigger kid, gets in the driver's seat of my car, puts the videocassette on the passenger seat, and backs my car into a grove of pine trees until it's covered with boughs and can't be seen from the narrow dirt road. Reemerging moments later through the branches, he says to the bigger kid: "Ok, Tim, let's get going."

The bigger kid, whose name I now know is Tim, shoves me toward the other car.

"Please," I plead with them, "you've got my car and my money. Please, just leave us here. I won't tell anybody."

"Shut up," Tim says, ramming his gun into my back.

They really aren't interested in my car, or my money, and I begin to worry they're planning to kidnap and rape me.

"Please, please don't do this," I beg.

"I said, shut up!" Tim yells, slamming me against their car, crushing Sarah between me and the window. She starts crying again.

"I told you, Mrs. Wolfson," the smaller kid says, "if you do as you're told, nobody'll get hurt. Now get in the car."

How does he know my name?

"You still want me to drive, Ott?" Tim asks.

"Yeah."

Now I know the smaller kid's name and that he's the leader of the two.

I climb in back with Sarah on my lap and try to comfort her. Ott sits beside us, digging his gun into my ribs. Tim takes the driver's seat and backs the car down the logging road the way we came, switching on the headlights when we reach the highway and turning south to Route 522, then Route 322 east toward Harrisburg. Sarah calms with the motion of the car and me holding her close. I'm trying frantically to remember the next exits, and whether there are any police stations, and what I've heard about self-defense—how the worst thing you can do is to allow an attacker to drive away with you in a car. While cradling Sarah, I slip my hand around the door handle to be ready to leap out at the first opportunity for escape; if I were alone, I might have jumped while the car was moving, but I can't take that chance with Sarah.

The miles go by. Ott and Tim say nothing to each other, or me, as we drive. Their actions are disciplined, efficient, and well-rehearsed, suggesting this is not some last second lark by a couple of teenage punks. I smell no alcohol on their breath and notice no slurring of their speech. Ott keeps checking to see if we're being followed. Eventually Tim turns the radio on low, tuning it into country music stations, and Sarah finally falls asleep; I'm thankful she has no idea what's happening to her. An uneasy peace descends upon the car. Ott relaxes slightly and sits a little less rigid but he's always on alert, jabbing the gun into my side whenever we slow down.

"I've got money in the bank," I whisper to him. "Lots of it. You can have it all, just let us go. If you stop now, you won't get in any trouble."

Ott says nothing. Five minutes pass, ten, and fifteen. We're on a four lane highway, driving farther south toward Harrisburg.

"Why are you doing this?" I ask.

"Why?" Ott asks, incredulous, without taking his eyes off the road ahead. "Because Holden Hurley was sentenced today; he got fifteen years because of your Jew husband, that's why."

"Holden Hurley?"

"Yeah, don't you watch the news? Your Jew husband was there at the courthouse, gloating in front of his TV cameras."

Shaved heads, camouflage fatigues…I begin to understand.

"You're members of The Eleven, aren't you?" I ask, more terrified than ever. I want to tell him my name is Brek Cuttler, not Brek Wolfson, that I'm a Catholic, not a Jew, and Sarah isn't Jewish either because it passes through the mother; but telling him this would be betraying my husband and my own beliefs; it would be betraying God. I wonder in that moment what I would have done if I was being questioned by the Nazis. Would

I tell them I wasn't a Jew to save myself and Sarah, and let them take Bo away?

A State Police car pulls around us to pass on the four lane. I don't feel the gun in my ribs anymore and I lift my arm to try to signal it. Ott sees me and says, "Look, Mrs. Wolfson, your baby likes the new toy I gave her." I look down and see the muzzle of his gun sticking in Sarah's mouth. I drop my arm.

"Why are you doing this?" I ask again. "The government won't let him out because you've kidnapped us, they don't negotiate criminal sentences with anybody."

"Because somebody's got to tell the truth."

"About what?"

"About the Holocaust…about my family."

"Are you Holden Hurley's son?"

"No, I'm just his friend. I'm Barratte Rabun's son, and Amina Rabun's grandson. Do you remember them, Mrs. Wolfson?"

My heart starts pounding. I didn't know Barratte Rabun had a son, or that the Rabuns had any connection to The Eleven. None of that came out in the litigation. I begin to realize this isn't about criminal sentences or making a political statement, it's about revenge.

We turn onto Route 283 at Harrisburg, then Route 30 at Lancaster, and Route 41 south toward Wilmington, Delaware. Fifteen minutes later, we're on Route 926, rushing past signs with arrows pointing toward Kennett Square, Lenape, and Chadds Ford. The gnarled, old oak trees along the two lane country road jeer at us, waving their limbs in the dancing shadows like the Damned welcoming our entrance into hell; leaves fall in eruptions of red, yellow, and orange flames as we hurl down the abyss. I'm nauseous with fear, and my mind is racing. *How long will it be before Bo calls the police? He'll expect us no later than eight, and he'll probably call work and the daycare to track us down. Maybe he'll figure we've gone to the grocery store or the mall. Ten o'clock—nothing could keep us out that late. He'll check first with my parents, then the television station to see if they've heard about any accidents, and then he'll call the police. They'll take the information, but they'll probably treat it as a domestic dispute and wait and see. Who knows when they'll start looking for us, probably not until tomorrow.*

The turns quicken and the pavement deteriorates. We're on a gravel road now, descending a steep ravine through woods and ending onto rutted dirt tracks leading through an open, overgrown field, and back into more woods, down an even steeper slope. There are no streetlights or power lines, and the sky is coal black, without the hope of stars or the kind solace of the moon. The last home passed from view miles ago, asleep in the cool harvest air pregnant with the scent of decaying leaves and apples. I start to panic again. *They're going to kill us! They've taken us out to the middle of nowhere to kill us!*

"Listen," I tell him, "I'm sorry about what happened to your mother and grandmother. I'll do anything I can to make it better. You've got to understand, it was the government, not us, who put her in jail. We had no control—"

Ott slams the gun so hard into my side that I lose my breath.

The road ends at a crumbling cinderblock building protruding from the ground like an ugly scab with windowless walls standing barely one-story tall, pocked with black streaks of mold and a leprosy of flaking white paint. It resembles the shell of an abandoned industrial building and looks out of place in the country. The cloying stench of manure and mushrooms make the air heavy and difficult to breathe.

We pull to a stop about twenty yards away. With the headlights illuminating the building, Tim leaves the engine running, pulls his gun, and goes inside. Ott waits nervously in the car with me until Tim reappears at the door and waves all-clear, then disappears inside again. Ott climbs out and orders Sarah and me out with him. Pretending to fix my suit jacket, I stall for time. *This may be our only chance.* Ott is standing at the end of the open rear door, his head turned over his shoulder looking at the building; the engine is running, but he could easily stop me if I tried to climb over the seat. *I have to get him away from the car.* I gently place Sarah into the footwell where she'll be safe. She stirs and looks up at me; under the dome light on the roof of the car, her eyes reflect back her love for me, as though she knows what I am about to do and she's thanking me for risking my life for her. She's trying to be so brave. I love her with all my heart. Tears fill my eyes.

I climb out of the car, shaking. Ott's waiting for me but still looking at the building. He's only a few inches taller than me and not nearly as intimidating as Tim. I decide what to do. I place my left hand on the door frame for balance and then, with all my strength, I thrust my knee up hard into his groin. He doesn't see it coming and instantly collapses to the ground with a sucking groan. *It worked!* I slam the rear door closed, jump in the driver's seat, and hit both locks with my elbow. As I reach around the steering wheel with my left hand to shift the gear selector into reverse, Tim comes running from the building at full speed, covering the ground so quickly that by the time I step on the accelerator, he's already even with my door and he's pointing his gun straight at me through the window. Time slows again, slicing the final moments of my life into small frames to be archived for the rest of eternity, decoupling memory from reality and reaching back to everything before—to the hands that bathed me when I was delivered from my mother's womb and hugged me as a young child, to my husband, my family, my friends, my daughter…to the moments and the memories that had become Brek Abigail Cuttler. But just as Tim is about to fire, Ott lunges up at him from the ground, causing his gun to bark harmlessly into the air.

Suddenly there is life, and perspective accelerates to real time, to the blur of adrenaline and the desire to live. The car roars backward, toward home and safety, toward all we had created. I'm racing backward so quickly and the path is so narrow that I lose control and we careen into a tree with a terrible jolt. Sarah starts wailing. I slam the gear shift into drive and stomp again on the accelerator, steering straight for Ott, who is on his knees aiming his gun at us. He fires four shots. The car slows and becomes less responsive, and I realize he's shot out one of the front tires. For a fraction of a second, I think of swerving to avoiding hitting him because he has just spared my life twice; but we are frozen in time, Ott Bowles and I, controlled by instinct and the will to survive. I accelerate straight for him but he rolls out of the way at the last second and the car plows into a manure pile. Determined to win our freedom, I rap the selector into reverse again and stomp on the accelerator. There's a loud explosion and the rear door window shatters into a hailstorm of glass pellets. Ott is sprawled on the trunk with half his body sticking through the rear window, his gun pointing down at Sarah in the footwell, both arms outstretched and locked, police style. I hit the brakes and bring the car to a stop.

"Don't make me do this!" Ott yells at me. "Don't make me do this!" His chest is heaving, every muscle tensed.

"Do it!" Tim shouts from the other side of the car, his eyes wide and crazed, intoxicated by the violence. "Do it now!"

Ott hesitates, and in that moment of indecision I shut off the engine and hand Ott the keys over my shoulder.

"Take it," I say, my voice quivering, just above a whisper, desperate to calm him down. "Please. She's just a baby. Take it."

37

"So, how long have you known Holden Hurley?" Ott Bowles asked the well-dressed, dark haired, bearded man seated across from him at the small cocktail table. He asked this question while sipping a beer and following the major league baseball game playing on a television over the bar.

"Two years," the man said, exhaling smoke from a cigarette, uninterested in the game.

It was late afternoon, on a bright, summer Saturday, and the bar was deserted. Ott was not yet of legal age to consume alcohol, but Trudy, the owner of the bar built against a mountain on Route 26 between Huntingdon and Altoona, served her customers without regard to age and, for this reason, Ott had been there many times. Trudy was a large woman with flaming red hair, and this afternoon she sat behind the bar watching the game and waiting for customers. The man sitting across from Ott was obviously of legal age but he sipped club soda through a straw.

"Yes!" Ott said, clenching his fist as a runner crossed home plate. "Bottom of the ninth, and the Pirates just scored, they're coming back!" He swallowed a gulp of beer and belched. "You got to admit, Sam," he said, "that Hurley's one weird dude."

"He is a bit eccentric," Sam said, "but he's one of the most talented people I've ever met. He could build a computer out of cereal boxes and sell steaks to vegetarians."

Ott studied Sam's blue eyes and dark complexion and laughed. "That's true," he said. "But, I don't know...I think he actually dreams he's Hitler when he's asleep. He's got some pretty extreme ideas."

"He's not such a bad guy," Sam said, taking another drag on his cigarette. "Everybody has dreams, and dreams sometimes become reality if you work at them long enough. He's been good to me. I owe him."

Ott picked up his beer and turned back to the baseball game. He didn't like talking about Holden Hurley and wished he hadn't even brought him up. He enjoyed the camaraderie of The Eleven enough, and the military training and the paintball war games they played—and the way everybody treated him like a celebrity because of his family's past—but he couldn't understand the president of The Eleven's rabid hatred of Jews and blacks—it was just this kind of extreme racism that made people believe the Holocaust actually did happen. Sam's defense of Hurley meant he was probably just as radical. "Where are you from?" Ott asked, changing the subject.

"New York."

"No, I mean your family. What kind of name is Samar Mansour...French?"

"No, it's Palestinian, actually."

Ott examined Sam more closely. He could see the Arab face now—the steep nose, beard, and dark skin, but where did those blue eyes come from? Ott had never known an Arab, and he couldn't imagine somebody like Holden Hurley doing anything to help one. Hurley hated anybody who wasn't white and a Christian. Maybe it was because Sam seemed more European than Middle Eastern, with his aloof attitude, articulate speech, and pressed blue cotton dress shirts and black pants—more like a Londoner or a Parisian. "When did your family come here?" Ott asked, looking back up at the baseball game.

"My dad came over when he was about your age. He was one of the Palestinian refugees…his parents were killed by the Jews during the war in 1948."

Ott glanced at him, then back at the game.

"Most Palestinians stayed in the Middle East," Sam continued, "but after the war my father got a job carrying equipment for an archaeologist on a dig in Jerusalem. He was a professor from over at Juniata College; Mijares was his last name. I think he was Argentinean. In any case, he was very wealthy, and very generous, and he liked my father; I guess he thought my dad was pretty smart, because he offered to send him to college here, all expenses paid. My father accepted. He attended Columbia University, married an American woman, and stayed. I was born in New York."

Sam waved for Trudy to bring them another round of drinks.

"Be right there, honey," she said, pulling two glasses from under the bar, grateful for something to do.

"Just another refugee story," Sam said to Ott. "Not very different from your own."

Ott was thinking the same thing. He finished his beer, accidentally dribbling a little onto his t-shirt. "You know my story?" he asked, reaching across to another table for a bar napkin.

"I know all about you," Sam said. "Brian and Holden told me a little, and I've done some research on the Rabuns too. I've spent a lot of time doing research in Germany, actually. People don't realize it but Germans and Arabs have a lot in common. *Das ist warum ich beginnen wollte, Sie zu kennen.*"

A look of surprise flashed across Ott's face. "*Sie sprechen Deutsches?*"

"*Wenig.*"

"*Wieviele Male sind Sie nach Deutschland gewesen?*"

"*Ich habe ein ungefähr Jahr dort verbracht.*"

They stopped speaking in German when Trudy brought the drinks to the table.

"You boys want anything from the grill?" she asked. "I can fix you some burgers."

Sam shook his head, no. "You want anything, Ott?" he asked, "I'm buying."

"No, thanks," Ott said.

"You boys just let me know," Trudy replied, a little disappointed. She returned to her stool behind the bar to watch the game.

"Too bad about Brian, wasn't it?" Ott asked.

"Yes," Sam said. "He was pretty young to have a heart attack, and in good shape. I guess you never know."

"The funeral was tough; Tim and his mom took it hard. On top of everything else, I guess Brian had everything mortgaged to the hilt and stopped paying his life insurance. They have to sell their house and the mushroom farm to pay off their debts. Tim's been staying with me for awhile."

"He's lucky to have you as a friend," Sam said. "It must have been hard on you when you lost your grandmother. She was a great woman; I admired her a lot. It wasn't that long ago, was it?"

Ott nodded uncomfortably, losing eye contact. "About a year now, I guess—less than a year after she got out of prison. Prison killed her. We were real close." He looked out the window painfully, filled with grief and pent-up rage, then back again at the baseball game. "How come I never see you at any of the meetings?" he asked, changing the subject.

"I'm not exactly a member," Sam said. "The Eleven supports what I'm doing, and I support what they're doing."

"What *are* you doing?" Ott asked.

"I'm making a documentary proving the Holocaust was a hoax."

The Pirates scored another run on the television. Sam looked up, but suddenly Ott was no longer interested in the game. "So *you're* the one?" Ott said, amazed. "Brian told me he knew somebody making a documentary about the Holocaust, but he wouldn't tell me anything more than that."

Sam turned from the television back to Ott and grinned like the player who had just scored the run. "It's been a secret," he said, "but now that I'm finished, Holden thought I should talk to you and maybe you could help. That's why I wanted to meet with you today."

"Can I see it?" Ott asked eagerly.

"Sure, soon."

"Are you some kind of filmmaker? How many documentaries have you done?"

"No," Sam said. "I was just finishing my Ph.D. in history at Juniata, actually—as a recipient of the Mijares Fellowship. The documentary is my first; it was supposed to be part of my dissertation, but the head of the history department is a Jew and, for obvious reasons, he wasn't too happy with my subject or my conclusions. He gave me the option of picking a new topic or leaving school without the degree. I left. Holden heard about it and he and The Eleven have been funding the project for two years. Now all I need is some money to get it distributed."

"Wow," Ott said. "I give you credit for taking on one of the most controversial issues in the world. But it's going to be pretty tough convincing people the Holocaust was a hoax. Don't get me wrong…nothing would make me happier than finding out it was a lie, but I've seen the pictures and read the histories. I've been to some of the camps too. My family built the incinerators. There's a lot of evidence out there to disprove."

Sam frowned. "But you don't really believe your family, or your countrymen, would murder millions of their own people in cold blood, whether they were Jews or not, do you? It doesn't make any sense; the Germans weren't barbarians, they were Europeans. I'm a student of history, Ott, and as a student of history, I've learned that the men who leave a mark on this world are the ones who turn black into white and white into black; it's along the border between opposites that we find the energy to create and to destroy." Sam crushed his cigarette in the ashtray on the table as if illustrating his point. "Atoms split and fuse into world-changing bombs; tectonic plates shift and new continents are formed; politicians make peace into war and war into peace; religions turn sinners into saints and saints into sinners. Have no doubt: the actions of men are good or evil depending upon which quality we choose to see."

The beer was hitting Ott now, and he was beginning to enjoy himself. He felt a warm tingling in his lips and forehead. Sam wasn't the extremist he feared after all; he was a rational thinker, a man who used logic and reason. Ott liked philosophical discussions, and the challenge of talking to educated people; he believed he could do well in college, and he was even thinking about going, maybe to a university in Germany. He hadn't done much of anything in the year since he graduated from high school, except hang out at the mansion in Buffalo or at The Eleven's training compound in the woods near Huntingdon. Most of The Eleven were just disgruntled local men, unemployed or underemployed; they drove pickup trucks, drank beer, loved guns, and hated Jews and blacks but couldn't tell you why.

Although Hurley was an extremist, he had taken Ott into his confidence and shown him how to use The Eleven's sophisticated satellite telephones, encryption technology, and remote computer servers that would ensure secure communication when the race war Hurley dreamed of finally started. Maybe, Ott thought, he would study computers in college. He liked the precision and unambiguousness of math, and computers gave him the unconditional acceptance he craved.

"Think about all the great men," Sam continued. "Einstein demonstrated that mass is energy and energy, mass—that's turning black into white and white into black. Galileo demonstrated that the earth orbits the sun. Columbus demonstrated that the earth is round. Moses demonstrated that the Law is the only way, then Jesus came along and demonstrated that love is the only Law, and later the Prophet Muhammad, peace be upon him, came along and convinced the world that the Law is the only love. All black into white and white into black. In the entire history of the human race, of all the billions of people who have lived and died, we remember only a few thousand at most. These are the men who demolished prevailing beliefs and formed new worlds using contradiction as their chisel. That's why they're remembered…and that's how I want to be remembered."

"Interesting," Ott said. "I agree with you, but that still doesn't prove the Holocaust was a hoax."

"Two outs," Sam said, glancing up at the television. "I know you, Ott," Sam said. "I know what you want. I'm just like you."

Ott looked down, embarrassed.

"I'm not a religious zealot, and neither are you" Sam continued. "We're practical men. My mother was a Roman Catholic, and that's how I was raised; I converted to Islam purely for authenticity. The simple reality is this: In 1948, the Jews evicted Arab families from their homes and re-created a state that didn't exist between the year seventy and nineteen forty-eight. Think about that. There was no Israel for one thousand, eight hundred and seventy-eight years. What happened to the Jews in the nineteen forties to change all that?"

"The Holocaust?" Ott said.

"See, I told you we think alike," Sam said. Ott smiled. "Now, the Jews base their claim to Palestine on a four thousand year old legend of self-serving hearsay—an alleged oral promise supposedly made by God to Abraham. There's no writing, no deed, no nothing; just a single Hebrew man's claim that God told him the land was his and his descendents'. God didn't tell the rest of the world about the deal; he didn't say a single word about it to the other people living there; he supposedly just whispered it to *one* man, who happened to be a Jew, who happened to want to live there. If that happened today, and this guy showed up in court to claim his land, he would be laughed out of the place; but since it happened four thousand years ago, and one of the guy's ancestors wrote it down in the Bible, some people believe it must be true. Amazing. That's a pretty thin reed to build a country on, but it's not by any means unprecedented. Every civilization, and every conquering power, has claimed their land as a matter of Divine Providence; that's what leaders need to say to motivate their people to kill other people, and that's what leaders and their people need to say to each other to soothe their consciences.

"Now think about this: For nearly two thousand years, this alleged promise from God wasn't enough to restore Palestine to the Jews. If God really wanted the Jews to have that land, don't you think he would have made sure they had it? He is, after all, *God*. So, again, any rational human being would conclude that the claim that God promised the Jews a home in Palestine is a fabrication, pure and simple. But the Jews have been clinging to it for two thousand years, because they really want that land. Then, in 1948, they finally get their chance.

"There's no dispute that many millions of people were killed during World War II; it was an ugly, horrendous war. And there's no doubt that the Nazis, like the Soviets, had prison camps and they did their share of mass killings of all sorts of people for all sorts of despicable reasons. It's also true that your grandfather's incinerators turned thousands of bodies at those camps into ash. But the big question everybody's eager to overlook in indicting an entire nation for genocide is what kinds of bodies were processed in those incinerators, and how did they die?

"Yes, there is significant evidence of anti-Semitism among Hitler and other Nazis, but that has been true of all of Europe and Russia for centuries. We must concede that, for centuries, Christian Europe greatly preferred that Jews find someplace else to live. We must also concede that, for centuries, Jews have resisted this; but, suddenly, they came up with a bold, new idea. Instead of demanding room in Prague, Berlin, Barcelona, Paris, Rome, and London, they offered to leave willingly if they could return to Palestine. And, guess what? The Europeans just happened to control Palestine after the war! How convenient! But there's a big problem: the Arabs who already live there. The Europeans are a people with high ethics and morality; they've just fought two world wars and they're not about to take part in the eviction of another people from their land. So, the Jews come up with yet another bold, new idea. They convince the world that they alone were singled out, above all others, for extermination by the Nazis, and that this will happen again and again unless they have their own state in Palestine. They also remind everybody that they lived in Palestine until the Romans—another European power—kicked them out in 70 A.D. So, the Europeans of today would only be righting the wrongs of the past by helping the Jews re-create the State of Israel. And, besides, they argue, using the same bigotry they claim led to the Holocaust, it's just a bunch of stupid Arabs on a worthless piece of desert! Who cares about them? Who cares about desert? It's genius, really. The Europeans gave up the innocent lives and lands of millions of Arab people as a burnt offering for their own sins. My family became the fatted calf for somebody else's sacrifice."

Sam lit a new cigarette, visibly angry. Ott was astonished. For the first time, he had met somebody like himself, with a legitimate reason to be angry at Jews. But it still didn't mean the Holocaust was a hoax. He felt sorry for Sam and called for Trudy to bring them another round.

"I never looked at it that way," Ott said. "I guess I've never thought of the Arabs as having so much in common with the Germans. So that's why your people are blowing themselves up in Israeli markets—because your land was taken from you?"

"No," Sam said, exhaling a cloud of cigarette smoke in disgust. "We do suicide bombings because we're stupid, uneducated, and don't know any better. That only hurts us, not the Jews. Do you see Jews blowing themselves up? Or Germans? Or anybody else? Of course, Jews have been working on taking back Palestine for two thousand years, while we've only been at it fifty; who knows, maybe the Jews were doing suicide attacks against the Romans in the first century? It takes time to see reality and the path from here to there; history is as much a function of the present as the past, and it's more a function of emotion than fact. History and truth are what we want them to be, Ott. For example, most historians now agree that fewer than one million people in total died at Auschwitz, not the four million originally claimed. Did you know that?"

"No."

"Okay. Did you know that many historians also agree that fewer than four million Jews in total died during World War II, not the six million in schoolbooks—versus twenty million Soviets, fifteen million Chinese, six million Poles, and nearly three million Japanese?"

"No, I didn't know that either."

"And no credible historian believes Germans turned Jews into soap and lamp shades."

"I never believed that," Ott said. "Germans aren't animals."

Trudy brought the drinks. She heard this last comment, raised her eyebrows, shook her head and walked away. Ott sipped his beer more slowly now. He was beginning to feel intoxicated, and he worried that he wouldn't be able to follow what Sam was saying.

"Did you know," Sam asked, "that more Jews died of disease and malnutrition in the camps than of unnatural causes? Why are the so-called 'facts' changing over time? Now consider this: standard disinfection and delousing techniques across Europe to control the spread of typhus and cholera in prison populations included fumigation of inmates with insecticide gases in the nineteen-thirties. So, yes, in a sense, the Jews were gassed, but not to kill them, to save them, and other prisoners, from infestation. And air raid shelters at the camps, and throughout the rest of Germany, utilized airtight doors for fear of chemical attacks after the terrors of World War I, and shower facilities at the camps often doubled as bomb shelters."

"Struck out," Ott said with a groan. "Game's over." Sam glanced up at the television, then back at Ott.

"Add to this that cremation has always been viewed suspiciously by the Jews, who thought of it as a sacrilege and means of concealing crimes. Then consider that the Soviets, more bloodied by the Germans than anyone else—and governed by pathological, Stalinist liars—captured the prison camps in eastern Europe and denied access to the west. Today, those camps are the only camps believed to have had gas chambers; even the Jews now agree no gas chambers existed on German soil. Now consider this: The eastern European Jews were the ones most insistent upon the creation of a Jewish state in Palestine before the war began; and they were the ones who claimed the Germans were gassing them. Motive and opportunity, Ott, motive and opportunity. All you have left to support the Holocaust stories are the tortured confessions of some Nazi officers and the inconsistent accounts of a few prison camp survivors about the general horrors of war."

Ott teased himself. *Could it be true? Yes, he thought, it had to be! The Jews weren't butchered and burned in the improved crematoria of Jos. A. Rabun & Sons!*

"And here's the clincher," Sam said. "I had a chemist do a forensic analysis at three of the so-called death camps. He detected high levels of Zyklon B cyanide gas embedded in the concrete walls of the delousing chambers in Auschwitz and Treblinka, but nothing—nothing—in the showers."

"Really?"

"Yes," Sam said, clinking his glass against Ott's. "If the showers had been used to gas millions of Jews, traces of cyanide would be all over the place. It's a hoax, and it's all in my documentary. By convincing the world of a German Holocaust, the Jews did in five years what even God couldn't do for them in two thousand—they created a Jewish state in Palestine that now has a military stronger than all of the other Arab nations combined."

Ott shook his head, thinking. He was convinced, but he was still trying to come up with a counterargument. "What about the pictures of all those dead bodies? What about the incinerators?"

"I'm not saying the Nazis were angels," Sam said. "The camps were terrible places, as are all prison camps during a war. People were killed, many Jews among them. As the Allies squeezed Hitler, Hitler squeezed the country, and the entire German population began to starve. The prisoners in the camps were the last to be fed or receive medical care. They were worked like animals, and disease was rampant. Many died in the camps, and there were, of course, many executions as well. Germany's 'final solution' for all the dead bodies piling up everywhere was to cremate them. But that's not the same as mass genocide."

"How are you going to get the documentary distributed?" Ott said. "What can I do to help?"

This was the moment Sam had been waiting for, the reason he had come to see Ott. "We need money," Sam said. "But the documentary is just the beginning of the story for me. You just want to clear your family's name, and we can definitely do that; but the misery of the Jewish occupation of Palestine continues for my people, all of whom now live like prisoners in concentration camps in the West Bank and Gaza with the Jews as Nazi guards and executioners. What the Arabs fail to understand is that suicide bombers and guns won't push the Jews back into the sea, any more than bombs and guns would push the Palestinians out of Palestine. The Jews will only go out through the door they came in—the revolving door of public opinion."

Sam was animated now, his voice raised, using his hands.

"When the world believed the Jews were liars, thieves, and murderers—responsible for everything from Jesus' death to economic collapse—the world contained them, enslaved them, scattered them, and hunted them down. There isn't a country that hasn't done it, from the Egyptians to the Romans, from the Crusades to the Inquisition. But when the world believed the Jews had been driven almost to extinction during the Holocaust, the world felt guilty about it, and created the State of Israel as a nature preserve to save them—a refuge for an endangered species. Anybody who hunts Jews now is punished, and the world is determined to protect them. It's like gray wolves. Do you know the story about gray wolves?"

"Yes," Ott said, immediately seeing the analogy. "When gray wolves were considered a threat to humans and livestock, the government funded programs to exterminate them, and they were hunted to the brink of extinction; but when there were only about four hundred left, we started feeling guilty about it and thinking they weren't so bad after all. Big nature preserves were created for them in Yellowstone, and we punished anybody who hunted them. It's been a big success; there are thousands of wolves roaming the wild again."

"Exactly," said Sam. "But now there are news reports that they're back to killing cows again, and scaring people in the middle of the night, and suddenly we're starting to remember why we got rid of them in the first place and realizing we were pretty stupid for letting them come back. They're back off the endangered species list again, and you can go out and shoot one any time you like. It's just the same with Jews. When the world sees them as a threat again—and it's happening, every day—then the beautiful nature preserve of Israel will fall. The Jews have been successful and prolific, like wolves, and the world is beginning to see them as a threat to peace in the Middle East. They can't control their appetites. They keep demanding more land and more settlements, and they keep hunting and killing Arabs. There's no peace. To get away with this, the Jews don't dare let the rest of the world stop feeling guilty for the Holocaust. So, they keep writing books, making movies, and building museums about it, and they keep shouting, 'Never again!' All the while, they, themselves, are perpetrating a Holocaust on the Arabs. It's been an effective strategy so far; it's what's been keeping the nature preserve open. Only when the world is able to relieve itself of the guilt and shame of the Holocaust can the hunting of Jews start again. For Arabs, the equation should be very simple: If you can erase the Holocaust, you can erase Israel.

Ott was excited. "You're right," he said, slurring his words slightly and slamming down his beer, slopping it onto the table.

"All we need to do is seed some doubt," Sam continued. "Doubt grows into skepticism, and skepticism changes beliefs. Truth is what we decide it should be. Look at what just happened. You believe what I've said just now because you want to believe it, because it sounds plausible, because nobody trusts the past, and nobody trusts governments, prosecutors, communists, or Jews. Scientists have convinced us that we can't even trust our own memories. The seeds of doubt are there, waiting to sprout. All we need to do is give them a little water to make them grow. And the best way to add water is with film, because seeing is believing. That's why I've done a documentary instead of writing a book. Nobody reads books, but everybody watches movies and TV."

Sam leaned back and stretched. Ott regarded him with envy and admiration, thinking that if he had had an older brother, he would have chosen Sam. They both turned toward the television. The Channel 10 Evening News was coming on now, with its triumphant music and flashing montage of scenes from central Pennsylvania, ending with the camera zooming in on the graying anchorman.

"Good evening," he said in an authoritative baritone. "Football star O.J. Simpson is questioned in the slayings of his ex-wife and her friend; President Clinton is set to announce a plan for national welfare reform; and, break out those tie-died shirts for Woodstock '94…but the big story tonight on Action News is our exclusive undercover investigation with startling evidence tying popular local charity Educate-for-Tomorrow, and its founder Holden Hurley, to a local white supremacist group."

"Oh my God," Ott said.

"Can you turn this up?" Sam hollered to Trudy.

"Here with the story is Action News investigative reporter, Bo Wolfson...."

38

Trudy turned up the volume on the television and the camera panned back to show Bo Wolfson, handsome and grave, sitting next to the anchorman.

"Thank you, Rob." he said, then turned and looked directly into the camera. "Every school district in central Pennsylvania now has computers and Internet access in the classrooms. Those computers are a gift from a local, non-profit corporation called Educate-for-Tomorrow and its founder, Holden Hurley. A native of Orbisonia, and a former computer programmer, Mr. Hurley founded Educate-for-Tomorrow—known as EFT—three years ago, and since then he has obtained more than five million dollars in grants from state and federal governments, private foundations, and charities, including the United Way, to bring computers and the Internet to rural schools. But, as a result of an exclusive undercover investigation, Action News has learned that an EFT subsidiary called TechChildren, Inc., paid more than seven hundred thousand dollars of those grant funds to an entity called EduSoft. According to the Pennsylvania Secretary of State, EduSoft is the registered alias of a white supremacist group known as The Eleven, which has a concealed and heavily guarded compound and training camp in the mountains just outside of Huntingdon. Over the past two months, Action News producer Bobby Wilson infiltrated The Eleven and videotaped Holden Hurley, the founder of EFT, speaking at meetings of The Eleven, making racist and anti-Semitic remarks. We confronted Mr. Hurley with that videotape in an interview conducted earlier today."

Sam and Ott looked at each other in disbelief as the screen filled with the sign and office building for EFT, the reception area, and finally Holden Hurley seated at his desk with a wide grin on his face, his slicked-back black hair shining like dashboard plastic. Bo Wolfson was seated across from him. It was a complete setup. Hurley had obviously agreed to the interview because he thought they were doing a story on the good things EFT has done for the community.

"Mr. Hurley," said Bo, after some preliminary questions, "EFT receives its funding from state and local governments, private charities and foundations. How is this money spent?"

"Well," said Hurley, with the soothing voice of a reference librarian, his big, beefy face frozen in a prideful smile. "We use the money to purchase computers at a discount for schools, and then we also provide networking services, Internet connections, and training to the teachers and kids. We've put twenty school districts, and over forty thousand children, online so far. I'm very proud of what we've been able to accomplish, but there's much more work to be done."

"What does TechChildren do?"

"Yes, well, TechChildren is an EFT subsidiary involved in developing educational software for kids. Our plans include developing software to help kids learn quicker and easier. Classrooms will look a whole lot different in the future. The blackboard and paper textbook days are coming to an end."

"Have you ever heard of a company called EduSoft?"

Hurley began looking around the room, stalling, searching for the answer. "Yes," he said, his smile forced now. "EduSoft is an educational software consultant."

"Do EFT and TechChildren do business with EduSoft?"

"That's a good question. I don't know."

"Have you ever heard of an organization called The Eleven?"

Hurley's face crimsoned, but the smile remained, like somebody who has just accidentally walked into a post in front of a crowd and wants them to believe he meant to do it.

"I don't believe this," Sam said to Ott, watching his dreams unravel in the bar. "I don't freakin' believe this."

"No, I can't say that I have," Hurley said. "Is it a computer company?"

"No," said Bo. "The Eleven is a white supremacist group. Are you sure you've never heard of them?"

"No," said Hurley, his voice rising. "What does this have to do with EFT and computers for kids? What are you suggesting?"

The camera switched to Bo, who stared down Hurley with calm contempt, hungry for the kill. "I'm suggesting, Mr. Hurley, that EFT is a front organization for a white supremacist group; that state, federal, and charitable funds have been used improperly to support this group; and that you, sir, are a white supremacist."

Hurley leered back at Bo. "That's an outrageous accusation, Mr. Wolfson, and you are doing tremendous harm to the children of central Pennsylvania by making it."

"I have a videotape I'd like to show you, Mr. Hurley, and then I'd like to give you a chance to comment on it."

A small television monitor is arranged on Mr. Hurley's desk. A dimly lit videotape with a muffled sound track, as if the camera were hidden inside a bag, shows Holden Hurley in front of a roomful of white men, pacing back and forth in front of a Nazi flag.

"My Aryan brothers," Mr. Hurley says, "today is a great day! Today we are ready to begin to Educate-for-Tomorrow the white youth of today on how we will win the coming race war, and we're going to do it by using EFT's computer intranet, built with the kikes' and niggers' own money, right under their own crooked and flat noses! And it all begins with this man, my brothers—our very special Aryan brother from the Arab world, Samar Mansour, who with our help, has just finished a documentary proving that the Holocaust was nothing but a Jew lie."

Ott looked at Sam in the bar, watching with his mouth open.

On the screen, Sam stands up to accept the applause of the members of The Eleven and thank them for their support. "It is time," he says, "for Arabs and Aryans to join forces against their common enemy. This documentary is the first step in what I hope will be a long and successful collaboration. My contribution to the battle will not be another suicide bombing like my brave Palestinian brothers, who are willing to sacrifice their own lives for the cause. No, I intend to demolish not just a few bricks of the State of Israel but the very foundation upon which the State of Israel was built. No gas chambers, no Israel!"

The room erupted into applause.

Trudy, the bartender, looked from the television to Sam and back.

"It's all over," Sam said to Ott. "They're probably out looking for me right now. I've gotta go." He left twenty dollars on the table and walked out with Trudy looking after him.

Ott turned back to the television to see Holden Hurley's face twisted into a shape as ugly as the Swastika behind him on the small monitor in his office. He said to Bo: "Sometimes people got to stand up for what's right and fix what's wrong. One day you'll understand that I've been doing both and you'll make me a goddamned hero. Now get the hell out of my office."

39

How bizarre it is for me to see life through a man's eyes, through my murderer's eyes.

How bizarre to experience his moods and obsessions, his sorrows and joys. How bizarre to see a baby and not ache to hold her but to see a beautiful woman and crave her with every nerve; how bizarre to flex muscles rather than stick out my chest, to talk tough with my buddies rather than share vulnerabilities with my girlfriends, to towel dry my hair and walk out rather than style my hair and apply makeup. How bizarre to be Ott Bowles as he shoots a bullet into the seat next to Sarah, and to hear me screaming; to feel the intense, almost sexual gratification of exercising complete dominance and control over me and seeing the terror in my eyes. How bizarre to see the small movements of my head as I drive down the road, to feel the softness of my body through the gun in the back seat, to feel contempt for me and everything I stand for but, at the same time, to be physically attracted to me and imagine what it would be like to make love to me, to listen to me pleading for my daughter's life and my own and, for an instant, to feel sympathy for me and to question whether I should have kidnapped a mother and her daughter and to search for a way out. How bizarre to feel the pain of a knee being driven into my groin. How bizarre to count down the last days of life on death row, to come to peace with death, to contemplate and confront its presence, and then to be delivered into it, strapped into a chair and electrocuted. And, in the end, how incredibly insignificant Sarah and I were inside Otto Bowles' life, how little we really mattered. We represented an unseen enemy, Sarah and I, the way words represent an unseen thought; and because this enemy could not be seen, we became the enemy, just as words are sometimes mistaken for the ideas they represent. To Ott Bowles, Sarah and I were primarily symbols, not human beings, a means to an end, nothing more than that.

And so, gazing back through my murderer's eyes, I could appreciate the logic of a kidnapping, because through those eyes I could see how all hope for the Rabuns of Kamenz vanished when my husband aired his tape of Holden Hurley and Samar Mansour carving their initials into the tree of history with the crooked iron spikes of a Swastika. Which was odd, actually, because those days had been so different, so magical and glorious for us. The story was picked up by the national network, and we threw a party to celebrate the launching of Bo's career. We never considered the impact of the story on Hurley, Mansour, or the other members of The Eleven, because they represented *our* unseen enemy: the bully around the corner, the false prophet behind the pulpit, the subversive thought rotting the fabric of society. Like a little David, my Bo had slain the beast, and we were proud. We had no idea that at the same time we were celebrating this great victory, Samar Mansour was sealing a videocassette copy of his documentary into a padded mailing envelope with the following note:

> Ott,
>
> The truth is what we want it to be.
> We may never see each other again.
> Plant the seeds.
>
> Your friend,
> Sam

By Sunday morning, the FBI had arrested Hurley on multiple counts of mail and wire fraud, tax evasion, and racketeering. A nationwide manhunt for Samar Mansour ended with confirmation that he'd fled the country, probably to Yemen or Afghanistan. Ott received the videocassette in Buffalo and inserted it into the tape player in his bedroom after his mother had gone to sleep.

Sam Mansour's documentary is actually a well-constructed and well-produced film, beginning with a grim river of historic black and white photographs appearing and disappearing on the screen: men in Nazi uniforms, the frightened faces of women and children being loaded onto train cars, electrified fences around concentration camps, prison barracks, showers, mounds of decaying corpses, smokestacks, incinerators. The images flash by faster and faster, finally trailing off to a screen of black. From this darkness, the mournful cry of an oboe emerges; it is the first sound we hear on the documentary, and it plays a dirge to accompany the slow march across the screen of hundreds of titles of books and films about the Holocaust—every title Sam Mansour could find during his research. As the last of these scroll across the screen, the oboe is swallowed by the symphonic roar of Wagner's *Die Walküre*, and the sneering face of Adolph Hitler consumes the screen. Finally, the title of the documentary appears in white letters superimposed over an aerial shot of Auschwitz, swooping down onto the reddish vein of rusting train tracks leading into the camp and the platform where millions of feet beat their last steps: *What Happened?* Sam Mansour stands on this platform as the camera zooms in; he is wearing the same black pants and blue shirt he had been wearing at Trudy's, the color of the shirt matching his eyes. His thick, dark hair is carefully combed, and he is waiting for us, the audience, to join him. His voice suits the role, educated, evocative, authoritative, believable; ironically, he looks and sounds more like a rabbi than a Palestinian doctoral student attempting to disprove the Holocaust, which only adds to his credibility. Smiling, he introduces himself as Sam Mansour, furthering the friendly academic impression, and he asks the audience a very serious question: What Happened? He talks to the camera as he walks toward the showers, explaining the purpose of the film and assuring us that he has no agenda other than the truth. As his proofs unfold, he asks us to leap with him the many gaps in logic and evidence that must be leaped, but keeps coming back to the "truth," always the truth, insisting on it, demanding that we believe he is acting in our best interest.

As a matter of cinematography, with the parabolic camera angles, haunting guard tower lighting, and echo chamber sound effects—as if everything is being spoken inside a concentration camp shower—the documentary is exceptionally good at creating the impression of actually being there during the dark days. Watching it for the first time in his bedroom, Ott is mesmerized. The filmmaker's skill, and Ott's own desperate desire to believe, help him to overlook the warnings in Sam's pleas for trust and the many discrepancies that strain reason as the documentary unfolds. Ott, of course, has never read the transcripts of the Nuremburg trials or the many Nazi documents admitting the atrocities; he has never visited the death camps in Poland, only Germany, or critically examined the evidence and photographs in the archives and museums; he is not told by the narrator that although Zyklon B residue cannot be found inside the showers, the chemical byproducts of the gas coat the walls; he is not shown the interviews of the survivors, with the horror still reflected in their eyes; nor has he read the books or seen the films that scrolled across the beginning of the documentary, if it can even loosely be called this and not propaganda. No, Ott Bowles sees only what he wants to see: the vindication of his family unfolding before him like a sweet dream.

Bo waited until after the story aired to tell me that the weekend nights he supposedly spent on call at the station were actually spent camped out in our car, in the woods outside The Eleven's compound, with a cell phone in his hand and one of my grandfather's shotguns across his lap, waiting for Bobby Wilson, his producer, to come out alive with the damning video—and ready to go in after him if necessary. I made him promise never to do anything that stupid again.

As a reward for their work and the risks they had taken, the station promoted Bobby to senior producer and offered Bo the anchor position on the morning news, with the promise of moving him up to the noon and five o'clock time slots as soon as his desk skills improved. We were ecstatic. People at the grocery store and mall began stopping Bo for autographs, and I was the wife of a local celebrity. These were happy times: my law practice was growing, our daughter was thriving, and Bo's dream of becoming an anchorman at a major market television station, or even on one of the networks, looked more promising than ever. How bitter to learn that the source of our triumph would soon become the cause of our tragedy, the end not only of our hopes and dreams, but of our family itself.

I also learned from Ott Bowles that Holden Hurley had made considerable progress in preparing his new computer network for war. The EFT intranet was powered by redundant computer servers and systems in Atlanta, Palo Alto, Dublin, and Madras, each equipped with military grade encryption software and scrambled satellite telecommunications access. He built multiple firewalls into the system, and everything could be operated with special codes from laptop computers by remote digital command.

Stored on the hard drives of these servers were the e-mail and street addresses and telephone numbers of Caucasian teens and young adults across the United States, cross-matched to demographic data taken, legally and illegally, from public and private databanks. Also on the hard drives were the names, addresses, and detailed biographical data of Jewish and African-American political, educational, media, and religious leaders. Other directories stored strategic information, including the locations, specifications, and computer access numbers for metropolitan water and energy supply grids, banking and financial institutions, air traffic control systems, military installations, and national telecommunications centers.

Hurley's great dream, confided to Ott as he showed him how to operate many of the EFT systems, was to disrupt the computer networks controlling public utilities, financial institutions, the Internet, and airline travel, but make it appear as though the commands to create all of this chaos had come from computers in Israel and certain American Jewish leaders and institutions. As the nation ground to a halt and panic ensued, Hurley would leak anonymous rumors that there was a plot by Jews to take control of the economic system, and e-mail messages to that effect would be sent to white teens and young people as a call to action. None of these rumors would be believed at first, but authorities tracing the hackers would follow a trail back to the computers of Jewish leaders, which Hurley would also infect with bits of anti-Christian e-mail, and e-mails about seizing control of financial institutions. The conspiracy would thus be proved. As Jews attempted to defend themselves, wide-scale violence would erupt, instigated by key assassinations perpetrated by The Eleven and other white supremacist groups encouraged by having their paranoia finally confirmed. Hurley would then send false e-mails to African-American leaders claiming that white supremacist groups were attacking African-Americans around the country, unleashing more racial violence and riots in the streets. In this way, a full-scale religious and race war would be started, and Holden Hurley—with The Eleven's advanced organization and secure communications—would emerge as a savior and defender of white Christian America and fundamental conservative American values. "It worked in Rwanda," Hurley told Ott, referring to the genocide of 800,000 Tutsis ignited just a few months earlier by a similar disinformation campaign, "and it will work here. Mixing hatred and fear always leads to an explosion." Holden Hurley's dreams were never nagged by a conscience, or constrained by reason or reality.

Ott Bowles regarded all this as the ranting of a madman, but during the confusion surrounding Hurley's arrest, and the void of leadership within The Eleven in the wake of Brian Shelly's death and Sam Mansour's flight from the country, he had the presence of mind to gather the EFT computer manuals, access numbers, and passwords and store them in a safe location. The idea for kidnapping Sarah and me to force the networks to air the documentary came later. To his credit, he never planned to harm us. That was Tim Shelly's idea.

40

The building in the woods to which Ott Bowles and Tim Shelly drove Sarah and me that Friday night in October, 1994, was the original mushroom house on the old Shelly farm near Kennett Square, built by Tim's great-grandfather, Clifton Shelly, in the nineteen-thirties when most mushrooms were harvested in the wild and people were just learning how to grow them commercially. Clifton Shelly, like his father and grandfather before him, was a dairy farmer, but he began experimenting with mushroom farming when he saw the demand for the edible fungi far exceeding the supply provided by the trained gatherers who roamed humid forests with sacks looking for mushrooms sprouting in the shaded, biologically rich compost beneath trees. To re-create and better control these conditions, and to make harvesting easier and less a matter of chance, he erected a windowless, block building at the bottom of an isolated ravine, away from prying eyes and near a pond where ice could be harvested during the winter to cool the mushroom house in the summer and water would be plentiful to humidify the air and moisten the compost soil. Soon he was producing sizable crops of the fungi and taking them to market, stunning grocers and mushroom gatherers alike with the volume and consistency he produced. As fungiculture techniques advanced and profits grew, he replaced his milking parlors and corncribs with mushroom houses and abandoned the original mushroom house at the bottom of the ravine because it was too small and remote for large-scale production.

Tim Shelly was certain the large California-based agribusiness conglomerate that purchased his family's mushroom farm at auction after his father died had no idea the old mushroom house at the bottom of the ravine even existed. Almost nobody did. It was far removed from the rest of the buildings and secluded deep in the woods, now overgrown with heavy brush. He suggested it to Ott when Ott told him about his plan to kidnap Sarah and me to force the networks to air the documentary. In such a remote location, he reasoned, there would be virtually no chance of detection, and with masonry walls and no windows, there would be virtually no chance of escape. Ott looked the building over and thought it would do, but to be certain he drove in and out at different hours of the day and night, and he even stayed for a few days in an outbuilding next to the mushroom house to see whether anyone would notice. No one did.

This outbuilding, which was basically an old wooden storage shed with a couple of windows, is where Ott and Tim stayed after they kidnapped Sarah and me. They stocked it in advance of our arrival with food for several weeks, plus a generator, two laptop computers, a satellite telephone, and several crates filled with assault rifles, ammunition, body armor, and rocket propelled grenades taken from The Eleven's compound. They covered the car we arrived in with a tarp and shoveled mushroom soil over it so it couldn't be seen from the air. It was from near this outbuilding, and from one of these laptop computers, that Ott sent an e-mail message to Bo when we arrived, attaching a digital photograph he had taken of Sarah and me in the mushroom house with a gun pointed at Sarah's head. Ott made no attempt to conceal his identity—he wanted the world to know exactly who he was and why he was doing what he was doing—but he did use the EFT computer servers and encryption software to conceal our location, routing his e-mail from server to server around the world, deleting the message headers and identification tags, and making it appear as though the transmissions originated from somewhere in India. Ott's only stated demand in the e-mail was to have Sam Mansour's documentary aired during primetime by a national television network; if that happened, he promised, Bo and the world would witness our safe return and Ott's voluntary surrender to the authorities. He explained in the e-mail that a videocassette copy of the documentary could be found on the front passenger seat of my car, which was parked in a grove of pine trees just off the old logging road in Ardenheim. He made no demands for money or even for Hurley's release from prison; asked only that the world consider the possibility that the Nazi gassings had been a fabrication, and that his family and the German people had been wrongly convicted of genocide. Since Bo was a television news reporter, this simple request shouldn't be too much, and he gave Bo three days to make the necessary arrangements. He made no express threat against our lives, and in his heart he never thought it would come to that; so convinced was he of the objective merits of the film that he believed the networks would jump at the chance to air it once they saw it. He fully expected a reply message from Bo within hours with the air date and time, and he had a portable television with satellite reception ready, from which he could watch the documentary when it aired and monitor news reports of our kidnapping.

Despite my attempted escape and being kneed in the groin, Ott was delighted with how well things had gone that first night. Sarah and I were locked away in the mushroom house, and an e-mail reply from Bo came within an hour, telling Ott he was doing everything possible to have the tape aired and begging him for our safe return. Two hours later, all the television news networks were carrying the story of our kidnapping with photographs of Sarah and me, and photographs of Ott, Holden Hurley, Tim Shelly, and Sam Mansour. The fact that Bo was a television news reporter and that I was an attorney—and that Sarah and I had been kidnapped by a white supremacist attempting to disprove the Holocaust—touched off a media firestorm, fanned hotter by the prospect of a mysterious Holocaust documentary, an international manhunt for a fugitive Arab, and Ott's skillful use of computer technology to communicate while concealing our location. By the next morning, the network and cable news programs were featuring experts on neo-Nazi groups, the Holocaust, hostage negotiations, and the Internet, together with mediated debates among Christian, Jewish, Islamic, and African-American leaders brought together to confront the underlying pathology of Holden Hurley. It was exactly the kind of international media sensation Ott wanted.

The only thing that worried Ott in all this was how his mother was handling the news. She refused requests to be interviewed by the reporters staking out the mansion in Buffalo; but, to Ott's surprise, by Saturday afternoon some of the networks were airing balanced and even sensitive background reports about Barratte, Amina, and the Rabuns of Kamenz, explaining how Amina had saved the Schriebergs in Germany, how the Rabuns had been gunned down by Soviet troops and Amina and

Barratte had been raped, and the litigation over the Schriebergs' theaters and property. Some commentators even began to create an almost sympathetic picture of why Ott might have kidnapped us for the sake of a Holocaust documentary, causing Ott to believe more deeply than ever that he had done the right thing. All he wanted in the end was justice. He even started comparing his actions to the courageous exploits of Amina herself in Germany—at an age not much younger than his—viewing Sarah and me the way Amina had viewed the Schriebergs, providing us with the necessities for our survival—water, food, baby formula, diapers, and an austere but safe shelter in the woods. He offered us some sweatshirts because the mushroom house had no heat, and he asked himself: "Am I not protecting this woman and this child from those who would harm them? From men like Holden Hurley and Tim Shelly who would one day hunt them down and murder them? Will they not be safer when the truth of the documentary is known?"

Sarah slept while I sat up awake worrying during our first day of captivity in the squalid, stinking mushroom house, the only light coming from small gaps and cracks around the door, and the only bathroom facility a bucket in the far corner. I knew nothing about the documentary and was convinced we had been kidnapped as part of a plot to extort Holden Hurley's release from prison. I assumed by now that the police and FBI agents would be searching everywhere; we just needed to hang on until they found us, and do nothing to provoke Ott and Tim any further. I prayed to the God of the Old Testament, the righteous and just God, to deliver us from our enemies. And to smite them.

When Sarah woke I fed and changed her and sang *Hot Tea and Bees Honey* to her over and over. I whispered stories to her about her daddy and her grandparents and great-grandparents, and even her great-great-grandmother, Nana Bellini. I hadn't thought of Nana Bellini in a long time, and her memory calmed me. We played patty-cake and cuddled in our sleeping bag. Sarah was so good and brave. She didn't fuss or cry. I think she enjoyed the close contact and the darkness, which might in some way have reminded her of being inside my womb.

Ott and Tim took turns checking in on us. Like the famous Stanford psychology experiment with college students assigned the roles of prisoners and guards, Tim Shelly reveled in the role of jailer; he shoved me around, barking orders and obscenities at us, throwing our food on the floor. He held no firm convictions of his own; he acted only on what others told him, but he would die for those people—for anyone to whom he could attach his childlike adoration in the vacuum created by his father's death and Holden Hurley's arrest. He was a mercenary, not a martyr; Ott understood this and took full advantage of it, playing on Tim's fantasies of battle and the camaraderie of men-at-arms. Ott needed Tim's help—his brawn and expert knowledge of weapons—to pull off his plan. To get it, he lied to Tim about almost everything. He told Tim they would hold us hostage until Holden Hurley was freed from prison, and said that from his jail cell Hurley had secretly instructed Ott to start the race war they had been preparing for so long to fight. Tim would become a great soldier in that war, Ott predicted, a national hero; and Ott promised Tim that if things went wrong, his family's contacts in Germany and elsewhere, who had helped SS Colonel Haber and other fleeing Nazis, would assist in their escape to South America where money would be waiting.

Tim believed Ott's every word and longed for his chance at glory, but by the second day of waiting for the real combat to begin, boredom set in. Tim got into the habit of conducting

FORGIVING ARARAT

hourly searches of the mushroom house with his flashlight, exam-
ining the walls and dirt floor to see if Sarah and I were tunneling
an escape. He would end his inspection with a pat down search of
my body, demanding that I lean with my face and arm against
the wall and my legs spread wide. I still wore my black skirt and
cream colored blouse from work, and the sweatshirt Ott had
given me; my stockings disintegrated on the rough surface of
the floor, and I had long since abandoned them. With each pat
down, Tim would linger a little longer around my crotch and
breasts, then call me a slut or whore and walk out. I made no
reply, worried it would only agitate him further.

Late during our second night in the mushroom house, Tim
performed his usual search but at the end walked up to where
Sarah and I were huddled in our sleeping bag and yanked her away
from me. I fought to hold onto her, but he hit me in the mouth
with his elbow, knocking my head against the block wall, then
carried Sarah to the opposite end of the building and plopped
her down in a corner. She whimpered softly for a moment and
then became quiet again. I tried to get on my feet to go after her,
still dizzy from my head hitting the wall, but Tim slammed me
back down onto the sleeping bag and in the dim yellow glow of
the flashlight began tearing off my clothes. I screamed for Ott
and tried kneeing Tim in the groin and scratching and biting
him, but even with two good arms he would have easily overpowered me. He was a large man—I no longer thought of him
as a kid—built strong and solid with a thick chest and arms. He
slapped me across the face and told me to stop screaming, and
when I continued, he started punching me over and over until
blood spurted from my nose and mouth and I fainted. When I
regained consciousness, he was on top of me. He had my panties
off and my bra pulled up, and his pants were off.

Ott slept for two or three hours at a time during the night and had just awoken to make his rounds. He was outside relieving himself when he heard my muffled screams coming from the mushroom house. Still half asleep, he had left his gun behind. When he burst through the door and saw Tim writhing on top of me, he thought at first that he was dreaming the same nightmare that had terrorized him as a child, of seeing his mother being raped and his Aunt Bette being raped and beaten to death. To toughen up her son, Barratte Rabun had begun telling Ott at an early age about the terrible things the Russian soldiers had done in Kamenz, sparing him no detail in recounting the story and repeating it over and over, as if to inoculate him by the horror of it against those same impulses that she believed coursed through every man, even her own son. She would not stop until he started to cry, which indicated to her that the vaccine was working. Thus, growing up, Ott Bowles had no basis for distinguishing between sexual crimes and sexual relationships. Intercourse was, to him, the ultimate evil act, and this led him to fear girls and withdraw from them, and to believe his attraction to them was shameful and a sickness. He never had a girlfriend, and when his friends talked about having sex, he recoiled from them with loathing and disgust.

Tim looked over his shoulder and laughed when he saw Ott standing in the doorway. "She only screws Jew boys," he said. "She thinks she likes them circumcised, but it's time for her to find out what a real man is like. You wait your turn outside and we'll see what she thinks. It won't take long."

Ott went wild. He charged Tim and kicked him in the head with his heavy boot as if he were knocking a humping dog off of a neighbor's leg. Tim was stunned for a second, and then he reacted like the male of any species when another tries to take his mate. He roared up from the floor, unleashing on Ott all those years of training for combat and the frustration of waiting so long for the opportunity. He beat Ott mercilessly, slamming his panicked body against the racks and walls inside the mushroom house as if it were a doll. The violence became sexual for Tim, a continuation of the act he was determined to consummate with me.

I crawled over onto my knees to get Sarah and run, but then I saw Tim's pants and holster piled in the corner. In his desire to destroy Ott Bowles with his bare hands, Tim had forgotten about his gun and me. My grandfather had taught me how to handle and fire guns on the farm; I knew how to chamber a bullet and remove the safety, although steadying the gun with one hand while firing was difficult for me and bullets often went astray. I found Tim's gun, rose to my feet, and fired a shot into the dirt beside me. The sound was deafening and immediately stopped Tim and Ott from fighting. They both turned toward me, astonished, and then, as he did with his father in Ott's museum in Buffalo, Tim lunged at me. I leaped back and squeezed the trigger three times into the darkness. Tim dropped face down onto the floor at my feet. His body heaved once and a pool of blood oozed out into the mushroom soil beneath his chest. His bare buttocks glistened with sweat in the flashlight, like Nero's loins after kicking Poppaea to death.

I pointed the gun at Ott, shaking, my finger on the trigger, trying to summon the will to shoot him too. He just stood there, waiting, almost hoping, still in shock from the beating he had sustained and, now, seeing Tim killed. But I couldn't do it. He had risked his life to stop Tim from raping me, and he had stopped Tim from shooting me when I tried to drive away; he spared Sarah's life when he could have shot her through the window. Somehow, even though he had put us through all this, I felt sorry for Ott and didn't want to hurt him.

"Why?" I screamed at the top of my lungs. "Why? All this for what? For what?" I backed away toward Sarah with the gun still pointing at him.

Sarah had started crying when Ott and Tim started fighting, but she had become quiet after I fired the three shots at Tim. I fumbled around through the darkness at the opposite end of the mushroom house to find her; she was curled up on her side and very wet, as though she had been perspiring and peed through her diaper. I just wanted to take her back home to her daddy and the life we had made, where we would all be safe again. Cradling her and holding the gun with the same arm, I made my way back toward the door. I could see Ott the entire time, illuminated by the flashlight and the small amount of light from the night-time sky. Ott watched passively, as though he had accepted the truce I offered and agreed that we were even; but when I stepped through the threshold, he moved toward us. I was ready for him and didn't hesitate this time; I turned and fired the gun. A bullet struck him low, in the leg; he collapsed, writhing on the floor next to Tim. I watched him for a moment, deciding whether to shoot again, trembling; and then I realized Sarah wasn't crying or moving even though I had just fired a gun close to her. I kneeled down to see her in the flashlight. Her clothes were soaked with blood and her tiny chest was ripped open. There was blood all over her beautiful cheeks and the creamy white perfection of her stomach. Her brown eyes were wide, staring out into nothing.

One of the three shots I fired at Tim Shelly had hit my baby, my Sarah.

I had killed my own daughter.

41

The skies open as if the bladder of space surrounding the earth has been punctured and an ocean of water falls from the heavens. I have never seen it rain so hard.

Through all this rain, Elymas and I scale the rock cliff of a shrinking island mountain, climbing higher and higher above a shoreline that only minutes earlier had been arid grassland and Mediterranean forest. The branches of olive, cypress, and pomegranate trees sway like seaweed fronds in the surf, collecting floating grasses, berries, wilted flower petals, pieces of dung, logs, pottery, and the distended carcasses of animals—the detritus of the earth over which these trees once reached toward the sun. And one might ask, what sun? For despite the noontime hour, only a hint of ultraviolet gloom passes onto the despairing planet below.

Elymas found me walking through the woods on my way to the Urartu Chamber to present the soul of Otto Rabun Bowles. "We have one more visit to make, Brek Abigail Cuttler," he said, "to meet others with an interest in the outcome of the case. Come with me, you will not be delayed long."

I assumed he would take me to see Bo and maybe my father and mother, but instead he opened the portal of his unseeing eyes upon the terrible flood of Cudi Dagh.

Lightning flashes and thunder cracks across the sky. Elymas is above me on the cliff. The water rises in feet, not inches, the waves below consuming the foothills and everything in their path.

"We're going to drown!" I call up to him on the cliff, rain streaming down my face.

"Do not worry, Brek Cuttler!" Elymas yells back down to me. "Cudi Dagh stands seven thousand feet. Noah found refuge here. Come along quickly."

Less than one-third of that altitude remains as we press our cheeks against the face of the mountain for the final assent. Elymas uses his gnarled fingers like a mattock, thrusting them into the crevices; he loses his grip only once, but it costs him his four-legged cane, which clicks against the boulders on the way back down to the roiling seas below. I keep my distance, afraid he will take me with him if he falls. I am as old and worn now as Elymas, moving slowly and cautiously, gasping for air and stopping often; I climb the mountain like a crippled goat, using the stump of my right arm for balance, barely able to see my next steps through the cataracts clouding my eyes. My clothes dissolve in the downpour into a paste of thread and dye that curdle into the wrinkles of my skin.

At the summit, we find a monastery constructed of mud thatch and thickset timbers; an annular rock garden sprinkled with chunks of sandstone, quartz, and veined blocks of marble rings the small building. Behind it, a narrow escarpment offers what in better weather would have been magnificent views of the lesser mountains and plains of Ararat. At the far end, a monument is chiseled into the gray basalt ridge; it is a carving of an immense wooden barge run aground in rough seas, waiting for salvage beneath the pensive wings of a raven and a dove. On the deck of the barge gathers a herd of animals fortunate enough to have escaped the floodwaters—pairs of lesser mammals and reptiles of every species—and at the bow stand the humble figures of a man and a woman.

Elymas nudges me inside the monastery, where we find a small chapel kept warm by a fire that burns without fuel inside a stone fireplace. A semicircle of crude wooden stools encloses the raised hearth, and between these and the flames stands a small rectangular table that serves the monks as both dining place and altar. At the center of this table sits an unusual bronze menorah, tarnished waxy black; a one-armed crucifix, like the one that hung from my Uncle Anthony's neck, is attached to the trunk and lowest branches of the menorah. The King of the Jews bends his left arm upward along the broad curve of the branch in a gesture of sublime exaltation.

Elymas ushers me through an alcove past one of the monks' cells, furnished with a bed of wooden slats suspended by iron straps above the floor. We enter the kitchen, which contains a small preparation table, a cistern overflowing with rainwater, and three wooden bins filled with dried fruit and nuts, as if the monastery has been recently inhabited. When we return from the kitchen into the chapel, we find that all but one of the stools in the semicircle around the hearth are occupied by monks wearing brown hooded robes. They face away from us toward the altar with its strange menorah, and on their laps they cradle laptop computers into which they stare reverently with their backs bent as if in prayer. Halos of fluorescent light from the computer screens give them the appearance of saints posed in a medieval painting.

We walk around them to see their faces, and I am stunned to discover that the first monk is Karen Busfield, wearing her blue Air Force uniform beneath her brown robe. Around her neck hangs the white linen stole I had embroidered for her by hand with a gold alpha and omega and presented to her at her ordination; it is a simple, conservative vestment, lacking the colorful ecclesiastical designs she preferred, but it was the best I could do with one hand. She wore it the day she married Bo and me and again the day she baptized Sarah; but she almost gave it back to me the day Bill Gwynne and I recommended that she accept the government's offer to drop all charges against her if she agreed to resign her commission and end her crusade against nuclear weapons. With tears in her eyes, she slid the stole across my desk but, suddenly, pulled it back.

"No," she said. "I withdraw my appeal to Caesar."

She fired Bill and me from her case, and she was right: the government dropped the charges anyway and gave her an honorable discharge, realizing that prosecuting a priest for trying to save the world from nuclear destruction would be a greater threat to the nuclear arsenal than freeing her and denying that any of it had even happened.

Now, sitting in the monastery on Cudi Dagh, the Reverend Karen Busfield's face, which was always loving and serene, gazes into the computer screen on her lap with an anguish even greater than the day when she came so close to giving up the priesthood. I approach her and touch her shoulder:

"Karen, it's me, Brek. What are you doing here?"

She looks up from her computer screen but doesn't recognize me in my old age; her cheeks are powdered with the brine of dried tears. Outside the storm rages on; the timbers of the monastery stiffen like the scourged back of a flagellant paying his penance. Karen closes her eyes and begins mumbling a chant beneath her breath.

Next to Karen sits my mother-in-law, Katerine Schrieberg-Wolfson, the second monk of Cudi Dagh. She clutches two photographs against the side of her computer. The first is a picture of Sarah, her granddaughter, and the second is a black and white photograph of her father, Bo's grandfather, standing in front of one of his theaters in Dresden. Katerine Schrieberg-Wolfson does not weep as she sits transfixed by her computer; she has witnessed too much sorrow in her life to weep anymore. She regrets only that she had never told Amina Rabun that it was her father, Jared Schrieberg, on that dark day in Kamenz, when God turned his face from Christian and Jew alike, who fired the shots from the woods that drew the soldiers' attention. He had met the same fate as the Rabuns, but she had refused to exploit this solemn repayment of her family's debt. She had even forbidden me from mentioning it during the litigation. Now she wonders if it could have made a difference.

"Poor Amina!" she cries. "But is it not a blessing that she didn't live to witness her only heir come to this? Oh, but now my precious granddaughter and daughter-in-law are paying for our sins! When will it end?"

Katerine gives no indication of recognizing me either; instead, she looks suspiciously at the monk seated to her left, Albrecht Bosch, who is typing madly on his keyboard with ink-stained fingers. Bosch weeps profusely, as a father weeps for a son, and he pleads in vain at the screen:

"No! No! No!"

Albrecht Bosch thought he had understood Ott Bowles' suffering, and that, by sharing his own sorrows with him, had shown him the way. He had been there for Ott as a friend, as the father he would never be in place of the father who never was; yet in recent months the letters and telephone calls went unanswered, and now his urgent e-mail messages are being left unanswered as well, begging Ott to free Sarah and me and return home to his family in Buffalo. From his stool in the monastery, Bosch frees another of these supplications into the ether of the Internet and looks frantically at his watch; it is too late, the time for Albrecht Bosch's final appeal has passed, leaving him alone again in a world that had never really welcomed him.

Sitting on the stools next to Bosch, Tad Bowles and Barratte Rabun follow the drama on their computers in disbelief, each concerned not for their son but for the difficulties that will be visited upon their own lives by his behavior. Tad's preoccupation is his reputation:

"My name will be forever associated with this outrage!" he bellows.

Tad is being humiliated by his own son, and, like his father before him, who was humiliated by his son in the bedroom of a lover, he vows with all his heart and soul never to forgive Ott this shame. In his rage, he tosses his computer onto the altar table at the feet of the other humiliated Son and walks out into the rain. Only when Otto Bowles' name has been replaced by a number, and then only when that number is to be erased from the Book of Life, will Tad reconsider this vow and seek to reclaim that which he has disowned; but by then he will discover, as did his own father, that what he disowned had long since disowned him.

Barratte Rabun, too, is consumed by names, but hers is a different complaint—she mourns an opportunity lost to resurrect a name rather than the urgent need to bury one. That name, Rabun, has now been soiled beyond all recognition, and dirtied with it is her dream of the family that lived so long ago breathing once again within the bodies of its children and grandchildren. She beseeches the heavens:

"How? How could I have lost them again? Twice in the same lifetime!"

The computer in her lap, where once she cradled this precious dream filled with such hope, sends back a message that the dream is indeed lost forever; and that message confirms for Barratte Rabun what her cousin Amina had understood and explained long ago—that the mercy of God will never shed its light upon the Rabuns of Kamenz. Barratte closes her computer and throws it into the fire. She will not grant the unforgiving God of that perverse, meaningless relic on the altar table another moment of satisfaction.

The stool at the apex of the semicircle sits vacant, and next to it sits Holden Hurley, wearing orange prison coveralls beneath his brown robe, smirking from ear to ear as if he is playing a computer game and winning with every move. Events have unfolded in ways even his grand dreams could not have predicted, lifting him higher and higher toward his goal. The scandal of Educate-for-Tomorrow has shoved Hurley's fascist drama onto the front page of every major newspaper, and into the lead segment of every news broadcast and talk show. Supporters have flooded the airwaves with words of support, and the mails with money; racist thugs around the world, emboldened by the new attention, have turned upon Jews and blacks in a giddy frenzy, torching their homes, businesses, and places of worship. Otto Bowles, the indispensable zealot toiling in the shadows, has secured for Hurley a place in the miserable history of the Holocaust by offering up as a blood sacrifice the family of the Jew who helped put Hurley behind bars.

Next to Hurley in the chapel sit my poor parents, eyes transfixed upon their computers in anguish and disbelief. They do not even notice me standing beside them. How can one begin to describe the agony of parents witnessing the murder of their own child and their own granddaughter? In their grief-stricken faces atop Cudi Dagh, I see the unfathomable joy of my first moments of life—the jubilant astonishment and wonder that rises up from the tender vulnerability of birth to declare again for a cynical world the existence of unconditional love. I could not bear the gift of that love as I grew older; I convinced myself I was not worthy of receiving it, even as I recognized it emanating from me with the birth of my own daughter. Yet here it is again, pouring forth from the shattered faces of my parents, flailing itself against the computer screens in a futile attempt to shield me from harm, to protect the dying object of an infinite grace. As if in a dream, all their hurts and hatreds melt away at that instant; the excesses of their marriage and divorce, the drinking and adultery, the intolerance, prejudice, and all-consuming self-centeredness fade, for one sacred moment, into the static background of life.

The digital clocks at the bottom corners of the computer screens on the laps of the monks of Cudi Dagh all display 4:02:34 a.m., 10/17/94. The screens flicker brightly, as if they are bursting into flame, then they show me holding Sarah, bloodied and lifeless, in the dim light of the mushroom house. I am screaming without sound, as if in a silent movie. The gun drops from my fingers. Ott Bowles, with a bullet hole in his leg, slides across the floor toward the gun.

The computer screens cannot show what Ott Bowles is thinking at that moment, but I know. His soul is mine now, and we are forever one. He is thinking about Amina, Barratte, and the Rabuns of Kamenz; he is thinking about the Schriebergs and how they have been ungrateful; he is thinking about the world and how it has been merciless; he is thinking about Holden Hurley and Sam Mansour and how my husband has destroyed them; he is thinking about Tim Shelly and how I have killed him and my own child; he is thinking about how he rushed forward to help us out of the mushroom house but how I shot him down in cold blood; he is thinking about how unjust and unfair life has been.

Most of all, Otto Rabun Bowles is thinking about justice.

He knows now the documentary will never be aired, and that he will be forever misunderstood, blamed, and convicted for Tim's and Sarah's deaths. The Rabuns have always been misunderstood, blamed, convicted for things they did not do.

The computer screens on the laps of the monks finally show what I have been unable to accept from the moment of my arrival in Shemaya. Ott Bowles raises the gun and fires three silent shots into my chest. I slump over on top of Sarah. Moments later, police officers storm the mushroom house. They had been able to trace the e-mails after all. The computer screens go blank.

42

The giant fist of the storm pounds the roof of the monastery of Cudi Dagh, demanding that the guilty appear for sentencing. When the storm is not appeased, the mountain itself begins to quake, and the sea overtakes the summit, bursting through the door of the monastery. The one-armed Savior on the menorah breaks free from his nails and tumbles head over heels into the water, but none of the monks dare to retrieve him—and it might be that none of them care—for he alone would spare the condemned, and there is no room left in the monastery of Cudi Dagh for forgiveness.

"Find him!" I scream, but I am not searching for the fallen Savior. I am hunting for the sinner, Otto Rabun Bowles, and I burn with the desire to become the instrument of his torture and within earshot of his shrieks. The thunderclap of electricity that too gently ended his life is only the beginning of what I have planned for him.

Holden Hurley leaps from his stool in a blind panic, believing it is his soul the storm hounds; and perhaps it is, for when he reaches the door of the monastery he is vaporized instantly by a bolt of lightning, leaving behind only the shape of his silhouette burned into the wood. Barratte Rabun, Albrecht Bosch, and Katerine Schrieberg-Wolfson look after him in horror but decide to follow him, if for no other reason than that it spares them the difficulty of deciding what to do for themselves. They, too, are disintegrated immediately by three more bolts of lightning.

The water is now up to my knees, and, for the first time, I see Bo and my Grandpa Cuttler sitting in a corner of the monastery, oblivious to the waters rising around them, staring at a single computer held between them. Grandpa Cuttler doesn't understand computers and is perplexed by the blank screen; together they press the keys, trying desperately to restart the machine like the police officers who raided the mushroom house that morning tried desperately to restart my heart.

After photographing the crime scene at the mushroom house, the coroner took Sarah and me to the Chester County morgue. Bo called Karen and asked her to be there with him when he identified our bodies. She was the logical choice, even though he was Jewish. Karen had baptized Sarah just six months earlier over the beautiful silver font at Old Swedes' Church—to give us options, I reasoned, and to keep peace in my family and hold theological doors open if Judaism didn't work out and I decided not to convert. Confident that beautiful morning that Christ himself had claimed Sarah as his own, Karen lifted her high for the congregation to witness the blessed miracle of faith and water, and beaming with a mother's own pride—because Bo and I had asked Karen to be Sarah's godmother—she carried her new goddaughter up into the pulpit with her to deliver the sermon. Sarah listened without a sound, as if she yearned to understand.

Karen prayed hard for Christ to be with Bo and her in the morgue that day when the coroner pulled the sheets back. She prayed for Him to reclaim the child He had accepted so recently and the woman, wife, mother, and friend who had been taken away. She anointed our heads with holy oil and pleaded for our souls. But Christ did not come, at least in a form Bo could recognize, and he howled at Karen in anguish:

"Where's your Savior, Priest? Goddamn Him, where is He?"

It was a taunt that the terrorized Jews in the death camps might have been heard to rail at the few equally terrorized Christians who shared their misery, a half-mocking, half-imploring cry.

"Where is He?" Bo's voice cracked; and with it cracked the Reverend Busfield's once durable faith.

A raging torrent of water fills the monastery. Cudi Dagh is being swallowed whole by the flood. Bo, my grandfather, and my parents flee in terror, but Bo sees the one-armed Christ bobbing in the water and looks back at Karen.

"There's your Savior, Priest!" he laughs maniacally. "Justice nailed Him to the cross, and now justice is setting Him free!"

Karen splashes after the broken Christ in the same way we chased after crayfish in the Little Juniata River. She lunges, but He escapes through her fingers, disappearing beneath the water.

"I can't find Him!" she cries. "I can't find Him!" Twice more she sees Him, and twice more He slips through her fingers as the waters rise, carrying Him out into the storm.

Karen is the last monk to leave the monastery. On her way out she pulls off the white stole I gave her and her winged Air Force insignia, and throws them into the fire on top of the charred remains of Barratte Rabun's computer, which is still burning. Karen does not see the rising waters quench the flames and carry the stole and the insignia back out of the hearth unharmed. They float freely together for a moment, like a dove and a raven in search of dry land. The stole spots the long branches of the menorah first, then the insignia comes, and together they cling to the branches until the waters engulf the menorah too. At the last second, as the menorah disappears beneath a whirlpool of water, the stole and the insignia take flight again, searching the waters for a sign of compassion.

The water is chest deep now. Elymas grabs my hand.

"We must reach the ark," he shouts, "before it is too late."

I look into his eyes, and the monastery disappears.

Suddenly, Elymas and I are standing on the deck of a great wooden ark in near total darkness. The storm lashes the boat, and we are being tossed about; but Elymas insists we must stay on deck and not seek shelter below.

I hear the anxious sounds of animals beneath my feet—the cacophony of an entire zoo assembled under one roof. Each time the ark pitches, the cries of the animals grow louder, but I begin to hear other cries too: awful, relentless shrieks and moans come from outside the ship, rising above the wind and thunder, overcoming the sounds of the animals. These are the most chilling, terrifying sounds I have ever heard.

"What is it?" I ask.

Elymas points a gnarled finger overboard and the clouds lift just enough for the sun's weak rays to illuminate the churning sea all the way to the horizon. Across all that distance, as far as I can see in every direction, the waters are covered with a slick of bloated bodies, human and animal, and each wave brings them crashing and grinding into the hull of the ark. Those humans still alive on this sea of horror are using the dead as rafts, clinging to the cadavers of their mothers and fathers, sons and daughters, calling out for mercy and forgiveness in languages I have never heard. The stench of decaying flesh is overwhelming, causing me to retch.

A deck hatch opens and through it climbs a young man with his wife, attracted to the surface by the brightening skies. They come to the rail and, looking out upon the carnage, begin to weep. Through the hatch behind them comes an old man, weathered, gray-bearded, and harried. He walks to the middle of the deck, raises his arms and proclaims:

"I PRESENT MANKIND…THEY HAVE CHOSEN!"

"But Father! Father!" the young man pleads. "We must rescue them, as many as we can! We cannot allow them to drown!"

The young man begins running around the deck tying ropes to the rails and throwing them over the side.

"No!" commands the old man. "Only we are righteous, and only we shall be saved!"

The young man's wife falls to her knees at the old man's feet. "Oh, please, father, please, let us help them!" she begs. "We cannot bear their suffering. Surely they are people born as you and I, who have done wrong and right as you and I. Surely you see that. You alone, father, were chosen as righteous, and the righteous, father, must take pity upon the wretched. Our ship is large and we could save hundreds, thousands. Please, father, we must try!"

"Ham, take this woman away!" the old man orders. "Take her out of my sight at once or I will throw her over with the others. I do not hear their cries. The time for weeping is past."

Ham looks upon his father with contempt. How can the great Noah leave them? How can the great Noah be so cruel? He crawls back through the hatch and returns to the deck with his brothers, Shem and Japeth. He leads them to the rail and shows them the sea of bodies, repeating to them what their father has said, expecting them to join him in convincing Noah to have mercy. But Shem and Japeth turn their backs on the people in the sea. They remove their cloaks and drape them behind their heads as curtains, and walking toward Noah they embrace him. Noah turns on Ham for questioning his judgment:

"A curse upon your descendants, the Canaanites!" he proclaims. "May they be the lowest of slaves to the descendants of Shem and Japeth!"

Noah orders them all below and seals the hatch tight. Like a linen shroud soaked with sweet oils and spices, the clouds descend onto the sea, compressing the putrid air into the waves and muffling the groans and screams. The grinding of flesh and bone against the hull of the ark continues for one hundred and fifty days.

And then the waters receded.

Elymas and I were there when Noah sent forth the raven and the dove, and we were there when the dove returned with an olive branch. Noah and his family were the only people to board the ark, and they were the only people to disembark when it ran aground on Ararat. No one from the sea was saved.

Noah built an altar and made a sacrifice to Yahweh that day, and on that day Yahweh was well pleased. Yahweh blessed Noah and his sons, telling them to repopulate the earth and vesting in them authority over all wild things. When Yahweh smelled the burning flesh of Noah's sacrifice, he promised never to flood the earth again. As a reminder of that covenant, rainbows appeared in the clouds.

After seeing all this, Elymas turned to me and said:

"Luas accused Noah of being a coward, but now you know the truth, Brek Cuttler. When lesser men would have faltered,

Noah made no excuses for humanity. The story is not about love, it is about justice."

And then, all at once, I was back in the woods behind Nana's house, on my way to Shemaya Station. Elymas was gone. I was a young woman again, dressed in my black silk suit covered with baby formula stains that turn to blood. I was on my way to the Urartu Chamber to present the case of No. 44371.

43

No. 44371 sits on the same bench where I found myself when I first arrived at Shemaya Station. It is as if no time has passed. My blood is still tacky on the floor, turning red the bottoms of No. 44371's white-soled prison sneakers.

He looks just as I imagined he would after the executioner sent four thousand volts of electricity crashing through his body. His scalp is bald and raw where it has not been charred into black flake and ash by the electrode; his skin and face are the color of stale milk; abrasions cover his wrists and ankle; his eyes bulge from their sockets; his trousers are soiled. He holds an object in his hands, but when he sees me, he hides it and looks down at the floor, hoping it will open up and devour him. No. 44371 knows that today is the day he will face his eternity.

Next to No. 44371, at the opposite end of the bench, sits a young girl who also stares at the floor. She looks familiar, like a young Amina Rabun playing with her brother in the sandbox, or a young Katerine Schrieberg walking with her father to the café in Dresden, or a young Sheila Bowles playing with a doll on her bed at the sanitarium. She is like all little girls—innocent, preoccupied, dreaming—but she sits naked on the bench, pale and emaciated like death.

What could she have done to be brought to this place?

As if in reply to my thought, she looks up at me and says: "God punishes children for the sins of their parents."

A low rumbling sound echoes through the great hall, a sound like the grinding of a train entering the station. I turn from the little girl to see Gautama, the sculptor of the sphere from the cocktail party. He is dressed in the same rainbow-colored dhoti wrapped around his waist and legs and he is rolling his magical stone sphere among the postulants. He smiles at them like a peddler, trying to convince them to buy his wares, but they pay him no attention even as the sphere nears them and flashes the patterns of their lives across its surface, mapping their journeys to now.

Gautama stops his sphere in front of No. 44371. It sands itself smooth before erupting into the grotesque rash of Otto Bowles' life, crisscrossing the sphere like a ball of yarn—here a young boy embarrassed and enraged, unable to forgive his father for striking his grandfather at the football game, there a man firing three bullets into my chest and demanding death by Electric Chair. In his arrogance, sitting here on the bench beneath the dome of rusted girders and trusses, which from far above Shemaya Station might appear to be a manhole cover in some forsaken back alley of the universe, No. 44371 does not notice his life drawn on the sphere, or think about the necessity of sewers to carry off the effluent of Creation. He stares stubbornly into the floor, daring it to rise up and seize him. I do not hear the cry of his soul as I did during my naïve moment of compassion in my office before lighting the candles. I hear nothing at all. I make a note to include his insolence in my presentation.

"Greetings, my daughter," Gautama says to me.

The surface of the sphere changes as I approach it, reproducing the pattern of my life's choices. I had seen only glimpses of them at the cocktail party, between the pairs of doors, but now they are displayed in great detail, like a street map on a globe. The trail begins with my birth at the top of the sphere and the earliest injustice of being forced from my mother's womb, separated forever from her unconditional love. The doors open next onto Nana's funeral and the injustice of being slapped by my mother—the mother who had created and loved me—for crying when I was forced to kiss her corpse. The sphere shows the nights when my mother was too drunk or depressed to care for me, and her vicious fights with my father, who was too selfish and preoccupied to notice. Through another set of doors, I am thrusting my right hand into the conveyor chain, offering myself as a sacrifice to my parents, and there, through yet another pair, I am an amputee, crying amidst a group of children who have tucked their arms inside their jackets and circled me with their sleeves flapping in the wind. Father O'Brien tells me justice is for God later, but Bill Gwynne tells me it is for us now, and I testify that the chain guard was in place but failed when I stumbled into it. Boys torture crayfish in buckets, and I put them on trial, deciding that day to become a lawyer because justice is the only salvation. The sphere rotates. Here I am again, worrying with my grandfather about fuel prices and recession during the nineteen-seventies, and reading from my other grandfather's treatises about equity and law. My father announces he is remarrying, and my mother celebrates this, and another anniversary of my Uncle Anthony's death in Vietnam, with a bottle of gin. I am not asked to the school prom; the boys are too afraid of me, and I of them. Karen, who is not asked either because God has not made her pretty, decides to become a priest.

The sphere rotates again and I am in law school now, meeting my first client on an internship at the welfare clinic, promising that I will find justice for her and her eight children who have not eaten in three days. I overwhelm the bureaucrats with legal papers and easily win the case. There I am later, an intern at the Philadelphia district attorney's office, meeting my first victims of crime and promising justice for them, too. I outprepare the overworked public defender and easily win the conviction. During the summers, I work at large corporate law firms with granite conference tables and expensive artwork on the walls; we promise the president of a chemical company we'll do everything possible to defeat the class action lawsuit brought by the heirs of those who died after being exposed to his company's pesticides. My legal research for the case is thorough, creative, and the partners of the firm are so impressed that they offer me a full-time position.

The sphere rotates again and Bo is in my bed asking me to marry him. I should be thinking about the beauty of our lives together, but instead I am thinking about the practice of circumcision and how each Jewish male child is given the mark of justice itself—indelible, binding, irrefutable. I say yes to him and weep with joy because my children and I will now receive that blessing and that hope; we will become third party beneficiaries of the contract between Abraham and God. Bo and I move to Huntingdon and decide to have a baby. I convince my mother-in-law to sue Amina and Barratte Rabun for her inheritance. I know now how to acquire and control justice, to make it do my bidding and to savor its many pleasures.

The sphere rotates a final time. I am scolding Bo because he has left his clothes all over the floor again. He does this all the time, even though I've reminded him. He has no defense. He just stands there in his shorts and t-shirt, looking confused. When he fails to apologize or concede the seriousness of his crime, I bring him to justice too. I am unwilling to allow even errant socks and underwear to pass unpunished for fear that injustice will tighten its grip around my life and my world.

"You think I'm your maid?" I shout at him at the top of my lungs. "Put here to run around behind you and pick up your clothes and wash the dishes you leave in the sink? You don't get up with Sarah during the night, and you don't get her ready in the morning! No, you're in way too big of a hurry to see the weathergirl! We can't go anywhere on weekends because you're always watching football, baseball, or basketball. If we don't talk about sports, we don't talk about anything! You haven't said a nice word to my parents in five years and you act like you can't stand them and then wonder why they hate you!"

My teeth bare and my muscles clench. I throw things around the room, seething with irrational, unjustifiable rage. Watching it being replayed on the sphere—every word spoken, and every object thrown, a passage through another pair of doors—I begin to wonder whether the pursuit of justice itself is irrational and unjust, as Karen had told me when we were kids. Then the sphere inches forward and shows me in my law office, writing a brief to help Alan Fleming escape repaying his debts on a legal technicality.

The sphere has come almost full circle now, displaying the final two choices of my life. The first is my decision not to shoot Ott Bowles in the mushroom house, choosing the door on the right. The second is my change of heart, my decision to shoot him as he steps toward me, choosing the door on the left. With that decision, the circle is closed and sphere has returned to the place of my beginning, to the place of unconditional love where I was separated from my mother's womb. Gautama rolls the sphere slightly toward No. 44371 and the sphere superimposes his choices over mine. Somehow we have taken similar paths.

Our meeting in the mushroom house seems mathematically certain, the inevitable result of a series of parallel equations and geometric principles. We spent our lives protecting ourselves from the unbearable pain of injustice. We spent our lives renouncing the inconceivable possibility of forgiveness.

The girl on the bench stirs. She is interested in the sphere and reaches out with her right hand to touch it but cannot because there is only a stump ending at the elbow. I remember her now: I had seen her in the great hall during the cocktail party, when Luas showed me the postulants among the shadows. I was unable to see inside her soul then, and, for some reason, the surface of the sphere reveals nothing more of her now.

The sphere erases itself again. Two pairs of doors appear. They look like miniatures of the doors to the Urartu Chamber. Above one pair is the word JUSTICE, and above the other, the word FORGIVENESS.

"Noah once stood before these doors," Gautama says. "And Jesus of Nazareth, too, was humbled by them. Now your time has come, my daughter."

The girl looks from Gautama to me, retracting the stump of her arm.

"You saw Yahweh butcher them," Gautama continues. "Mothers, fathers, babies. You sailed with Noah upon the sea of horror, you smelled their rotting bodies and heard their pathetic cries."

"Yes," I say.

"And when the waters receded and the sun returned, you saw Noah look up at the Murderer. You saw him with your own eyes, my daughter, and yet, you still do not see."

"I saw Divine justice unfurled in rainbows," I respond in my defense.

"Rainbows are not the colors of justice, my daughter. They are the colors of forgiveness."

"God forgave no one."

"That is true, my daughter. But Noah forgave God, and the colors of God's joy burst through the clouds. Thousands of years later, on one dark and terrible afternoon, the people tortured and murdered God. God forgave the people, and the colors of our joy burst through on Easter morning. Love is shown to be unconditional, my daughter, only when it embraces that which is least deserving of love. What you do not yet understand is that justice is the exact opposite of all that love is and all that you are. The longer you pursue it, the farther you run from the place you wish to be. The Kingdom of God cannot be entered along the path of justice."

No. 44371 rises from the bench and walks across the train station, leaving behind the young girl and the object he had been holding in his hands.

"But love is justice," I say to Gautama.

"It is not so, my daughter," Gautama replies. "Cain murdered Abel for justice. God flooded the earth for justice. The people crucified Jesus of Nazareth for justice. Terror and murder are the way of justice, not the way of love. Every war waged, and every harm inflicted, has been for the sake of justice. Soldiers kill because they believe their cause is just; assailants attack because they believe they have just cause. Justice drives the abusive spouse, the angry parent, the screaming child, the feuding neighbor, the outraged nation. He who seeks justice is harmed, not healed, because to obtain justice one must do that which is unjust. God experienced perfect justice when he flooded the earth and destroyed the possibility of evil, but the price of achieving perfect justice was unbearable; all creation was destroyed and God was separated from all that God loved and all that could love God in return. This is why the story is told, my daughter; it is a warning, not an invitation. Rainbows contain God's covenant never to seek justice again."

"But not to seek justice is to allow others to harm us, to become victims."

"No, my daughter. Not to seek justice is to love those who harm us and become victors. Love is not passive or submissive; it is the determined application of opposite force to hatred and fear, demanding the highest effort and skill. The warrior who fights back with weapons is honored and celebrated, but what bravery is there in meeting gun with gun? True bravery is displayed in meeting gun with arms wide open, refusing to submit to hatred and fear, even under pain of death. Those who mistake such bravery for cowardice do not see clearly and are forever doomed to the cycle of suffering and violence. At times, an assailant will be conquered by such love and stop attacking, but at other times he will ignore such love and continue to cause pain. Is this not also true of justice? At times, an assailant will fear retribution and stop attacking, but, at other times, he will ignore the threat of retribution and continue the onslaught. Has justice prevented the crime? People cannot be controlled; they are all born with the freedom to choose. The wise man who chooses love over justice controls himself. Experiencing unconditional love, he ends his suffering and reenters the Garden from which he came. Reuniting with his Creator, he knows, at last, what it means to be God."

I reach down and pick up the object Ott Bowles left on the bench. It is the small figurine of the one-armed Christ that fell from the menorah on Cudi Dagh. The young girl stirs and reaches out timidly with her left hand. I allow her to have it. She takes it and walks across train shed to Luas, who has just entered and is seating himself on a bench next to a new presenter who has just arrived at the station and is sitting all alone, looking perplexed. I had not seen him there earlier. The girl offers Luas the figurine, but he waves her away and she wanders off. Luas smiles at the new presenter the way he smiled at me when I first arrived, as if to say: *Yes, my son, I see. I see what you are afraid to see, but I will pretend not to have noticed.*

44

The man on the bench tries to deny and conceal his wounds, as I had done when I first arrived, but I am a presenter now, and I can see them, and with them I see the last moments of his life.

The man's name is Elon Kaluzhsky. His abdomen is torn open, and pieces of his face and forehead are missing, along with both arms and legs. Twenty minutes before he arrived at Shemaya Station, when his body was still whole, he kissed his beautiful wife and three beautiful children goodbye for the day and walked the two blocks from their apartment on a quiet street in Haifa to the bus stop. Rosh Hashanah would begin at sundown that evening, and Elon Kaluzhsky was thinking about the festive meal they would share. He loved dates, and as he walked down the street he contemplated the Rosh Hashanah prayer that must be said before eating them: "May it be your will, G-d, that our enemies be finished."

With this thought fresh in his mind, Elon took the last available seat on the Number 35 express bus, which would bring him to the downtown offices of the profitable Israeli export business where he maintained the accounts. He was full of goodwill this morning and offered a pleasant hello to the oddly overdressed man seated next to him, wearing a long overcoat on an eighty-five degree day. The greeting was not returned, but even this did not spoil Elon's happy mood. He smiled kindly at the elderly couple sitting across the aisle from him, and next to them a pretty, young secretary. Further down the aisle sat several businessmen reading newspapers, a group of high school students, and a young mother cradling her infant son.

The express bus gathered speed and the buildings of Haifa flashed by. In the middle of the journey, in the middle of a street, the overdressed man stood calmly, braced himself against a support pole for standing passengers, and from beneath his long coat pulled an automatic assault rifle. Without uttering a word, he opened fire on the passengers, sweeping the bus in an arc. Brass shell casings rained down, and a fine spray of blood filled the air as bodies collapsed onto the floor, including the elderly couple, the secretary, the businessmen, the high school students, and the young mother cradling her infant son. Elon Kaluzhsky, who had been thinking about dates and their meaning, was an athletic man and reacted bravely. He tackled the man with the gun and pinned him to the floor.

"You Arab bastard!" he screamed at him in Hebrew. "You son of a bitch!"

The man spit in Elon's face and said, "*La ilaha illa 'llah.*"

Then he detonated the suicide bomb strapped to his waist.

Luas embraces Elon, who has just recognized that his own blood is flowing through the gaping wound in his abdomen and is sobbing uncontrollably on the bench. Luas leads him away, to what

Elon believes is the house outside Moscow where he was raised, to be cared for there by a tender spirit he believes is the soul of his mother, who died ten years earlier of cancer. Elon does not notice on the way out that seated on the next bench over is the Arab man who blew himself and Elon down the tracks into Shemaya Station. I can see the last moments of this man's life too, and I recognize his face and his thoughts. Samar Mansour was not thinking about passengers or dates when he boarded the Number 35 express bus in Haifa. He did not even see the faces of those around him. He saw only Israeli soldiers firing bullets into the bodies of Palestinian children.

It had been hot the day before in Ramallah, and the customers in the café had been irritable from the heat, the humiliating Israeli checkpoints, and being penned into their neighborhoods like animals. When Samar Mansour heard the shots, he raced up the blockaded alley and into the line of fire to see if he could help. Children who had been throwing stones at the Israeli soldiers were running back down the alley toward him, but when he arrived he saw three boys lying in pools of blood on the ground. The soldiers aimed their guns into the crowd from the walls and rooftops. Samar lifted one of the boys and carried him to an arriving ambulance. The boy had a leg wound and was not hurt badly. Sam tried to comfort him.

Other men arrived at the same ambulance, carrying the other two injured boys. Samar heard a woman wailing behind them, "Hanni! Hanni!" as she tried to reach one of the boys. Samar could tell instantly the little boy was dead. Military ammunition does unspeakable violence to a child's small body.

Something changed in Samar Mansour at that moment. He thought of his father, orphaned by the Israelis and forced to carry the bags of an American archaeologist to survive. He thought of his Holocaust documentary, which had changed nothing at all, and of his theories, which had liberated no one. He thought of the little boy, Hanni, whose life in Ramallah had been full of misery, and of Hanni's mother, who would never forget the horrifying image of her son that day. He thought of the ranchers on the great plains of America who find the mauled carcasses of their livestock and go hunting gray wolves. And so, on the Number 35 express bus in Haifa that morning, Samar Mansour saw only Israeli soldiers and gray wolves, not human beings living their lives.

Luas returns to the train shed after leaving Elon with his mother and sits down on the bench next to Samar.

"Welcome to Shemaya," he says. "My name is Luas."

Like Elon, Samar tries to conceal and deny his wounds, but there is not much left of him to conceal actually, just a head and some torn pieces of flesh and bone plopped in a grotesque pile on the bench. But in Samar's imagination, he is whole. Luas smiles at him, as if to say: *Yes, my son, I see. I see what you are afraid to see, but I will pretend not to have noticed.*

Across Shemaya Station, Gautama rolls his stone sphere forward, toward a muscular young man sitting all alone on a bench. I recognize this young man as Tim Shelly. He is covered with sweat and has no pants, exactly as I had last seen him in the mushroom house. The surface of the sphere changes, but I cannot look.

"The choice is yours, my daughter," Gautama calls out to me. "You are standing before the doors, as all people who have come before you and all who will come after. Which door will you open?"

45

I do not remember anymore.

Were my eyes blue like the sky or brown like fresh-tilled earth? Did my hair curl into giggles around my chin or drape over my shoulders in a frown? Was my skin light or dark? Was my body heavy or lean? Did I wear tailored silks or rough cotton and flax?

I do not remember. I remember that I was a woman, which is more than mere recollection of womb and bosom. And for a moment, I remembered all my moments in linear time, which began with womb and bosom and ended there too. But these are fading away now, discarded ballast from a ship emerged from the storm.

I remember unlocking the doors and entering the Urartu Chamber to present the soul of Otto Rabun Bowles. I was met there by Legna and denied passage to the presenter's chair.

"This way," she said, pointing to the great monolith itself.

I followed her, through a fissure in the sapphire wall and up the stairs, climbing several stories to the triangular aperture at the top through which light enters but does not exit. We came to a small balcony from which I could see the glistening, amber floor of the Chamber below and other similar Chambers to my right and left, thousands of them, with thousands of sapphire monoliths rising up like chimney stacks across a city skyline, extending to the horizon and beyond.

In one of the Chambers closest to mine, Mi Lau, the Vietnamese girl, stood at the presenter's chair and, extending her arms, announced:

"I PRESENT ANTHONY BELLINI... HE HAS CHOSEN!"

The energy from the walls of her Chamber surged through her, washing into the Chamber a dirt tunnel beneath a village, Mi Lau's family, my Uncle Anthony, a grenade, and a horrific explosion. Legna ended the presentation when Uncle Anthony put a gun to his own head and squeezed the trigger, but God did not pass judgment upon Anthony Bellini's soul from the balcony of the monolith. God had not even been there to watch. The balcony was empty.

In another Chamber nearby stood Hanz Stossel declaring:

"I PRESENT AMINA RABUN . . . SHE HAS CHOSEN!"

I had seen this presentation before and knew the ending. Again the balcony was empty. No one heard Hanz Stossel's cries for justice from his Israeli prison cell.

In yet another Chamber, young Bette Rabun raised her arms and screamed:

"I PRESENT ALEXY PETROVITCH... HE HAS CHOSEN!"

The Chamber turned into little Bette's bedroom in Kamenz where Alexy held her arms down while another Russian soldier beat and raped her in the darkness. No one stood on the balcony of the monolith to witness the crime or to convict the prisoner.

In another Chamber, Elon Kaluzhsky raised his arms and cried: "I PRESENT SAMAR MANSOUR...HE HAS CHOSEN!"

Into his Chamber roared the Number 35 express bus, the sounds of gunfire and the concussion of a bomb. Again, the balcony in the monolith was vacant. No one saw the last terrible moments of Elon Kaluzhsky's life.

From a Chamber behind me came Luas' voice:

"I PRESENT NERO CLAUDIUS CEASAR...HE HAS CHOSEN!"

I turned to see Luas being brought in chains before Nero. At the emperor's instruction, a Roman soldier raised his sword and decapitated him. Luas' bald and bloodied head rolled within an inch of the emperor's foot. He kicked it away, then motioned for the mess to be cleaned. Legna ended the presentation and Luas walked back out of the Chamber. No one watched from the balcony, and no one condemned Nero to the hell he deserved.

Moments later, Luas appeared inside my Urartu Chamber, accompanied by Samar Mansour. They took their places on the observer chairs. Samar Mansour looked around the Chamber in fascination and awe, as I did on my first visit.

"Brek Cuttler will be presenting the case of Otto Bowles," Luas whispered.

"I'm up here!" I called down to Luas, but he couldn't hear me.

Then Haissem entered the Chamber, the young boy who had presented the soul of Toby Bowles. Luas was visibly disappointed, as he had been when Toby failed to appear to present the case of his father.

"Oh, it's only you, Haissem," he said, frowning. "We were expecting Ms. Cuttler.... Well, here we are anyway. Haissem, this is Samar Mansour, the newest lawyer on my staff. Samar, this is Haissem, the most senior presenter in Shemaya. I must say, Haissem, that Samar has arrived not a moment too soon. We just lost Amina Rabun and now, it seems, Ms. Cuttler."

"Welcome to the Urartu Chamber," Haissem said, bowing politely. "I once sat here to witness my first presentation. Abel presented the difficult case of his brother Cain. That was long before your time though, Luas."

"Quite," Luas said.

"Little has changed since then," Haissem said. "Luas keeps the docket moving, even though the number of cases increases. We're fortunate to have you, Samar, and you're fortunate to have Luas as your mentor. There's no better presenter in all of Shemaya."

"Present company excepted," Luas said.

"Not at all," said Haissem. "I handle the easy cases."

"Few would consider Socrates and Judas easy cases," Luas said. "I'm just a clerk."

Haissem winked at Samar. "Don't let him fool you," he said. "Without Luas there would be no Shemaya." He took Samar's hand. "I must enter my appearance now and prepare myself. We will meet again, Samar, after your first case. You'll do well here. I'm certain of it."

Haissem moved to the center of the Chamber. Legna emerged from the monolith and whispered something to him, then returned. Haissem stood, raised his arms in a graceful arc, and in a voice much louder than the other presenters, almost an explosion, he said:

"I PRESENT BREK ABIGAIL CUTTLER...SHE HAS CHOSEN!"

I remember hearing the sounds of water rushing and wind blowing, of dolphins laughing and birds singing, of children talking and parents sighing, of stars and galaxies living and dying...the sounds of the earth breathing, if you could have heard it from the other side of the universe. I remember hearing God in those sounds, crying out for forgiveness from Cudi Dagh, and I remember hearing humanity in those sounds, crying out for forgiveness from Golgotha. And there, too, in the music was the ineffable joy of Noah, reaching up from the littoral to forgive his Father, and above that the ineffable joy of God, reaching down from the cross to forgive His children. And somewhere still, more faint, but it was there, I heard the cry of Otto Rabun Bowles, and with it the song of another soul, so joyous it could be heard above all these sounds, singing three words over and over:

"I AM LOVE! I AM LOVE! I AM LOVE!"

It was the song of unconditional love—the song of Eve returning home to the Garden after such a long and terrifying journey. The song grew louder as the presentation of my life continued, and in this song I heard Divine perfection, because in it I heard all of Creation: my birth into the world was in that song and my mother's first embrace; flowers were there, and music, sun, and rain; mountains and oceans were there, and books, sculptures, and paintings; boyfriends and girlfriends were there, and brothers and sisters on porch swings, children at play in sandboxes, and a young man running to the defense of a woman; horses, sailboats, and babies were there, apple trees and cattle too, and mothers nurturing their young; bread, water, and wine were there, eyes and ears, skin and hair, lips and arms and legs; air was there, and water and blankets, sunsets, moons and stars, work and play, heroes and heroines. The generations were in that song, and generosity and selflessness too. And love was there. But fear was there too: a parent's abusiveness and a child's selfishness, a dishonest lawyer and her dishonest client, an adulterer and his lover, a soldier and his gun, a death chamber and an incinerator; racists, liars, drunks, rapists, and thieves. Boys who tortured crayfish were in this song, and the God who slaughtered His own children, and the children who slaughtered their own Father, but even this sounded sweet, because out of it came the Light—the Light and gift of God.

Legna joined me on the balcony and asked if I had reached a verdict or wished to see more evidence. I told her I had seen enough. She returned to the floor of the Chamber and ended the presentation. Luas and Samar Mansour left the Chamber, but Haissem stayed behind.

He entered the monolith, and I could hear him climbing the stairs, but the soul who appeared on the balcony to greet me was not Haissem, the little boy. It was Nana Bellini. And she was holding Sarah!

Through my tears, squeezing Sarah close, I could see the Chamber below filling with souls. Tobias Bowles was there, and Jared Schrieberg, and Amina Rabun, all radiant and beautiful. Behind them came Claire Bowles, and Sheila Bowles, and between them Bonnie Campbell. Henry Collins was there, and Helmut Rabun, and Amina's mother and father, uncle, grandfather, and cousins. My Uncle Anthony was there, and behind him, Mi Lau's family. And then the crowd parted, as if to allow someone important to pass. A young man carrying a tray made his way through the crowd.

He entered the monolith and climbed the stairs, but he hesitated at the top when he saw Sarah and me. I didn't recognize him at first. He looked so different with all that hair and his eyes so clear and blue. Sarah smiled, and he came closer. He knelt and placed the tray before us. It was a silver tray with a silver teapot and three silver cups.

"Hot tea and bees honey," Ott Bowles said, his eyes filling with tears, "for three we will share."

GITA NAZARETH lives in the farthest corner of the imagination, where hope triumphs over despair and miracles happen. This is Gita Nazareth's first novel written from that place.

www.forgivingararat.com

1/28/2011

LaVergne, TN USA
04 December 2010
207383LV00003B/1/P